LUCKY'S
Beach

Also by Shelley Noble

A Beach Wish
Lighthouse Beach
Christmas at Whisper Beach (novella)
The Beach at Painter's Cove
Forever Beach
Whisper Beach
A Newport Christmas Wedding (novella)
Breakwater Bay
Stargazey Nights (novella)
Stargazey Point
Holidays at Crescent Cove
Beach Colors

LUCKY'S
Beach

A NOVEL

SHELLEY
NOBLE

wm

WILLIAM MORROW

An Imprint of HarperCollinsPublishers

LUCKY'S BEACH. Copyright © 2020 by Shelley Freydont. All rights reserved. Printed in the United States of America. No part of this book may be used or reproduced in any manner whatsoever without written permission except in the case of brief quotations embodied in critical articles and reviews. For information, address HarperCollins Publishers, 195 Broadway, New York, NY 10007.

HarperCollins books may be purchased for educational, business, or sales promotional use. For information, please email the Special Markets Department at SPsales@harpercollins.com.

FIRST EDITION

Designed by Diahann Sturge

Library of Congress Cataloging-in-Publication Data has been applied for.

ISBN 978-0-06-295353-7

20 21 22 23 24   LSC   10 9 8 7 6 5 4 3 2 1

To Janice
Ardent supporter and friend

LUCKY'S Beach

Prologue

Julie Barlow looked over her students' heads to the wall clock behind them. The minute hand clicked forward.

It was the last day of school, the last five minutes to be precise, and Julie was the only one in her fourth-grade class at Hillsdale Progressive Elementary who was watching the clock.

Sixteen nine-year-olds, heads bowed, were finishing up the last of their work: a questionnaire about their summer goals.

Travel, enrichment classes, chess clubs, special workshops—even in summer, they were adding to their résumés. After all, they were in fourth grade and time was passing.

She jumped when the bell buzzed. Watched the children she'd tried to guide and nurture for the last year gather up their iPads, iPhones, and backpacks. They filed by her desk, leaving their questionnaires in her inbox.

The last to leave was Jimmy Marcuse, a quiet boy who had surprised them all by winning the county spelling bee. Spelling wasn't really emphasized at Hillsdale Progressive. That's what spell-check was for.

"Looks like you'll be having a busy summer," Julie said, glancing at his questionnaire.

"Yes, Ms. Barlow. I leave for space camp next week."

"Space camp, that sounds exciting."

"I have a lot of studying to do first. They don't usually take fourth graders."

"That *is* an achievement. Is your family planning a vacation?"

"My parents are taking my brother to look at colleges, so he can decide where to apply for early admission. I'm staying home and taking a digital media workshop while they're gone."

"Oh, you don't want to go see the sights?"

"He already knows where he wants to go. I don't see why they have to go look at them."

"There are probably some other great things to see and do."

He gave her a look so sympathetic that Julie flinched.

"Well, maybe I'll see you at the pool this summer."

"We have our own pool. Besides, in August I have soccer boot camp."

"That sounds fun. What position do you play?"

He shrugged. "I don't know. Defense, probably. It's really hot in August. You get sweaty and there are bugs."

"True."

"But Dad says it's important to have a well-rounded résumé if I want to get into a top school."

Julie smiled. She wanted to say, *But you're in fourth grade.*

There's time—you should be having fun over the summer, but she didn't. Julie had been just like him at his age, always achieving, always with the future in mind. She was like him now.

She followed him down the hall to the exit, held the door open while he stepped into the sunshine.

"Jimmy."

He looked back over his shoulder but didn't slow down.

"Never mind, have a good summer."

She stood at the door watching as he walked down the sidewalk and got into the front passenger seat of a silver BMW. Watched as the car drove away, Jimmy's head already bent over his phone or his tablet, school and last year's teacher forgotten as he planned for the next step toward a brilliant future.

Julie wanted to run after the car and say, *There's more to life. Hard work doesn't guarantee a perfect future. Spend time with your family; they're the most important thing in the world.*

But who was she to give him that advice? She'd been raised by a single mother and a sometimes uncle.

Her mother had worked her whole life to give Julie a secure future, but Julie hadn't had the advantages of most of her students, certainly not the same technology at her fingertips. At nine, most of them had more experience in the world than she had.

She'd always wanted to be a teacher, guiding young minds, introducing them to the world of possibilities, and giving them the tools to achieve their dreams.

But had she done anything this year beyond the syllabus? Opened them to any new ideas? Showed them something they couldn't see without her? At least bring a balance to their lives? She was afraid she knew the answer.

That's why she'd applied for an educational leave of absence for the following year. She knew if she just had new experiences, a fresh outlook; if she could just broaden her own horizons, learn new methodology, she could make a real difference in their lives. Their whole lives.

But her application had been denied.

And now Julie Barlow was about to do the most reckless thing she'd ever done. Because she had to do something to fulfill her own dream.

She returned to her classroom, opened her desk drawer, and with trembling fingers took out the letter of resignation she'd written the night before.

Her mother would be disappointed. But she would understand. In time.

Julie marched resolutely down the hall toward the principal's office.

Halfway there, Sara Olins came out of her classroom. "Oh good, you're just who I need. You have a minute, don't you?"

She didn't wait for an answer, but steered Julie inside.

"I can't get this mural down by myself without tearing it, which would be such a shame."

Julie looked at the wall. Ten feet of second-grade depictions of "People in Our Neighborhood." She pulled over a stepladder. "I'll release the tape, you hold the edges."

By the time they'd rolled it up, wrapped it in plastic, and found a place for it in the closet, the principal had left for the day.

Julie stood outside his door, half defeated, half relieved. What had she been thinking? She'd worked her whole life for this.

She tore up the letter right there.

But the original was still in a file on her laptop. And she wouldn't delete it. Not just yet.

Chapter 1

Two Weeks Later

Vacation. It couldn't get here soon enough, thought Julie, but looking out the window wouldn't make Kayla and Aggie arrive any earlier; her two best friends since forever were always late. Notoriously late.

Girl Scouts, soccer camp, junior prom, the vacations they'd been taking together since college—they'd never yet arrived anywhere on time. Even as teachers the two of them were always running into the classroom along with the bell.

Julie had been doing a lot of waiting lately, for school to end, for vacation to begin. For something to happen. She needed this vacation to figure out how to get her life back on track.

She turned from the window and made one last mental sweep of her living room. Lamps unplugged, laptop packed, cell in purse, extra chargers in her suitcase. Printer off. Desk . . . not cleared.

The stack of travel brochures she'd been collecting for the last two years and that she'd meant to recycle the night before still sat there, a painful reminder of all the places she wouldn't be going during the next school year. She'd put them out in the bin now.

She wouldn't need them anymore, now that she'd been denied a leave of absence, and it was time she stopped thinking about what might have been.

Recycle bin, she reminded herself.

A prolonged honk jarred Julie back to the here and now.

At last. Vacation had arrived and—she glanced at her watch—only seventeen minutes late, practically early.

She hurried across the room and opened the door just as an electric-blue SUV stopped at the curb and Kayla and Aggie jumped out of the car. They were both in vacation mode, in short shorts and tees. Kayla was beanpole thin with shoulder-length dark hair, today tied back in a ponytail that she'd pulled through the back of a hot-pink baseball cap.

Aggie was unselfconsciously poured into a pair of stretchy short-shorter-shortest cutoffs and a tight T-shirt, proud to sport her hourglass-in-a-post-Twiggy-world figure.

Julie was wearing new shorts from Aritzia and a Freddie Mercury T-shirt. She'd attempted to clip up her curly hair into a twist with tenuous success. She'd even done a pre-vacation sit out in the backyard so she wouldn't look like rice on the beach. Still, she felt not quite ready for prime time.

Kayla stopped at the back of the SUV and opened the hatch; Aggie made a beeline for the front door.

"Hurry up. Happy hour's waiting! Is this all your stuff?" She breezed past to pick up Julie's laptop. "Kayla's making more space in the trunk. Good luck with that one." She spotted the brochures that Julie had left on the desk.

"Oh goody, plans for our next vacation."

"No! They're not . . ."

Aggie shoved the brochures into Julie's beach bag just as Julie lunged for them. "Man, this is heavy, what do you have in here?"

"Beach stuff and a few books."

"Better be juicy romances and not a textbook."

"My Contemporary Trends class starts in three weeks."

Aggie rolled her eyes. "Another three points toward your master's degree. I'm impressed, but I may be moved to toss it out the car window."

"Very funny. I'm putting it in the trunk."

Though right now Julie wouldn't cry if Aggie did toss it. She was the only one of the three working on her master's degree. Better salary, better job security. *Better do it now,* her mother had advised. So she had.

She hadn't told Kayla and Aggie about her request for a leave. At first she didn't want to share it in case it didn't happen. Now that it had not happened, she wondered if she should mention it at all. She knew they would commiserate, be disappointed that she didn't get it and angry that she'd been passed over, but they would also be relieved because they would still be together like always.

Well, she wasn't going anywhere but back to school. No reason to mention it ever almost happened.

Aggie headed toward the open door. "Chop-chop. Time's a'wasting."

"You guys are the ones who were late," Julie groused.

"We're always late," Aggie said cheerfully.

"True, and I love you anyway," Julie said, following her out the door.

Kayla had even been late to her own wedding, but that was because the limo had had a flat tire on the way to the church. Not her fault. But it had probably been one of those signs that no one ever paid attention to until it was too late.

Seven years later, her two kids spent two weeks each summer with her ex-husband, and Aggie and Julie always planned their vacation accordingly.

Julie stopped to double-lock the front door and rolled her suitcase out to the SUV.

"I think we may need your organizational skills," Kayla said, staring under the open cargo door.

It was a mess. Julie nudged Kayla aside and began removing the haphazardly balanced bags, cases, coolers, beach umbrellas, and backpacks. Several minutes later, she'd repacked and secured every piece while managing to leave a full view out the back window for the driver.

"Pure genius," Kayla said, and slammed the hatch.

"All righty, girls, let's rock 'n' roll." Aggie stuck up her hand. They all high-fived and jumped in the car, Aggie riding shotgun and Julie in the back.

They hadn't gone two blocks before someone's cell phone rang.

Kayla turned down the radio while they all listened.

"It's mine," Julie said, recognizing the "By the Seaside" ring-tone she'd downloaded for the summer.

A few seconds of rummaging in her bag and she extracted the phone, looked at the caller ID. "It's my mother."

"I thought she was on that nurses' cruise."

"She is." Julie connected. "Hey, Mom."

"Hi, Louise," Kayla and Aggie called from the front seat.

"What's up? Everything okay?"

"No."

Julie sucked in her breath. "Are you okay?"

Aggie turned around in her seat, looking worried.

"I'm fine. But Lucky's missing."

Julie shook her head. Tony Costa. Her mother's younger brother—by seven minutes. Julie's sometimes surrogate father. Always entertaining, often irresponsible, never reliable, Uncle "Lucky" was a favorite with her friends. For Julie, the jury was still out.

She relaxed and gave her companions a thumbs-up. "Oh, Mom, you know how he is."

"I do and that's why I'm worried. We talk every week without fail."

"I'm sure there's nothing to worry about. Maybe he couldn't get access to your cell while you're on the ship."

"Of course he could."

"Maybe his cell phone died or he doesn't have reception on *his* end." *Maybe it fell in the ocean while he was out catching the big one.*

"He's in Delaware."

"Delaware?" Julie glanced at her friends as a creeping sense of inevitability stole over her. She vaguely remembered that he had settled there . . . somewhere.

"Honey, you remember; he opened up that bar in wherever they have the big waves."

"In Delaware?"

"Well, they're biggish. And I'm sure it's right on your way to Rehoboth."

"We're going to Dewey Beach."

"It's just a few minutes out of your way. He's my twin brother. I can tell when something's wrong."

Leave it to her mother to pull the twins card when she was determined to have her way.

"Mom."

"What's wrong?" Aggie asked.

"Or maybe I can get them to airlift me off the ship . . ."

"Oh, Mom."

"Put her on speaker," said Kayla.

"Is that Kayla?"

"Yes. I'm putting you on speaker."

"Hi, girls, I'm so glad I caught you. You don't mind taking a little detour, do you?"

"It's a four-hour trip," Julie argued from the back seat, but no one paid any attention. She already knew they'd be detouring to check out Lucky's "retirement" venture. Some surfer bar in some beach town that was not the beach town they were going to.

But Julie could never hold out against her friends or her mother—or even Lucky.

"Not at all," Kayla said. "We've got this covered."

Julie rolled her eyes heavenward. Her mother was an intelligent woman, hardworking. She'd raised Julie solo and done a good job of it, while also saving enough money to send Julie to college. But all that rationality and self-reliance flew out the window when it came to her twin brother.

Julie tried not to audibly sigh. "Okay, text me his number and address. I'll phone you tonight." She ended the call and sank back against the seat.

In the last two weeks, she'd been denied leave, almost quit her job, and in the midst of her existential crisis, they were driving not to their planned vacation but to look for her disappearing uncle. Okay, one more little detour, and her duties would be done. Then ten whole days of lying on the beach. Fun in the sun. Drinks with little umbrellas. Dancing in the moonlight.

A few minutes out of their way. What could possibly go wrong?

Though when her uncle was involved, you never knew. *Uncle Lucky.* Julie remembered the first day he'd shown up at their door, tanned to a crisp and wearing cutoff jeans and a Grateful Dead T-shirt. With a gigantic nylon duffel bag by his sandaled feet and a surfboard tucked under one arm, he was the strangest creature Julie had ever seen. He looked nothing like his sister, except for his sun-streaked hair that fell well beyond his shoulders.

He'd missed her father's funeral. He'd been in India or some-

where at a surfing competition. But he was here now, he said, and he was staying to take care of his sister and niece.

Her mother said, "Oh, Tony, we're so lucky to have you." And from that moment on, he became Uncle Lucky.

And he did take care of them. Sort of. Whenever he wasn't riding the waves. When the other parts of his life or friends didn't get in the way.

Her phone pinged: a text from her mother. "Oh man, listen to this address. Route One and Daly's Junction." She keyed it into her map app. "I don't think it's even a town. Good thing we have a long drive. It'll give me time to find it."

"Haven't you been to visit him?"

"Nope. He used to move around all the time. I figured he still was. I mean, why would he settle down in Delaware? How challenging can the waves be?"

Kayla frowned at Julie in the rearview mirror. "He *is* getting older."

"Fifty-two is not that old. Anyway, sorry we're losing a beach day for what is most likely a wild-goose chase. We'll probably find him lying on the beach with an open beer and an uncharged cell phone stuck in the sand."

"Huh," Aggie said. "Maybe it's a sign."

"Of what?" Julie said. "Annoyance?"

"No, that it's time you broke radio silence."

"The phone works both ways," Julie said defensively.

"Maybe, but you started it."

"Are we really going to beat this dead horse on our first day of vacation?"

"Oh, come on, Jules. It will be great to see him. We all loved him."

"Yeah," added Kayla. "He was like a . . ."

"A father?" Julie finished for her. She'd hoped he would be. He'd been like a father to all her friends, but Julie had wanted a father all her own.

"Well, he was . . . kind of," Aggie said.

"She's still bent because he missed her college graduation," Kayla said.

"Am not. And he missed *both* my graduations," Julie reminded them. "And I haven't thought about that in years. We just fell out of touch."

"No, you didn't. He called to apologize. You told him you never wanted to see him again and hung up on him, remember?"

She did remember. She pushed the vague sense of guilt that she'd neglected him firmly back where it belonged. He was a grown man. He could have tried harder.

"I remember he sent you that huge bouquet of pink roses to make up for it," Kayla said. "We were all so envious."

"Yeah," Aggie said. "All I got was dinner at Benny's Pizzeria because that's where my brothers wanted to go."

Roses. There had been two dozen and they filled the entire entryway of their house. But Julie hadn't wanted flowers. She wanted Lucky to be there with the other fathers, beaming proudly as she took her diploma.

"We really had some fun times with him, didn't we?" Kayla said. "And he saved our bacon more times than I can count."

"I'll say." Aggie twisted in her seat to see Julie. "Remember when we drank the punch at Susie Connor's party? We didn't know it was spiked. We called Uncle Lucky to come get us and he sobered us up before he took us home."

Julie remembered. He'd even fooled Louise on that one. And saved them all from big trouble.

"Yeah," said Kayla. "And when we decided to paint our camp cabin and you poured paint all over us."

"The can fell off the ladder," Aggie insisted.

"We had green hair for weeks," Kayla said, laughing.

"I thought Louise was going to make me shave my head," Julie said. "But he convinced her that everyone would think I had head lice." She laughed. "I'll never forget her face when he said that."

"He taught us the hula." Aggie wiggled in the front seat.

"And how to skateboard," Kayla added.

And he'd taught Julie how to twirl a baton. Because for some irrational reason, the serious, studious, did-what-she-was-told Julie decided she wanted more than anything else to be on the middle school twirling team.

She didn't even tell Kayla and Aggie. They were busy planning which outfits to wear and picking out the cute boys whom they might meet at their new school.

Her mother discouraged the idea—Julie didn't know how to twirl; she didn't have a baton. And there were all the reasons she didn't say: they couldn't afford the uniform or to send Julie on trips if she did make the squad.

Lucky didn't argue, but the next day while her mother was

at work, he took Julie into the backyard and pulled out a baton he'd bought at the local dime store. It had white and pink streamers on each end.

Every afternoon, they practiced in secret, Lucky imparting what little knowledge he found at the public library and by consulting Mrs. McCleary, an overweight matron who lived down the street and who had been a majorette many decades before.

All summer they practiced. Then school started and the day of tryouts came.

"You'll be there, Uncle Lucky. Promise."

"Wouldn't miss it. You'll be great. They're gonna love you."

The telephone rang. Lucky talked a few minutes. Julie didn't notice his expression when he came back. She was too busy visualizing herself on the squad.

"Bring me one of those hair things," he'd said. "We'll put it up like Mrs. McCleary showed us."

The afternoon of the tryouts, Julie came to the field where they were being held. All the girls had their hair piled in curls on the tops of their heads and had real batons, none of which had streamers on the ends. And they had cute little skirts and matching tops and were doing all sorts of fancy moves as they practiced.

They all watched Julie take out her baton from her backpack, then exchanged looks with one another. Julie looked down at her best shorts and T-shirt, looked for Lucky, but she couldn't find him seated with the parents along the side of the field.

One after another the girls' names were called and they showed what they could do. Some even had music to go with their act.

And still Uncle Lucky didn't come.

Then it was Julie's turn. She took her cheap baton out before the judges, took her pose, but without Lucky's encouragement, her fingers turned to clay. She tried to roll the baton in her fingers but couldn't get the rhythm; it went round and round limping like a flat tire. She couldn't make anything work. She turned and the baton hit her in the leg, and she almost dropped it. Everyone was watching; she heard someone snicker. Several girls rolled their eyes.

She couldn't do it. Nothing was working. Where was Lucky? She threw the baton in the air. Her big trick. It went up but arced away from her; she tried to run after it, to stretch out her arms and catch it, but she couldn't move. The baton bounced and rolled out of reach.

Murmurs from the parents.

Even the judges looked away. They didn't ask her to line up with the other girls.

Lucky was wrong. They didn't love her. She should never have tried out. It was stupid to think she could make the team.

She grabbed her backpack and raced from the field. Ran all the way home and burst into the kitchen.

Her mother was at the sink.

"Good heavens, where have you been? Have you been crying? Why is your face all streaked with dirt?"

Julie ran her arm across her eyes. "He said they would like me. He said he would be there, and he wasn't. He's a liar. I hate him."

"Who? What's happened?"

And the story came pouring out.

"Well," her mother said when Julie had gasped and hiccupped to the end. "It's just as well. Those girls have far more experience than you. It was silly of Lucky to give you false hopes. And besides, they have to practice almost every afternoon. Better to spend your afternoons studying."

And with that, her mother brushed away the dirt and Julie's dream in one single swipe of her dish towel.

"He promised. I'll never believe him ever again."

"Go upstairs and clean up, things will look better after dinner."

But Julie didn't go upstairs; she went out the kitchen door and hurled the hateful baton into the garbage can. Then she ran to the very back corner of the yard and cried until she was afraid she was going to throw up.

She could never show her face in school again. They had laughed at her. And worse, they'd felt sorry for her. Even the grown-ups.

She felt something nudge her knee. She moved her hands away from her face to see the bulb of her cheap baton, its streamers crumpled and broken—and a dirty hand holding it. It was the boy Lucky had brought home a few days before. He'd been the dirtiest boy she'd ever seen.

"Here." He thrust the baton at her. "Don't quit. You're good at it."

"No, I'm not. I should have never tried. Lucky's a liar."

The boy's fists clenched. "No, he's not."

"Oh yeah? He left you, too. Maybe he won't even come back for you."

His eyes blazed black; she stepped back from the intensity of his rage, then ran into the house and up the stairs and locked herself in her room.

She said she would never trust Lucky ever again. But she had, over and over. Sometimes he was there, sometimes he disappeared for days or weeks at a time, like he'd gone out and forgotten how to get home. He'd come back, looking tired and saying he was sorry, and she'd believe him, until the next time he let her down.

Missing her college graduation may have been the last straw, but it was missing her baton tryout that hurt the most.

"Hey, Jules," Kayla said. "Are you sleeping back there?"

"Huh? No," said Julie, her cheeks flushed with remembered humiliation. Maybe she *was* asleep. Maybe she'd been asleep for a long time.

They stopped as soon as they crossed the Delaware state line, long enough for Kayla to pass out ham and cheese sandwiches and bottled iced tea that she'd packed in one of the coolers.

When they hit the road again, Julie began scrolling the internet for information about Lucky's Beach Bar and Grill.

She searched the usual "Ten Best Beach Bars on the Delaware Coast"–type sites. No Lucky's BB and G.

She went on to the less popular sites. "Eureka. Number twenty on the 'Other Places' list. One dollar sign. Why am I not surprised? One review. 'The shore's best-kept secret for those who long for the old glory days of surfing.'"

"What about the current glory days of surfing?" Aggie asked. "Do you think there will be any surfers? That could be fun."

Daly's Junction turned out to be miles south of Rehoboth *and* Dewey Beach and a drive through a national park where the land was so narrow you could sometimes see the ocean and the bay merely by turning your head.

Julie was about to tell Kayla to turn around and head back to their motel when the GPS announced they had arrived at their destination: a four-way stop consisting of a convenience store, an empty lot, a gas station, and a boarded-over one-story building with a FOR LEASE sign in the window. But no Lucky's.

"This doesn't look promising," Julie said.

"Well, the ocean's on our left, so if it's a beach bar . . ." Kayla made the turn onto a two-lane road only to be immediately surrounded by marshland.

"Really not promising," added Julie.

"It's an adventure," Kayla said, sounding skeptical.

"There better be surfers at the end of this road," Aggie said.

"I just hope there's a way out," Julie said. *In more ways than one,* she added to herself.

A few minutes later, they rounded a bend into a neighborhood of saltbox cottages lined up side by side and arranged in square blocks perpendicular to the main street.

Two blocks later they crossed over a narrow bridge, passed a modest-looking marina, and drove into a downtown area of colorfully painted Victorian storefronts.

"This is more like it," Aggie said.

"Cute," Kayla agreed. "Somebody should put up a sign on the highway."

Even without a sign, it was fairly busy.

Kayla drove slowly, while Aggie and Julie scanned each side of the street for Lucky's Beach Bar and Grill. There was a post office and Poppy's Fish Market on the right. On the left, a yellow cottage had been repurposed into a convenience store. They had just passed a red-striped ice-cream stand at the end of the first block when Aggie pointed. "There it is!"

An opening between two buildings with a sign that said BEACH. And below it a sign for SURF'S UP. And below that BEACH BAR AND GRILL. The first word had been x-ed out and LUCKY'S had been painted over it in bright red lettering.

Julie slid a little lower in her seat, though the seat belt kept her from sliding out of sight. Which was what she'd like to do. He probably wouldn't be there. But if he was, what was she going to say?

Maybe he didn't even want to see her.

Kayla made the turn through a thicket of beach scrub and onto a wedge of hard-packed parking lot. Beyond the parking lot, a beach of white sand slid into a sparkling blue ocean stretching in both directions to the horizon.

"Wow," Kayla said. "Talk about uninterrupted landscape."

"Just look at that view," Aggie added, her eyes following two surfers on their way to the water. "I'm thinking it doesn't get much better than this." She glanced at the other two. "And the beach isn't bad, either." She flashed them a cheeky grin.

It *was* beautiful, thought Julie.

"Now you can understand why they don't advertise," Kayla said. "They want to keep this all to themselves."

Other than several cars parked around a small beach shack at the edge of the sand, the parking lot was mostly empty.

"There it is. Lucky's Beach Bar and Grill." Kayla hooked a right and brought the car to a stop next to a rusted-out dune buggy and a battered Jeep.

Julie just stared. Lucky's BB and G was little better than a beach shack. It was a wide, sprawling wooden structure with a front porch and unpainted steps with a side area sheltered by a tattered canvas tent top that probably served as an outside bar. A wooden sign over the door was so faded that Julie didn't know how Kayla had picked it out of the general malaise.

"Oh, come on," Aggie said, opening her door. "It's not that bad."

Bad enough, Julie thought. And for a surprising second she felt a stab of compassion for the young surfer who had grown too old to compete and, as far as she knew, had never learned to do anything else. *That's what happens when you don't prepare for life.* Julie wondered if her mother had told Tony the same thing.

Julie had followed her mom's advice. *She* was prepared, and she was miserable. And she still hadn't told her two best friends in the world what she'd almost done. Though to quote her mom, *almost didn't count.*

She and Aggie climbed out and joined Kayla, who was standing like Ponce de León searching for the Fountain of Youth.

"It's really beautiful here." Kayla let out a long sigh. "Calm."

"It is," Julie agreed. Would Kayla have rather gone to someplace quiet instead of a party-scene beach like Dewey? She'd never mentioned that.

Kayla dropped her hands to her sides. "Let's go find Lucky."

"Tony," Julie corrected her. She'd determined long ago not to call Uncle Tony "Lucky" ever again. He'd fallen off her "Lucky" list, and he wasn't doing much this trip to reestablish himself. He hadn't been so lucky for her.

Aggie threw out an arm to stop her. "Whoa. Cute surfer dude alert at ten o'clock."

Julie looked in spite of herself. Aggie's radar never failed. Not one, but three cute surfers were coming out of a shack as dilapidated as the bar but nearer to the beach. Its wooden sign was painted in bright blue, yellow, and green.

"'*Surf's Up.*' And so am I." Aggie gave them a saucy grin. "Maybe we'll get lucky while we're looking for Lucky."

Julie and Kayla rolled their eyes.

"Oh, come on, guys," Aggie said. "What's wrong with a little fun while we're looking for Mr. Right?" Aggie had always loved to party, but lately some of her enthusiasm covered what she really wanted: a house, a husband, and her own kids. But Kayla and Julie went along with the ruse.

"Fine," Kayla said, "but our Lucky first, that lucky later." She nudged Julie up the splintered steps to the screen door, where a sign read NO SHIRT, NO SHOES, NO PROBLEM. An orange crate of mismatched flip-flops sat beneath it.

"It's going to be fine," Aggie said, and pushed Julie through the door.

Chapter 2

The three of them had to stand for a few seconds while their eyes adjusted from the brilliant sun to the dingy bar light, whose only source seemed to be from neon scripted beer signs that littered the walls and cast everything into deep shadows. At least the music was turned low, so low that Julie could barely recognize the twang of a country-and-western singer.

At first it was impossible to tell if there were any customers besides the three guys sitting at the bar, whose heads had turned to see who had just entered, their grins glowing green from a neon MILLER TIME sign above them.

"Not so cute," Aggie said under her breath.

"Middle-aged regulars," Julie guessed. "The surfers probably come in later." She walked forward and shouldered her way between the guy on the right, thin-faced with a gray chin beard, and the dark-skinned, chubby-cheeked guy in the middle who was wearing a cap advertising Corey's Electronics.

The bartender turned away just as she reached the bar rail, and she addressed the back of his head.

"I'm looking for Tony Costa."

Was that feeling of sudden cold from the fridge he'd just opened, or was it emanating from the change in mood as the three men turned back to their beers?

The bartender turned to face her.

"I take it back," Aggie whispered from behind her. "Now that's cute."

"I believe this is his bar," Julie said.

The bartender just looked at her. She looked back at him. Aggie was right. He was pretty decent in a scruffy bartender way. Dark eyes and dark beach-bum-length hair that curled temptingly at the ends. She tried to ignore that fact. Why wasn't he answering?

"Well, is it? Is he here?"

"No."

"To which? He doesn't own it, or he isn't here?"

The three men continued to drink their beer. Not one of them looked up or offered an explanation.

Kayla pulled off her cap and leaned on the bar, letting her hair swing seductively over the polished wood. "We're just passing through and thought we'd look him up. Julie is his niece, and Aggie and I are Uncle Lucky's two biggest fans."

A flicker of interest from all four men as Kayla moved back and ceded the standing space to Julie. "So do you know where he is?"

"Huh. So you're Lucky's niece," the bartender said, giving Julie a quick, scrutinizing look.

She scrutinized him back. She guessed he was younger than he looked, midthirties maybe, possibly even younger with some hard living in his past. "Yeah, so can you tell me where I could find him?"

"Nope."

"You're Lucky's niece?" asked the guy in the electronics hat. "Well, I'll be." He stuck out his hand. "Corey Washington. I own Corey's Electronics in town. Anything from earbuds to home security systems, I'm your man."

Julie smiled, but before she could continue, the man on the far side of him stretched his hand across his companion. Julie shook it, too.

"Ron Petry. Retired. Twice. Glad to meet you."

The bartender seemed to have lost interest and was smiling slightly at something—someone over her shoulder. Probably flirting with Aggie.

The man on her right stuck out *his* hand. "Ike Gibson. Lucky and us go back a long ways. Glad we finally get to meet you."

"Do any of you know where he is?"

Simultaneously the three heads snapped back to the bartender.

"He's out of town," he said, dropping his smile. "But I'll tell him you came by and to give you a call when he gets back. Just write your number on the chalkboard over there." He thumbed a gesture across the room to where a large, much-erased chalk-board was balanced precariously against the wall.

Julie turned around just in time to see three heads snap back to contemplating their beers. "Do any of you know when he'll be back?"

The three men looked at the bartender.

"Nope," he said.

Julie was beginning to think she was being punked. It would be just like Lucky to be hiding behind the bar waiting to pop up like a demented jack-in-the-box. She resisted the urge to lean across the bar top to look.

"Is Tony out of town now, or just not at the bar? Maybe he's still at home. Can you give me his address?"

"Why don't you just give him a call when you get a chance?"

"My mother talks to him every week." She started to say that he hadn't called her and that she was worried, but some-thing held her back. "My friends and I are on our way to Dewey Beach and told her we'd drop by to say hello."

"Dewey, huh? Tell Louise he's fine."

Julie's eyes narrowed. "How do you know my mom's name is Louise?"

He cracked a nanosecond grin. "Because she calls him ev-ery week." He leaned toward her. "Look, Lucky's fine. I'll tell him to call her when he gets back. Go enjoy your vacay, there's a drink with an umbrella there with your name on it. I'll even call ahead to tell them you're coming."

She turned to the beer contemplators. "What about you three? Do you know where he is?"

"Nope."

"Can't say."

"Not a clue."

Julie gritted her teeth. "Well, it's been a real pleasure." She turned to leave. The three men lifted off their seats in a show of respect before returning to the contemplation of their beers.

So be it. This surly jackass and his three-man goon squad weren't the only people in town who might know where Uncle Tony was.

Aggie and Kayla followed her out, followed by the three men from the bar, who stopped on the porch and watched for a few seconds before melting away in the direction of Main Street.

"Gee," Aggie said. "I feel like we've just been run out of Dodge. What was with those guys?"

"Too much beer and time on their hands," Julie guessed.

"What do you want to do now?" Kayla asked.

Julie really wanted to go on her vacation, to hang out with her friends, drink sweet cocktails out of glasses with little umbrellas in them—and not worry about Uncle Tony or her life or what came next.

"Maybe you two should just go on. I think I'll ask around town. At least find out where he lives and leave him a note. It's not fair to have Mom stuck on a cruise ship worried about her irresponsible brother." Plus Louise wouldn't leave them alone until Tony was found or if she came to see for herself.

"And how are you going to get to Dewey if we leave?" Kayla asked.

"I'll take a car service. They must have one."

"Don't be ridiculous," Kayla said. "It might cost hundreds of dollars if they even have services. We can spend a couple of hours here. And we'd like to see Uncle Lucky, too."

"There's no reason for you to give up your—"

"Stop it. We're staying," Aggie said. "What do you want to do next?"

"I want to take another shot at the bartender now that his posse's gone."

"Good idea," Kayla said.

Julie retrieved her purse from the back seat of the SUV.

"You planning to try some of your strong-arm elementary school teacher tactics on him?" asked Aggie.

"Hey, I've brought some hard-core fourth graders to their proverbial knees," Julie said.

"And with a smile," Kayla added.

"True," Aggie said. "Who ever thought Jimmy Marcuse would win the county spelling bee?"

"That *was* pretty weird," Julie admitted.

"That was pretty you. Take some credit."

Julie shrugged. "Right time, right place." Though it struck her that the "Jimmy Miracle," as it was called in the faculty lunchroom, had been pretty cool. But her feeling of triumph hadn't lasted.

"And you didn't get teacher of the year for nothing."

"That was weird, too."

"You deserved it."

So why wasn't she satisfied? "I'll hurry."

"Sure you don't want us to come with?" Kayla said.

"I'm sure. I haven't been on the receiving end of recalcitrant children for the last six years to be stymied by a recalcitrant bartender with a third-grade sense of humor."

"You go, girl." Aggie gave her a thumbs-up. "We'll hit the surf shop. If anybody knows where Tony is, it will be his fellow surfers. Meet us back here in a few."

Kayla and Aggie went off in the direction of the surf shop. Julie really wanted to go with them, but she knew where her duty lay. She turned and strode up the steps and back into the bar.

With his customers gone, the bartender had moved to a table near the side door and the best available light. An open battered briefcase sat at one elbow and several thick manila folders were stacked at the other. He was bent over, studying a single open folder.

He looked up when Julie stopped in the center of the room. He was wearing glasses just like an actor in one of those commercials, where the intense, handsome nerd and the femme fatale with ridiculously shiny hair and long legs are brought together by some product that no one paid any attention to. Cue music.

Only Julie was no femme fatale, and he'd turned off the music, which had left the bar eerily silent.

He closed the folder he'd been reading, returned the stack of folders to the briefcase, and carried it back behind the bar.

Julie followed him over. "Can you *please* help me?"

"Sure, but I'll have to see some ID." A smile. One he obviously saved for flirting and manipulation.

Julie had to admit it was very effective. She concentrated on looking over his shoulder at the row of bottles along the wall.

"What would you like? You don't look like a beer drinker. I'm thinking pinot grigio."

"You have a wine list?" Julie asked, temporarily taken off guard.

"Sure we do. Red, white, and pink. Pink is a favorite with you gals."

Gals? What decade was he living in? Or was he just trying to piss her off?

There was a thumping sound from the other side of the bar.

Maybe Tony *was* hiding back there after all.

He reached under the bar and brought out an industrial-looking wineglass that he began polishing with the same cloth he'd been wiping the bar with.

He couldn't be as clueless as he was acting. So why the belligerence?

"Look. My mother is worried. All I want is to know for certain that my uncle hasn't met with some accident . . . or worse."

That earned her a sharp look. Something odd was going on here. Everyone thought schoolteachers were pushovers, but nothing could be further from the case. They just had fiercely honed endurance and infinite patience, though she had to admit hers was being sorely tested as she felt her vacation slipping into one of those what-might-have-beens, just like her leave of absence.

"He's fine."

"How do you know?"

"What's with the questions? I told you I'd have him call you."

"Can you call him?"

"Why would I be able to call him if you and your mother can't?"

Good question. Julie's mind was beginning to go places it shouldn't. Tony's body floating in a vast ocean, bleeding in an alley where he'd been attacked trying to save a stray dog . . . or boy. Her uncle, turned to crime to keep his bar afloat.

Maybe she was being overly alarmist—chalk that one up to her mother. Julie had also inherited her curly blond hair and dimpled knees. You couldn't choose your genetics.

He was probably just on the lam, looking for bigger waves than those found at his own beach. Maybe some things never changed and he still came and went at will, not bothering to tell his staff, just like he had when he'd lived with Julie and her mom.

"You really and truly don't know where he is? And you aren't worried?"

The bartender shot her a grin that was dazzling. "Nope."

He put the glass he'd been polishing this whole time on the counter before her. It didn't look any cleaner than when he'd started.

He reached into the bar fridge and brought out a bottle of white.

More thumping from behind the bar.

"Pinot grigio, safest bar wine there is. It will usually err on the side of no taste than bad taste." He poured a tiny amount into the glass, nodded at it, and raised his eyebrows at her.

He wanted her to taste it? What was he going to do, pour it back into the bottle if she didn't like it? The situation was getting more ridiculous by the minute.

He nodded again, ludicrously attentive.

She took a minuscule sip just to move things along. "It's good," she blurted out.

"Told you." He filled her glass.

Thump. Thump. Thump.

"What's that knocking?" Julie stretched to see behind the bar.

"Huh? Oh, it's just Dougie. Dougie, go introduce yourself to the lady."

There was groaning and snuffling and the sound of someone or something getting to his feet.

Julie lifted her own feet off the ground. Dougie could be anything from a barboy to a boa constrictor.

A huge, shaggy head with a lolling tongue and slobber hanging from substantial jaws appeared around the edge of the bar, followed by what must have been a shedding nightmare of fur.

Julie considered climbing onto the bar top.

Dougie lumbered toward her, stopped at the stool, and snuffled her knee, leaving a wet, gooey trail of doggy drool on her thigh.

"You're not afraid of dogs, are you?" the bartender asked belatedly.

Julie forced a smile. "Not at all. I just—"

Dougie was looking for more interesting places on her person to snuffle; she tried to push him away. He just opened his jaws in a chasmic yawn and put his head in her lap, pinning her to the barstool.

"He likes you."

"Great," Julie said, trying not to move. "While we're doing introductions, what's your name?"

One eyebrow dipped. "Scatter," he said.

"What?" Her head automatically snapped toward the door in a primitive reflex of fight or flight—or one too many attack drills at school.

She laughed, dispelling that momentary reaction, only to have it followed by a flash of recognition. But it was probably a surfer handle like Hanger, Slick, Ace, or Moondoggie.

"What's on your driver's license?"

"Alex."

"Ah." She absently took a sip of her wine. It was certainly more sophisticated than its surroundings. "I guess Dougie is one of my uncle's strays?"

Dougie commented with a sound that would have been a bark if he could have worked up the energy to lift his head off her lap.

The bartender had taken out another glass, which he was giving desultory swipes with the bar cloth. But it stopped suddenly. His frown was fast, angry, and unexpected. "What do you mean by that?"

Had she just struck a nerve? "It's what my mother always said. Tony used to live with us and he was always bringing home stray animals, down-and-out surfer buddies, scruffy run-aways . . . all sorts of unsavory characters."

She'd definitely struck a nerve. Maybe Alex/Scatter was one of them.

"You're not drinking your wine."

"I didn't actually order it."

He picked it up, took a sip. Looked at it. "Not too bad. Light, dry, but with surprising body. Crisp with a hint of pear."

Julie rolled her eyes.

He finished it off and put the empty glass on the bar.

"Glad you enjoyed it," she said.

"I did. And I'm glad you didn't ask for white zin. I order the reds and whites, but I let the distributor decide on the pinks. If you ask me, pink drinkers don't know the difference."

He was definitely trying to piss her off, but he didn't know the resilience of a fourth-grade teacher. His attitude paled in comparison to eight hours of booger and butt jokes.

"Do you have an opinion on everything and everybody?"

"Pretty much. But I try not to show it."

"Ever consider trying harder?" She wouldn't learn anything from this guy, and she had begun to think he was purposely keeping her from her uncle.

Julie pushed the empty glass toward him. "Put it on my tab."

She eased Dougie's head away and slid off the stool. Then she extricated her purse from beneath Dougie's massive paws, trying to ignore the dirty prints marring its brand-new surface and making a note to self never to leave her purse on the floor while she was in town.

The bartender stopped, stared at her. "A tab?"

"Yeah, I'll settle up when I leave—after Tony returns and we've had a chance to visit."

She grinned at him. That should give him a few seconds of WTF.

"See ya." And willing herself not to brush at the slobber drying on her legs, she sashayed out of the bar.

"FYI," he called after her. "Around here, he's called Lucky."

$\mathcal{A}$lex watched Julie Barlow walk across the floor and out the screen door. Dougie padded after her but stopped as the door slammed in his path. He lolled his head back toward Alex.

Alex gave him a quick nod, and Dougie nosed the door open and padded outside.

Then Alex reached beneath the bar for his cell. Pressed speed dial. Walked to the door while he waited for an answer. Lucky's niece was standing in the parking lot, talking to her two friends.

"Get in the car," he urged under his breath. "Just take your friends and get out of here."

Dougie slowly snuffled his way down the steps and toward the three women.

Someone answered on the other end of the line.

"It's Scatter. We may have a problem."

Chapter 3

$\mathcal{M}$arie Simmons ended the call and sat down at her kitchen table trying to assimilate this new information into her already overloaded mind. Julie Barlow had come to visit her uncle, which would be wonderful if it wasn't the worst possible time for her to finally show up.

Lucky had hoped for a reconciliation for years, though he would never say so. He was hurt, Marie could tell, though he never mentioned it and she would never ask. He'd just give her some brush-off, like "Julie will figure it out." Sure, Marie thought. Someday . . . maybe, when it was too late to matter. He might never know why she'd stopped confiding in him or communicating with him at all.

Marie thought she knew. She even sympathized. Lucky had always been a free spirit, even as a child. A citizen of the world, not someone you could pin down and own. Marie had learned that early on, but Louise never had, and evidently neither had her daughter.

Lucky was who he was and would be until the day he died.

Marie quickly crossed herself. She was no longer a practicing Catholic, but she was still superstitious. She'd honed that superstition at the feet of her mother and grandmother on the boardwalk at Asbury Park.

And Marie had a bad feeling. Her nerves were raw.

Not good, she reminded herself. Nerves were the first things to betray you. She took a deep breath, held it, let it out.

Lucky had been gone for four days. No communications, as they'd agreed, but she could sense that something had gone wrong. How wrong, she couldn't tell.

She reached for her coffee cup, ignoring the deck of cards stacked beside it. The coffee had grown cold. She put down the cup, and with a sweep of her hand, she spread out the cards.

But she wouldn't turn them over, not yet. She was afraid of what they might tell her.

*J*ulie met Kayla and Aggie coming from the surf shop. "Any luck?"

"Not really," Aggie said. "The best we could get was that he should be back any day and to go check at the bar."

"We did get a few weird looks," Kayla added. "You'd think they'd be used to seeing tourists."

"I'm beginning to think it's because we know Uncle *Tony,*" Julie said.

"I guess it was a dead end with the bartender?" Aggie said.

"Big time. I can't remember meeting someone that clueless and obnoxious."

"Who's your friend?" Kayla asked at the same time something bumped against Julie's leg.

Julie looked down. "It's Dougie, the slobbering bar dog."

Dougie rubbed his matted ear against her thigh.

Julie edged away. "You probably have fleas, and your bartender friend is a pain in my butt."

"He needs a haircut," Kayla said.

"He needs a total makeover," Julie said.

"What?"

"Oh, you mean Dougie."

"He's friendly," Aggie said, and bent down to scratch his ears. Dougie backed away.

Aggie stood. "I guess he's a one-woman dog."

Oh, great, Julie thought. Now *she* was picking up strays.

If Alex/Scatter had just answered her questions, they would be on their way by now. Back on schedule. Sans her new man's best friend.

She wasn't really concerned about Uncle Tony. He'd show up eventually—he always did.

Julie had planned the ten days meticulously, at first leaving time to make plans about what to do with her leave of absence and then, when that fell through, leaving as little time as possible so that she wouldn't get depressed about going back in the fall.

She'd set up the hotel reservation and had lists of great places to eat, nightspots, and music venues for the next ten days. Keeping busy would prevent her from lying on the beach nursing her disappointment. She knew it would go away. It always did, and she'd soon be back on the path to a "responsible life with a secure future." Something her mother had groomed her for since the year her father died.

Julie shook herself.

Dougie did the same, and Julie wiped her arm on her T-shirt. "At least *I* don't slobber," she told him.

"Don't look now," Kayla said, "but the bartender is on the porch and watching us."

Julie forced herself not to look. Aggie didn't bother. She smiled, wiggled her fingers at him. Laughed. "That got rid of him. Too bad he's such a grouch. He definitely has vacation potential."

"I'm not sure he's safe," Julie said. "Do you mind if I check out the town for a few minutes? Someone must know where Tony lives. Then we can leave him a note and be on our way."

Simultaneously they all looked back at the bar, and Julie knew they were all thinking the same thing. She didn't want to imagine her uncle camped out in a back room with a sleeping bag, though she was pretty sure it wouldn't bother him at all.

It's what happens when you don't plan for your future—her mother's words, uttered years ago when Julie had asked her why Uncle Lucky didn't have his own house and wife and little girl.

Julie and her mother had planned for Julie's future. It had all gone according to plan, so why couldn't Julie be content? Maybe she was more like her uncle than she wanted to believe.

"Why don't we all go?" Kayla said. "We can split up and reconnoiter in time for lunch."

"It's way past lunch," Aggie pointed out.

"Early dinner," Kayla said. "Let's go."

They started across the parking lot toward town, the sun beating down on their backs and Dougie doing his best to trip Julie up along the way.

When they reached the street, they split up, and Julie turned left along the row of colorful storefronts.

The first store, La Mer—a boutique that sold women's fashion, none of which looked very beach appropriate—had a CLOSED FOR LUNCH sign on the door.

Next to it, the Knitting Knoll was open. Julie stepped inside. The store was unevenly lit, and yarn was stacked seemingly at random without regard to color or content.

A squat, high-shouldered woman with dark hair curled in a tight perm sat behind a counter covered with baskets overflowing with skeins of yarn.

"Can I help you find something?" The woman crossed her arms as if daring Julie to mention that it would be nearly impossible to make a color choice in the stingy light.

"Thank you, but I'm looking for Tony Costa. I was told he lived in town, but I don't have his address. I was hoping you might know him."

"Tony Costa." The woman huffed. "Don't talk to me about Tony Costa. Lucky, my foot. Nothing but trouble if you ask me."

Julie didn't ask, just thanked the woman and hurried outside. Dougie was waiting. Ignoring him, she took a second to regroup and saw Aggie going into a store across the street. She wasn't having any more luck than Julie.

The next store, Claire's Beachables, was a white-shingled

cottage trimmed in sky blue. Julie opened the front door, setting off a tinkle of seashells strung above her head. Claire's was bright and filled with an overwhelming array of beachwear, beach chairs, beach Christmas ornaments, books, jewelry, even little nylon bags of sand with LUCKY'S BEACH printed on them.

As Julie stood taking it all in, a heavyset woman wearing a voluminous colorful muumuu came from the back, wiping her mouth with a paper napkin. She had a round face topped by a nimbus of fine curly red hair. "Sorry, just grabbing a quick bite during the lull. How can I help you?"

"I . . ."

It occurred to Julie that she might have more success if she bought something. She pulled a couple of postcards from a display carousel. Did people even send real postcards anymore?

"Just these."

The saleswoman tilted her head, took the cards, and carried them to the glass counter.

"Actually, I'm looking for someone."

The woman's hand froze on the cash register key. She looked up with a friendly, but assessing, smile.

Julie hurried on. "I believe he lives in town. Well, I know he does. He owns Lucky's Bar out by the beach." Receiving no answer, she added, "He's my uncle."

"You're Julie?" The woman came out from behind the counter. "I'm Claire. Claire Doyle." She clasped Julie's hand in her soft fingers. "Don't look so surprised. Lucky's always talking about you and your mother—Louise, isn't it?"

Julie nodded. "You're friends with my uncle?"

"Oh Lord, yes, me and half the town." She chuckled. "The other half doesn't count."

"Oh good, I was worried."

"You stopped at the Knitting Knoll first, didn't you?"

"It was on my way."

"Stella Killready. A fitting name if ever there was one. Pay her no mind. She's always upset about something. Every town has one," she added cheerfully.

"Can you tell me where I can find him? I went to the bar, but the bartender said he was out of town."

"Is he?" She tapped her chin with a beringed finger. "Come to think of it, I haven't seen him this week. Well, that is a shame. Did you come here to visit him?"

"Oh, no, I'm on vacation with my friends and we thought we'd just stop and say hello, but I don't have his address . . . for some reason." Maybe because she'd never had it.

"Didn't Scatter give it to you?"

"The bartender? No. He wasn't very friendly."

"Really." Claire glanced toward the front door. It was a strange thing to do since no one had entered. "Never mind Scatter. That's just his way. I guess since you're Lucky's niece . . ." She hesitated. "He lives in a cottage on Dune Lane."

At last, thought Julie. "Great. Is it nearby?"

"A few minutes' walk. Turn left out of the store, past Marzetta's—she's our local fortune teller—past the hotel, and you'll come to Dune Lane. Turn left and go along the side of the hotel, then"—she closed her eyes—"one, two . . . the third, no, the fourth house on the left. Yellow shutters. Green door."

"Thank you so much." Julie quickly paid for her postcards.

"Lucky will be sorry to have missed you," Claire called as the door closed behind her.

Success at last, Julie thought, and nearly tripped over Dougie lying across the sidewalk. He clambered to his feet in slow motion.

"Are you still following me?"

Dougie lolled his tongue and shook his head. Flying slobber ensued.

Julie stepped back to avoid the spray. "That's an unfortunate habit you have."

Julie narrowed her eyes. Did Dougie just smile at her? Did dogs smile?

"You can go home now."

She looked across the street, but not seeing Aggie, she decided to go to Lucky's on her own.

She turned left and headed down the sidewalk, studiously ignoring the dog, under the theory that if she didn't encourage him, he would lose interest and go back to the bar.

She passed the psychedelically painted Madame Marzetta's Psychic Readings. Thank goodness for Claire, or she might have been tempted to go in and ask for advice from the fortune teller.

She smiled at the idea. Her mother would not be amused.

The hotel was a simple, shingled building that rose three stories and had to be a hundred years old. There was no one sitting on the four rockers on the front porch.

At the corner, she found the sign for Dune Lane and hooked

another left. She cut a quick sideways glance behind her. Yep, Dougie was still there. But he was moving slower, tongue hanging out.

It must really be hot beneath all that fur. It was uncomfortably hot for Julie in shorts and a tee. You'd think they would have gotten him a summer cut, though from the bartender's attitude, she wasn't surprised that he hadn't thought of the dog's comfort.

Dune Lane was narrow, too narrow to drive down; there were no cars in sight. The street, paved but not curbed, was lined with rows of semi-identical beach cottages, like the ones they'd seen on their way into town.

They were painted white or in pastel beach colors. Some of the postage-stamp-sized front yards were planted with grass. But most were covered with either white stones or a combination of sand and weeds.

The third cottage on the left was surrounded by a white picket fence holding back a thriving perennial border of brightly colored blooms and luxuriant greens, which gave privacy to a small grassy lawn and the cheerfully painted cottage.

Pink hibiscus, purple amaranth, and zinnias of all colors nodded above the pickets; trumpet vines trailed up the sides; and blue periwinkles peeked out from the ground. Julie stopped just to admire it.

A stone walk led up to the front door, which, as far as she could tell through the blossoms, was painted white.

Number four had yellow shutters and a green door and was a serious contrast to its neighbor. It did have a picket fence, but it only extended across the front of the yard, yielding at each side to a chain link around the rest of the perimeter. An eyesore at best.

Julie tested the gate, then pushed it inward. Dougie preceded her inside, knocking her off-balance. By the time she recovered, he had lumbered up the three front steps to the porch and was sitting by the front door.

Julie followed more slowly. When she reached the door, she gave a perfunctory knock. Waited. Heard nothing from inside.

"Well, Dougie?"

Dougie's answer was unintelligible.

She walked over to one of the two front windows, cupped her hands, and peered inside. Curtains blocked most of her view, but she saw a swath of faded patchwork quilt that she recognized. It had once been red, blue, and kelly green. Her mother had one just like it, but in pastels of lavender, pink, and yellow. Her grandma had made one for each of her children.

Her mother's quilt had gone into a chest in the attic years before and probably still held its original hues. The fact that Lucky had kept his all this time, still used it and slept beneath it, was poignant and, somehow, sad.

She stepped away, and tripped over Dougie, who was now stretched out in the shade of the porch eave. She peered in the second window. Living room: an overstuffed, sagging couch; several chairs crammed together in order to fit in the space; a desk shoved into one corner; a file cabinet; and a work lamp. It was hard to see anything else.

There was a mailbox hanging next to the door. She looked

back to the street, and since no one seemed to be about, she opened the flap and looked inside. Empty. She dropped the flap, thought, *What the hell,* and tried the doorknob.

It was locked.

She went down the front steps to the yard and walked around the side of the house. Had to stand on tiptoe to see in the side window. Didn't see much.

At the back fence, a mesh gate opened onto an alley that ran behind the cottages. And if she wasn't mistaken, she was standing across from the rear of Lucky's Beach Bar and Grill, with a dumpster, big trash cans, several small outbuildings, and wooden stairs leading to an upper story all screaming fire hazard.

But convenient for Lucky.

There was a small stoop at the back of the cottage, and she could see the kitchen table through the window and a stack of unopened mail on the counter. Someone had been bringing in the mail while he was away.

She retraced her steps to the front of the house, where she scribbled a note: *Sorry we missed you. Please call Mom. She's worried about you. Julie.* She tore it off the notepad she always carried and slipped it into the mailbox.

"Come on, dawg. It's time for you to belly up to the bar."

Dougie rolled his head.

"Come on, you can't stay here. I can't leave the gate open." Julie nudged him with her toe. "Dougie, please."

Dougie rolled over onto his back, feet up.

Julie sighed. "That's a very unprotected position. It's a good thing I'm a dog lover." Actually, she'd never had a dog. Tony had brought plenty of them home, but they'd always stayed outside in the garage. Her mother thought they were untrained and possibly dangerous. And Julie had to admit that the ones Tony brought home were, at best, extremely dirty. But sometimes he'd take Julie out to visit with them . . .

She braced her hands on her knees and leaned over Dougie. "I bet that Scatter dude has a nice bowl of water for you. Maybe even a bone."

No reaction.

"I'm leaving." She stomped down the porch steps, looked back.

Dougie merely turned his head to watch her.

She continued to the gate and caught sight of a woman's head over the hibiscus next door. The woman saw Julie and came across the lawn to the fence. "Can I help you?"

"Actually, yes. I'm looking for Tony—Lucky—but he doesn't seem to be at home."

The woman's eyebrows lifted. They were dark, though her hair, cut short around her face, was pale blond, almost white. She was wearing a navy linen dress and carrying a wicker basket and a pair of pruning sheers.

"I believe he's out of town."

Her voice was cool, and her linen dress was unwrinkled in odd contrast to the pervasive heat. Definitely not gardening togs; perhaps she'd come out only to cut a few flowers for inside—or to spy on whoever was poking around Lucky's cottage.

She tilted her head, obviously studying Julie while waiting for her to formulate an excuse for trespassing.

"I don't normally help myself into someone else's yard. I just wanted to leave him a note, and now I can't get this stupid dog to leave."

"Dougie," the woman said in the same cool voice and only a smidgen louder.

Without hesitation, Dougie hauled to his feet and padded down the porch steps, across the yard, and out to the lane.

Julie hurried after him and closed the gate. She caught up with him as he was about to enter the neighbor's garden.

But the gardener was already waiting for him.

"He's Lucky's dog," the woman said, by way of explanation.

"I was pretty sure he was."

The gardener broke into an amused smile. "Lucky will be sorry he missed you. You look like him. Though more like Louise. She got the delicate features of that family." She smiled slightly. "You definitely inherited Lucky's curiosity."

Julie blushed, not that anyone could tell, since she was already flushed with heat. "You know who I am?"

The woman looked surprised. "It's pretty obvious. Julie, right?"

"How did you—? Did the bartender at Lucky's call you and tell you to watch out for me?"

The woman raised her dark—and expressive, Julie noted—eyebrows. "Scatter is someone who minds his own business."

Not exactly an answer to her question, Julie thought, but she brushed her suspicions aside; she was beginning to see conspiracy everywhere, and both Claire Doyle and this woman seemed perfectly friendly.

"I don't suppose *you* know where he is, so I can call my mother, tell her not to worry, and get on with my vacation . . . not here."

The slightest, almost imperceptible tightening of the woman's full lips. A smile or show of concern?

"*Is* there something to worry about? Do you know him well?" Julie asked.

"Hang on for a second and I'll walk you back to the street."

She turned and Frisbee-tossed the basket to the porch, a good ten feet away. She sent the secateurs after it in a gesture that reminded Julie of a knife thrower at a carnival, and just as accurate. The pruning shears landed neatly in the basket.

The woman had already turned back to Julie, either knowing or not caring about the outcome. She headed toward Main Street, Dougie falling in step beside her—Julie could hardly call it heeling—until he finally ceded the pavement to her and wandered to the side of the street to lift his leg.

"Marie Simmons," the woman said as they reached the corner. "Tell Louise Lucky is fine. Now your duty is done and you can go enjoy your vacation."

That stung. It made Julie sound like she didn't care about her uncle. Maybe that's what everyone here thought. But that wasn't true. Not exactly. "Where is he? Have you talked to him? If you know my mother, you know she won't be content without hearing his voice."

Marie chuckled. "Sounds just like Louise. Some things never change."

"How do you know them?"

"We grew up in the same neighborhood in Asbury Park. We were pretty close as children. And Louise was just as over-protective then as she is now."

Julie bristled, but she knew it was true. Julie still sometimes chafed under her mother's all-encompassing care.

"Tell Louise not to worry. He had some business meetings. He's probably in one of those big conference rooms where there's no decent reception. Those places are often dead zones. Lots of dead zones around men in groups, if you know what I mean."

Julie guffawed and slapped her hand over her mouth.

"Or his phone died. You know how men are."

Actually, the men Julie knew would never let their phones die. Their business or their students might depend on getting through to them.

They'd stopped at the corner when Julie noticed that beneath her crisp linen dress Marie was wearing fuzzy house shoes.

Marie looked down the street and huffed out a sigh. "Not again. Excuse me, there seems to be a slight altercation ahead."

She abruptly strode off down the sidewalk toward the knitting store. Dougie took off after Marie, and Julie, left by herself, followed. As they passed the front of the hotel, three men who had been rocking on the front porch stood and moseyed down the steps to join them. Corey, Ike, and Ron from the bar. They did seem to get around.

Two preteen boys sprinted across the street, passing Aggie as she made her way toward Julie.

A thin young woman in short shorts and a tank top stood next to an overturned sandwich board sign, yelling at Stella

Killready, who was shaking a broom at the retreating boys. "Leave them alone, they weren't doing nothing!"

The older woman turned the broom on the younger one. "Don't you tell me they weren't doing nothing. They're a menace to all of us. So don't you go sticking up for them. You're on thin ice as it is."

"Me?" The young woman jutted her face closer until she was nose to nose with the broom wielder—though she had to lean over to accomplish it. "Thin ice? I can walk on water, you old bag, so don't mess with me or you'll—"

"CeeJay!" Marie barked, moving in on the two women and expediently defusing the situation by slicing her arms between them and parting them like Moses and the Red Sea.

Julie stayed a safe distance away, but Corey, Ike, and Ron formed a semicircle around the combatants. They didn't interfere, seeming perfectly content to let Marie handle the situation.

The old woman staggered, and Marie caught her by the arm and righted her without missing a beat. Her other hand had managed to grab CeeJay's scrawny arm and was holding her in place.

And Julie got a ridiculous image of a boxing match with Marie Simmons as the referee.

Both of her captives began yelling at once.

"She tried to hit them," CeeJay said, straining toward Stella.

"They're taking over the whole town. Any more and people will be afraid to come here shopping, much less stay overnight. Look at the streets, they're damn near empty. How are we supposed to make a living?"

"It's a sweltering midafternoon," Marie said calmly. "People are either at the beach or napping inside. I imagine traffic will pick up later in the day. Same as every day, Stella."

"All I know is that it isn't safe on the street with those—those no good—"

CeeJay lifted her fist, careful, Julie noticed, of her purple polished nails. "They weren't doing nothing."

"They were stealing my sign. Those kids are robbing me blind."

"No, they weren't. They were playing and tripped over your stupid sign, because it was in the middle of the sidewalk where it shouldn't be."

Finally Corey of Corey's Electronics piped in. "CeeJay. Aren't you gonna be late for work?"

"Aw, shit." CeeJay shot a parting glare at Stella, then ran off down the street.

Stella turned to the others. "First of all, Mayor Atkins shoulda never let Tony Costa talk him into adopting those two boys. Nothing good ever comes out of the system."

Julie's ears pricked up.

"And second of all, letting that CeeJay babysit every child in town is setting a bad example."

"Aw, Stella," Corey said. "That was the mayor and his wife's idea; they'd been trying to adopt for years. Lucky just facilitated them getting through the paperwork."

"Well, he's responsible for all that riffraff down on the beach."

"You talking about us?" said twice-retired Ron. "We just

enjoy having a postprandial beer at Lucky's; doesn't mean we're riffraff."

"You know full well I wasn't talking about you."

Ike, who had so far been silent, gave her a playful nudge. "Come on, Stella. They're just kids. They weren't doing any harm, nothing more than we all used to do on a hot summer day. Remember?"

"You're a fool, Ike Gibson. They're just the beginning. Pretty soon we'll be overrun with 'em. They'll scare all our customers away. I've seen it before."

They had begun to attract attention. Two women coming out of Claire's Beachables saw the altercation and hurried off in the opposite direction. Claire, who had accompanied them to the door, sighed and went back inside.

"You're the one scaring people away, Stella," Ron said. "You've been listening to those conspiracy people again. There are no gangs marching into Delaware. There's nothing to be afraid of."

"Except getting old and helpless," said Marie, who Julie noticed had left the confrontation as soon as the others joined it. "She's picking on the kids because they can't fight back. Unfortunately, when people get afraid of whatever it is they're afraid of, they get angry."

Dougie bumped Marie's leg.

"Not you, Dougie." She scratched the matted hair under his neck. "Dougie here was starved, infested with fleas and open sores, and left on the side of the road to die. But he never lashed out, never tried to bite the hand that was trying to help, didn't even growl when Lucky and Scatter struggled to get him in the back of the truck. Did you, Doug? He was too far gone to even be afraid." She raised her eyebrows at Julie. "Which one is worse, do you think? Anger or fear?"

Julie looked at her in surprise. "I . . . I don't know. Anger, I guess."

"Really? Interesting."

The fight was over. Corey righted the sandwich board sign and placed it nearer to the curb, and the three men saw Stella back inside the knitting shop.

"What was that all about?" Aggie said, coming up to Julie.

"Some kids knocked over her sign. Oh, here comes Kayla."

"Any luck?" Kayla asked as soon as she reached them.

Aggie shook her head.

"Well," Julie said, "I found his house and met his neighbor. This is Marie Simmons. She's a childhood friend of Lucky and Mom from when they lived in Asbury Park in New Jersey."

"Lovely to meet you both," said Marie. "I'm sure you're anxious to get to Dewey Beach. Rush hour has already started. Tell Louise that things are fine and Lucky will call her as soon as he returns." She smiled and turned to walk toward the opposite end of town.

Julie exchanged looks with Kayla and Aggie.

"That was abrupt," Kayla said.

"Is she wearing house shoes?" Aggie asked. "That's weird."

Julie nodded. "But what's really weird is . . . how did she know we were going to Dewey Beach?"

Chapter 4

"You didn't tell her about Dewey Beach?" Kayla said.

"No," Julie said, watching Marie Simmons's retreating form. An ordinary woman would have looked silly walking down Main Street in a dress and furry house slippers, but not Marie. She looked like a woman on a mission.

"Did you tell anyone else?"

Julie thought back. "No . . . just the bartender."

"Maybe he called her," Aggie said, then frowned. "But why would he do that?"

"Maybe he knew I wouldn't give up and he warned her to be on the lookout. She lives right next door."

"But why would it matter?" asked Aggie. "Why wouldn't they want you to find Lucky or his house?"

"The same thing I've been wondering since we got here."

"I don't get it," Kayla persisted. "Somebody has to know where he is. It's like the whole town is conspiring to keep us from finding him."

"Maybe he told them he doesn't want to have anything to do with me." Julie supposed he had every right. She'd pretty much cut him off without an explanation.

She hadn't meant for it to be so final. Had she?

"I'm sure that's not true," Aggie said. "He was always there for us."

Not always, thought Julie. And a memory came back to hit her hard in the face. The first time he'd let her down. She was eight and she'd run down to the basement to remind him of the father-daughter square dance that night only to find his gear—and Uncle Lucky—gone.

His red bandanna, one of two her mother had bought them special for the occasion, made it all the worse, and she crumpled it in her hand. She would have torn it to pieces if she'd had the strength. She dropped it on the floor and ran upstairs to her room.

Her mother waylaid her on the stairs. "I'll go with you."

"I'm not going."

"He couldn't help it."

"It doesn't matter."

She did go to the square dance. Aggie's and Kayla's fathers stepped in to save the day. Fathers did that, Julie guessed. Friends did that. Uncles didn't.

Although her friends' fathers tried to fill the void left by Lucky, she'd hardly danced at all that night. She couldn't dance, couldn't remember the steps, even though they'd been practicing them in music class. She was using all her concentration to keep the tears at bay.

It had been the first of many disappointments.

"Julie?"

Julie started. "What?"

Kayla was looking at her with concern. "What do you want to do now?"

"I don't know. Maybe I should try harder."

"Because you're worried about him?"

"Not really. It's like him to come and go at will. Mom's been worrying about him for as long as I can remember, and nothing has happened to him yet. Maybe we should just forget it and go on to Dewey. I just don't want her to have to cut her first-ever sort-of vacation short because he's inconsiderate."

"And she will," Aggie said. "You want to keep trying?"

Lucky may have been a rolling stone, and he may have been *indiscriminate*—her mother's word—with his friends and protégés, but he was *a good man at heart.* Also her mother's words.

Julie shook her head. "I don't know. Maybe I should come back, but I don't want you guys to miss another day of vacation. What would we learn that we don't already know? But if I don't, what do I say to Mom? I promised I'd call her tonight."

Kayla frowned. "What's going on with you? You never have trouble making decisions. You must have apologized to us ten times today for taking this detour. If you're that worried about Uncle Lucky, we'll drive back tomorrow and canvass the town until we find someone who'll talk."

"I—I just—" Julie bit her lip. *Just what?* Wanted everything to work out like she'd envisioned and it hadn't. She ended with a shrug.

"Maybe we should discuss this over a drink," said Kayla.

"Or dinner," said Aggie. "It's getting late."

"Okay," Julie said, "but first let's take Dougie back to the bar, and I'll call the motel and tell them we're going to be late. Then dinner's on me."

$\mathcal{M}$arie Simmons made it halfway down the next block before she realized she'd left the cottage wearing house shoes and without her purse. She'd panicked. She'd seen Julie Barlow peering in Lucky's windows and she'd panicked.

Marie picked up her pace. They'd just have to put up with her house shoes. If she went back home to change, she'd be late. As it was she would be early, and the last thing she wanted was time on her hands.

She strode forward, trying not to worry about Lucky's niece showing up unannounced.

She hesitated in front of Darinda's Luncheonette, peered in the window. It was closed for the day, but she could see Darinda and her three boys scrubbing the counters and booths. They worked hard, and if the diner cuisine was a little heavy on the curry, no one had complained yet.

Darinda looked up, waved, said something to her eldest, Vihaan. He turned his mop over to one of his younger brothers and disappeared into the kitchen. Darinda hurried over to unlock the door.

"He just has to take out the trash and he'll be right with you. Would you like a cup of tea while you wait?"

"No thanks, but I will sit down."

"Please." Darinda hurried away.

Marie slid into the closest booth where she could watch the sidewalk. Tried to steady her nerves. *Face it,* she told herself. *You're getting soft.*

Well, that was what retirement was about, wasn't it? Living a schedule-free life, enjoying the peace and quiet of the shore, and sliding gracefully into old age.

Ha. The reappearance of Tony "Lucky" Costa had put paid to that. He'd needed a favor that she was in a position to give. He'd showed up and he never left.

And in the ten years that had passed, this little corner of the beach had become Lucky's Beach. Actually, he had swept into town, and the locals, most of them anyway, had collected to him like iron shavings to a magnet. A bunch of retirees with time on their hands, teenagers with too much energy on their hands, the lost, the found, the clueless—it didn't matter to Lucky.

Then one June, Les arrived. Scatter came a few months later. Others began to spend their summers here, even though the surfing was middling.

It wasn't about the waves or the surfing.

There was something magic about Lucky, though he'd laugh himself silly to hear her say so. She'd recognized that the first summer they'd met, when he'd sneaked into her family's stall on the boardwalk and motioned for her to meet him outside.

"I'm a surfer," he said as soon as they were well away from

the stall. "Is it true what they said about your mama? Can she really know the future?"

"So can I." Marie had read his cards that night, sitting cross-legged on the sand in the moonlight. They'd been ten. And she knew then that their fate was sealed.

They became inseparable—the three of them, because though Louise didn't approve of Marie, she was already the self-designated guardian of her brother. And consequently jealous of Marie and afraid that she would steal him away like a baby in the night.

The only time he was ever free was when he was riding the waves—Louise was afraid of sharks—or when he'd sneak out after everyone was in bed and he and Marie would spend hours talking on the beach.

Marie's family didn't like him. *Beach bum,* they called him. *He'll never amount to anything,* said the people who worked from a derelict wooden storefront on a beach that had seen better days and clientele.

It was a total lie, of course. Tony Costa could do just about anything he set his mind to, except help the ones he cared for most.

Marie had been sitting in a diner booth just like this one when he'd left to follow the sun, the summer they were eighteen.

Louise had burst into the diner. "This is your fault!"

"Mine?" Marie said. "You're crazy." He'd left Marie, too, but she'd seen it coming for a long time, and she hadn't needed a crystal ball to understand.

Louise dropped into the opposite banquette. "How could he leave me?" she cried. "Surfing. He might as well have run off to join the circus."

Marie agreed. And if she didn't do something soon, she'd be stuck in the sideshow that was her future forever.

By the time Louise had finally calmed down enough to go home, Marie had made a decision. A few days later, with all her worldly goods stuffed into a backpack, she climbed out the window and joined the world.

She hadn't seen Tony or his sister for years after.

Marie had done her share of good in the years since. And some questionable things. Most days she thought the good outweighed the bad.

But there were others when she didn't know if she'd done any good at all, if she'd helped make the world a better place or a worse one.

That's why people have children, her good friend and colleague Alice would tell her. *So there will be a next generation to keep up the fight when we get too tired.*

Well, Marie was tired. She didn't want to think about fighting—not for justice, much less for the future.

That's why she was waiting for Vihaan. He was the next generation. And he also aspired to do more than work in the family luncheonette. Marie glanced back to where Darinda was folding towels to be laundered and wondered if she had any idea what was in her son's head. Or if he would ever be able to take that chance and leave the family business behind.

Vihaan burst through the kitchen door, slinging his backpack over his shoulder, and hurried over to meet Marie.

Darinda let them out, casting one quick glance at Marie. Marie smiled her reassurances. Vihaan's future would have to work itself out in time.

At the moment she had a problem much closer to home.

Julie, Aggie, and Kayla started down the sidewalk back toward the beach. Dougie plodded alongside Julie, his body knocking her off-balance with every other step.

"Wow, would you look at that?" Aggie said.

The parking lot had filled considerably in their absence. Kayla's SUV was still there, but now it was surrounded by other cars and motorcycles. The music was pumping. Julie could hear the buzz of conversations and laughter coming from the cabana at the beach side of the bar.

Dougie stood perfectly still, looking up at Julie.

"Yep, this is where you and I part company. It's been swell. You guys coming?"

"We'll wait here," Aggie said, perusing the beach.

Julie went up the steps and opened the door. Dougie shoved her aside and squeezed through ahead of her.

"Just like a man," Julie said.

"Ain't it the truth," said a buxom brunette wearing a lace beach cover-up and high heels. "I'm leaving that one"—she nodded toward a skinny guy laughing with his buddies at the bar—"to figure out the meaning of life. Before I make his shorter, if you know what I mean."

Julie was afraid she might.

The temperature had dropped by double-digit degrees. Lucky's was air-conditioned, at least during happy hour. And boy, was it happy. The din was close to deafening.

Dougie disappeared into the crowd, and Julie headed to the bar, dodging several barmaids carrying trays through the clusters of drinkers, only to be delayed when a longhaired man grabbed her around the waist and tried to steer her toward "my friends over there."

She smiled and peeled his arm off, stumbled over Dougie, who had made a miraculous, if somewhat clumsy, appearance, and fell headlong into another guy who at least had a soft paunch to land against.

"Pardon me, I'm so sorry," she said, rebounding off the man's stomach.

"Any time, pretty lady, any time. Buy you a drink?"

"Thanks, but no." She had to raise her voice to make herself heard.

She finally made it to the bar, where she managed to squeeze in between a man and a woman who were definitely on their way to something later.

"Sorry," Julie said at the top of her voice. "I'll just be a second."

There were now two men working the bar. One of them was Alex/Scatter. He saw her and, true to form, turned away.

"Alex!" she called. "Alex!" she tried again, only louder. "Alex!" Exasperated, she yelled, "Scatter!"

Two men at the end of the bar hit the floor. Several people ran for the exits.

Scatter turned around, his eyes rolled so far back in his head that only the whites showed. "Perhaps I should have warned you," he said. "You probably shouldn't yell my name in a crowd."

Julie opened her mouth, but words failed her.

At least the noise level had diminished somewhat, and the waitresses continued to move through the crowd as if nothing had happened.

"I could see where that might be a problem," she said. "Well, not to worry. I don't think I'll have occasion to use it again. I've done my duty. Tell Lucky to call his sister if he can rouse himself."

Her sarcasm was wasted on Scatterbrain.

"What?" he said cluelessly.

"Oh, nothing. I brought your dog back."

Dougie leaned against her, threatening them both with toppling over.

"Oh. You're leaving? Have a nice vacation."

"Sure. Thanks. Well, see ya . . . or not."

She looked down at the dog. He returned her look with big, lugubrious eyes and a particularly large string of slobber.

"Dougie."

She walked toward the door, turned back. Dougie's head drooped.

"Oh, what the hell, you stupid old dog. I know when I'm being conned." She walked back, squatted in front of him, and scratched the matted fur behind his ears. "See ya, Dougie." She stood up, wiping the slobber that she hadn't managed to avoid, and leaned over the bar. "You should really get this poor dog groomed."

She walked quickly away without waiting for an answer, feeling the oddest sense of wanting to burst into tears. Definitely time to get to the beach and away from all responsibilities, real, imagined, or left behind.

Aggie and Kayla were standing where she'd left them.

"That was quick."

"I just dropped off his dog. Actually, it's Lucky's dog." She reached in her bag and extracted her phone. "Let me just confirm with the motel we're coming in late, then let's eat."

Julie called the motel and was immediately put on hold.

They started walking back toward the street, and had almost reached the sidewalk, when a harried voice said, "Reservations."

"This is Julie Barlow and I'm calling—" She didn't even get to finish.

"You're on my list to call . . ."

Julie stopped. "What list?"

"What's happening?" Aggie mouthed.

Julie shook her head. Held up a finger. Listened. "But I booked that room three months ago."

Kayla lifted her hands in a what-gives gesture.

"Oh, don't worry, we will. And you'll call me as soon as you know? Fine." Julie ended the call. "They walked us."

"They can't take our room," Kayla said. "We're confirmed."

"Well, they did. They have a wedding party that needed

extra rooms and they've taken over the whole hotel. Ugh!" Julie dropped her head in her hand. "This is all my fault for making us late. And for nothing."

"Wow!" Aggie said.

"I know. I'm so sorry."

"No, I mean, who has a wedding at an economy motel?"

"My guess is a lot of people on a budget?"

"So do they have a plan?" asked Kayla.

"The usual. They're very sorry and are trying to book equivalent rooms elsewhere."

"But probably not near the beach," said Aggie.

"Well, they aren't exactly that close to the beach, either," Julie said.

"Maybe it's a sign," said Aggie.

"A sign that my uncle has managed to screw up our vacation without even being here. No, I take that back, I should have had you drop me off here and had you go on to the hotel."

"Oh, right, so you could be stuck here without Lucky." Kayla frowned. "And they might have walked us anyway."

"Maybe we could just stay here and send them the bill," Aggie suggested.

"Is there a hotel nearby?" Kayla asked.

"I saw one downtown," Julie said. "But it looks pretty old."

"It *is* a nice beach," Kayla said.

"And Surf's Up is having a special on surfing lessons," Aggie said. "Les told us when we went to ask about Lucky. I've always wanted to learn to surf."

"Since when?" Julie asked.

"Since she met Les." Kayla shrugged. "He is kinda cute. And very nice."

"Okay, let's go ask and then I'm taking you guys to dinner."

"Oh, come on, Jules, none of this is your fault. But we'll definitely have dinner and a few drinks, and you can tell us what's been eating you lately."

Julie smiled. Sort of. She wasn't ready to share. She wasn't even clear in her own mind—how could she explain it so it would make sense to her friends?

They had to move to the side when a red Jeep with a roll bar rumbled up behind them. And stopped.

"Les," Aggie said, so brightly that Julie expected her feet to leave the ground.

"Wow. You must be Julie," a man said from the driver's seat. He leaned over and shook her hand. "You and Lucky have the same hair, cool. I'm Les, owner of Surf's Up."

"Nice to meet you."

"You guys decided to stay?"

"We might have to," Aggie said. "We just got dumped from our room through the weekend in Dewey because of an overbooked wedding."

"Man, that sucks. You have a place to stay?"

Julie tensed. *Please do not offer us a place on your living room floor.*

"I can call over to the hotel and see if they have any vacancies." He grinned. "I have a deal rate with the owner."

"Sure, that would be great," said Aggie, before Julie could tell him thanks, but they were on their way there now.

He pulled out his phone, pressed speed dial. "Julie, yeah, Lucky's niece. Yeah, sure, but I've got that meeting." He smiled and held up one finger.

Two minutes later they had rooms at the Dunes Hotel.

"Wow, thanks," Julie said.

"Think nothing of it." He shifted into first, turned to Julie. "You surf?"

She shook her head.

"Lucky didn't teach you to surf? I can't believe it."

Les had obviously never met her mother.

"Come in tomorrow at ten, all three of you. I have a free slot for a lesson. I'll have some nice beginner boards all picked out." He saluted. "I'll have you riding those waves before Lucky even gets back."

"You know where he is?"

Les's mouth turned down. "Not a clue. See you tomorrow. I'd stay and buy you a drink, but I have a . . . someplace I need to be." He stepped on the gas and the Jeep took off.

"Let's go check out the hotel," Kayla said. "If we like it, we'll stay and call Louise tonight."

"And then get some dinner." Aggie clutched her already tan midriff. "I'm starving. This is gonna work out fine. And while we're doing your duty to Louise and Uncle Lucky, we can all lie out in the sun, do beach things, and party."

"Okay," Kayla said. "But no selfies with surfers in compromising positions. You don't want your photo plastered all over the internet for unsuspecting parents to see."

"Not to worry, we got this."

"Come on, Jules. Now you can relax and have some fun. And we'll be here when Lucky gets back. You deserve a little fun, sun, and who knows?"

"Yep," Julie said, and fell in step with her two friends.

Maybe losing the hotel *was* a sign. A time to trust her friends, reconnect with Lucky, and stop acting like not getting the leave of absence was the end of the world. She might even have time to look through the brochures of all the places she wouldn't be going to.

Chapter 5

The hotel was old like its exterior had promised. But the lobby held an old-timey beach charm, with white-painted wainscoting and wicker chairs with slightly faded floral cushions.

Henry Nix, the proprietor and manager, was waiting for them at the registration desk and hurried out to welcome them. He was well over six feet, youngish, hip, and enthusiastic.

"Welcome to the Dunes," he said, and pumped each of their hands. "So glad we could accommodate you."

"Thanks," Julie said. "Les explained what happened?"

"Yes, yes. Overbooking. The bane of the modern-day traveler. You won't find anything like that happening around here. We honor our commitments."

He looked at Julie as if his comment had been meant entirely for her. And she did feel that maybe she deserved it. *Okay,* she told herself, *I'll make amends . . . maybe.*

"I have three rooms on the third floor." His eyebrows dipped.

"They're not together, but it was the best I could do on short notice. They're in the back, so it's quiet. I hope that's okay."

"Yes, and we really appreciate it," Julie said at the same time Kayla asked, "How much are the rooms?"

"Whatever that other hotel compensates you."

"But we only had one room there," Kayla confessed. "Maybe . . ."

Henry's hands flew up. "Hey. Lucky's niece and friends. Least I could do."

"It's a deal," Julie said, thinking they'd have to come up with a way to compensate him for his help.

"And I'll throw in the last unmetered parking place in town. It's out back by the dumpster, but it's next to the service door, and if you're like most vacationers, you'll be glad not to have to carry all your stuff back and forth from the parking lot. It's two blocks away."

They signed for three rooms, retrieved the SUV from Lucky's parking lot, and drove the hundred feet to the alley at the back of the hotel. The SUV fit neatly into a spot between the dumpster and a vintage Chevrolet.

Henry was waiting by the open service door.

"Your car?" Julie guessed, indicating the Chevy.

"My dad's. He doesn't drive that much anymore."

They piled the bags, the coolers, and Henry into the elevator, which had creaked and moaned on its descent to the lobby, and decided to climb the stairs to the third floor.

Julie's room was spacious, with a double bed, a casement

window, and a wall air conditioner. She put her suitcase, purse, and laptop on the dresser while she checked for cleanliness, a habit that her mother had ingrained in her. *You never know who stayed here last.*

Other than the usual musty smell of beach hotels, it seemed fine. She went over to the air conditioner and turned it to high. It jumped and ground into gear, then settled into a rattling work mode. A few minutes later, cold air was pouring into the room. Her one window opened to what was—if she didn't look down—a partial view of the dunes and ocean in the distance. So ocean-view-ish. More than they would have had in their economy hotel.

If she *did* look down, which she did, the alley curved past the dumpster and Kayla's SUV and continued along a row of backyards. She pressed her nose to the window and peered as far down the alley as she could.

She was pretty sure she recognized the trash bins at Lucky's about halfway down the block. And the cottages across the street. Actually, if she sat here all weekend she might be able to see Tony's return.

Fortunately she felt no need to be so scrupulous. She wasn't the FBI, the local police, or even her mother.

Still, it might be nice to stay here and to see her uncle again.

That thought set off a flutter of nerves in her stomach. Why had they grown distant? Was it really because he hadn't come to her graduation and she'd stopped talking to him? It seemed silly now. But it wasn't just about his no-show; it was because he hadn't filled the void she thought he would fill.

She should have known better, even then. He would never be her father. But he could always be her uncle. Except she'd sort of wrecked that possibility herself.

She unzipped her bag and began hanging her clothes in the closet, and got a sharp memory of visiting her grandmother in Asbury Park. Her closet had also smelled slightly of cedar.

A phone rang. Julie jumped and looked around for the source. A red button was blinking on the room phone. She picked it up.

"Isn't it just the cutest?" Aggie said. "This phone. A cord. When was the last time you saw one of these?"

Julie thought they had them in the principal's office but she didn't mention it. "You guys ready?" she asked.

"Yep. Kayla is here and we're on our way to your room."

"Okay. See you in a few." Julie hung up, rummaged through the rest of her clothes, and quickly changed into capris and an off-the-shoulder sailor-striped tee.

She went into the bathroom, a larger-than-necessary space that must have been converted from another room or designed with hoopskirts in mind. A quick glance in the mirror told her that her makeup had faded and her hair had curled into corkscrews.

Well, hell, it was the beach. She grabbed her cosmetics case, slapped on some lipstick, and squeezed out a daub of Curl Stay. She'd just finished fingering it through her hair when there was a knock at the door.

A couple more scrunches and she went to answer it, wiping her palms on a hand towel and tossing it back toward the sink. She grabbed her purse from the dresser on her way out.

"So what do you think?" Aggie asked as they walked down the hall toward the staircase.

"Charming?" Julie guessed.

"And a whole lot cheaper than Dewey," Kayla added. "Three rooms for the price of one? Do you think there's a catch?"

Julie hoped not. "You okay with it, Aggie?"

"Sure, you know me . . . Where the boys are . . ."

Julie and Kayla laughed. Aggie was always making jokes about her dating status, though lately the jokes had had a ring of seriousness to them. Julie suspected that she was beginning to tire of her constant fun, fun, fun lifestyle and longed to settle down with Mr. Right. And her "Who needs kids at home when I face sixteen of someone else's every day?" was beginning to sound a little wistful.

Alex cut out the side door of the bar, nodding to several locals but not stopping to shoot the breeze. He had only a half hour for dinner, a few minutes of quiet and calm before he had to be back at the bar.

He walked out past the dining deck and between two storerooms and took the shortcut—a narrow, almost unrecognizable path over the dunes—to his current residence: a modern beach house. A house he could never have afforded to maintain, much less buy. It had been loaned to him by a grateful old man. Alex didn't deserve that kind of thanks. He'd never been a very good person. He'd been a terrible kid. Really terrible.

Seeing Julie Barlow today made him painfully aware of just

how bad. Not that anything he had done since meeting Lucky had been as bad as what happened before. Well, not much of it.

He paused at the crest of a dune, equidistant between the bar and his house, the music of the bar behind him and peace ahead. But first he checked his phone again. Another thing he could credit to Julie Barlow and her crazy mother. He hadn't been worried until she'd shown up. At least not much.

Lucky knew what he would be doing could be dangerous. Alex had offered to go instead of him. He had the skills, long buried but not forgotten, in case there was real trouble. But Lucky refused. Wouldn't even let him ride shotgun.

Alex had argued. This was bound to turn out to be more than a one-man operation. There were bound to be repercussions, serious ones.

And now Henry Nix had called to say that the niece was staying at the inn instead of going on to her scheduled vacation.

What the hell was he supposed to do about that? The girl was stubborn as ever and just as uppity. And still doing exactly what her mother told her to do. Julie Barlow should really grow up. Go off to her damn vacation and leave Lucky alone. It's not like she'd made any familial overtures to him in the last six years. She'd cut him off and then got on with her life as a suburban elementary school teacher, too busy to even bother to see if he was alive or dead.

Well, her spite was not his problem. Keeping her away from Lucky until this was over was.

If he only knew when Lucky would return.

Behind him the sun was hanging heavy in the sky; ahead of him the sea shimmered with reflected light. Alex gritted his teeth. They had a situation on their hands, and he was standing here like some moonstruck poet, pondering the landscape. Poet, he was not. The only things he read were the newspaper, the bar's accounts, and a never-ending stack of caseloads.

He checked his phone again. He knew nothing had come in but he checked anyway.

Alex shoved the phone back in his pocket and trudged over the rise of the dune and down the other side. Suddenly the din from the bar subsided, replaced by the breaking and rolling of the waves. Alex took a deep breath, and another, and went up the steps to the deck. But there, he hesitated.

He could see Rosie, his housekeeper, putting his dinner on the dining room table. He would have been happy to eat at the kitchen table while she worked, her rolling accent lifting him, calming him. Bringing him peace.

She'd taken care of Lucky's Beach Bar and Grill since it had been Sam's Beach Bar and Grill. When Lucky took over, she became indispensable to him. When Alex rolled into town a few years back, she started taking care of him. Now *she* needed *them*.

She saw him and motioned him to hurry inside.

He put on a smile of sorts and opened the door. The aroma of beef and peppers wafted around him.

His stomach growled, and he hurried to where she stood waiting to lift the top off a yellow earthenware dish.

"Sit down, sit down, you are late."

"Sorry."

"Hmm, sorry." She snapped a napkin at him. He caught the other end and put it in his lap, while she ladled rich, thick stew into his bowl. It could make a grown man cry, the way she spoiled them, going from one house to the other, helping at the bar. She was indefatigable. She was loyal. They could trust her with everything.

Alex, in his more pitiful moments, wished she had been his mother. He took a bite. "I must be in heaven."

She quickly crossed herself. "Heaven forbid. Eat. I will get you milk."

Alex ate another spoonful. She was going all out tonight. Not breaking into tears or prayers. Not asking if he'd heard anything. Just smiling and taking care of him. Like always. Keeping up a good front better than he was.

The waiting was getting to him. Like the old days, the very old days, but for entirely different reasons. And like the old days, the more time passed, the more agitated he felt. He tried not to show it. Tried to tamp down the sense of inevitability that this might be the thing that undid them all.

She returned with a big glass of cold milk. It was crazy; she'd been a part of his and Lucky's lives for so long now, she knew what made each of them happy. Milk. Something he never had enough of as a kid. Something he never thought of now except in times of stress. And suddenly there would be Rosie with a big glass of cold milk. Like tonight. Reminding him that things would be okay.

He hoped she was right.

He hoped to God they didn't fail her.

$\mathcal{T}$he Fish Fry," Henry said when Julie, Kayla, and Aggie stopped for dinner recommendations. "The food is good, plentiful, and it's where all the locals eat. Plus it's on the water. Great view. *And* a breeze!"

"Do we need reservations?" Julie asked.

"Nah," Henry said. "Turn right out of the hotel and walk toward the marina, then turn right to the water. You'll see the sign."

It would have been hard to miss. They had just turned at the marina when they saw THE FISH FRY in big neon yellow cursive across the entrance to a gabled and turreted Victorian house, painted in green, blue, purple, peach, and yellow and sandwiched in between the marina and the beach.

"This looks good," Aggie said, and picked up the pace. "Are those palm trees?"

Two artificial palms decorated with strings of colorful lights and inflatable parrots stood at either side of a wide set of steps that led up to the covered porch. There were several occupied tables on the porch, and the smell of grease hung in the air.

Kayla wrinkled her nose.

"He did say it was where all the locals ate," Aggie reminded her, and led them up the steps. "Yum, fried oysters," Aggie added, reading the chalked specials on the easel next to the hostess stand. Her eyes widened as a waitress passed by carrying a tray laden with platters piled high with every variety of fried food. "Girls, get out your antacids. I feel some mighty fine cuisine coming on."

They were led through a filled-to-capacity dining room, which must have been converted by combining the original parlor and dining room, and out an archway to a screened-in porch that looked over several narrow wharves and a handful of modest boats that made up the town's marina.

"Henry at the hotel said you were coming," the hostess told them. "So we saved you a good table."

It was a perfect table, set back in the far corner by the panorama windows with a view of the marina on one side and the ocean on the other. It was a clear night; stars were just beginning to sprinkle the sky, and a quarter moon hung low above the horizon.

"Henry must have a lot of clout," Kayla said. "The place is packed."

They ordered drinks—Island Sunsets, recommended by their waitress—and more food than they would ever eat. And Julie tried to settle into vacation mode.

Their drinks arrived, pink concoctions served in curved goblets with an orange slice and a paper umbrella sticking out the top. Kayla lifted her glass. "To a kid-free and unfettered vacation."

They toasted and drank. The combination of sugar, fruit, and alcohol was guaranteed to put Julie under the table if she didn't watch herself.

Kayla put down her glass, leaned on her elbows. "Okay, Jules, what gives?"

Julie lifted out the umbrella from her glass and put it on the table. "What do you mean?"

"What the heck's going on?" Aggie said. "You've been acting weird since school's been out."

"I know."

"Then what?" Kayla said. "What's wrong with you?"

Julie bit her lip. "It's nothing really."

"Jules? You're not acting like a girl on vacation. Are you that worried about Lucky?"

"Not really." She was, but that wasn't what she needed—wanted—to tell them. She knew she couldn't enjoy their time together if she was holding back something this important to her.

"So what is it?"

"Actually, there is something I've been meaning to tell you."

Aggie and Kayla leaned closer and Julie squirmed.

Aggie gasped. "Oh my God, you're pregnant."

"No-o-o-o. I'm not even seeing anyone."

"We noticed." Aggie let out a big whew. "That would have been awkward."

"Your mom?" Kayla asked tentatively.

"No, she's fine, thank God," Julie said. "Oh crap. I forgot to call her. She'll be frantic." She pulled out her phone, calculated the time difference. "I should call her now."

"What are you going to tell her?"

"I don't know, that no one seems worried and we've decided to stay a couple of days to see if he comes back? Does that sound plausible?"

"Tell her that it's cheaper than Dewey," Aggie said. "She'll understand that."

"Good idea," Julie said, and made the call. It went to voice mail. She left a message saying Lucky was out of town but expected back any day, and they had decided to stay and say hello.

"It's really great here and . . ." She didn't want to sound too happy; her mother would get suspicious. "And much cheaper," she added.

Kayla and Aggie nodded their approval from across the table.

"Love you. I'll call tomorrow." Julie ended the call just as a platter of fried calamari appeared on the table.

"Another round?" the waitress asked. They still had half-filled glasses, but they nodded. It was vacation, after all.

"Now what were you going to tell us?"

Caught off guard, Julie choked on her Island Sunset. "I just . . . just . . . remembered a bit of lunchroom gossip. Did you hear about Lenora Jenner?"

"Lenora?" Kayla asked. "The sixth-grade teacher? What about her?"

"I heard," Aggie said. "She's leaving teaching to go into business with her husband, selling some kind of herbal homemade candy."

"She's the one with the frizzy hair, isn't she?" Kayla asked.

Aggie and Julie nodded.

"She must be crazy to take a chance like that. I'm fairly certain homemade candy making doesn't offer a pension or decent retirement insurance."

Julie's mouth went dry. A leave of absence would have added

one measly year to her retirement requirements, but quitting outright would have been disastrous. What had she been thinking?

"Yeah, it's pretty wild," Aggie said. "Gail Richards didn't even take her full maternity leave, she was so afraid her sub would try to stay. Especially at Hillsdale. There has to be a waiting list of applications a mile long. We're lucky we were all hired."

"Maybe someone died and left them money," Julie said, feeling worse at each comment.

"It better be a lot. I can't believe she would desert her students for a crapshoot." Kayla cocked her head at Julie. "Wait. You've been worried about Lenora Jenner?"

"Uh, no. Not really. Just makes you think." It was certainly making Julie think.

Kayla and Aggie continued discussing Lenora's resignation, while Julie stared out into the dark marina.

She didn't want to desert her students or make candy; she just wanted to take a year to figure out how she could make a difference, be inspired, so she could come back to inspire her students.

Sure, that's why you still have your resignation letter sitting in a file on your computer.

And if her friends thought a teacher they barely knew was crazy to have quit her job, what would they think of her?

They left two hours later, filled with everything fried, along with coleslaw, pickles, and three rounds of Island Sunsets. They moseyed down the street back toward the hotel. Julie knew she should be having a good time, but between this Lucky detour and her job worries, not to mention those three rounds of Island Sunsets, her head was spinning.

And when Aggie and Kayla stopped at the beach parking lot entrance, Julie balked. "I'm going to bed."

"It's not even midnight. You can't spend your first night in Lucky's Beach without having a nightcap at Lucky's," Aggie complained.

"It's been a long day," Julie said. "And I don't want to take my first surfing lesson with a hangover. You guys go ahead."

"Okay, but tomorrow you better be ready to go the distance."

"You're on." Julie walked back to the hotel and went straight upstairs. The air conditioner was rattling away in her room. She'd turned it lower when she'd left for dinner; it was still doing its best to cool the room but was losing the battle. She immediately walked over and turned it up; the rattling got louder but at least the air got cooler.

She changed into shorty pajamas, brushed her teeth, and, barely able to keep her eyes open, crawled into bed. She yawned, pulled the coverlet up to her neck. And waited for sleep to overtake her.

And waited.

And waited.

Suddenly her exhausted mind was firing on all cylinders. Jobs, and uncles, and questions about her future tumbled over one another, clamoring for her attention. She turned over, hoping some of the worries would get buried underneath the others.

No such luck.

She heard Aggie and Kayla return to their rooms around one o'clock. By two, Julie had had enough and she was freezing. She pushed back the covers, padded across the room to turn off the air conditioner, and pushed open the window.

A refreshing ocean breeze wafted into her room. She could hear the waves in their rhythmic rush and recede. That was more like it. Soothing. She leaned her elbows on the sill and looked out into the night. Lucky's had closed and the alley behind it was dark. The rooftops of the houses on Dune Lane rose like black silhouettes against the night.

She pulled over the desk chair, sat down, and let herself be lulled by the waves. She began to nod and was about to sneak back to the comfort of her bed when a new sound brought her fully awake.

An engine below her window. Someone was returning late from a night on the town. The sound came nearer, but no headlights pointed the way. Odd.

She peered over the sill. A van, its headlights turned off, moved slowly past the hotel and continued down the alley. It slowed to a stop behind Lucky's Bar and right across from Lucky's cottage.

Could it be her uncle? What was he doing, driving without lights?

Julie leaned out the window to get a better look. But with only the sliver of moon and stars lighting the night, it was hard to tell exactly where the van had stopped.

The driver's door opened. At the same time, the back door to the bar opened and someone stepped out; a third person came out from one of the cottages.

What the hell were they doing? Traveling under the cover of darkness, no headlights. Conspirators waiting for the signal?

A man got out of the van. Julie squinted, trying to recognize some feature that would tell her it was Tony Costa. But it looked like an old man. He was bent over and hobbled toward the back of the van, holding the side for support. So not her uncle—someone else.

The old man waited for the other two to join him. The man from the bar—Julie was almost certain he was Lucky's bartender—stopped, said something. The old man shook his head and opened the side door. The bartender reached inside and pulled out a bundle covered in a tarp or blanket. It didn't look like a box or crate, but Julie couldn't be sure.

It must be some kind of contraband. Was he cheating her uncle while he was out of town? Was that why he'd been so unwilling to let her get in touch with Lucky?

The man carried his load, not back into the bar, but several feet to the far side, where he dumped whatever it was into the bushes. He hurried back to the van for a second load, this one larger and heavier than the last, and dumped it behind the bushes with the first. The old man closed the van door; the person who had come out from the cottage took his elbow and led him into one of the cottages. The bartender jumped into the van and drove it away.

Great, Tony. With friends like those . . .

In her rapt curiosity, Julie had hung really far out the window. Now she pushed herself back inside, keeping her eyes trained on the alley, waiting for someone to take the contraband from the bushes. But no one appeared. The van didn't return, nor did Alex/Scatter, if it was indeed him.

She waited for a good half hour until the sky began to lighten, but there was no further activity.

Julie finally moved from the window and crawled back into bed, only one question looping in her mind.

Had she, Kayla, and Aggie just wandered into something they shouldn't?

Chapter 6

The sun and the threat of another sweltering day coming through the open window roused Julie from a too-short sleep. She blinked several times. She felt achy and her eyes were gritty.

Morning. She groped for her phone and checked the time. Seven thirty. She'd gotten maybe three hours of sleep. She could go back to bed, or . . . Something was knocking at her foggy brain: the image of a van, no headlights . . . She bolted upright.

Had it been a dream? Just what had she witnessed last night in the alley?

She threw the sheet off and padded over to the window. Below her, the alley looked perfectly normal. But it hadn't been.

She pulled out a pair of shorts and a tee from her suitcase, put them on without a care for how they looked, slipped into sneakers. A quick stop in the bathroom and she shoved her room key in her pocket and went downstairs.

She hesitated in the lobby, then decided to go all the way back to the beach entrance rather than take the shortcut through the service door. She wanted to see just where that van had come from. And if it was parked in Lucky's parking lot this morning.

All the stores on Main Street were still closed and there was very little activity. There were several cars already parked at Surf's Up and a few others nearer the bar, probably left by people who were too drunk to drive or had hooked up during the evening. But no van.

The Jeep that had been parked at the side of the bar yesterday was still there, but the bar was closed.

She turned right into the alley, followed the curve past the back doors of La Mer, the Knitting Knoll, Claire's Beachables, and the fortune teller's; past the dumpster where Kayla's SUV was parked and the hotel's service door.

She continued until she was standing behind the bar, made a slow turn, and perused the ground.

Julie was almost positive this was where the van had stopped. And though she couldn't see the break in the bushes where the bartender had dumped the goods, she was pretty sure Marie Simmons's cottage was where the third person had led the old man.

Maybe her mother had been right all along, because it appeared that Lucky's current posse was up to no good.

She quickly looked around, just as the door of one of the shops opened and someone hurried out and down the alley in the opposite direction.

Nerves jumping, Julie quickly stepped into Tony's backyard. She climbed up the two steps to the stoop and peered into the kitchen. The pile of mail was still there. No one had been home to pick it up.

She searched the room for any other signs that her uncle had returned but found no shoes left on the floor by the door, no jacket slung over a chairback, no used glass sitting on the counter by the sink.

Hopefully that meant he wasn't involved in whatever nefarious activity the others were involved in. But Marie and the bartender certainly were. With Tony's knowledge or without?

Maybe she should just turn around and pretend like she hadn't seen anything. She'd really hate having to tell her mother that Uncle Lucky was a crook.

She winced as she realized she had just slipped back into calling him Uncle Lucky.

She returned to the alley and took a good look at the back of the bar and grill, then walked down the alley searching for the place where they'd unloaded the "goods."

She passed the trash cans and the sheds at the back of the bar, peered into the beach shrubs looking for any signs that something had been dumped there.

And found it several yards along—an opening to a path that led over the dunes.

She didn't hesitate but turned into it. The running shoes she'd worn for the occasion immediately began to fill up with sand. Which was to be expected at the beach but could get annoying really fast if this was how deliveries were made to the bar. But this was no ordinary delivery path. It wasn't leading her to the side of the bar but over the dunes toward the beach.

She trudged onward and upward.

Had Scatter come back for his load and carried it over the dunes to a waiting boat? Didn't smuggling work the other way, from boat to land? At least it did in the historical romances she read, which she sometimes blamed for never finding anyone who quite lived up to the heroes of fiction.

An image of her uncle standing wild and larger than life in their living room doorway tried to steal its way into her mind: she pushed it out. He'd looked the part, but he was no hero.

He'd come to help her mother, but even then, Julie had seen that her mother had been the one to take care of him. Images of abandoned dogs in the garage and scruffy runaways tried to weasel their way into her thoughts, but she pushed them aside, too. Lucky should have taken care of family first, not run off to take care of others, not brought home ragamuffins who demanded all his energy and attention. He hadn't helped her mom; he'd put an extra burden on her.

She kept walking, the sand heavy and giving way beneath her sneakers. A path not taken often, she surmised. At least not by human feet. It was narrow, flanked on both sides by high-growing seagrass, bush pines, and beach roses.

Quiet, beautiful—and lonely.

What if whoever they were were waiting for her on the other side of the dune? That made her pause, but only for a second, because she saw the top of a roof ahead.

Relief washed over her. It had been a delivery for the people in this house, not a smuggling operation. Her relief turned to wariness. Surely there was an easier way to get to the house, a driveway or a finished walk.

Why drive with the headlights turned off?

She should turn around and mind her own business, but she trudged on, curious now and, she had to admit, a little excited . . . until she came to the sign. NO TRESPASSING. No explanation, no "private property," "turtle crossing," "protected environment." Just a threatening NO TRESPASSING.

She looked around; there was only one path, no secondary way to avoid trespassing without turning back and going the way she'd come. And she wasn't going to do that . . . yet. And she couldn't very well walk across the dunes.

A bunch of little birds ran out almost across her feet and disappeared into the grasses on the other side of the path.

She hesitated, then stepped past the sign. Waited for someone to come running and yelling at her to go back. Considered the chances of that someone carrying a BB gun, a shotgun, possibly an assault weapon—and her determination faltered. For a second. All the more reason to get to the bottom of this and get to a beach where they welcomed vacationers and there were no missing relatives to worry about.

She did attempt to make herself smaller, by bending her knees and hunching her shoulders as she crept up the path.

The house came into view without warning. One moment she was surrounded by sand and seagrass, the next she stepped out to a modern wooden stilt house that took her breath away. A rambling construction of dark weathered wood and a lot of glass, it seemed to perch between the edge of the dunes and an endless blue sea. Warm and cold at the same time. Remote as if she'd stepped over a time divide.

No wonder the owners didn't want people tromping up to their house on their way to the beach.

Especially if they were up to no good.

A door opened and a woman stepped out, carrying a garbage bag. She was small but sturdy, with thick black hair coiled around her head. Julie was so surprised that she froze for a second. The woman looked up and she froze, too.

They stood staring at each other before Julie managed to step back into the cover of an overgrown beach rose. Too little too late.

The woman dropped the bag and ran back inside.

Getting a gun, calling the police . . . or warning her partners in crime that they had been found out.

Julie didn't wait to find out, but turned and ran back across the dunes, spewing sand with each step. It wasn't until she was in the alley, legs throbbing, that she stopped to catch her breath.

Just someone carrying out the trash. Though it seemed to Julie that the woman had been more than startled. In that brief moment when their eyes met, Julie hadn't missed the terror in the other woman's eyes.

𝒮he was here, outside!"

Alex heard the words. At first they didn't register. Even as he dragged himself from exhaustion and Rosie's worried face came into focus, he wasn't sure what they meant. "Wha . . . ?"

Rosie grabbed his shoulder. "Just now. She was here. Julietta. She looks like Lucky."

"Juli—" He sat up. "Lucky's niece? Mother—"

Rosie crossed herself.

"What was she doing? Did she say anything?"

"She say nothing. Just stand on the dune and look at me."

"And did she see the—?"

"No."

"Good."

He leaned over the mattress, snagged his jeans off the floor. "I need coffee."

Rosie nodded and hurried away. He slipped on his jeans and searched for a T-shirt while he called Marie. He'd left the two of them last night without learning anything about why things had gone so wrong and not knowing what had really happened.

It took a while for Marie to answer, and when she did he could hear the fatigue in her voice. He warned her about the roving Julie and told her he planned to come down as soon as the coast was clear. She rang off without even a goodbye.

Rosie was waiting for him in the kitchen. Steam rose temptingly from a ceramic mug on the table. But he went straight to Rosie and put his hands on her shoulders. "Mi querida Rosie. All is well. She was probably just exploring. You know how these tourists are."

Rosie put on a brave smile, nodded, placing her complete trust in him—and Lucky.

"What did she do when she saw you?"

"She ran away. Over the dunes."

"See? She probably just didn't see the sign and realized she was off the right path." He hoped that was the truth, but he was dubious himself. From the minute Julie Barlow walked into the bar, he knew she was going to turn their lives upside down. Now she could destroy it all.

"Sit, have your coffee."

He did, though he'd totally lost interest. He just needed to talk to Marie—now. But he sat down and drank while Rosie watched, both of them pretending that it was a normal day.

But the look in her eyes told him everything. She knew that it wasn't over yet, and she was frightened. His stomach turned over. He knew that gut-wrenching fear. He'd felt it often enough in the past. It would sometimes hit him even now that he'd gotten his life together.

He hated seeing it on Rosie's face. "It's going to be fine," he said in what he hoped was a soothing voice. It sounded like gravel to his own ears, but Rosie nodded. He stood, gave her a quick hug. She smiled, but when he looked back as he left, there were tears forming in her deep brown eyes.

*M*arie ended the phone call and pulled the kitchen curtain aside just enough to see a sliver of the alley. She felt more like an old snoopy neighbor than a middle-aged conspirator, but whatever.

She saw Julie run out of the bushes and onto the alley pavement. Stop long enough to look frantically around the alley. At first Marie thought she'd been scared away from Scatter's house; she'd bolted into the alley fast enough.

But it wasn't fear.

Marie was pretty certain it was speculation that had her head turning back and forth like a submarine periscope. *With a target in sight?*

"What's she doing?" Lucky grabbed the edge of the table where he was sitting and tried to push to his feet.

"Stay put," she told him without taking her eyes off the girl in the alley. "You don't want her to see you like this."

He slumped down again. She could hear his painful exhale and she wanted to cry, but not as much as she wanted to knock some sense into him. She'd spent the night pacing in her small bedroom. Watching him sleep. Afraid to sleep herself in case his injuries were more serious than she thought. Alternating between relief and fear, love and anger.

"What does she look like?"

"She looks young with her whole life before her."

"Why now?"

"Because you didn't call Louise."

"I was afraid to give my location away."

"I know," Marie said, finally letting the curtain drop. "Nobody's fault, but it is inconvenient. Are you sure no one recognized you?"

Lucky gingerly adjusted in his seat and pulled the mug of coffee closer with both hands. "Nah, why would they? They don't know me. Besides, I'm pretty sure these guys were just a bunch of faceless hired thugs. And just a stupid coincidence. I'm not even sure they were after us. Or even knew what I was doing. I think they wanted to steal the van. Like I said, stupid."

"At least you got away with the, uh, merchandise." God, she was talking in code. How easy it was to slip back into the past.

"Barely." He grinned at her through a swollen jaw. "Not as young as I used to be."

Marie snorted. "Middle age is a bitch. At least you're in shape."

"Some sort of shape." He leaned on his elbows.

Marie slammed her palms down on the wooden table. "You could have been killed, you stubborn son of a bitch!"

"I'm sorry. What was I supposed to do?"

"You could have taken Scatter with you."

"No, I couldn't, you know that." He made another attempt to get up. "Is she still out there?"

Marie growled.

Dougie, who had been keeping guard at Lucky's feet, growled in return.

"Hush, Doug," Lucky warned. "We're already in the dog-house."

Marie scowled at them both. "Just stay put. I'll make you some breakfast, and we'll decide what to do when Scatter gets here. And no, Dougie. Get away from the door, you'll just have to hold it until we're sure she's gone."

The knock sounded like artillery fire. They all jumped, including Dougie. Marie hurried toward the door, peeked through the sheers, then opened it wide enough for Scatter to squeeze in and Dougie to squeeze out.

Scatter placed a paper bag on the table. "Three burner phones, compliments of Corey's Electronics. Call your sister.

Tell her everything's just peachy, tell her to send her daughter and company on to Dewey Beach, then get rid of it."

"I know what to do with a burner phone," Lucky said at his driest.

Scatter reached in the bag and pulled one of the phones out. "Sorry. But between you and that niece of yours, I'm so spooked I could—"

"Julie always had that affect on you," Lucky said.

"Bullshit. She was a kid." He handed Lucky the phone. "Jesus!" he exclaimed, seeing Lucky's face.

"Did she recognize you?" Lucky asked.

"Of course not, I don't think so. Are you sure you don't need a doctor?"

"It's not that bad."

Marie and Scatter exchanged looks.

It was bad enough, Marie thought. And it could only get worse.

*J*ulie walked slowly back to the hotel. She had no idea what to make of her morning or the night before. Maybe there was nothing to be made. But if there was she sure as hell didn't want her mother to get involved in it.

Lucky had always surrounded himself with a bunch of unsavory characters, and if last night was any evidence, he still did. That they'd waited until Lucky was out of town to do whatever they were doing just proved what a mess he was in. Especially if his employees and his childhood friend, who was also his next-door neighbor, were conspiring against him. Julie wasn't sure where the old man fit into this. He might be married to Marie. Maybe he lived in the house on the dunes and that's why the housekeeper was afraid.

Her mother had always warned him that befriending the down-and-out would bring him trouble. He'd always laugh and say, "Lou, they're my posse."

Lucky hadn't heeded her then or obviously now. Julie just hoped he wasn't in any serious danger from them.

Maybe it was true what they said about twins, that they could sense when the other was in trouble. She'd actually seen it herself when she was a kid. Her mother had known when Lucky broke his leg and collarbone in Hawaii. And when her mother was hospitalized with a ruptured appendix, Lucky had traveled all day and night from the coast, missing his big tournament to be by her side when she awoke from the anesthesia.

Julie had forgotten that. There *had* been times when Lucky had been there for them. Plenty of times. She'd just refused to remember them. Maybe there was something wrong with her that she had been remembering only the times he *wasn't* there.

But there *had* been those other times, when her feelings had been hurt, humiliated by one of the popular girls or a boy she liked who'd ignored her. She would slink down to the basement, stick her head around the doorjamb, and wait until Lucky noticed her and flicked his head, telling her to come in.

He'd reach into the fridge her mom had bought for him and pull the tab off a cold Coke for her, take a beer for himself. He'd sit in the lumpy reading chair brought in from someone's curb while she sat on the couch and poured out her woes. And later when she climbed back upstairs on a sugar high, with her self-esteem restored, she felt like everything would be all right.

There had been those times and she'd forgotten them. Of course he'd never really given her much advice. He was single, in his thirties, never been married. Always on the go, looking for a bigger wave, a larger challenge, and picking up hard-luck stories on his way: down-on-their-luck fellow surfers, stray dogs, and runaways.

"There you are!"

Julie jumped. Kayla and Aggie were coming out of the hotel, loaded down with beach chairs, bags, and a cooler.

"We were worried," Kayla said.

"Yeah," added Aggie. "We called your room several times, knocked on the door, and were about to call the cops until Henry said he saw you leave the hotel earlier this morning."

Julie looked at her watch. "This is a first. It's not even nine o'clock. I thought you'd still be asleep."

"We can sleep for the next two months." Aggie winced. "Well, I can."

"The kids woke me up already complaining that they're bored," Kayla said. "I don't know why he insists on making them ride around in the golf cart all morning while he plays golf."

"Anyway, we have our surfing lesson this morning," Aggie reminded them.

"I forgot," Julie said.

"Don't even try to get out of it. Go put on your suit. We've got a cooler full of muffins, fruit, and cheese. We can stop on the way to the beach for coffee. Ten minutes."

Julie left them on the sidewalk and hurried upstairs.

She was back in eight minutes. Suited up, covered up with a knee-length beach shift in case they decided to have lunch somewhere that required something besides a bikini. Aggie handed Julie her beach chair and they started down the sidewalk.

When they turned into Lucky's parking lot, Julie couldn't help but look down the alley, but seeing nothing out of the ordinary, she decided not to give it another thought until absolutely necessary. If ever. Maybe Lucky would return and everything would be fine. She tripped on nothing as her mother's voice bubbled up from the past. *When Lucky gets back, he'll fix it. Things will be fine . . .* When Lucky gets back.

Well, Uncle Lucky, let's hope that still works for you now.

Chapter 7

*I*t's going to be a perfect beach day. Hold my coffee." Kayla handed her cup to Julie and wrestled with her beach chair. "I can never remember how this thing works."

"You say that every year," Aggie said, and took it from her. The chair slid open. Aggie twirled it around and stuck it in the sand. "Just have to have that magic touch." She dragged her own chair over to form a neat semicircle with the others.

Julie had nestled her cup in the sand and was slathering on sunscreen, trying not to think about the upcoming surfing lesson. It wasn't fear exactly. She knew how to swim . . . well enough. She did great in the town pool, but she could see the bottom there. The idea of other things that you couldn't see swimming with her . . . She would happily sit on the beach for the next nine days reading and sleeping and never getting wet above her ankles. *Face it,* she told herself. *You're a wuss.*

She was; she didn't have to remind herself. Just witness her last day of school.

She reached over to get her paperback, realized it was on the other side of Aggie's beach chair. "Can you hand me my bag?"

"Sure." Aggie tossed the bag over to Julie, dumping the paperback and a slew of brochures in her own lap. "Sorry." She picked up the paperback. "*Her Pirate's Heart*? I haven't read that one." The paperback followed the bag. She straightened the brochures, started to hand them to Julie, then pulled them back. "I get Mexico and Italy, but"—she held up two of the sleek trifolds—"a safari? The Peace Corps?"

Kayla sat up. "What are you blathering about?"

"Julie's planning our next vacation."

"I'm not going on any safari. And I can't afford Italy."

"None of us can," Julie said, reaching for the brochures.

"So . . . what is all this?" Aggie held them just out of reach.

"Well . . ." Julie hesitated. You didn't keep friends if you were afraid to confide in them. Still . . . "You know what we were talking about last night at dinner?"

Two blank faces looked back at her.

"About Lenora Jenner quitting."

"Yeah?" Kayla said. "What does Lenora quitting have to do with us going on safari?"

"Nothing," Julie said, "if you must know. The brochures are not for vacation. I applied for a leave of absence."

Both women sat up, turned as one to Julie.

"You're taking next year off?" Kayla asked.

"They turned me down."

"Whew," said Aggie. "I mean, that's awful, but we'd miss

you. They turned you down? How could they do that? You won teacher of the year last year."

"Probably because she won teacher of the year," Kayla said. "They'd be crazy to let you go, even for a year."

Julie tried for a smile. "Well, it's academic now."

"Jules, we're sorry," Kayla said.

Aggie nodded. "But what were you planning to do? A world tour?"

"I guess that was the problem. I wanted to broaden my horizons. Learn something new."

"How broad do your horizons have to be to teach fourth grade?"

Julie opened her mouth, closed it, at a loss for any answers. Whatever they were, she obviously didn't have them.

"It doesn't matter." Julie took the brochures and stuffed them back in the beach bag, lifted up her paperback.

Kayla plucked it out of her hands. "Not so fast. What's going on?"

Julie looked out to sea. The water was sparkling like glass or diamonds . . . shards of discontent. "I don't know. I'm just not sure I want to be a teacher anymore."

"What happened?" Aggie asked. "Did someone complain?"

"You know how these parents are," Kayla added.

"No. It's something else. I've been feeling this way for a couple of years now. Like I'm not where I should be, not doing the job I should be doing."

"You're a great teacher."

"I'm a decent teacher. I can teach the material, maybe get them to understand it. But I'm not making a difference."

"Well . . . sure you are." Kayla frowned. "We all are."

"You are. Aggie is. Don't think I'm saying that teachers can't make a difference. It's just not for me. I don't blame the kids or even their parents. It's just . . . not for me."

"Of course it is, you've always wanted to be a teacher," Kayla said.

"That's what I thought, too. I thought I would inspire them, excite them, open them to new worlds." Julie huffed out a sigh. "Most of them already have more experience in the world than I do."

"You just have end-of-the-year burnout," Aggie said, looking concerned. "I was ready to brain every one of the little buggers. That's why we go on vacation."

"Maybe I should have been a nurse."

Her two friends stared at her.

"The two things Mom encouraged me to do."

"We remember," Aggie said. "Nursing and teaching, job security, steady paycheck, and retirement benefits."

"And we all listened," Kayla added.

"You love teaching," Aggie said, but Julie heard her voice waver.

"I *want* to. I just feel so ineffectual. The kids don't need me. They have social media; I can't get them interested in anything that isn't trending. They're in the fourth grade. They hardly even look out the window. Sometimes I just want to take their phones away, herd them outside in the rain. Get their feet wet, play in the mud." She sighed. "But muddy shoes won't get you into a top college."

"Definitely burnout," Kayla said.

"I'm not even sure that I want to go back."

"What do you mean?" Aggie asked. "Not go back this year?"

"Not go back at all."

"Hell," Aggie said. "What about your pension? Another seventeen years and you can retire with a full salary. You'll only be forty-five, and forty-five is the new thirty."

"I thought forty was the new thirty."

"Whatever. But think, only seventeen years."

Julie shrugged, trying to quell the panic that was rising in her gut. "We could all be hit by a bus before we get there, then what? I'm turning thirty and I feel like I've never done anything, you know, important or interesting."

She used to dream about seeing the places Lucky would tell her about, but her mother always said, *There's enough time when you've established yourself and saved some money.*

But even back then, she could hear what her mother wasn't saying—*a frivolous waste of time and money.* She was too busy keeping them afloat and doing with less so Julie could have more.

Her mother had never had time for fun.

But Lucky had.

"So what," said Aggie. "At three o'clock you can go home."

"And grade papers and make lesson plans that have to conform to everyone else's lesson plans. I feel like an imposter—have felt that way for a while now."

"Well," Aggie said after an uncomfortable silence. "I say there's no better place to be in a career crisis than at the beach. We'll chill and hang and learn to surf, and things will look better. You'll see."

Kayla reached over and put her hand on Julie's arm. "Don't do anything crazy."

"Me?" Julie laughed. "Have you ever known me to do anything without planning ahead?" And maybe that was just what was wrong with her.

"And in the meantime, we have a surf lesson. I can't believe Uncle Lucky never taught you . . ." The rest of the sentence was muffled as Aggie's head disappeared into the cooler. She tossed out apples, which Julie barely was able to catch.

She handed one to Kayla, who was already stretched out, a wide-brimmed straw hat sheltering her eyes from the morning sun.

Kayla studied the apple before taking a bite. "Yum. Remind me to go for baked or steamed tonight."

"Agreed," Julie said. "I think I ate ten days' vacation worth of grease last night."

"Well, I for one plan to eat my way through every seafood known to the Delaware shore." Aggie passed out breakfast bars. "Eat up."

Well, thought Julie. She'd wanted adventure. Here it was.

Julie lifted her sunglasses up to look out to the water, where a surfing lesson was already in progress. A young woman lay on her stomach on a board while one of the buff instructors stood beside her waist-deep in the water. Julie had noticed them when they'd first arrived at the beach, and they'd been in the same position ever since.

I can do that, she told herself optimistically, and took a bite of apple.

Twenty minutes came all too soon, and Julie, feeling not quite so optimistic, followed her two friends across the sand. The beach was already filling with people: families setting up camp for the day, kids playing Frisbee, younger kids digging in the sand.

Julie took a deep breath, tried to channel vacation feelings, and was surprised to feel it working. She guessed that confession really was good for the soul, or at least good for bonding with your friends.

Les came outside to meet them and he flashed them a white-toothed grin. "Morning, ladies."

Julie could see why Aggie was already smitten: sun-streaked hair flopping over one eye, tight abs, impressive biceps, board shorts riding low on narrow hips, and a good face to put the bow on it.

Aggie lit up like next year's Christmas tree. He seemed pretty happy to see her, too. Well, good for her. Aggie knew how to have fun wherever she was, something Julie had never perfected. Always shoulder to the grindstone, making contingency plans for everything. Like her mother.

Until recently. Julie had been floored when her mom had announced she was taking an island cruise. She couldn't remember a time when her mother had done something frivolous for herself. At first she'd been afraid that it might be a bucket list thing, that her mother was terribly ill and was going to live it up before she went.

But Louise had quickly put an end to that. It was a nurses' conference that several of her colleagues had decided to go on and talked her into going, too. Off-season, cheap, and a learning experience to make them better nurses and further their careers. Her mom's dream vacation.

Les led them over to where three boards lay in the sand. "We always start on land," he said. "Since there are three of you, I've asked Bjorn to help out."

Bjorn, blue eyed with blond hair tied back in a ponytail, stood up to an impressive height. "Good morning, ladies." He had a delectable Scandinavian accent.

"Bjorn came over for the summer," Les explained.

Julie looked from Bjorn to the ocean, where gentle waves broke near the shore. Delaware seemed an odd place to come if he wanted to surf.

Julie didn't know squat about surfing except what she'd gleaned by hanging around listening to Lucky and his cronies. They talked about the Pipeline in Hawaii, Oaxaca, Tahiti, and California. No one ever said, *Man, do you remember the big one in Delaware?*

See, she told herself. *These are the kinds of things you learn when you're not hermetically sealed inside your own expectations.* For all she knew, Delaware was the "in" place to surf.

Les explained the mechanics of surfing, then under the enthusiastic tutelage of Les and Bjorn, they spent the next fifteen minutes lying on their stomachs and pushing to their feet.

Not as easy as it looked, Julie had to admit, and they weren't even in the water yet. When her thighs began to scream in protest, Les finally gave them a break and explained how to fall off.

Get up, fall off. Got it.

"You're doing great. For your next lesson, I'll give you a board leash, but today we'll be staying in white water."

He showed them how to carry the boards into the water.

As they passed Surf's Up, Les called out. "CeeJay!"

A skinny blond girl stuck her head out the door. It was the same girl who had been arguing with the knitting store lady.

"You're in charge."

The girl gave Julie, Aggie, and Kayla the once-over.

"And don't help yourself to the till while we're gone."

CeeJay scowled at everyone in general and disappeared back inside.

They slid their boards into the water and guided them, more or less, to where they all stood waist-deep in the surf. Julie was already feeling the strain.

Bjorn helped her to slide onto her board and gave her a push. She made it about six feet before a breaking wave drove her right back to shore, where she sprawled in the sand and her board squirted out to sea where it had refused to go while she was on it.

"Fall to the side," Bjorn reminded her, and reached out to retrieve her board.

Kayla kept paddling like crazy and managed to stay put. Aggie toppled over. Les lifted her, spluttering and laughing, out of the surf.

Bjorn glided the board back to Julie with an ease that made her grit her teeth. "Okay, try it again. Don't fight the waves. Work with them."

She hit the next wave head-on and got a mouthful of salt water for her trouble. When it passed, she found herself still a few feet from the shore. *Progress,* she thought optimistically. She was feeling pretty smug when the next wave carried her right back to where she'd started. She remembered to roll off before she got too shallow and the fin got damaged by the sand.

She stood up, dragged the board through the water. This time she walked it out as far as she could, jumping over the waves that continued to roll in. When she was chest-deep, she scrambled onto the board. Not an easy feat.

Bjorn and Les were busy with the other two, so Julie grabbed and splashed and finally managed to slide her stomach across the board. She wriggled to the side and hauled both legs onto the board. Huffed out a breath and met Bjorn's grin.

"An interesting technique," he said.

"Whatever works," Julie said.

"But you're facing the wrong way."

Julie looked up. Everything was blue ahead. She sat up.

"I mean you're facing the back of the board, which is facing the wrong way."

She felt the board move. Her first reaction was to pick her feet out of the water, until she realized that Bjorn had the board by the nose and was turning it to face the open sea.

"Now you."

Julie groaned, then scooted around until she was facing the ocean again.

"Good, now paddle." He gave the board a push. "Keep your head down. I'm right behind you."

It was exhausting work, and by the time Les said, "Okay, now you're ready to try standing," Julie was thinking about lunch and a piña colada.

The next eternity was spent with the three friends climbing to their feet only to be dumped in the water. Kayla managed to stand for a few long seconds. Julie and Aggie hooted and began to applaud, when a larger swell hit Kayla from behind, tossing her and her board into the air. Julie and Aggie screamed as she disappeared into the water.

Bjorn and Les both dove in and pulled her out.

She spluttered and shook her head. Her hair sprayed water. "That was so much fun!" she exclaimed. "Where's my board?"

After a few more attempts with varying degrees of success, Les called it a day. "Tomorrow we'll go deeper and you can ride the big ones."

Julie glanced out and saw the waves were suddenly looking a lot bigger than they had earlier. *Maybe it will rain.*

Julie's arms and legs were shaking as she wrestled the unwieldy surfboard across the sand to its rack.

"So, you game for another lesson?" Les asked them, but he was mainly looking at Aggie, who, wet and bedraggled, still exuded sex appeal. Julie didn't know how she did it. She wished she had some of it herself. As it was, she was just wet, bedraggled, and wishing she could lie down for a nap.

They agreed to another lesson in the next day or two, then staggered across the sand to their beach chairs.

"That was exhausting," Kayla said, flopping onto her chair. "But what a rush. For those couple of seconds I was standing on water. It was so cool."

"Definitely fun," Aggie said. "And invigorating. I wonder if Lucky's is open for lunch."

Kayla checked her watch, the only one of them with a waterproof timepiece. An extravagance for the usually frugal kindergarten teacher that she'd bought as a necessity "because of bath time." Fine by Julie. Kayla deserved some extravagance, since her deadbeat ex didn't do anything but obstruct her and disappoint the kids.

Kayla sat up. "It's almost noon. Man, that went fast."

"But do we dare eat the food?" Julie wondered.

"Good point," Kayla said. "There's bound to be a good restaurant in town."

Aggie gave her a look. "I'm not going back to the hotel, taking the time to shower and change clothes, just to eat a hot dog, rewind, and get back to the beach before the sun goes down. Lucky's must be able to throw a burger on the grill. I'll ask Les."

She wandered off, weaving like she'd already had a few too many girlie drinks.

Julie planned to look like that herself by the time lunch was over. Then she was going to spend the afternoon reading under the umbrella that still lay crammed into its plastic case.

Aggie returned a few minutes later, looking incredibly smug.

"Well?" asked Kayla. "Does Lucky's serve food and will it give us food poisoning?"

"Yes, and Lucky's has a Thai chef."

Julie snorted. "I think 'chef' is probably a stretch."

Aggie shrugged. "Maybe, but Les says he makes a mean burger and the best pad thai in twenty miles."

"Sounds like lunch," Kayla said, and leaned over to brush the sand from her feet before slipping them into her thongs.

Julie closed the book she'd barely opened and stood up. "Think it's safe to leave our stuff here?"

"Oh sure," Aggie said. "Les will watch out for it."

"So when did you have time to get so chummy with Les?" Julie asked as they trudged up the sand to the bar. "We haven't even been here twenty-four hours."

"More than enough time to par-ty," Aggie said, and shimmied, setting off the aqua waves printed across her beach cover-up.

Lucky's was blessedly cool after their morning in the sun, and they decided to opt for a table inside. Corey, Ike, and Ron were sitting at the same places they'd been sitting when Julie and her friends had arrived the day before. Probably sat there every day, on the same stools, drinking the same beer on tap.

They turned simultaneously and nodded at the three women, then turned back to the bartender.

Scatter zeroed in on Julie. He did not look pleased.

Well, neither was she. And she was dying to march right up to him and say, *I know what you did last night.*

But she didn't really know. And he might be dangerous. Actually, she was pretty sure he was. And not in a sexy pirate way.

She just hoped her uncle wasn't involved. Because if he was, her mother would somehow get dragged into it. What if she had to use all her savings to get Lucky out of jail? Or pay for his attorney fees? What if something had happened to her uncle and her mother blamed her?

Kayla and Aggie had already snagged a table near the dartboard. From the look in Scatter's eyes, Julie didn't think that was the best choice, but she sat down anyway.

A stocky young waiter brought water and three menus, which consisted of a typed paper slipped inside a sheet protector.

"Our lunch menu," the server said with a smile that showed crooked, discolored teeth. He nodded and walked away, limping slightly. Another one of Lucky's strays, no doubt.

"Strange choice for a waiter," Kayla said.

"Not at all," Julie said. She had just been thinking the same thing, but defense of Lucky's choice came unbidden and unwanted to her lips. "Lucky always helped people who needed it."

"Well, look who's sticking up for Lucky for a change. And just so you know, I agree," Kayla said. "Still, you have to admit that most places have cute college people manning the front end. Think about it."

And, of course, Julie did. And what Kayla said was true. Look at them, three almost thirty-year-old teachers, out for fun and ogling cute surfers and talking about partying. They were just ordinary schoolteachers. And they were looking for fun just like everyone else.

They started with nachos and piña coladas as a test of Lucky's cuisine. They were both so delicious, they ordered sliders, the pad thai, curry coconut shrimp, and another round of drinks.

The drinks didn't come with umbrellas, but they were frosty and tangy and sweet, and Julie found herself musing on how someone as un . . . -couth? -finished? -communicative? as Alex/Scatter could make such a refreshing girlie drink.

With the second round of drinks came the rest of their lunch and Alex/Scatter himself. He wasn't carrying a tray but had three plates lined up along his arm. Julie automatically moved out of spill range, but he neatly placed them on the table with an ease that impressed her. Then he stood at attention.

"Enjoying your stay?" His smile wandered from Kayla to Aggie and landed on Julie.

She tried to read his expression beyond the bland smile and the colorless question, without success. "Yes," she said tentatively. Did his question have a double meaning? Did he know she'd seen him last night? Ridiculous. "Yes," she repeated, recovering herself. "The beach is lovely."

"Fantastic," he said in the flattest voice she'd ever heard. "Oh, by the way, I heard from Lucky this morning. He said he's sorry he missed you and he'll call Louise right away. His phone died and he didn't have time to get a new one. So no worries, you're free to continue on to Dewey Beach."

"Oh, we love it here," Aggie said. "We're learning to surf."

"So much better than fighting the crowds at other beaches," Kayla said enthusiastically. "But still close enough to visit if we get bored here."

"Which we won't," Aggie said cheerfully. "This is just perfect, isn't it, Julie?"

Julie narrowed her eyes. Why were they being so chipper? Trying to cheer her up? Or just putting it to the bartender?

"So we've decided to stay for our whole vacation," Aggie continued.

Since when? They hadn't decided that. Had they?

The bartender turned to Julie with a scowl so intense that, instead of dissuading her as she knew he meant it to do, it just got her back up. She didn't know why her friends were acting so enthusiastic, but she smiled, shrugged, and said overbrightly, "And you can't find a better piña colada than at Lucky's Beach Bar and Grill."

She heard a muffled growl and looked past him to the bar to see if Dougie was lumbering toward them. But Dougie failed to appear. Julie looked back to Scatter. The growl must have come from the surly bartender.

"So you'll be seeing a lot more of us," Kayla said as if someone had just announced Christmas in June.

"Huh." He suddenly looked tired. Well, who wouldn't after the night he'd had?

Maybe she should have told her friends what she'd seen in the alley. Of course she might be overthinking the situation. Kayla and Aggie would be the first to point that out. But still, she had a responsibility to her friends. *Always prepare for the worst, and you'll usually be pleasantly surprised.* Another gem from her mother.

She was not the type to go looking for trouble. She usually avoided confrontation at all costs. But lately, something was bringing out her most impulsive urges. One of those urges had just tempted her to jettison her security and her future for the unknown. If it hadn't been for Sara Olins asking her to help with her student mural, Julie would be unemployed instead of on vacation.

"What about *him?*" Aggie said.

"What?" Julie asked, watching Alex return to the bar. "What him? What are you talking about?"

Aggie gave her a long-suffering sigh. "You and"—she tilted her head toward the bar—"the scrumptiously brooding bartender."

"I think he knows more about Uncle Lucky than he's telling."

Kayla lifted an already perfectly arched eyebrow. "Is this still about Lucky, or do I sense some other reason for this tension between you and the mysterious—"

"It's about Lucky, period."

"Dangerous, like a romantic hero," Aggie intoned. "With an intensity that makes you wonder what he'd—"

"Not me," Julie said. His intensity was creeping her out. "He's a beach bum who knows how to pull a beer tap—okay, and makes a mean piña colada, I'll give him that."

"Come on, Jules. Even you have to admit he *is* kind of cute in a rough-and-tumble way. He might be just the distraction you need."

"Even me?" Julie asked, distracted. "Why even me? I date."

Kayla rolled her eyes. "You'll never find someone if you're always prejudging them."

She was right. They were both right. Her social life sucked. She went out with men who didn't challenge her, because she was so busy trying to make her life work that she didn't have time to make a relationship work. You didn't need a sabbatical to figure that one out.

Alex/Scatter *had* been looking their way; actually, she got the feeling he'd been trying to figure her out since the moment they'd met. He'd been totally unhelpful, not to mention he might be a crook. But she had to admit there was something about him . . .

"Ugh." Julie slumped on her elbows.

"Well, he's certainly interested in you," Aggie said. "He keeps looking over here."

"Maybe he just wants to make sure we enjoyed our lunch," Kayla said.

"Probably making sure we don't stiff him with the bill."

As Julie said it, Scatter looked straight at her. She looked away.

"That's just what we mean," said Aggie.

She'd definitely have to tell them about what she saw last night in the alley. But maybe she should talk to him first. "Maybe I'll go talk to him."

"Ask him what time he gets off work tonight," Aggie said. She nudged Kayla and the two of them pushed back their chairs and gathered up their bags.

"Wait. You're leaving?"

"You can do it. We'll settle up later. We have every faith in you. Toodles." They made a beeline for the front door.

Julie gathered up her stuff and took the check over to the bar to pay up. She slipped in between Corey and Ron and placed the check and her credit card on the bar top.

"Hey, Scatter," said Corey. "Julie here would like to pay her bill."

On his far side, Ron nodded and winked at Julie and went back to his beer.

Ike just grinned and pulled on his chin beard.

Scatter's head appeared at the far end of the bar and he walked over to them.

She slid the check and her credit card toward him. He took it without a word and went to the cash register.

All three men were giving the transaction their full attention.

She signed the returned bill and left a tip in cash. "For our . . . other . . . waiter."

"I'll see that he gets it," Scatter said, and slid it over to the side.

She'd meant to wheedle a confession out of him, but he was always insulated by the comedy team of Corey, Ike, and Ron. Or maybe they were hired to run interference. They did seem to be everywhere.

Now you're just being paranoid, she told herself. "Well, in case you're wondering, we enjoyed our lunch."

"I'll tell the cook."

"Scat," Ike said. "What's wrong with you? If this lovely lady was chatting me up, I'd be on my best behavior."

"I'm not," Julie began.

"I don't think that's what she's doing," said Alex.

"Sure she is," added Corey.

"Sorry, let me start again." Scatter smiled at her, flashing white teeth and two rather sharp canines.

Which reminded her. "Where's Dougie?"

"I don't know. Around somewhere."

"He's probably with—ouch!" Corey shot an accusing look at Ike and reached down and rubbed his leg.

"Anything else?" Alex looked at her pleasantly, vapidly, but she hadn't missed that one spark of light that might have meant anything . . . or nothing.

"No thanks." She turned to leave, changed her mind, turned back. "Actually, there is."

He raised one dark, forbidding eyebrow.

"Why are you so mean?"

Three heads snapped toward her. The bartender's didn't move. His expression didn't change. Three heads snapped back to him.

There was dead silence and Julie got a creepy-crawly feeling up the back of her neck.

"It's a legitimate question." She had to force the words out. "It can't be good for business."

"Aw, Julie, Scat's bark is worse than his bite," said Ron.

"He is a little rough around the edges," Corey admitted.

"But he's got a heart of gold," added Ike. Everybody, including Scatter, stared at him. "You just sometimes have to dig a bit."

Julie snorted. "I guess I'll have to take your word for it." She started to leave.

"You want to know why?" Alex moved slowly until he was leaning over the barrier of the bar.

She nodded. She had to fight the urge to step away.

"Because you cut Lucky off. Didn't bother to make contact for years. And suddenly you show up out of the blue with your attitude and your demands."

"He deserted me," she said feebly.

"Bullshit. He moved the earth to do whatever Louise allowed him to do, which wasn't much. Dropped everything to be at all your recitals and parties, even when there were people who needed him more."

His knuckles were white where he gripped the lip of the bar. Corey, Ike, and Ron leaned away, opening like scruffy human flower petals.

"I don't remember it like that." Julie wanted to step away, to unhear his words, unfeel the intensity rolling from him across the bar.

"That's because your memory starts and ends with 'me.'" He turned away.

Finally, Julie stepped back.

Corey, Ike, and Ron slowly righted themselves on their barstools.

"Anything else?" he asked, without turning around.

She stepped farther back, her mind racing, the thoughts

random, her excuses never finding a place to land. "I—" She grabbed at the one question that rose from all the others. "What is your real name?"

"Alex. Alex Martin." He looked over his shoulder. Their eyes met, his growing almost black. Then he turned away—but not before Julie saw a flash of something so deep, so painful, so profound, that it sucked the breath out of her.

And she reeled as a strange sense of déjà vu enveloped her, only to tumble into a more immediate sense of wariness. And she knew in that moment she would never, ever want to make him really angry.

Alex Martin was not a man to be crossed.

Chapter 8

$\mathcal{M}$arie pushed away one clothes hanger after another.

"You're going to be late," Lucky said from where he lay on the bed, his feet with their Peruvian sandals hanging off the side because, as he always said, his mama raised him right. One sandal had fallen to the floor as he leisurely rubbed the top of Dougie's head. The dog lay on the ground alongside his fallen idol.

She'd covered Lucky with a quilt of wisteria flowers for luck and devotion. He didn't need it, but her mama raised her to be superstitious, and a double stint in government service hadn't managed to completely bury that strain.

Especially on days like today.

She pushed another hanger aside and lifted a deep purple caftan out of the closet, tossed it lightly on the bed.

"I like that one," Lucky said. "I like your red one better."

She gave him a look. She was still mad at him. How stupid could he be to think he could have managed by himself? It had nearly gotten him killed. That's why she was mad. That's why she'd given him hell when he'd returned. She'd yelled just to quell the fear, the bone-chilling, blood-freezing, gut-spewing fear that said maybe he wouldn't make it back this time.

She'd paced her small bedroom last night, watching him sleep, and remembering. Marie didn't like looking back. Somehow the fond memories often were wound up with the bad ones, the ones she'd rather forget.

But last night they'd stayed away.

She remembered the night they'd met. Sitting on the dark beach, his hair reflecting the moonlight.

They'd all been ten that summer. And they became inseparable until eight years later, when Lucky—he'd still been Tony in those days—left in search of the big one, Louise went to nursing school, and Marie joined the army, to get as far away from life on the boardwalk as she could get.

She remembered the day he'd shown up at her door ten years ago. It had been twenty-four years since she'd seen him or heard from Louise. Her parents had closed up shop and moved to Florida years before.

She remembered him just standing there in the doorway, grinning. Older, deeper, honed to toughness. He needed a favor. A young protégé wanted to join the force. Do something about drugs on the street. Something that Lucky had saved him from. Like he'd saved Scatter.

She gave him a name to call. He stayed four days, then left again. She had an email address; she'd expected nothing more.

Then Sam Delaney decided to close his bar and grill and retire. On a whim, she emailed Lucky. He was interested and came to check it out. This time he stayed.

As much as Lucky ever stayed.

She shook herself. This feeling, the sense of acute awareness and wariness, would pass. It always did. It had to. That or she would be the one moving on. And she wasn't going anywhere. Because for the first time in her life, Marie Simmons had something she was afraid of losing.

She opened the door to the second closet, where a system of shelves and baskets organized scarves, jewelry, shawls, belts, bells, headpieces, and whatever extra touches would round out each ensemble to make it most effective . . . to beguile her customers in and keep her demons away.

It was a job—two jobs—she'd never intended to return to. She didn't need to work. Her cottage was paid off. She had a pension and savings and one day, if it still existed, Social Security. But she couldn't dig in the garden all day. She couldn't say no when she was needed, and her storefront gave her a good view of the street.

She pulled the madras shift over her head, felt Lucky's toes slide up her thigh.

"You probably have broken ribs or something."

"Nah," but his foot stopped moving. Lucky looked at her with what could only be disappointment.

She exchanged her floral summer dress for the long caftan, went back to the closet and chose a wide red scarf to wind around her middle. Took out a pair of Toms canvas shoes—no one said she couldn't be comfortable while she worked. And besides, no one ever saw her feet. She grabbed a handful of bangle bracelets and slipped them on her wrists. The tinkle they made for some reason set her teeth on edge. She didn't want to go in today at all, but life didn't stop when you got cold feet.

As she pulled the last article off the top shelf, she heard the covers shift. She turned on Lucky just as he was trying to sit up. "Stay," she ordered.

Dougie lumbered to a sitting position.

"That wasn't for you, but you stay, too."

"I need to get home. I'm fine."

"You're not going home. You're not leaving here until we know that you haven't been followed."

"And if I was, I'll have led them right to you."

She tilted her head at him, and her heart filled with that stupid loyalty and love that women had felt through the ages. "I can take care of myself," she said, and leaned over Dougie to kiss Lucky's forehead. "I mean it. Stay put."

She let herself out the kitchen door. It was barely noon and already the pavement was hot beneath her feet. The heat might drive some people off the beach and indoors, and if it didn't, her front window still had the best view of town.

Fortunately it was just a short walk down the alley. She let herself in the back door, cranked up the air-conditioning, and walked through the dark paisley curtains to the front room.

A quick look around to make sure everything was in order and she turned the CLOSED sign to OPEN and unlocked the door.

Madame Marzetta was open for business.

*J*ulie stepped out of the bar and grill into bright afternoon sunlight and stopped to take a few fortifying breaths while she deliberated. She wasn't absolutely sure it was Scatter—Alex Martin—she saw last night in the alleyway. She'd toyed with the idea of confronting him but decided she should wait until Uncle Lucky got back and let him handle it. In the meantime, she'd keep her eyes open.

But she had to tell Kayla and Aggie her suspicions. They would either heed her worries or talk her out of them. Either way, their safety might be at stake—probably not, but maybe—and she had to let them know.

She marched over the sand to where her two friends were already stripped down to their suits and reapplying sunscreen.

"Well?" Aggie said. "How did your little talk go?" She batted her eyes at Julie.

Julie stiffened her resolve. "There's something you should know."

Aggie flopped back in her chair. "Now what? If it's something that prevents you from flirting with the bartender, we don't want to know." She stretched. "Let your hair down a little."

Julie had twisted it into a French knot before leaving the hotel that morning.

"If you don't like Scatterman, I bet Bjorn will be more than willing."

"It's something important. Maybe."

Kayla sat up. "Is this about your sabbatical? Hit us with it."

Julie pulled her beach chair to face theirs and sat down on the edge. "Last night I couldn't sleep—"

"Well, you would've if you'd—"

"Hush, Aggie, can't you see that she's serious?"

"Sorry, what is it?"

"I couldn't sleep and I went to turn off the air-conditioning, and while I was looking out the window . . . now this is going to sound weird, but a van pulled into the alley behind the hotel and drove halfway down to where Lucky's house is, or near to it."

"He's back?" Aggie said. "Why didn't you tell us?"

"No. I don't think so. It was pitch black. The van had its headlights off."

"Probably some dude sneaking home after staying out too late."

"That's what I was hoping. But he stopped at the back of the bar, which is right across from Lucky's cottage and Marie's. A man came out of the back door of the bar, I'm pretty sure it was the bartender. And another person came out from one of the cottages. The driver got out and they unloaded the van and dumped whatever it was in the bushes."

"Wow," Kayla said. "Maybe they were smuggling liquor or something."

"Or dumping trash illegally," Aggie said.

"There's a dumpster right there," Julie said irritably.

"Well, speak of the devil," Kayla said. "There goes the bartender now."

They all turned to watch Alex "Scatter" Martin stride across the parking lot. He was carrying a briefcase and a backpack. He threw them both into the Jeep parked at the side of the bar, hopped in after them, and drove away.

The three women exchanged looks.

"A briefcase?" Aggie said.

"Definitely not the briefcase type," Kayla agreed.

"Unless . . . it's payoff money. What if Julie saw them dealing drugs or something?"

Kayla jerked around. "Aggie, stop it."

"Really," Julie agreed. "I don't think you get to smuggle on credit. It has to be a cash-and-carry business." She shook her head. "Besides, I can't believe that Uncle Lucky would ever get involved with something like that."

"Me neither," Kayla said. "He always warned us against drugs, remember?"

"But who knows what has happened since?" Julie said. "How did he afford to buy this bar? It's right on the beach, prime real estate. He never had two pennies to rub together."

"Maybe they're substituting cheap liquor and putting it in bottles with more expensive labels," Aggie said. "I saw that in a movie once."

"That would make sense."

Kayla looked dubious. "But surely Lucky wouldn't allow that."

"Who knows?" Julie said. "We lost touch. He could have gone off the deep end for all I know."

Kayla's eyes rounded. "I think you should stay out of it."

"What?" Aggie asked. "You think Scatterman and the neighbor might be dangerous?"

"Not really," Julie said, "but on the off chance, maybe you two would—"

"Absolutely not!" Aggie said. "We're not deserting you."

"What about you, Kayla?"

"We'll stick together," Kayla said. "But I have kids. If it gets dicey, I'm outta here."

"If it gets dicey, we'll all get out, but I'm sure I'm blowing this all out of proportion. And there's some totally reasonable—" Julie's phone rang. "Mom," she told the others, and answered it. "Hey, did Uncle Lucky call you yet?" Julie cringed at how easily she'd fallen back in the habit of calling him Lucky.

"Yes, he's at some kind of conference. Imagine Lucky at a conference."

Julie couldn't.

"He said his phone died. Won't hold a charge and he hasn't had time to get a new one. Just like Lucky to let something like that happen."

Sounded like a bunch of bull to Julie, but she wasn't about to say so. "So he's fine?" she asked.

"Yes, and he's sorry he missed you."

That was it? Like she dropped by all the time and he just happened not to be home. "When is he coming back?"

There was a pause over the phone. "He didn't say. Why? Is

something wrong? There's something wrong, isn't there? I can tell in your voice."

"Uh, no. I'm still recovering from partying last night." She made a face at Aggie and Kayla, who were straining to hear the conversation. "Just thought since we're here, it would have been nice to say hello."

Aggie and Kayla nodded.

Her mother was silent, no doubt remembering Julie's usual attitude toward her uncle.

"I mean it's been a while," Julie said contritely, and to her surprise felt it.

"Are you sure *you're* okay?"

"Of course I am. It's vacation."

"Well, don't burn the candle at both ends."

"We won't. And, Mom, have a good time."

"Call if you need me."

"I will."

"Say hi to the girls."

"Mom says hi."

"Hi," Kayla and Aggie called.

Julie ended the call, tossed her phone in her beach bag. "So we're off the hook. Lucky's safe, all is right with Louise's world, and we can get on with our vacay."

"What about the dead-of-night delivery?" Kayla asked.

"None of our business. And no reason to stay here longer than the weekend."

"Oh, I can see a few," Aggie said, waving to Les and Bjorn, who had just stepped out of Surf's Up. "You know, if you don't fancy Scatterman, we can save him for Kayla and you can take Bjorn."

Kayla reached over to smack Aggie's thigh. "You're totally mercenary."

"Hell, we're on vacation . . . Time's passing, and, well, look at us. Kayla's a single mom with kids, good luck with that one. Julie won't settle for good enough. I would but I can't even find a good-enough who will commit."

"But you don't want commitment," Kayla said. "You want to have fun."

"Who says I can't have both?"

"Yikes, I'm stuck for something to say," Kayla said.

"How about 'the world doesn't revolve around men'?" Julie said. "As we all should have learned by now."

"Of course it doesn't," Aggie snapped back. "Even I know that. But it's a lot more fun with them around."

$\mathcal{A}$lex stopped the Jeep in front of the town bowling alley. The sign hadn't been lit since he'd moved here.

He slipped his backpack over his shoulder and reached for his briefcase, which had been getting heavier instead of lighter since the school year ended and as harvest season reached its height.

He was running late, the camp van was already there. Well, it couldn't be helped. He'd already moved his regulars to tomorrow. He was doing double duty this week, triple since today was also his day for swimming lessons. Something he was actually looking forward to. His shirt was sticking to his back just from the three-block ride from the bar. He crossed to the door and pulled it open. He could hear activity from the right, the ESL class in the now defunct food court.

A men's group crowded into two of the old banquettes, listening to someone talk about retirement investment. The unused bowling balls were still lined up in the trough as if in expectation of the next game. There would be no next game. The land was owned by some development firm that had no intention of reopening the alley or even paying to have it torn down, having bought it at auction for a pittance and rented it out to the homeowners' association for more than it was worth.

Fortunately the people of Lucky's Beach were civic-minded. Sometimes too civic-minded for Alex's liking. He turned to the left, away from the activities, and walked past the rental station with its rows of shoes still in place. No one manned the reception desk, as they hardly ever had anyone to watch over things unless there was a big event.

To the far side of the shoe racks was what had once been the manager's office. Now it was his office. He unlocked the door and went inside.

It was stuffy but not unbearably hot, thanks to the concrete block construction. He'd cleared out the bowling alley detritus, painted, and put up some colorful pictures. Added an activity table and several chairs donated by a juvenile furniture store that was going out of business.

He swung his briefcase onto his desk and turned on the old window air conditioner, just as the first knock came. He tucked the briefcase out of sight and went to answer the door.

Desiree Hoyes stood smiling in the doorway. Young, bright, fresh out of college, Dee was ready to change the world one kid at a time. She ran the overflow migrant children's day camp just outside of town practically single-handedly.

She was also very pretty, which set her young charges at ease and made Alex's job much more bearable.

"Good morning, Mr. Alex," she said brightly, and nudged a scrawny nine-year-old, Alberto Nunez, into the room in front of her.

Alex held out his hand for their Alex and Alberto—"Dos Als"—ritual handshake, but today Alberto hung back. Alex didn't miss the bruise under the kid's eye or the cut on his lip. Most likely there were more bruises under his shirt.

Alex squatted down until he was eye-level with Alberto. "Que pasa, amigo?" he said quietly. It wasn't really a question. They all knew what had happened. Alberto was running with a rough set of kids; when they got angry at anything they took it out on Alberto because he was the smallest, the newest, and he hadn't learned how to fight back—yet.

Alberto just shrugged, looked at the ground. Alex sat him down at the activity table, reached into the minifridge he kept behind his desk, got out a juice box, then reached in his desk for a bag of Goldfish crackers.

Dee made herself invisible in one of the chairs across the room.

Alex jabbed the straw in the juice box, probably with more force than necessary, then opened the package and poured the Goldfish out onto a napkin. He knew Alberto would never reach inside the bag on his own accord. That's how cowed life had made him at nine.

And Alex knew just what it felt like. Those feelings ~~never~~ faded, never got completely buried.

"So, my man," Alex said once Alberto had started on his snack.

It all came out eventually. The same story, week after week: Alberto talked funny, he was small for his age, and kids could pick out weakness faster than they could make a friend. It was the easy way out, the beginning of a life of tormenting others. And the bullied either perished or became bullies themselves.

Alex could only sit, let Alberto take his time, wait for him to say something—anything—that Alex could use to help guide him toward an answer. Hell, he was that arrogant to think he could do some good.

The only good you could really do was what Lucky had done with him. Dragged him out of an alley before he was dead, gave him a safe haven, which Alex hadn't appreciated at the time. He'd known only how to fight—to the death if he had to. He hadn't, thanks to a stranger who wouldn't give up on him.

He'd been eleven maybe, not that much older than Alberto. He'd run away; Lucky would come after him. Every time. Determined to knock some sense into Alex's bruised and unloved psyche. Until finally Alex gave in.

He still didn't really understand why Lucky fought so hard to save him from the street and an early grave, but Alex was grateful that he had. He doubted whether he could ever pay Lucky back. He didn't have whatever drove Lucky to keep saving people. And he was beginning to doubt if he could make a difference to all the kids he saw. His bulging briefcase was an affidavit to a crisis that was going unchecked. He was one man with his finger in the dike.

The half hour was over too soon. Alberto, once he warmed up, didn't want to leave. As Dee guided him to the door, he broke away and threw his arms around Alex's legs. Alex bent down. Hugged him for all he was worth while the boy shook within his arms.

You weren't supposed to touch your cases—too many lawsuits and accusations of abuse. But hell, how could he turn this kid away? Once he had been that kid. He didn't remember crying, but he must have, like Alberto was doing today. But Alex had had no one to cling to, no one with a soothing touch. Alex couldn't remember if he ever had. He just remembered Lucky dragging him over the pavement of that dark alley, while he kicked and bit and cursed Lucky for saving his life.

Chapter 9

The sounds of children's squeals and laughter woke Julie from a deep sleep. A nightmare, surely; this was an adults-only vacation. She cautiously opened her eyes. She was on the beach, but there were still squealing children. She sat up. The two beach chairs next to her were empty.

She'd convinced Kayla and Aggie to move the chairs closer to the dunes so the grasses and scrub oaks could shelter them from the afternoon sun. Which had been a good thing at least for her, because several pages into her book, she'd fallen asleep. The book had slid to the sand.

But that laughter . . .

She lifted her sunglasses and scanned the beach until she found the source of all the hilarity. In a roped-off area between the lifeguard tower and the hook of rock jetty, a dozen kids splashed and carried on in the surf.

Bjorn sat on the lifeguard tower. Two lifeguards, Les and . . .

Aggie? . . . stood ankle-deep in the surf overseeing the only other adult in the water.

Julie craned her neck. No, it couldn't be. Alex Martin was standing up to his knees in the waves, several little people clinging to his legs, his hands, his swimsuit.

"I know," a voice said above her. Kayla handed her a cold soda. "I had to go see for myself. That bad boy may be a lyin', cheatin' crook, but he's good with kids." She raised both eyebrows.

"Not something I really care about at the moment."

"Which? The bad boy or the kids?" Kayla sat down and twisted the top off her drink. "Listen, if you want to talk, work through some stuff . . . I mean, you always loved kids."

"I still do, I guess." Julie shrugged. There was no way to explain what she was feeling. It would be like a betrayal of all their plans, of their life choices. Teaching was working out for Kayla and Aggie. Just not for Julie. "It's no big deal. I just thought maybe I could get a new perspective. Learn something to teach them that they couldn't get off the internet."

Now Alex was surrounded by children jumping up and stretching their arms to him.

"Are you unhappy?" Kayla looked like she might cry.

This was just what Julie had wanted to avoid. "Not at all. I'm happy as a clam. And even if I weren't, I don't think getting it on with the buff, possibly criminal Alex 'Scatterbrain' Martin will make the difference."

"No, but it might help for a minute or seven. And you have to admit he looks pretty damn good in jammers."

Yeah, he does, thought Julie. Underneath that sloppy T-shirt and those stretched-out jeans was a beautiful body. Damn, it just wasn't fair.

"And the kids seem to love him. A person could do worse . . ." Her last sentence ended wistfully.

Julie squeezed her arm. Of the three, Kayla had the fewest choices. With two kids, she couldn't quit her job because it wasn't satisfying. She couldn't go out and meet new people on a whim. Her social life consisted of the gym on the weekends and ten days every summer, ten days that were being eaten up with Julie's obligation to her mother.

"Well, couldn't you?" Kayla prodded.

"With Scatter? The idea is growing on me. Well, not his personality, and that's sort of important to me."

"Yeah, me, too. That and liking kids."

Julie nodded, looking at her friend in a new way and realizing that she'd been so self-involved that she hadn't noticed that both her friends were also searching for something.

"Well, I'm going to get closer to the action." Kayla started pulling her beach chair over the sand. "Coming?"

"I think I'll stay here and read about romantic pirates for a while." She retrieved her book from the sand, but instead of opening it, she watched Kayla cross the beach to the others. Her eyes wandered down to where Alex was now tossing children into the water, though without ever really letting go.

Ugh, how was she supposed to concentrate on a fictional pirate when Alex/Scatter was right in front of her face? *He's not a pirate,* she reminded herself. A smuggler maybe. And that wasn't good.

But Kayla's questions had started up her worry thoughts. Her life wasn't going as planned—not her career, not her personal life. She didn't even have a personal life at the moment. She tossed her book aside. It was impossible to concentrate on pirates and damsels in distress when she was the one stressed.

She walked to the edge of the water, determined not to look down the beach to where Alex Martin stood like the Colossus of Masculinity. That would not solve anything.

Besides, he was a jerk.

She turned away, walked along the shoreline in the opposite direction. The tide was out, and she crossed a rivulet of water that had been invisible before. On the other side was another smaller white beach. It was totally isolated; no human footsteps marred the sand.

She saw the ridges of a pink shell and picked it up, cleaned off the sand. Held it up to the light, a perfect fan. And then she saw it, the same dark wood and glass house she'd stumbled onto that morning. A railed deck wrapped around the long front of the house, and from the beach side, it didn't seem so ominous.

It did look totally unoccupied. Maybe the housekeeper had just come in to clean. Besides, beaches were public, right? Owners had to allow access. She was sure she had read that somewhere.

She walked on, but more slowly, looking for more shells. Keeping one eye on the house to make sure no one was there, just in case she was trespassing.

Someone *was* there. Looking through the slats of the deck

rail, small fingers grasping the wooden balusters. Then a set of eyes appeared. Two sets of them.

As she watched, a head popped up over the top rail: a young boy, black hair cut in bangs straight across his forehead above big dark eyes, his chin barely reaching the top. Beside him, the crown of another dark head rose just above the rail, too small to see over.

Julie waved. At first she got no response. But as she turned away, a tiny hand lifted in the air to wave back. Even though she was on a no-kids vacation, she felt sorry for these two, stuck up there, isolated. She could hear the laughter of the other children from where she stood. She was sure they could, too.

Julie held up her shell, not even sure they could tell what it was. Then the two heads moved down the deck rail toward her.

They didn't get far. The woman Julie had startled that morning appeared and hurried the two children inside.

Poor things, left in the care of the housekeeper when they probably longed to be out in the surf with the other kids.

Julie turned around and splashed through the ankle-deep rivulet, back to her beach, kicking water and sand in a rage against something she couldn't even name. That's what education—her life—was missing. The kids never got down and got dirty.

At least not at Hillsdale Progressive. How could they possibly be satisfied with that? How could she?

*A*lex trundled the last of the camp kids onto the old mini-bus. It was getting harder and harder to send them back, and it would get even harder as the summer wore on and they grew more used to the water. Even though the younger ones were practically blue from staying in the water so long, they would stand defiant, teeth chattering, until Alex bodily lifted them up and carried them to the sand.

And he could feel the change, from loud, boisterous, joyful, to the quiet, accepting children who lined up to be driven back to the migrant workers' camp, where they would live for this harvesting season, before moving on to the next fields where their parents hoped to find work.

He stood as the folding door creaked shut and the bus swayed out of the parking lot, a row of hands sticking out the windows, waving furiously. He waved back, and a beer bottle was shoved in his hand.

Alex took it gladly.

"They were a handful today," Les said.

"Better than not being a handful."

"I'll drink to that." Les lifted his beer and took a long pull. They both stood watching as the bus veered around the corner, headed back to the field where the kids would be dropped off to weary parents and left to their own devices until bedtime. Half of them would rise early to work in the fields; the other half would be bused off to day programs provided by the state and county. And then to people like Les and him, who, growing up, hadn't had after-school programs or even school for that matter.

Lucky often said the two of them were his toughest cases. And Alex knew in his case that must be true. But they'd made it through—all three of them—to land here, Les and Alex totally loyal to the old surfer who took them off the streets and into his life.

He'd helped Alex make it to college, set Les up with Surf's Up. Lucky didn't take credit for it, he never did. Like he wouldn't take credit for what he'd done last night. Alex shuddered. He could have been killed. He was beat up pretty bad. But he insisted on going solo so he wouldn't involve others if the mission went south.

The town was filled with people whose lives he'd touched, no matter how little. They wouldn't let him down. Just like Les and Alex, Bjorn, Mike the regular barman, Rosie, and others would lay down their lives for him.

Not that Alex thought it would ever come to that. Well, not until last night.

"Crazy little blighters," said Bjorn, coming to stand beside them.

The bus disappeared and they turned back to the beach, where Julie's two friends, Aggie and Kayla, were sitting in the sand. It didn't escape his notice that Julie wasn't with them. Alex didn't know if that was good or bad—if she was merely making herself scarce because she didn't like him, or taking the opportunity to poke around where she shouldn't.

Bjorn raised his beer to the others. "I can't think of a better place to spend the summer."

And pay allegiance to Lucky, thought Alex, though none of the three former tough guys standing there would ever admit it out loud. Inside, they were still kids looking for a bed, a hot meal, and someone to watch their back.

Lucky had met Bjorn in Hawaii, a long way from Sweden, which as far as Alex knew didn't have much surfing. But Bjorn, an avid snowboarder, had wanted to learn to surf, so he hitched, stowed away, trekked, until he ended up on the beaches of Oahu, picking up a nasty drug habit along the way.

"Hey, hey, hey," Les said under his breath. "Look who's headed this way."

Julie Barlow was walking toward them from the far side of the beach.

"She is a beauty," Bjorn said.

Alex agreed, but he'd never say so. "Better watch your step."

"Oh, I would never. Lucky would have my guts for breakfast. Kayla's nice."

"Just keep an eye on them until this is over."

"You gonna join us?" Les asked.

Alex shook his head, though he was so tempted. "I don't think so. Lucky would have my guts, too."

"If you're not up to the task . . ."

"Someone has to stay alert."

Les slapped him on the back. "We're alert, man. Don't worry."

Julie had ignored the three of them and joined her friends. They'd gathered up their gear and were heading inevitably, inexorably, toward them.

"Hey," said the flirtatious one, Aggie. She'd been coming on to Les in a big way, and Les, used to attention from women, was acting curiously not like himself.

The three women stopped, though Julie hung back as he'd expected. Lucky had always said she had the spark of the devil in her, but Alex couldn't see it. Certainly not when she was nine. Then she'd been one of those perfect little girls with Shirley Temple hair and clean fingernails, and always polite, except when it came to Alex. All she could do was gawk and turn up her nose at him.

But she seemed fascinated by Lucky, fascinated but not warm. Her mother had done a number on her.

Not that Alex didn't like Louise. She was kind, but . . . What was the word he was thinking of? Fearful. That was it. She was afraid of what life might bring if she wasn't prepared. Man, she had no idea.

Hell, how did you prepare for life anyway?

"You guys really handled those kids great," Aggie said, reserving the brightest part of her smile for Les.

And damn if he didn't smile back. Not his usual friendly, slightly flirtatious smile he used with clients, even ones he wanted to get in the sack.

While Alex was frantically trying to get rid of them, Les was giving at least one of them every reason to stay. Not good. What the hell was Les doing?

"Who were those kids?" Julie asked.

"Part of a town program for migrant workers' kids," Les said.

"Oh, that's cool."

Les shrugged. Bjorn as usual said nothing.

Alex wished they would just keep walking. He was wound tight today, between Lucky and Alberto and the hour he'd spent making sure the kids had fun without slipping past the buoyed ropes and out to sea.

"Do you have other kids' programs?"

"Some," Les said.

"Why?" Alex asked. He couldn't stop himself.

"Just curious. I just saw some kids who live in that house over on the other side of the dunes."

Alex's blood ran cold as he and Les and Bjorn all followed her glance to the dunes—and beyond it, out of sight, Alex's house.

"They were outside watching the other kids, but the house-keeper hustled them inside."

Alex felt a totally inappropriate sense of disappointment. He should feel panic that she'd seen the children, but he wanted her to butt in, do something outside her comfort zone—turn into the woman Lucky had predicted. But so far she'd lived up to her mother's expectations completely.

He almost didn't want Lucky to see her. They had lost contact since she'd graduated from college. Alex knew Lucky was hoping for better things from her than being a schoolteacher in some posh suburban school where they probably didn't even need her. But he bet she fit right in, toed the line, taught the book, made good citizens who would follow the rules when it didn't inconvenience them. It made him . . . what? Angry? Disgusted? He didn't even know what he was feeling, but he knew he had to stop her from further questions.

"They were probably just visiting for the day. There are no kids there."

He saw Les's eyes widen before he caught on and managed to nod. "Hey, see you at Lucky's later?"

Alex gritted his teeth, grabbed his backpack, and left them to it.

*J*ulie decided either she was developing a serious case of paranoia or people were acting strange. She tried to shove the feeling away. They were not just a bunch of deadbeat beach bums following the sun. They were helping migrant kids. That had to speak well in their favor.

And she had to admit, as both Aggie and Kayla pointed out several times on their way back to the hotel, that Scatterman was looking good and was good with children. A plus for any woman their age. And he was definitely giving Julie his full attention.

"I don't think he's flirting," Julie said.

"No," said Aggie. "But he's definitely interested in you."

Julie had noticed it, too, but what his reasons were remained a mystery. Unlike Les and Bjorn, he was not trying to endear himself to her or her friends.

They parted at their respective doors and went to change for dinner. Julie went immediately to the window and looked down to the alley while she shed her beach cover-up and suit. But there was no activity, no sign of life anywhere.

As she dressed to go out, she found herself returning to the window, looking out as if she could will her uncle to return. Somewhere in the last two days, checking on him for her mother had segued from slight annoyance to determination. She didn't know how it had happened, but responsibility had turned to curiosity.

They opted for an early, healthier dinner at one of the small restaurants downtown, then strolled the sidewalk in the lingering light peering into store windows and arguing with Julie about whether she would join them in their next surf lesson. They'd just passed the Knitting Knoll when Aggie stopped them.

"Look, Madame Marzetta's is open. Want to know what our futures are going to be?"

Julie would, but she didn't think she'd be learning it from a crystal ball. She told Aggie so.

"Why not? What harm could it do? You might have a tall, dark stranger in your future." Aggie wiggled her eyebrows suggestively.

"Doesn't everybody?" Julie groused.

She remembered the only time she'd gone to the traveling carnival. Uncle Lucky had taken her. A real treat. Her mother ordered him to hold her hand at all times and not to take her to the sideshows—so he took her to the fortune teller.

She'd had nightmares for a week. The woman said she could tell people's futures and that she could see that Julie was a smart girl. But when she took Lucky's hand and turned it over, she sucked in her breath, said, "Good luck, my friend," and sent them on their way.

"What did she mean, 'good luck'?" Julie had asked.

"Just what she said, wasn't that nice?" he'd said.

It didn't sound nice to Julie. It sounded like something bad was going to happen. And it did, in a way. Soon after that

Lucky made the first of his disappearances. For weeks, Julie was afraid he was dead because they'd disobeyed her mother.

Weeks later, when he finally showed up at the door late one night, she wanted to throw her arms around him and beg him to never leave them again. But he had a scruffy kid by the arm. The kid looked half dead, until he saw Julie and her mother; then in a burst of feral energy, he tried to bite Lucky.

Her mother had said, "I'll get some fresh towels. Julie, go to bed," and hurried away.

Lucky struggled to get the kid down the stairs, and Julie stood there, relieved and sad and feeling totally alone.

"Maybe Madame Marzetta knows where Uncle Lucky is," Aggie said.

Julie dragged herself back from the past. She really had no desire to find out from a fortune teller if her fears had at last come true.

"Well, she might. And besides, I want to see if I should put any more energy into getting to know Les or not."

Kayla rolled her eyes, Julie hung her head in resignation, and they went inside.

Chapter 10

The first thing Julie noticed about Madame Marzetta's was the dark and the smell. Deep purple variations on lava lamps were placed on fabric-covered tables along the front window. Fabric was draped down the walls and formed a curtain across the back of the claustrophobic waiting room. Pillows topped a cushioned bench along one wall.

And it all was cloaked in a heavy, earthy incense.

As they stood in the tiny waiting room, the curtains across the back parted in a wave of paisleys. A remarkable being stood in the opening, arms outstretched like a Wagnerian soprano, but actually merely holding the curtains apart.

She was swathed in deep purple, a sash of vibrant red encircling her waist. Ropes of beads hung from her neck, and a store's worth of brass bangles jangled on her arms. An iridescent turban sat low on her forehead, an exotic feather arcing forward to create a shadow over her face.

It was all a bit much. But what the hell, it was vacation.

"Welcome to Madame Marzetta's."

She lowered her arms, setting off a noisy waterfall of bangles as the curtains fell behind her.

"Have you come for a reading?" The voice was contralto, deep, mysterious, and surely put on for effect.

Next to Julie, Kayla had picked up what appeared to be a price sheet and held it close to one of the purple lamps, attempting to read it. She let out a sigh, probably worried about how much this little escapade would cost them.

"We want to have our fortunes read," Aggie volunteered.

"Tarot? Palms?" Madame Marzetta lowered her head and looked out from beneath what had to be false eyelashes, though it was hard to tell anything about her in the obscure light. "Crystal ball?"

"What do they cost?" Kayla asked.

"Sixty dollars for half an hour."

Kayla put down the price list.

"For a group of three, twenty each."

Julie rolled her eyes, but they all took out twenties and handed them to Madame Marzetta. The bills quickly disappeared into the folds of her robe.

"Come this way." She turned in a dramatic display of fabric and, brushing away one side of the curtains, motioned them to come through. Aggie stepped boldly forward, followed by Kayla, then Julie.

The inner chamber was more fabric, obscurely lit from unseen sources and just as claustrophobic. A round table in the center of the room was covered by a shimmering cloth that glowed iridescent purple in the eerie lighting. It was surrounded by several straight-backed chairs and one "throne"—the first word that came to Julie's mind—a heavily carved Victorian armchair that added a touch of horror to the otherwise exotic effect.

Madame Marzetta motioned them to sit in the chairs, gesturing Kayla to go to the far side, Julie in the middle, and Aggie to her left. They sat down, though Julie was wishing she could get a better look at the furnishings; they looked like they'd seen many years and very few cleanings.

Madame Marzetta ensconced herself in the "throne" across from them. It put her several inches higher than the others, and the light from above cast her features into mysterious shadows. It was very effective, and Julie couldn't resist the shiver of anticipation that wormed its way into her rational thought.

"Now," Marzetta intoned. She splayed her long, supple fingers over the tabletop; the globe that sat at the center of the table, and had been dark a second before, pulsed with a milky light.

Kayla and Aggie gasped in delighted awe. Julie frowned at it, wondering how she'd turned it on with her hands empty in front of them. A foot switch probably.

Madame Marzetta closed her eyes and her body began to sway. Her hands moved gracefully in the heavily incensed air. Circling and coming together as the globe turned from white to pink to aquamarine, finally settling on a dark burgundy.

Suddenly the fortune teller let out a *huh* sound that shattered the silence and made the three women jump.

The red color dissipated in the globe to be replaced by glittering silver particles. *Like a snow globe,* Julie thought. And very pretty, though Julie was determined not to be taken in. Then ruined it by thinking, *Please, nothing scary, just give us the tall, dark stranger bit.*

"You have been friends for a long time."

A good guess, Julie thought.

"I see water, a stream perhaps. A cabin."

Julie glanced up.

"A bucket of paint?"

"OMG!" Aggie exclaimed. "Girl Scout camp. I almost fell off the ladder and knocked the paint bucket off. It poured all over Julie and Kayla, who were holding the ladder steady. We were just talking about it."

"I don't think you're supposed to give her clues," Julie said, totally exasperated, except for a tiny niggle of doubt that asked, *How did she know about the paint?* It was such an odd and ancient fact for Madame Marzetta to have pulled up, even if she'd seen them in town, marked them as tourists who would probably come to have their fortunes told on a lark, gone to the trouble of finding out their names, and googled them. But what were the chances that she'd learned about the paint fiasco?

Madame Marzetta suddenly took on more interest. Not that Julie believed that she could really tell the future, or the past for that matter.

"Friends formed in youth can withstand the trials that befall us later in life."

Was that a warning? Was something bad going to happen

after all? Julie pushed the thought away and steeled herself not to fall under the spell of this exotic charlatan. It was just an ordinary platitude delivered with panache.

"What kind of trials?" Kayla asked.

Marzetta reached out as if she were going to touch the globe, but it suddenly lost its light, gray swirls of clouds filling the inside, then growing opaque, inert, and dark.

None of them moved or even breathed.

"The future is a mystery. As always. But this future . . . Now is not the time to rest." She slowly shook her head, stretched her fingers, and placed her palms near her ears as if symbolically shutting out some sound she didn't want to hear.

Julie didn't hear anything. The room must be acoustically enhanced, because they could be on a deserted island for all the noise from the street she heard.

"Don't move," Madame Marzetta said, and swooped out of her chair. She stopped before a heavy cabinet that Julie hadn't noticed in the shadows and came back with a deck of cards.

She was going all out. They should have checked the add-on prices. Julie had heard of these people charging hundreds of dollars for a reading. She shifted in her chair, but she had to admit Marzetta was putting on a pretty good show.

But Madame Marzetta seemed to have forgotten them as she spread the cards on the table before her, gathered them into a deck, and held them in her hands until Julie could swear they began to illuminate.

Holding the glowing cards in front of her, she turned her

head first to Kayla, then to Aggie, then to Julie. Scoping them out? Reading their auras or something? Julie couldn't even tell if she was actually looking at them; her eyes appeared as black crescents in the eerie light.

Slowly she turned over a card and placed it in front of Kayla. She nodded to herself as if what she saw was as she suspected. Julie and Aggie both craned their necks to see. Julie had seen tarot cards before, even had them read at a party. But this deck was unlike any she'd seen.

"Is this tarot?" Aggie asked.

"Shh." Marzetta's command was sharp and definitive.

Aggie's eyes widened; Julie practically held her breath. Kayla was staring at the card so intently Julie wondered if Kayla was seeing something different from what she was seeing.

"Many responsibilities," Marzetta intoned. "Do not rush."

Kayla blinked.

"Trust in yourself, not someone else. All will be."

Will be? Julie thought. *Will be what? Fine? Well? A big fat riddle forever?*

Marzetta turned to Aggie. Laid down a card. "It is time."

"Time?" Aggie squeaked. "Time for what?"

"For what you truly want."

Aggie's eyes bugged. "You mean . . ."

Marzetta slid the card away from her and returned it to the stack. "I mean it is time."

She turned to Julie. Tapped the deck of cards twice with a pointed fingernail. Turned a card over on the table. Looked at it for a long time without speaking, so long that Julie began to fidget. She looked at the card but couldn't tell anything from the bird and tree portrayed there.

Marzetta took a deep breath. "You are not where you should be."

No kidding, thought Julie. Was she so obvious in her dilemma? Feeling dissatisfied with her life but not knowing what to do about it.

"It isn't here," Marzetta said, as if she were answering Julie's own question.

Julie looked up from the card, tried to see the fortune teller's face, but her head was lowered as if she'd fallen asleep, the feather creating a curtain across her features.

"But it isn't behind you."

Julie had to fight the urge to turn around and look. Even though she was pretty sure Marzetta didn't mean literally, it was a little spooky. What *did* she mean? She cautioned herself that this was the way they operated, saying something vague and leaving their victim to make up a story around it. Julie had just fallen into that trap.

Marzetta sucked in a long breath. "You must look elsewhere. And soon."

Kayla and Aggie were both staring at Julie.

"Now," said Marzetta with a flourish of hands and fabric. "Your half hour is finished. Heed the signs as you will, it is your choice."

Perhaps, thought Julie, but her pronouncement sounded more like an enter-at-your-own-peril warning.

The girls hastily got up and slipped through the curtains into the waiting room, Marzetta hot on their heels, as if she couldn't wait to get them away. Or just anxious to get on with her next paying customers?

Kayla and Aggie were already out on the sidewalk talking to two women who were looking in Marzetta's window.

As Julie stepped past the fortune teller into the fading light, her eyes met Madame Marzetta's. A momentary flash of recognition as the light fell across the woman's face.

"You."

"Me. Good evening, Julie."

Madame Marzetta nodded and shut the door behind her.

"So she was worth it?" asked one of the newcomers.

"Yeah," Aggie said. "She was."

"Yeah," Kayla added. "It was kind of scary what she knew."

"Thanks." The two women hurried inside.

The three of them walked down the sidewalk, each lost in her own thoughts, but for different reasons.

Madame Marzetta's scam could have just been augmented by things Lucky might have told her. They *were* friends. But the "you must look elsewhere soon" had more ominous overtones.

For a friendly town it sure seemed like a lot of people wanted to get rid of her.

"She was so real," Aggie said. "How did she know all that stuff about me? And the paint thing?"

"Did you tell Les about any of our childhood escapades?" Kayla asked.

"No. The past was the last thing on my mind. And I certainly wouldn't share about me dumping paint on your heads. Do you think she read our minds? We were just talking about it in the car."

"Of course not," Julie said.

"Then how did she know?"

Kayla shrugged.

"Because Lucky must have mentioned it since he's been here . . . for some reason," Julie said. "Everyone in town seems to know who I am and they didn't know we were coming. *We* didn't even know we were coming."

"And we forgot to ask about Uncle Lucky," Aggie said.

"I don't think she would have been helpful there."

"Why not? Because he wasn't with us?"

"Because she doesn't want us to find him."

Kayla and Aggie both stopped.

"That's crazy," Aggie said. "She doesn't even know why we're here."

"Actually, she does. We met her yesterday. Only then she was wearing a linen dress and house shoes."

"That was the woman in the house shoes?"

Julie nodded.

"She can be a housewife and have extrasensory perception," Aggie said, her enthusiasm taking a nosedive.

"Sure," Julie said.

"You think she's a fake?"

Julie shrugged.

"But her message to me was so spot on," Aggie said.

"That it was time?"

"Yeah."

"Oh, come on, Aggie. Time for what? It was so vague it could mean anything. Time to pay your rent? Get your hair cut?"

Aggie shook her head. "No, she knew."

"Knew what?"

"Nothing, it's just . . . just weird. What about you, Kayla? What did she mean 'trust yourself'?"

"I don't know, but . . . my ex is always behind on his child support, though he's making plenty of money. My mother is determined to find me a new husband. My father thinks I should sell the house and move in with them so they can help with the grandchildren. They're sweet, but God, no. My brother is trying to talk me into putting my savings, such as they are, with his investment firm. I'm torn, but I think Madame Marzetta's right, it's better to just trust myself."

"See, she *was* right," Aggie said.

Julie made a face. "Oh puh-lease."

"What about what she said to you? I didn't understand it at all."

"Well, I did. She wants us—me in particular—out of here. I'm not where I should be. More like not where she wants me."

"Where's that?" Aggie asked.

"Away from here—and Lucky."

Kayla huffed out a sigh. "It did sound that way, now that you mention it. But why?"

"Because I think she's involved with whatever shady things are going on here. She wants us out of the way. She lives next door to Lucky. She said she'd been friends with him and my mom since their childhood in Asbury Park. That's probably how she knew about the paint and stuff; she's probably heard stories about us from him."

"But still. She helped me," Kayla said.

"Me, too," said Aggie.

"Oh, she helped me, too," Julie said. "But not in the way she meant. Because no way in hell am I going to leave Uncle Lucky to walk into this without backup."

"We're going to stay for the duration," Kayla said.

"Yeah," Aggie said, and grinned. "It's time."

Yeah, it was time. And first thing tomorrow morning, Julie was going to have a little tête-à-tête with Madame Marie "Marzetta" Simmons.

Shall we hit Lucky's for a nightcap?" Aggie suggested.

"Lucky's isn't the only bar in town," Julie said.

"But it's the only happening one," Kayla said. "Come on, Jules, don't be a party pooper."

"You know me so well," Julie said sourly. She did. Julie had never learned to party comfortably. "Oh, all right. Come on."

They walked next to each other down the sidewalk and had to move over only once to let some other strollers pass. Julie could hear the music pulsing from Lucky's before they turned into the drive. Amazing that it didn't get a ticket for disturbing the peace.

Evidently it was fifties night at the bar. The beach crowd had been joined by an assortment of people of all ages in vintage dress that could only be a cross section of the town. Tables and chairs had been pushed to the sides or removed altogether, clearing a wide area of the wooden floor for dancing. The dance floor was packed, with additional waitresses skirting the gyrating couples to deliver their drinks safely to the tables beyond.

The outside area was just as crowded, so they ordered drinks at the bar and stood at the edge of the dance floor watching the couples.

It wasn't long before a guy with a crew cut and sleeveless tee that read BEACH BUM took the drink from Aggie's hand and led her to the dance floor.

Kayla began talking to a couple on her other side, though it was impossible to carry on much of a conversation since they were standing in front of a speaker.

Julie sipped her drink and swayed a little to the music, trying to look nonchalant and wishing she could disappear.

Gradually she gave up any pretense of enjoying herself, finished her drink, and put it down on a nearby table that was monetarily empty. When she turned back, Kayla had disappeared. Julie looked around, finally spotted her out on the dance floor. Julie began to edge her way toward the exit.

A glass of white wine appeared before her downcast eyes.

She looked up to see Alex "Scatter" Martin smiling at her.

He said something she couldn't hear.

"What?"

He took her elbow and pulled her out the door to the patio. "I said, 'Not in a partying mood?'"

Julie shrugged. "Not my scene."

"What is your scene?"

"Actually, I'm not sure I have one."

The pounding music wound to a stop to be replaced by a slow ballad. He tilted his head.

Julie had a moment of panic. Surely he wasn't going to ask her to dance. He was on the clock.

"Always a bridesmaid, never the bride?"

Well, that was a dash of reality. "I guess, now that you mention it. Something like that."

He turned to her with popping eyes, an over-the-top expression that any other time would have made her laugh. "You want to be the bride?"

"No, well, not the bride, but not the extra person all the time." Damn, why had she said that? Maybe because she'd already downed a third of the glass of wine he'd just handed her, just because he made her nervous.

"You could try harder."

"I am."

"No, you're not. You have to put yourself out there."

"I hate doing that. It seems so artificial."

"Well, forget finding that here. We're about as laid-back as you can get."

"Really." She gave him her best I-know-what-you're-up-to look.

It didn't faze him.

"Or you can learn to enjoy your own company."

"I do. Besides, I have other things on my mind."

"Not a multitasker?"

"Why are you so obnoxious?"

"Am I?"

"Yes."

He grinned.

"I saw you last night," she blurted out.

He gave her a look. "You and half the town. I was here until almost two closing up."

"Until three."

"Was it that late?" His tone was casual, but she hadn't missed that split second of quiet, the telltale sign of guilt whether you were eight or thirtysomething.

She took a sip of wine, though it was more like a gulp for courage. She probably shouldn't do this. If he was a crook, he might do anything. *Except ask you to dance, idiot.*

She plowed on. "I saw the van—in the alley. I don't suppose you know who was driving it?"

The bartender made a dismissive gesture. "Lots of people use the alley. You said it was around three? What were you doing up? You don't strike me as the type to stay out that late."

"Don't try to distract me."

He cocked his head.

"I couldn't sleep—I was worried about my uncle."

"Well, now you don't have to be worried anymore."

"Who was driving the van?"

"I have no idea. Probably a fisherman coming home from trawling."

"Driving with his lights off?"

He looked slowly down at her, grinned. "Maybe he has a bitchy wife."

His smile was smug. So clever, but it didn't fool her. Alex Martin's eyes were as hard as obsidian. The sudden change sent a chill down her spine and she took an involuntary step away from him.

But she'd gone too far to back down. It was her duty to family, and part of her hoped it was something innocent that she had misperceived.

"An old man was driving; he stopped behind the bar. Someone came out the back door and unloaded whatever was in the van and dumped it in the bushes."

"Oh, that." He looked around.

At last, she thought.

"Trash," he said. He made another show of looking around. Bent down close to her ear. "Look, we have a lot of off-the-book workers, everyone does, so don't pass judgment. They need the work. And we pay decently. They're usually supporting several family members with inadequate living arrangements. Sometimes they need a place to dump their garbage and are afraid to go to the dump for obvious reasons. You have to show ID to prove you're a resident. So if they want to use our dumpster, we look the other way. It's no big deal. Lucky doesn't mind."

She scrutinized his face. He was an awfully good liar, but he was lying. She was almost certain.

"You're not going to turn us in to the environmental board, are you?" His smile was back to charming.

She could almost believe him, but that smile was just too good, too nonchalant. And she'd seen it before, the last time he'd been trying to snow her.

She took another step away from him.

His smile broadened.

She conjured up her most foreboding fourth-grade teacher look, hindered by one too many glasses of wine. "Garbage is one thing, but if you're doing something illegal, like substituting cheap liquor, to cheat Uncle Lucky, I won't stand for it."

The ubiquitous, multi-duty smile faltered for a second, then snapped back in place. "You won't? Glad to hear it. There's hope for you yet." He took the now empty glass out of her hand and walked away.

"What? You don't know me," she said, just as the music cranked up again. "And this isn't about me," she yelled.

He turned. "What? I can't hear you." And with another annoyingly cocky grin, he headed back to the bar.

$\mathcal{M}$arie pulled off her turban and threw it on the kitchen table. "They came to get their fortunes told."

"Julie?" Lucky closed the latest issue of *Surfer* magazine. "That's promising."

"Would you be serious?"

"I am serious. I wish . . . but this is not the time for wishes, is it?"

It never is with you, Marie thought.

"I did the best I could. Aggie, the vivacious one, was pretty easy to read, major aura, major stuff going on inside, not the obvious first impression." It hadn't been a surprise. The most "out there" people sometimes had the most to protect inside. "Kayla, the brunette, has children and is in a tough financial situation, or I missed my guess."

"I didn't think you ever guessed," Lucky said.

"Huh. I'm second-guessing you all the time."

"Come here." He pulled her down to sit on his lap, which was never comfortable. He was all bone and sinew and muscle. But she humored him.

"I *don't* guess. Just some people are easier to read than others. And in those cases, I do have to extrapolate.

"I made a few pertinent predictions on my initial readings, conjured up the story you told me about the camp paint disaster to add a little veracity to the session. It impressed the other two. Julie was not amused, so I drove it home with a little card turning, instilling the idea that they should leave. Told Julie her future wasn't here."

"Where is it?"

"Hell, I don't know. You come back beaten to a pulp with the possibility of a drug lord on your tail, say you really need Julie out of the way in case the shit hits. I did what I could, wearing a damned turban and enough clanking bracelets to give me a headache."

"I'm sorry."

"No, you're not. And neither am I. I just don't know what's best to do."

"Do you think you convinced her to leave?"

"I don't know. She's a hard nut to crack."

Lucky sighed. "Like her mother. Who I could never face again if any harm were to come to her daughter."

Marie sighed as well. "Besides, she remembered me from yesterday morning. That was a mistake. I shouldn't have gone out when I saw her snooping around. But I was worried." She perused his face. "Is it really as bad as that?"

"I hope not. But we all know that sometimes people get caught in the cross fire. It's what we live. But innocent bystanders? Julie? No, I couldn't bear it."

"I know, love. Neither could I."

Chapter 11

Julie, Kayla, and Aggie decided to try Darinda's Luncheonette for breakfast the next morning. Julie thought they all might be feeling the effects of too much partying and possibly, at least on Julie's part, having their planned vacation hijacked and having second thoughts about the outcome.

Darinda's evidently was the place for breakfast in Lucky's Beach, and they had to stand in the doorway to wait for a table.

The dining area was painted in a yellow tone that bordered on ocher. The far wall had a colorful mural of a many-armed goddess surrounded by flowers, birds, spiraling designs, and geometrical edgings.

Not your typical diner.

Ceramic mugs and cutlery rattled on the Formica tables that ran along both walls and were spaced evenly apart in a domino pattern in between. A melodious Indian raga played a quiet accompaniment to conversations, laughter, and a bustling wait-staff.

An Indian woman—Darinda herself?—wearing an orange tunic over black flowing trousers hurried forward, picking up three menus on her way to greet the newcomers. Her hair was pulled back in a low bun, and big hoop earrings hung from her ears.

"Welcome to Darinda's. This way, please." She waited for a waitress carrying a heavy tray of plates to pass by and then for a very young and skinny busboy, also Indian, to cart a rubber container filled with dirty dishes in the direction of the kitchen. Then she led them to a table for four a narrow aisle away from the row of booths that ran along the wall.

Julie was in the process of pulling out a chair when a trio of "Mornin', Julie" got her attention. Corey, Ron, and Ike from the bar. They seemed to turn up everywhere she went.

She smiled over at them. "Good morning. I see this is the place to be for breakfast." She finished sitting down.

"You sounded just like an elementary teacher," Aggie said.

"Ugh." Julie reached for a menu. "I'll try not to be so chipper in the future."

"The best in town, ain't that right, Darinda?" said Ike.

Darinda, who had just handed Aggie and Kayla their menus, nodded.

"This here's Julie," Ron said. "Lucky's niece."

There was a sudden lull in the luncheonette. Darinda's face lit up and she took Julie's hands in both of hers and squeezed them. "Lucky's niece. Welcome. Welcome. Are you comfortable at this table? I can find you one less busy."

"Thank you, but we're fine here. These are my friends, Aggie and Kayla."

"Welcome, welcome. Vihaan, bring coffee." She snapped her fingers. A slim boy, older than the busboy but definitely of the same family, bustled over with the coffeepot and three mugs dangling from his fingers.

With Darinda's keen eyes upon him, he poured three mugs without a drip, and with a "Please, enjoy your breakfast," they both departed.

A quick look around assured Julie that most of the diners had returned to their breakfast, except for Corey, Ike, and Ron, who were still beaming at her. Friendly, avuncular, perhaps, and . . . feeling guilty? *About what?* she wondered. She'd seen those innocent smiles before, usually when she'd caught young miscreants up to no good. And if ever there were three boys in grown men's bodies feeling guilty about something, it had to be these three.

In the booth behind them two women prepared to leave: the irate knitting lady, Stella, and Claire of Claire's Beachables. Julie would never have thought of them as breakfast buddies.

Stella heaved herself out of the booth. She was dressed in a light rose twinset, which would soon be unbearable in the heat. Julie supposed it was advertising. Stella adjusted a black leather purse across her shoulder and reached back onto the banquette for a plastic shopping bag filled with a newspaper and what appeared to be mail. She stopped long enough to glare at Julie.

Julie smiled, hoping to ward off any ill will, but it was ineffectual.

"You tell your uncle . . ." she began.

"Oh, Stella, give it a rest," Ike said.

Stella's top half twisted toward him. "You mind your own business, Ike Gibson. Someone broke into my store last night."

Claire nudged her toward the exit with an apologetic smile.

"Well, why didn't you say so?" Ron said.

"It weren't Julie, if that's what you're thinking." Corey chuckled. "We can vouch for her."

"Ha, 'cause she's Lucky's niece?"

"That's reason enough. Did you call the police?"

"Why bother?"

"Well, what did they take?"

"How could I tell? Everything was moved around so I couldn't find anything this morning. Yarns all out of place."

"Think they were looking for something special?" asked Ike. "I hear Sally Tierney's baby is gonna be a girl. Any pink yarn missing?"

"You probably just rearranged things and forgot," Corey said. "Happens to us all, don't it, guys?"

"Uh-huh."

"Yep."

"I would expect that attitude from you," snapped Stella. She swiveled back to Julie. "It's those delinquent children Lucky keeps bringing to town. I know he thinks he's doing good, but it's ruining the town."

Ron slid out of his seat and wrapped his arm around Stella's shoulders. "Aw, Stella, nobody wants to hear that nonsense this morning. Why don't me and Corey and Ike come over and help you get things back to normal."

"It's those darn kids, they're everywhere. You mark my words. There's bound to be trouble."

"Now, now, we wouldn't let anything happen to you." Ron waggled his eyebrows over her head and ushered her out of the diner.

"Don't let her upset you," Claire said. "We all have our cross to bear. Stella just sees hers as bigger than anyone else's. I try to be a friend, but I can tell you, sometimes it takes a lot of energy. You three have a good stay." She followed the others out.

"Looks like Uncle Lucky hasn't changed," Aggie said.

Julie sighed. "Sounds like it. Still bringing home strays."

"Well, good for him," Kayla said. "If my kids ever ran away, heaven forbid, I hope they would find Lucky or someone like him."

Julie considered Kayla. All her friends had adored Uncle Lucky. She had, too, until he started disappointing her. It was like the case of the cobbler's children going without shoes. Maybe she hadn't needed him as much as the others did. At least maybe he'd thought she hadn't. But she had.

She shook herself. *Oh, boohoo.* She'd had a good life, and she'd never had to live on the streets; she'd never even threatened to run away, much less actually carried it out. She had a lot to be thankful for, so why had she felt so resentful toward her uncle?

"Don't look," Kayla said. "But these two guys in the booth next to our friendly welcoming committee keep looking this way."

"Are they cute?" Aggie said, glancing over Julie's shoulder.

Julie turned to see for herself.

"I said don't look. Anyway they're getting up."

As they watched, two men walked past them to the door. They were wearing slacks and short-sleeved button-down shirts. Slicked-back hair. They looked more like salesmen than surfers, and strangely out of place.

*B*reakfast lasted longer than usual, as people came up to say hello and welcome them to town. It seemed everyone in the diner knew Lucky. Even Mayor "call me Billy" Atkins stopped by to introduce himself and his two young sons—the same two boys whom CeeJay had saved from the irate Stella.

When they'd finished their meal and finally drained the last drops of their delicious dark roasted coffee, all four members of Darinda's family walked them to the door.

"I can't believe everyone is so friendly," Kayla said.

"I can't believe we ate all that food," Aggie said with a groan. "It was delicious, but now Les will see me with breakfast belly in my new bikini."

"He saw you in it yesterday," Kayla said. "He'll give you a pass."

"Not that old thing. Another new one. I'd been saving it for tonight. They're having a bonfire on the beach. And I saw this other really cute one in the window of that boutique we passed last night . . . maybe I'll go try it on."

Kayla rolled her eyes. "Well, I've got to call the kids, make sure they survived another day on the golf course. And then I'm for the beach."

"I'll meet you guys there," Julie said. "But first I'm going to pay a visit to Madame Marzetta . . . at home. Ask her a few questions and then I wash my hands of the whole Lucky situation. This was way more trouble than it was worth."

"Yeah, but you have to admit, this is sort of better than the big beach crowd."

"I guess." It was more laid-back, which was much better for Julie's temperament. And now that they knew Lucky was fine, she could start enjoying herself. Though she was curious about what Marzetta had told her last night, not as a real fortune, but as a way to see Julie gone.

Aggie went off to the shops, Kayla returned to the hotel, and Julie headed toward the alley that ran behind the stores and cottages. She had considered walking down Dune Lane, but she thought showing up at the back door of Marie's cottage would seem more informal, less obvious.

She nodded to Claire and the three guys who were standing outside the Knitting Knoll talking to Stella. Julie picked up her pace and was soon walking down the alley. She was passing the back entrances of the shops when one of the doors opened just wide enough for someone to slip out: a girl, tall, thin, blond. She eased the door closed and took off at a run.

Right into Julie.

"Shit, sorry." She looked up and Julie recognized CeeJay from Surf's Up. "I'm late. Don't tell anyone you saw me. I'm gonna tell 'em I had a flat tire."

"Sure," Julie said, still recovering, and watched CeeJay race toward the parking lot. She looked back at the door CeeJay had come from. There must be apartments above the stores.

Julie turned back to her own business and walked on, though her steps slowed as she reached the row of cottages and her usual indecision took over. Maybe she was making too much of this. She really shouldn't bother the woman this early. Maybe she had a day job.

So what if she did? *Stop being such a nervous Nellie. Learn to assert yourself. It's just a few harmless questions. The worst she can do is say no. Call the police?* Julie had already been attacked by a resident once today. *Oh hell. Grow a pair.*

She forced herself forward. She'd reached the house next to Marie's when her door opened. Julie automatically stepped back.

Dougie bounded out the door, sniffed around, saw her, and galloped toward her. Julie raised her head to call out to Marie to stop him, but she froze in her tracks.

The face staring back at her wasn't Marie's. Neither of them moved or even blinked. Then Lucky stepped back inside and closed the door.

Julie just stood there, disbelieving, waiting for it to open again. For him to invite her inside. But it didn't. He didn't. He'd seen her. Recognized her. And closed the door on her. He'd been hiding from her all along. He didn't want to see her.

And something inside her imploded.

Fine, it didn't matter. She'd just go back to the hotel—but her feet wouldn't move. *He shut the door practically in my face.*

Dougie had stopped a few feet away, his sweeping tail tucked low, his ears drooping against his head.

Turn around. Leave.

She forced her body to turn away, began to retrace her steps to the parking lot.

He must have been here the whole time and told everyone to get rid of her. Well, fine, she was leaving, now. She would never search him out again. Because you couldn't depend on good old Uncle Lucky, even when you gave up your vacation just because your mother was worried.

She made it as far as the steps of one of the shops before her knees gave out. She sank down and buried her head in her arms trying to breathe. All this trouble. All these feelings. And he didn't want to see her. She just didn't understand. What had they ever done to him?

A slobbery wet nose nudged her knee.

"Go away. He doesn't want to have anything to do with me. Go back to where you belong."

Dougie plopped down, stretched, and rested his head on her feet. She tried to nudge him away but he didn't budge.

"He didn't even have the courtesy to say hello and send me on my way. He didn't have to hide. From me. Why didn't he just call my mom like he's supposed to do? Then I would have never even come here."

Dougie didn't seem to have an answer, but she suddenly did. Lucky—Tony—was in hiding because he was a common criminal. A part of whatever they were smuggling the other night. It hadn't been an old man driving the van; it had been Lucky—Tony. He did sort of look old and bent over this morning.

It all made sense now, why he had never invited them to visit. Why he missed this phone call. He'd been busy robbing somebody. Maybe Stella was right: he was not the great man they all seemed to think he was but a crook.

"What am I going to tell Mom?"

Dougie had the grace to roll his eyes toward her and whimper.

"Yeah, me, too." She began to absently rub Dougie's back. "I just won't tell her. I'll just forget everything I've seen." She sniffed. "But why, Dougie?"

Dougie rolled over to have his stomach scratched.

She stood up, eliciting a low moan from Dougie. "Go get Lucky to rub your stomach. I'm leaving." She stomped away, Turned back. "And don't follow me."

Dougie looked up from where he was still lying on his back.

"Ugh." She stalked off, kept up her righteous indignation until she reached the parking lot and her face crumpled. She gave herself a stern talking-to and managed not to cry.

She reached the sidewalk and turned left toward the hotel. She'd just calmly tell the girls what had happened and that their duty was over and they could leave as soon as their room at the economy motel was free. Though neither Aggie nor Kayla seemed at all discontent. How had things gone south so fast?

Two words: Uncle Lucky. Well, Tony Costa could just go live his life. Julie Barlow didn't care. Not anymore.

I couldn't help it," Lucky said. "I saw her and I just panicked. Is she still out there? Maybe you could—"

"She's gone." Marie turned from the kitchen window.

"Dammit. This has been an effing mess since the get-go."

"So what do you want to do?" Marie knew they were in over

their heads. There had been some iffy cases in the past, but none like this. You didn't mess with Joseph Raymond without the inevitability of retribution. He would be swift and ruthless. All the preparations they'd made could unravel in a heartbeat.

"You'd better go after her," Lucky said.

"And do what? Bring her back? Tell her to pay no attention to that man behind the kitchen curtain? She deserves more than that; she's been on a mission to find you."

"Because Louise was being Louise, worrying about stuff that is none of her business and that she can do nothing about. And because she has a total hold over her daughter—she always has. I tried to give the poor little thing a chance, but she was always so afraid of upsetting Louise."

"Louise was not an ogre."

"No, just overprotective. Of me and of Julie. It was suffocating for me but downright debilitating for Julie."

"Because she's worried about you both. And she knows the harsh reality of having to depend only on yourself."

"No, Mar. *You* know that harsh reality. Louise had plenty of support. She just refused to accept it."

Like someone else I know, Marie thought. They were twins in more ways than Lucky realized. But that was another story. In his case, it had led him to take the chances Louise had refused to take. It also placed him in harm's way more times than was good for his or Marie's health. "Louise is what she is, and I know that it looks like Julie's turning out to be just like her, but—"

"I should just leave them alone to be who they are?"

"Perhaps, but remember, you once told me that Julie had a tiny streak of you in her, if she'd only listen to it."

"She's better off the way she is."

"Maybe. No, I don't mean that. It's only because you put yourself at risk on this last trip."

"And everybody else, too."

"Are you sorry you did it?"

He took a long time to answer, while Marie held her breath. She was worried about him. Lucky was a man who took things in stride, the good, the bad, the ugly. It's what made him the man he was and effective at what he did.

"We all know you had to do it. And we're all grateful, but we knew going into it that you can't protect everyone, though you think you can. And that's the little streak of Louise in you."

She stilled, not sure how he was going to take that last jab. He at least looked better today than he had two nights ago, bloodied and beaten. It had scared the bejesus out of her. But her training, begun at her mother's knee and honed in the service, had taught her to show no emotions, whether it was telling fortunes or telling lies.

"We'll just have to see it through together."

Lucky shook his head. "I tried to get Rosie to go to a safe house, but she feels safe here. I should have insisted. Raymond's bound to have men looking for her, and I may have led them right to her. If the authorities aren't able to pick them up first . . ."

"They will," Marie said. "They won't let us down."

He gave her a look that pierced to her soul.

"They won't. And Raymond's men might have found Rosie regardless. That couldn't be helped, and we all agreed."

"But Julie didn't. I can't risk her getting caught in the cross fire."

"There won't be any cross fire if we stick to the plan."

"Oh hell, Marie, I don't know what to do."

"You always know what to do. And if you don't, you know how to fake it. But Julie's got to be warned not to say anything."

"And enmesh her in this mess? She can't stay here."

"It's better than keeping her clueless and having her snatched off the beach and held for ransom."

Lucky rubbed his chin, winced as his fingers passed over the yellowing bruise. "No. The less she knows the better. Scatter says she thinks he's smuggling cheap liquor. It's a pretty good cover story." He shook his head, laughed softly. "I'll die without ever salvaging my reputation with those two."

Marie slipped behind his chair so he couldn't see her face and put her arms around him. "Don't even put that out into the universe."

He turned his head to kiss her cheek. "I'll go talk to her, if she'll listen."

"I'll go. You stay put." Marie grabbed her purse.

"First call Scatter, we'll have to get our story straight. I won't have her getting hurt. Not for me, not for anybody."

Chapter 12

*B*y the time Julie reached the beach she'd pretty much re-signed herself to accepting the fact that her uncle didn't want to see her. She could live with that. It's not like she'd given him any reason lately to care about her.

She wasn't mad at him—not anymore. Didn't blame him for not stepping in to fill the emptiness of not having a father. It all seemed beside the point today. And too late to make a change.

She'd done what her mom had asked. Checked on Uncle Lucky. He was fine. There was an end to it. She would never have to tell her mother the humiliating story of having the door slammed in her face. Well, to be truthful, she'd actually been one house away. But dammit, she was tired of always being truthful, being fair, caring about others. Her duty was done.

Now it was her turn. For once she would be carefree, unreli-able, creative, flamboyant . . . She looked down at her sensible shorts and tee. Well, she could be—at least for the summer, at least a few weeks—until she had to start her coursework toward her master's, toward a better salary, toward a better retirement . . .

Then rounding up supplies for next year's classes and going in early to decorate her classroom, because even though they might be hermetically sealed from outside distraction, she could at least make it a kid-friendly environment.

And it would all start again. She'd be standing at the front of the room looking at the expectant faces of another year of promising fourth graders. Maybe next year . . .

Who was she kidding? It would never change. *She* would never change.

Except maybe for the next week. And dammit, she was going to make the most of it.

But not here. Dewey Beach would be filled with distractions of its own. No chance of running into relatives who didn't want her. She was going to suggest they confirm with their original hotel for the rest of vacation.

Aggie and Kayla were standing around the entrance to Surf's Up, talking with Bjorn and Les. While she'd been running around looking for her uncle, they had been doing what you did on vacation.

Kayla saw her and motioned her over.

That's when she noticed CeeJay standing in the doorway, leaning up against the frame, arms crossed, and looking daggers at Aggie. The girl was definitely not happy about that blossoming relationship.

"Les and Bjorn are taking us out on their boat," Aggie said.

Julie smiled. "Great. Have fun. I'm—"

"You're going, too."

"Thanks, but listen. I saw Tony. He's here. He's been hiding from me this whole time. He saw me and he shut the door on me."

"No way, that doesn't sound like Uncle Lucky."

"Well, it's true."

"Then let's go find out why," said Kayla.

Julie shook her head. "I know where I'm not wanted. I'm going to Dewey. I know you guys are having a great time, so you can stay here if you want."

"Wait a minute," Aggie said. She glanced at Les, who had stepped sort of out of hearing distance. "Come sit down and tell us what happened."

Julie sat on the bench that ran along the front of the surf shack. Aggie and Kayla sat on either side of her, leaning in, a human shield of sorts. And Julie felt immeasurably grateful. Her friends never let her down.

"Now, tell us everything," Kayla said.

"I was going to see Marie, Madame Marzetta, to ask her what she knew. Obviously she wasn't telling us everything. I'd gone down the alley and was next door from her house when her door suddenly opened and Dougie—"

"The slobbery dog?" Aggie asked.

Julie nodded. "He came out, and I was about to wave to Marie and tell her to wait, but it wasn't Marie. It was Lucky. He looked right at me. Then he stepped back and shut the door."

"Well, did you go and ask him why?"

"No. I know where I'm not wanted."

"He probably just didn't recognize you," Kayla said.

"The sun was probably in his eyes," Aggie added.

Julie thought back. Was it possible? It *was* sunny. But she was grasping at straws. "No. He knew it was me. Our job here is done."

"Don't you want to try again?"

Julie shook her head.

"If you want to leave, we'll all go," said Aggie. "But not until tomorrow after the bonfire."

"And not until the wedding party clears out and we have a room," Kayla pointed out. "And in the meantime, we're all going for a boat ride. Maybe things will seem better on the salty sea."

Aggie nodded vigorously. "Please?"

"Okay, but tomorrow I'm going." *Just like Marzetta had predicted. Man, what a racket.*

Aggie and Kayla exchanged looks.

"Fine," said Aggie. "Les, we're ready when you are." She looked around, but only Bjorn stood there looking uncomfortable. "Where's Les?"

"He had to, um . . . he'll be right back."

CeeJay lifted her chin in the direction of the bar, and they turned to see Les bound up the steps and go inside.

*A*lex looked up as Les burst into the bar. The screen door slammed behind him.

He tensed. "What? Is it—"

"No," Les said, and glanced over his shoulder. "Julie saw Lucky. She thinks he's been hiding from her. She's upset, she wants to leave—"

"Excellent," Alex said, ignoring the rock in his gut.

"But the other two are talking her out of it. What do you want me to do? I'll take all three of them for a boat ride, but you guys need to decide what to do. I do have a business to run, and I don't trust leaving CeeJay to actually 'mind the store.' I'm pretty sure she's helping herself to the cash register."

"Okay, I'll take care of it, but you need to deal with CeeJay."

"I've kind of been busy."

"I don't know why she doesn't get a second job."

Les gave him a look.

Alex sighed. He'd seen a lot of fake IDs in his life. Had used a few. And CeeJay's was not even the most realistic. It would pass as long as it wasn't overly scrutinized, because he bet she wasn't a day over sixteen. He just wondered whose Social Security number she was using. Alex shook his head. "If she screws up, we won't be able to help her."

"She knows that."

"Then you'd better have a heart-to-heart and soon."

"I will as soon as this shit is over."

"Let's hope it's soon," Alex said. "You keep Julie and her friends occupied, I'll try to get this sorted." He waited for Les to stride out the door, then went through the kitchen and out the back door.

Alex got CeeJay. He'd talked to her only a few times, but she was tough, and he was afraid if he pushed too hard, she would run. She'd obviously been on the run for a long time. He recognized the signs. What she needed was a stable home life, not camping out with a handful of other girls in a one-bedroom apartment.

But at the moment, CeeJay wasn't his problem. Right now he wanted a definite game plan on what to do with Julie Barlow. Because the situation was about to get dicey.

He gave a perfunctory knock on the cottage door, then opened it to Dougie. Standing guard? That string of saliva would scare the most determined adversary away.

Except for Julie Barlow, he thought with a wry smile.

Marie and Lucky were sitting at the kitchen table sipping coffee out of two heavy blue ceramic mugs. An ordinary morning in a beach community when your life was in danger.

Alex went over to the coffee maker and poured himself a cup, turned to face the other two. "Here's the deal. She knows you saw her, she thinks you've been hiding from her the whole time and don't want to see her. And she wants to go on to Dewey tomorrow."

"Good," Lucky said, staring into his mug.

"Her friends are talking her out of it."

"Oh," Marie said. "How do you know this?"

"Les. He's taking them out on his boat, but he stopped off to give me a heads-up. I told him to keep them as long as he could, but he does have a business to run, and there is the bonfire and barbecue tonight, which means I have work to do, too."

"I should come help," Lucky said.

"No!" Alex and Marie said together.

"I'm beginning to wish I had never agreed to do this. It's causing a lot of trouble, with probably more to come."

"Maybe not," Marie said. "Hopefully, Raymond will decide to cut his losses and move on."

"Joseph Raymond? They don't call him La Cobra for nothing. He's just as interested in vengeance as he is in keeping his workers," Lucky said.

"That's *how* he keeps his workers," Alex said. He'd learned that much as a gang member. "And he'll use Rosie and whoever else gets in his way to get to Rosie's niece. She knows too much. He can't afford to let her go."

"Well, it's a little late to worry about that," Marie said. "He may not even know that Lucky's involved."

"But they'll be looking for Rosie as Ana's nearest relative."

"True," Marie said. "Is it too late to move her to a safe house of some sort? I can make a call."

"She won't go," Alex said. "She's afraid they'll find her. She feels safer with all of us."

"As she should," Lucky said. "There are no completely safe houses. No one's been around asking questions?"

"Only Julie." Alex smiled. "I don't think she's a member of Raymond's gang."

"Not funny," Lucky said, and cradled his head in his hands.

"I think," Marie began, "that if you want to see her, then you should. Just don't tell her you're involved in something that is currently way out of our control. Maybe you could explain to her that you're really busy, but you'll come up to Dewey for dinner—or better still, invite her for Thanksgiving, but now just isn't a good time."

Both men looked at her.

"Then you two come up with a lie that works."

Alex paced toward the door, but Dougie blocked his way. He paced back. "How's this: you are in hiding, but not from her."

"I can't tell her that. Ugh. Of all the times for her to show up."

"Then just tell her you don't want to see her and be done with it."

"But I do want to see her, and I don't want her to think that I don't care about her."

"You've hardly seen her in the last ten years. Another few weeks won't make any difference."

Marie stood up. "God, let's hope it isn't that long." She went to pour herself more coffee, held up the pot. Both men shook their heads.

Alex put his mug down. "Look, Lucky, she's everywhere, asking everyone stuff. Just her questions could give us away. You have to tell me what to tell her. Not that she's going to listen to me."

Marie came back to the table. "Say he was in a fight and he's lying low for a few days."

"Why?"

"I don't know. He's embarrassed to be seen with the shit kicked out of him? How about he's afraid the guys who beat him up aren't finished with him. That's pretty close to the truth."

"She'll think I'm a coward," Lucky complained.

Alex nodded. "She'll think he's a coward."

"Well, I'm sorry if you two macho men can't take a little ego bruising for a good cause."

"Me?" Alex said. "What did I do?"

"Nothing. But I'm scared," Marie said. "Not for myself, not for Rosie, but for you, Lucky. They'll kill you if they find you."

Now Lucky stood up. "You're right, maybe I should leave town for a while."

"Christ Almighty," said Alex. "Will you two get a grip and come up with a story? Who gives a shit about the truth, just make up something we can all remember."

He was met with silence.

"Okay. Then how about this? She already thinks I'm smuggling contraband while you're obliviously out of town. What a laugh. She saw the van. Saw an 'old man' get out. I guess it was dark and you were bent double with those ribs. She saw us dump something in the bushes.

"Let's make her right. She always wants to be right anyway. Let her."

Lucky cut Alex a look and smiled.

Alex narrowed his eyes at him.

"I always thought you—"

"Don't. Just don't."

"—kinda liked her," Lucky finished.

Alex snorted. "I was bowled over. She was the prettiest, cleanest girl I'd ever seen. But you have to consider my twelve-year-old lifestyle." The reminiscent laughter died on his lips. "You've taken care of us all. We'll take care of her if we have to."

"Yeah, but having her here is spreading our resources thin. I wish he'd just make a move."

They put their heads together and came up with some story about a fight and illegal liquor sales. About Lucky being too embarrassed to be seen with a black eye. It wasn't all that black, but Alex wasn't going to quibble.

"Do you think she'll buy it?" Lucky asked.

"Of course not. She might be straight as all get-out, but she's not stupid."

"She was never stupid."

"Nope," Alex agreed. "But she's pretty straitlaced and she might consider turning us in for moving contraband."

"That straight?"

Alex made a face.

"As bad as Louise?"

"I would say . . . yes."

"And I had such hope."

So had Alex.

Julie felt immensely better once they had left the marina and headed for the open sea. She wasn't sure if it was the reassurances of her friends or the fresh ocean air that seemed to blow the cobwebs away. For a few minutes she wasn't even worried about her future or what the next year would bring.

She felt free.

She didn't even feel seasick—something good to know. This was heaven.

"Having a good time?" Les yelled over the motor.

"Wonderful," she yelled back.

"Come take the helm."

She hesitated, then straddle-walked her way toward the steering console. "What do I do?"

"You drive a car?"

She nodded.

"Same thing." He turned the wheel over to her but stood nearby. Hair blowing back from his forehead. Sturdy, good-looking. Amiable. No wonder Aggie liked him.

Julie liked him, too. But . . . she just liked him. She glanced over at Bjorn. Nothing wrong with him, either. Of course Kayla was giving him her full attention. Well, so what? Julie was content to drive the boat. Sort of.

The sun had dipped toward the horizon when Les took over the wheel and steered them back into the marina. He jumped onto the pier and tied up the boat, then reached back and helped the three women out.

They decided against stopping for a drink at the Fish Fry, since there were things that needed to be done for the bonfire and barbecue. Les and Bjorn dropped them off at the hotel.

"Meet downstairs in an hour," Aggie said when they left Julie at her door. "And wear something sexy."

"Right," said Julie.

She went straight to the window and pulled down the shade.

She'd spent a delightful day without worrying about her life, her uncle, or anything else. She wouldn't do any more spying. From now on, she was going to enjoy her vacation. She opened the closet and peered inside, looking for something remotely sexy.

She was going to have a good time tonight if it killed her.

Chapter 13

The sky had turned to a deep mauve by the time Julie, Kayla, and Aggie, laden down with beach blankets and other paraphernalia, reached Lucky's parking lot. The parking lot was full. An area near the beach had been roped off and was crowded with food trucks surrounded by picnic tables. What looked like the entire kitchen of Lucky's had been moved outside, and the canopied seating area had been extended across the sand.

People were lined up at the trucks and waiting for seats at Lucky's. Beyond them the flames of the bonfire leaped over their heads. It wasn't an old-fashioned bonfire, Les had explained to them during the boat ride. The fire was contained in a steel ring—easy to put out and cart away without leaving the sand charred and filled with debris. Only plastic was allowed at the event, no glass or metal, though they would have the beach swept the next morning in case any detritus slipped through.

There was a small group crowded around Surf's Up. They'd

be pulling beer and pitching surf lessons for most of the evening.

"What shall we eat?" Kayla asked.

"I don't care. I'm starving," Aggie said, looking around.

"What about ribs from that truck over there?" Julie suggested. "Or there are tacos over there. Kielbasa?"

They agreed to ribs and joined the line waiting to order. Ten minutes later they walked away with plates—each piled high with ribs, corn on the cob, a boiled potato, and a slab of cornbread—and four guys named Cliff, Brad, Petey, and Hanger.

They were surfers and ready to party. They found a table that was just being vacated and all squeezed in, Julie between Cliff and Hanger, Aggie and Kayla on the other side with Brad and Petey. They chatted and ate and drank.

Cliff and Petey went for another round of beers, and Julie began wondering if Lucky's kept a good full-bodied cabernet under the bar.

They'd seen Les and Bjorn working the Surf's Up stand when they arrived, but even though she looked, she didn't see Scatter at the Lucky's area. Maybe he was inside. Maybe that was the real reason she was longing for a cabernet—as an excuse?

If she was completely honest, a part of her was hoping that she'd see him tonight. She hadn't been lying when she'd told Kayla that he was growing on her.

Hell, it was vacation, after all; she was single, along with all the other single women up and down the coast looking for fun. Was that pathetic? Aggie didn't seem pathetic, just lonely sometimes. Kayla was too stressed all the time—so what if she let herself have a little fun at the beach?

And Julie? What was it about her that she just couldn't seem to "let her hair down," as her mother would say, and just give in to impulses with no worries about tomorrow. Something her mother would *never* say.

She glanced from Cliff, who had moved closer to her when he'd returned with the beer, to Hanger. They were both perfectly nice. She laughed and tried to be part of the conversation, much of which was lost in laughter and guzzles of beer.

And Julie wondered what Bjorn and Les would think if they were to see Kayla and Aggie having fun without them. Maybe nothing. Maybe they were out flirting with potential surfing students at the same time.

They were on their third, maybe fourth, round of beers. Cliff had his arm around Julie's waist and was beginning to nuzzle her neck, when Hanger said, "We'd better give up our table. We have blankets over there."

Cliff gave her a squeeze before he stood and gathered up his plate. They all got up and threw away their trash. Julie swayed on her feet as she slid her plate, cup, and plastic utensils into the oil drum that said TRASH.

Fun, she reminded herself. *You're here to have fun, not save the planet.*

But she wasn't having fun.

So when Cliff said, "We better get one more round before we settle in for the night," Julie pulled away.

"Excuse me, I'll be back. You guys go ahead."

Cliff didn't want to let go, but she managed to slip out of his arm.

"Later."

And she fled, killing all her fun intentions for the evening, because she knew she wouldn't be going back to take up where they had left off.

She walked away from the crowd, not toward town, but toward the water, toward, she realized, the private beach where she'd seen the kids on the deck. If there were a bunch of lovers there she'd just quietly leave and go back to town. She had plenty of reading material to keep her busy.

She did turn back once to look at the bonfire and wonder just for a second if she was missing out on someone special.

Dimwit. Hadn't she learned anything over the last decade of not-so-great attempts at love? That there are no soul mates? No one you could totally depend on. And if you found someone who came close, he died or left you to catch the next big wave.

There was a new sign at the rivulet of water that separated the public beach from what Julie assumed was the beach that belonged to the house in the dunes. She couldn't see the actual warning, and she didn't stop to try to read it from the light of the quarter moon. It had probably been put up because of the bonfire and said something like "Trespassers Will Be Shot."

Well, it wasn't like she was going to show herself or make noise of any kind. She'd just sit out of view of the house and think about her life.

The mere thought made her want to howl with frustration.

She slipped out of her shoes, waded across the stream, and trudged over to a rock she'd noticed the other day near the dunes. She sat down, wrapped her arms around her knees, and stared out at the dark ocean.

The Great Leveler. Someone had once called the ocean that. She couldn't remember who. The name usually was given to death, but Julie could see how the ocean might be the Great Leveler. Even outside of hurricanes and tsunamis, it was just so vast, so strong; nothing and no one could withstand the ocean in the end.

She could see the aura of the bonfire over on the public beach, hear the music and laughter over the crash of the waves.

She was so screwed. She was tired of her past and kind of dreaded her future. And as for the present? She was sitting here on a romantic beach, alone.

"What are you doing?"

Julie let out a squawk at the same time her heart skipped a beat . . . or two. She recognized the voice; she just hadn't heard him approach.

"I—I was just sitting here for a minute. Do you think they'll mind?" She nodded toward the house.

He moved forward. His body created a great silhouette, tall and strong and . . .

"How much beer did you drink?"

She shrugged. "I dunno. You didn't answer my question."

"They won't mind . . . as long as you don't get close to the house," he added.

"Oh good."

"And you didn't answer mine."

"Your what?"

"My question."

"I forgot it."

"Oh brother."

His face disappeared. She was looking at him, then he was gone. She looked down. He was sitting on the sand beside her. It put her above him physically. An advantage, but she had the strongest urge to slide off the rock and snuggle up beside him. She pushed that idea away.

"Actually, I was looking for you," he said.

"You were?" Did she sound too hopeful?

"About Lucky."

"Oh. It doesn't matter, I've decided to leave."

"Oh, well, in that case . . ."

"You don't have to sound so happy."

"I'm not. It's just . . ." He hesitated. "Oh hell, about Lucky. He wants to see you, only he got in a fight and is lying low. He said to tell you he'd come over to Dewey Beach next week when the coast is clear."

She peered intently down at him. And pitched forward.

He caught her as she slid and moved over to make room for her on the sand. "I think you should cut out beer completely. Stick to a nice pinot grigio."

"Actually, I prefer a dry red."

"Well, why the hell didn't you say so in the first place?"

She shrugged, looked out to sea. "You didn't ask me. Does it matter?"

"It should to you."

"You're right. It should. It does. But I never seem to . . . What's wrong with me?"

"Give me a sec while I hang out my shingle. I mean—"

"Oh, shut up. I didn't ask for your sarcasm." Julie pushed to her feet, staggered a bit.

"Hey, wait." He grabbed her elbow.

She shook him off. "I'm fine. It's just the sand shifted."

"Right." He pulled her back down.

She landed with a thud on the sand.

"Okay, sorry, I'm a bartender, I get told a lot of stuff. So the guy was hitting on you and it turned you off."

"What? What are you talking about? Life is not all about men." Her head snapped toward him; he went out of focus before his scowl resettled on his face. "How did you know some guy was hitting on me?"

"I saw him."

"I didn't see you."

"You were busy."

"Not that busy."

"Yeah, you didn't look like you were that into it."

"You were watching?"

He shrugged, shifting her weight, which made her realize she was leaning against him. She thought about moving away, but it was awfully comfy.

"I just happened to . . . well, yeah. Anyway, Cliff's not your type."

"Oh, so now you know what my type is."

He looked out to sea.

"Well, what is it?"

"You know, I see a lot of hookups in the bar. That one wasn't going anywhere. Louise would never go for it."

"My mother? Jeez. We're talking about one night on a beach, not happily ever after. And in case you're wondering, I realize there's no such thing."

"You do?"

She rolled her eyes at him. It made her feel woozy. "I'm not stupid."

"Just not interested."

"I guess."

"You got somebody waiting at home?"

She gave him another look. "That's hardly an excuse in these modern times."

"True. But do you?"

She sighed. "No. It just seems like a lot of trouble knowing it isn't going anywhere. And that's stupid. I should live for the moment."

"You're telling me."

"What?" Not getting an answer or even a look, Julie plowed on. "I just wanted to be frivolous for a change."

"You?"

"Why not?"

"You were never frivolous." He finished the statement with a chuckle.

"You don't know me."

He stopped laughing. "No. I don't." After a second he said,

"So why aren't you out there being frivolous instead of sitting here alone?"

"You wouldn't understand."

"I might."

"It's kind of hard to be frivolous when you're having an existential crisis."

"You're having one of those?"

"If you must know. Yeah. My dad died when I was little. My mom spent her whole life working double shifts to keep us afloat and saving money so I could go to a good college. She always told me to be a nurse or a teacher or to work for the telephone company because they had good benefits. No way was I going to work in an office cubicle. And after seeing her work herself to the bone nursing, I chose teaching."

"And?"

"And I hate it." There, she'd said it. She hated teaching. "Oh my God. What kind of horrible person am I? Who could hate teaching kids? Inspiring them? Helping them to succeed?"

"Opening up a whole world to them?"

She stopped. Looked at him. Looked away. "But I didn't. Maybe I couldn't. I tried, but . . . Why am I telling you all this?"

"Because I'm a bartender?"

She laughed. "People do tell bartenders their innermost secrets, don't they?"

"Yeah. So what didn't you like about teaching?"

"It was the same, day after day. Study, test, labs, more tests. They were perfectly nice, well-behaved children, they never acted out in class, never were late with their homework, never even got caught staring out the window or reading a comic book folded inside a textbook." She sighed. "Kind of hard, considering most of the day they were looking at their laptops or phones instead of me."

"You felt superfluous."

"Yeah." She turned to him, her knees touching his thigh. "I felt like I was turning to stone. They have so many opportunities. They're stuffed with opportunities. They're nine years old and already working on their résumés. When we went on field trips, instead of looking out the window of the bus, they were all on their phones.

"Even recess, which is not called 'recess' but 'gymnasium,' after the Greeks—we're a very progressive school. Every minute is overseen, organized with teams and matching uniforms, new equipment. And score keeping, and strategy, and good sportsmanship. Sometimes I just wanted to take them out in the rain, have them stomp in puddles, sling mud at each other, but of course when it's raining we stay inside and play Nerf ball or watch a video. I just wanted to give them something special."

He was grinning at her.

"Great. I'm glad to see I'm amusing you. But it isn't funny to me."

"I'm not laughing. I'm just glad to see a spark of the devil in you."

"What? What devil? I've done everything I was supposed to do. And I feel terrible. I saw kids playing today in the water, and I thought, *Why can't teaching have some joy in it?*"

"And it doesn't?"

"Not for me." Julie bit her lip. "I know. I'm lacking something. Maybe I just don't like kids. I don't know what it is, but my mother is going to be so disappointed."

"And you never wanted to disappoint her."

"What?"

"Nothing. Just that a person doesn't want to displease their parent. So why don't you quit?"

"What? I couldn't." But she'd come so close, that last day of school.

"Why not?"

"I don't think . . . I'm just . . ." She groped for what she was feeling.

"Scared?" he volunteered.

The breath stuck in her lungs. She gave him a long, hard look. "I guess I am."

"There are a lot of scarier things than being out of a job."

She shuddered. "Not to me. Maybe I should have been a nurse."

He burst out laughing. "If you don't like teaching why on earth would you want to be a nurse?"

"My mother. Nurse, teacher. Job security." She sniffed.

"Job security, a pension. If those are the only reasons you chose teaching, maybe you should rethink your motivations."

"What do you mean?"

"Well, here I was thinking you were into helping others, and really you're only worried about yourself."

It was like a smack across her face.

"No, I . . ." Maybe she was. But she wasn't ready to face that possibility. She lashed back. "What do you know about it?"

"You'd be surprised."

She sighed, moved away from him. Staggered to her feet. "Sorry, it must be the beer making me talk so much. I guess between this and Uncle Lucky I just got a little overwhelmed. Sorry."

She started to walk away. Still weaving, *damn beer.* She wouldn't be drinking too much again. It just led to embarrassing yourself one way or the other.

A spark of the devil in you. Why had he said that? No one had ever said that about her before.

She reached the rivulet of water, realized she'd forgotten her shoes. She couldn't go back. She couldn't even turn around to see if he was still there. To hell with them, if they were still there tomorrow, she'd retrieve them. If they were gone . . .

A spark of the devil. She was standing in the hallway. Lucky and her mother in the kitchen. Lucky saying, *Give her a chance to grow, Lou. She's got a little spark of the devil in her, give it a chance.*

Her mother had put paid to that in no uncertain terms.

And Julie, just like her fourth graders, had been the perfect daughter, the perfect student. Then, and as it turned out, even now.

She became aware of someone walking beside her. She didn't need to look to know it was Alex Martin, aka Scatter. She ignored him. She'd made a fool of herself, spilled her guts to a shady bartender who might or might not be ripping off her uncle or abetting him in illegalities.

She skirted the edge of the beach and expected him to leave when they reached the entrance of the bar and grill, but he didn't even slow down.

"You don't have to make sure I get back to the hotel, if that's what you're doing," she said at her most sarcastic. But her heart wasn't in it.

"I know."

He said nothing else and neither did she until they got to the hotel. "Thanks for seeing me home."

He snorted. She stumbled over the threshold. He caught her elbow. "Where's your room?"

She raised her eyebrows at him. Okay, maybe she could be frivolous after all. There was no one at the desk, but it wasn't like she'd have to explain anything; they were probably used to things like this.

She opted for the elevator, since she wasn't all that steady on her feet and she had to pee. He stayed by her side, waited for her to fish for her key. Took it from her and unlocked the door. She stepped inside. He was still standing in the hallway.

"Aren't you coming in?"

He was smiling but he shook his head. "I never hit on a woman when she's drunk."

"I'm not drunk. I never get drunk."

"Well, you're doing a damn good imitation of it. Here are your shoes. I'll take a rain check."

She took them and he reached past her to shut the door. She stood and listened to him walk away. The whole beach was full of drunk people carrying on, and here she was in a hotel room alone. What was wrong with her?

Five minutes and three aspirin later, she fell into bed. Had he said he'd take a rain check? She was pretty sure he had, but did he mean that, or was it just a polite way of saying no thanks? She turned over, pulled the sheet up to her chin. He'd also said she had a spark of the devil in her. She distinctly remembered that, and that was the thought she clung to as she fell asleep.

Chapter 14

Well, that had been close, Alex thought as he walked back toward the beach. Too close—or not close enough. He had been so tempted. Lucky would've killed him. Still, she wasn't as boring as he'd expected. Naive, a little cautious. But so tempting.

Maybe it was wishful thinking that she would actually break out of that Louise-imposed shell. She'd done exactly what her mother wanted her to do, the thing that made Lucky crazy, and she wasn't even happy.

And you should stay the hell away from her, he reminded himself. Too complicated. Too volatile. Too not for him.

He let out a long exhale. Right now, he had more urgent matters to deal with.

He looked both ways down the alley. It was usually quiet by this time of night, since the residents had made it perfectly clear when Lucky had bought and reopened the bar that their privacy and peace were important. And Lucky had done what he could to make sure their wishes were respected.

Tonight with the bonfire, several groups of revelers were walking down the passageway, most likely taking a shortcut to the parking lot at the other end of town. Still, Alex kept a watchful eye on their movements, if any of them lingered too long to look around or took particular interest in one of the cottages as they passed.

A patrol car drove by, and Alex stepped into the shadows to watch. Some things you never forgot; they became a part of your being, whether they were wanted or not.

The cruiser stopped at each group, which quieted down before it drove on.

Alex stepped back onto the pavement. Tonight the only reason he was avoiding the cops was that he didn't have time to chat.

Marie's cottage was dark, but he knew that she planned to keep Lucky at her house until he was back to fighting condition and they were sure no one else was snooping around his cottage.

This situation had been inevitable. They'd made contingency plans for all the variations they could think of. They had support from Marie's former colleagues. And the town. But not one of them had thought that Lucky's niece, after a radio silence of almost six years, would choose this week to make amends.

Actually, Alex wasn't sure Lucky had taken into account Joseph Raymond's reputation as a ruthless drug trafficker. He wasn't called "La Cobra" for nothing. It burned Alex that this son of a bitch used a Spanish nickname while he was an American, born and bred, without a drop of Latin blood in him. Alex wanted him so bad, he could taste it. Until now no one had been able to bring him in. *Until now.* That was about to change.

With God as his witness, if Marie's people blew this and Rosie came to harm, Alex would finish the bastard himself.

And he really, really didn't want to go there.

He knocked at the kitchen door.

After a minute or two, the kitchen light came on, and Lucky peered out the curtains that covered the windowed door. Some fortress. They'd be safer at Alex's house. At least his glass was hurricane-proof.

The door opened and Alex slipped inside.

"Where's Marie?" Lucky asked first thing. It was obvious he'd been asleep.

Alex glanced at his watch, almost laughed. It wasn't even midnight. It felt like much later. They were all getting old. "She's probably still working."

"Wanna beer?" Lucky's head disappeared into the fridge.

"Sure, why not?" Alex had planned to take the rest of the night off and find some fun for himself at the bonfire. But that hadn't worked out so great. By the time he got to the bonfire, it would be nothing but cold ashes.

Lucky handed him a bottle and they sat down at the kitchen table. Alex had to make himself not go to the window and check the alley one more time. Funny how old habits, when they came back, came back in spades.

"Did you talk to Julie?"

Alex took a long pull at his beer. "Yeah." *Though she'd done all the talking.*

"What happened?"

Where to start? "I told her you'd been in a fight and you'd come over to Dewey Beach next week to see her."

"What did she say?"

What didn't she say? And none of it had much to do with her uncle. "Oh, she said she was leaving."

"Whew. That's okay then."

"I guess."

"You think we should keep her here?"

Alex stared at him incredulously. "No. I don't know. I just don't like it."

The door opened. Marie stopped on the threshold. "Don't like what?"

"You're late tonight," Lucky said.

"The bonfire. I had people trickling in all evening and night. Finally I just turned off the lights, put up the Closed sign, and sneaked out the back door."

"You must be exhausted," Alex said, "dealing with the mysteries of the universe all night."

"I'll take no lip from you, mister. I'll go toe to toe with you against the universe any day. So what don't you like?" She pulled off her turban, threw it on the table, and scratched her head with both hands. "Well?"

"Scatter doesn't like Julie being here. But he also doesn't like that she's leaving. I guess she ruffled his feathers."

She'd ruffled more than his feathers, Alex thought, but he wasn't about to tell Lucky that.

"None of us like her being here," Marie said. "You told her to leave."

"I didn't have to," Alex said. "She told me."

"And?"

"And nothing."

Marie reached under the counter and brought out a bottle of Scotch. Alex wasn't the only one feeling the stress tonight. She poured a couple fingers' worth into a tumbler.

"I guess it's for the best. She's already wasted several days of her vacation for nothing." She paused to shoot a look toward Lucky over the rim of her glass. "She probably has to go right back, start preparing for the school year. Whoever thinks teachers get three months off every year doesn't know teachers."

"That's the other thing," Alex said, jumping into the fray. "She hates her job."

Lucky and Marie both stared at him.

"At Hillsdale Progressive?" Lucky asked.

"Yeah, that, too. But she doesn't want to be a teacher anymore."

"But she's great with kids. She won all those awards."

"How do you know? You don't know what her life is like."

Lucky gave him one of his deceptively mild, but cut-you-to-the-quick, looks. "I've kept up . . . through Louise . . . It's just that Julie . . ."

"The phone works both ways," Marie said, sipping her Scotch.

Yeah, they were all feeling the pressure all right.

"You don't have to remind me." Lucky switched his focus to Alex. "Oh man. Does Louise know?"

Alex took a long breath. "That's not exactly the point."

Marie reached for the Scotch bottle, pulled out a chair, and sat down. "Can we just stick to the problem at hand?"

"Which problem?" Alex asked.

"I don't want her to leave," Lucky said. "It's just—"

"Don't want her to get caught in the cross fire when it comes." Marie finished off her Scotch.

"I don't want any of you to be harmed."

She slammed her glass on the table, hard enough to make Alex jump. "You big— Ugh. When will you ever accept that we're in it for the long haul? We have been for a long time, before you even wandered back into my life."

"Maybe we should just explain it to her," Alex said.

"Oh no," Marie said. "Don't even think about it. She's malleable. Easily swayed. Probably why she's stayed in a job she hates for so long. What if she can't keep a secret? What if she feels compelled to notify the authorities? The wrong ones. Face it, Lucky, you don't really know anything about her, do you?"

Alex stood, looked out the window. Marie was right, but damn, a part of him was kind of wanting for her to stick around. And he thought it would be good if Lucky had a crack at her.

The girl was seriously messed up. But hell, hadn't they all been there? Some of them, like Alex, more than once.

Alex looked away from the window to find Marie staring at him. "What?"

"Nothing."

"She's really gotten under your skin," Lucky said.

"She scares me shitless."

Lucky chuckled. "Good for her."

"Not in a good way. It's all bolloxed up."

"How did you learn all this?" Marie asked. "I thought we agreed to avoid contact as much as possible."

"I ran into her on the beach at the bonfire. I came right over here once I saw her back to her hotel."

Alex didn't miss the exchange of looks between Lucky and Marie.

"She'd had a couple of beers too many—obviously not a drinker. I wanted to make sure she made it back okay. Nothing happened."

Lucky expelled a breath he'd probably been holding.

"But, Lucky, it is the twenty-first century. Women know what they want. Most of them," he added, mainly to himself.

"I'll drink to that," Marie said.

"Not with my niece, it isn't."

Marie barked out a laugh. At least Alex had the good sense to hide his grin behind his fist.

Lucky's eyes narrowed. "Did you tell her who you are?"

"She knows I'm the bartender at your bar. She thinks I'm robbing you blind while you're away. Isn't that enough?"

"Ha. Did you tell her who you *were*?"

"Hell no. It will just complicate matters."

"How?"

"It would justify her distrust."

"No, it won't. You're scared."

"Don't be ridiculous. It's just more information that she doesn't need to know. What if she begins to wonder why you and I are both here, and Marie, and the others? Don't you think she'll be suspicious?"

"What's there to be suspicious about? If we were all painters and sculptors living in one town, people would call it an artistic community. And come buy stuff for ridiculously high prices."

"Yeah, and what would they call ours?"

"People of like minds."

"A philosophic community? Like Walden Pond? Good luck with that."

Marie leaned forward on her elbow. Alex saw that her second drink was gone. "Look, fellas, decide how to deal with this. Maybe we're being too cautious, and it's all over but the paperwork."

Alex and Lucky both gave her incredulous looks.

Marie threw up her hands. "Then either tell her you don't want to see her or . . ." She yawned.

"What's the other choice?" Lucky asked.

"Invite her to dinner and tell her everything. I'm going to bed."

*D*ay four of Julie's vacation and it didn't seem like she was seeing any relaxation. Even last night when she'd actually gotten buzzed, she'd spurned one guy's advances and been shot down by another. Some track record.

Her vacation was slipping away. Her future loomed like a big dark cloud. She blew out air, sucked in more, blew that out—she was not feeling calmer.

She felt awful and she didn't even have a hangover. Or maybe this was the Julie Barlow hangover and she just didn't realize it.

She looked over at the suitcase she'd pulled out of the closet a few minutes before. Was she really going to pack her bags and leave? Just because her uncle was embarrassed to have been in a fight? A barroom brawl? A poker game dispute? Partners in crime?

She should have pushed Scatter for more information the night before.

If only she'd stuck to getting info, instead of being so self-involved and moany—and kind of interested in the arrogant bartender.

And that was another humiliation she'd rather not face today. Not that she could exactly avoid him for the next week.

She closed the suitcase and returned it to the closet. Looked at herself in the mirror. She didn't look bad, considering. She'd just bluster her way through. *Chin up. Smile on the face.*

There was a rat-a-tat-tat on the door. Julie opened it, and Aggie and Kayla practically tumbled into the room.

"I'm surprised you guys are up already. I'm running late." Julie pulled her alternate swimsuit out of the drawer.

"Where did you go last night?" asked Kayla.

"Yeah, one minute you're all hot and heavy with Cliff, then poof, vanished." Aggie grimaced. "Please tell me you didn't come back here and read."

Julie deliberated. To lie or just to prevaricate a little, that was the question. "Well . . ."

"What?" Aggie and Kayla leaned in attentively.

"I kind of met up with Alex Martin."

"Alex . . . ?" Aggie broke into a full grin. "Scatterman? You go, girl. You go, girl," she chanted, and began to dance around in the limited floor space.

"It didn't go anywhere—well, not where these things normally go."

"Oh," Aggie said, deflated.

"But," Julie added before they started feeling sorry for her, "he said I was drunk and he didn't take advantage of drunk women"—*or close enough*—"and that he'd take a rain check."

"And are you?" asked Aggie.

"Going to take a rain check," Kayla added.

Julie shrugged. "It's a long way between going to and did it."

Aggie groaned. "Spare us technicalities. We're on vacay. Go change, the beach is waiting."

*I*t was going to be a scorcher, Alex thought as he sped down the road away from the beach, past the town and the main highway and into farm country. He didn't envy the laborers who dotted the fields to either side of the road, backs bent over or kneeling in the soil picking strawberries. It was the end of strawberry season, and soon they would move on to tomatoes, then watermelons—truly backbreaking work—then corn, until they picked up and moved to the next harvest zone, then south again, ending up in California or Florida for the winter growing season.

He'd picked apples one year, when he was still being a useless drag on Lucky. It was monotonous, grueling work. He'd been one of a handful of local guys along with a bunch of day pickers that the truck brought in early in the morning, when the frost was still on the ground. They were driven to an orchard, where they maneuvered three-legged ladders into the trees.

There was one guy who kept passing out on the ladder. He always fell forward, must have trained himself to do that so he didn't break his neck. One day they had to call an ambulance to take him to the hospital. Alex thought that was the end of him for sure, but he showed up a few days later back at work. Alex never did find out what was wrong with him.

Alex had lost his appetite for apples ever since that fall. He couldn't pick one up without thinking of that old dude, draped over his ladder, somewhere between dead and alive.

People, he figured, never thought about where strawberries came from when they oohed and aahed over their shortcake, or the potatoes that came with their filet mignon, or the cherries in their cocktails.

Sometimes when Alex saw a maraschino left in the bottom of a glass, he wanted to say, *Someone picked that cherry, breathed pesticides, cracked their hands, passed out on ladders, for you to ignore it.* Though he didn't really blame them for leaving the blanched, artificially colored, and sweetened fruit uneaten.

He never ate them.

The sun beat down on his neck. He raised his hand in greeting as he passed several workers close to the road. Most didn't even look up. A couple waved back, kids too young to be working twelve-hour days in the heat of the sun.

At least the county provided a day camp for the younger children whose families qualified where they taught them English, math, reading; fed them nutritious enough meals; did art, music, games; took them on field trips to the beach or the county pool.

And though it was a well-meaning program, Alex often dealt with the resentment from those who were too old to attend, who didn't have the papers to make them eligible, or who were just needed in the field or at home to care for those who weren't old enough or able to work.

That was one of the reasons he was doing what Dee Hoyes called his "house calls."

He pulled into the parking lot of the concrete building that housed the program. Beyond it, cornfields stretched out in all directions. He jumped out of the Jeep and buzzed the front door.

It took a few minutes before it opened and Dee let him in. "Hey," she said. "We weren't expecting you."

"Playing hooky from office appointments." Alex smiled.

Dee ran the center, did the paperwork, taught, oversaw the field trips, and made certain that those who needed counseling got it. She was enthusiastic, nonstop energy, and never acted frazzled or tired. Her lipstick always looked like she'd just applied it, bright red, a beacon of hope—not in a sexual way, but in a yes-we-can kind of way—that everyone—children, women, and grown men alike—found reassuring.

"I just thought I'd check up on Alberto," Alex said as they walked down the hall to the activity rooms.

"And see what the situation is here?" Dee shook her head. "You know we don't allow bullying of any sort here or between our kids and the local kids when they have group programs. We have no control over what happens to and from the center.

"But Alberto isn't here. I haven't seen him since the day we came over to town. I had one of the aides drive over there. The grandmother said they're not sending him anymore."

They stopped at her office, a cheerfully painted room with children's artwork covering every square inch of wall.

"Did the grandmother say why?"

"She wouldn't let her in. Just yelled through the door, 'Vete! Vete!'"

Go away. "Document problems?"

"No. They had to present their papers to be accepted into the program."

That rubbed Alex the wrong way, but he didn't say so. He remembered what it was like to live under the radar. And he was born in Baltimore.

"I think I'll ride over and see what I can do."

"Good luck. Do you have time to visit?"

"Not today, but I might be back soon. And bring a friend if that's okay."

"Sure, the more hands the merrier." She walked him back to the front door. "Let me know what happens. I hate to see him miss out on coming. Alberto's a good kid." She smiled. "Dos Als. You're a good kid, too."

Alex blew out air. "I don't know about that. But I won't lose this kid if I can help it."

"Good luck." Dee closed the door.

Alex found the road with its rows of square stucco houses without much trouble. It took some time to find where Alberto lived, about three-fourths of the way down the long stretch of neglected buildings.

He knocked on the door but got no answer. He looked around, knowing that there would be eyes watching him from behind the windows, those too old or too young or too infirm to work. He knocked again, felt more than saw a curtain pulled slightly aside.

"Abuela! It's Alex Martin. Alberto's . . . friend."

The curtain dropped and he waited for her to answer the door. She didn't.

He knocked again. "Abuela. Por favor."

The curtain lifted again, but this time the face looking out was not the grandmother's but Alberto's. Alex smiled, held up his hand in greeting. The curtain dropped.

He heard whining and a string of rapid-fire Spanish, then the door opened. Alberto ran out. "Dos Als!" He grabbed Alex's hand and pulled him toward the door, where the grandmother stood, tiny but formidable, in the shadows.

$\mathcal{M}$arie held the bouquet of fresh-cut flowers from her garden before her like a middle-aged flower girl at a wedding. Or like Madame Marzetta warding off evil spirits. Hospitals were never her favorite places, even at the best of times, and this wasn't even good—barely passable.

They'd put Rosie's niece in a restricted ward at the far end of the hall. She wasn't contagious; she was the victim of a violent crime. And her attacker was sure to try again. But she had no insurance, so they'd placed her among criminals and the destitute with an armed guard at the entrance of that wing.

She nodded to the guard, Officer Nickels, and wondered if he got a lot of meter maid jokes. But she didn't say any more than necessary, just handed him her ID, waited for him to scrutinize it, and kept going.

Anger bubbled up before Marie could stop it. She tamped it back down. *Good thoughts, peaceful thoughts. Never waste your energy on anger that doesn't change things.* Lord, she'd wasted a lot of energy over the years.

But some of it had paid off big time.

At the end of the hall she paused at the door of a four-bed room. Fortunately two of the beds were unoccupied. She'd tried to get Ana into a single room, mainly for her safety. But it was a no-go.

She put on her best-under-the-circumstances smile and went inside.

Ana Lopez lay still as the dead beneath a light beige blanket tucked into the mattress. A thick white bandage was wrapped around her head, covering most of her forehead, like a latter-day mummy.

It wasn't the first time Marie had visited victims of abuse, many worse off than Ana. It didn't make it any easier. She'd seen enough battered bodies growing up, some of them her own brothers'. Eddie killed even, wrong place, wrong time, bad luck.

But Ana was still alive, so far. Marie sent a quick prayer to Saint Christopher for her continuing to be so. Though she was no longer a practicing Catholic, she still believed in the saints. And Ana needed the protection that perhaps only Saint Christopher could provide.

A nurse came in to check out the visitor. She recognized Marie and took the flowers out to find a vase.

Marie had meant to show them to Ana first, but it was clear she was still not awake. *Induced coma,* they'd said. *Swelling in the brain.* Where that damned—where her "fiancé" had beaten her with a golf club. Broken ribs, broken arm and collarbone. Bruised so badly that her face was a purple swollen moon above the crisp white sheet folded beneath her chin.

If he found her he would kill her, because she was going to cooperate to bring him to justice. She'd phoned Rosie to tell her the night before she disappeared.

Joseph Raymond. They'd been after him for years with no success. But finally, in retirement, Marie was going to bring him down.

She moved closer. "Ana," she whispered, then a little louder: "Ana, it's Marie Simmons. Rosie's friend."

She would have taken Ana's hand to reassure her, but it was captured beneath the blanket.

"Rosie is fine," she continued in her Jersey-accented Spanish. "Your children are fine. We got them back. They are with Rosie. They miss you and send their love." She pulled a visitor's chair over to the bedside and sat down. "They wanted to visit you, but we must take precautions for their safety. I hope you can hear me, Ana. Everything is fine."

Marie opened her bag and pulled out a folded piece of paper. A message from Rosie. Marie read it off dutifully, word for word, though her accent left a lot to be desired.

She thought she saw Ana's eyelids flicker, but she was probably mistaken. She continued on in Spanish. "Things are proceeding, so you only need to get better. There's a lawyer working on your behalf. My friend Ike Gibson has filed the paperwork for you to be granted an extension on your visa. It will take some time, but we are helping the authorities with capturing the man who did this to you. You must get better."

The nurse came back, carrying a vase and the flowers. "Aren't these lovely, Ms. Lopez? I'll just put them here so you can see them when you wake up."

Marie blessed her for not resenting this woman who was found left for dead in the street, no identification and undocumented. It was just by chance that she had been brought here, where a friend of Marie's was an ER nurse.

She sat a few minutes longer, talking about nothing in particular, just to give Ana a chance to hear a voice that might give her comfort. When the nurse returned to check Ana's vitals, Marie said goodbye.

She automatically checked the hallway for anything out of the ordinary, anyone who looked out of place. An old habit.

She'd learned to recognize minutiae from her mother, the third-generation Madame Marzetta, on the boardwalk of Asbury Park. She'd put her skills to good use for the government. Until they pissed her off one too many times. And then she'd found Lucky's Beach . . . and Lucky found her.

She took a circuitous route home. Residual habit maybe, or the real possibility of being followed by some unsavory characters. And she had to admit, beneath the outrage and empathy for Rosie and her niece, she felt a little rush of excitement. She tried to push it away: this was not a game. These were people she cared about.

Times like this Marie wished she could really see into the future. Actually, she was afraid she could see into this future, and she knew from experience things here were bound to get worse before they got better.

Chapter 15

*J*ulie had decided that catching and riding the "big one" could not be harder than trying to balance on a surfboard in the middle of a totally calm sea. She'd succeeded in standing fairly consistently. Even managed to stay upright for a few seconds before the tiniest swell shot the board out from under her.

Kayla was paddling out farther under the watchful eye of a guy named Petewaller, which was some surfing moniker and not an odd children's book character.

Les and Bjorn were in Ocean City on "surfing business" and hadn't asked the girls along. But they promised to be back in time to take them out on the boat.

Julie had every intention of ducking out and spending a lazy day on the beach reading her pirate romance and maybe just taking one last peek at all the brochures she'd collected.

She fell off her board. Splashed, coughed, and grabbed the side.

That's what you get for letting your mind wander, for daydreaming when you should have been paying attention, while someone else got ahead, won the prize, got the job, ended up with a pension. By paying attention.

She'd spend the afternoon dutifully looking at her *Trends in Contemporary Education* textbook, though it didn't seem fair. The days were ticking away, and soon she would be back at home. She wasn't looking forward to spending most of the remaining summer in a classroom as a student, only to go back in the fall as a teacher again.

She rested her arms on her surfboard, her body dangling in the water, until the tide had brought her almost to shore and she could touch the ground.

She dragged her board out of the water, aware that CeeJay was watching her from the doorway of Surf's Up. She'd been left in charge, Julie guessed, and she didn't appear to be happy about it.

Well, join the club, thought Julie. Today, even a job working at a surfboard rental joint had its merits over a classroom.

She immediately stopped long enough to chastise herself for not being grateful. She was grateful . . . just not excited about her work. Surely that was the kind of disconnect that she shouldn't have.

"What?" asked CeeJay in a bored voice.

Julie turned to look at her.

"You didn't take your full time."

"I know, but I'm done."

"You don't get a refund."

"Not a problem. I had a lovely time. I'll just put this away now."

"Suit yourself."

"Thank you." Julie refused to be goaded into this altercation. She didn't know why CeeJay was taking out her frustrations on her, unless maybe she was jealous of all the time Les and Bjorn were spending with Aggie and Kayla, or could it be Petewaller? Julie couldn't resist looking over her shoulder, half expecting CeeJay to be watching the kid with dreamy eyes, but she was still scowling at Julie.

So maybe not Petewaller.

And not her problem, Julie reminded herself.

She left her board, picked up her beach chair and bag, and trudged across the sand, past blankets and umbrellas, sunbathers and Frisbee players, and staked out her place on the beach as far away from CeeJay and her anger as she could get without trespassing onto the property of the unfriendly house owners.

When she'd set up her chair and placed her water bottle and snacks where she could reach them, she opened *Her Pirate's Heart.* Now this was the life.

She was reading when Aggie and Kayla came over to say Les and Bjorn were back and taking them out on the boat.

"Man, you've been reading for hours."

"Have I?" Julie looked down at her book. Page 186. She'd been oblivious.

"Hope you remembered sunscreen," Kayla said.

"I did. Thank goodness for SPF 30, or I'd be the color of a ripe tomato."

"You sure you don't want to go?"

"Thanks, but I just got to the good part." She held up her paperback.

They didn't argue but hurried away, and Julie felt a rock drop in her gut. She'd never been good at socializing, even as a kid. That's what made her friendship with Aggie and Kayla so special. But she had to admit that the two of them had more in common with each other than Julie had with either of them. And it occurred to her that maybe they'd outgrown her.

Is that why she hadn't told them about how unsatisfying teaching had become? Not because they might think she was making a judgment on them, but because she was afraid that she might lose them forever.

Maybe they had already given up on her and just kept planning vacations together out of habit. Now that she thought about it, Julie had always been the one in charge of the plans.

Was that why they were so enthusiastic about staying here, not because they were concerned about her uncle, but because it was more fun than the things she'd researched?

She turned her paperback over on her stomach, rubbed her temples, trying to drive out the insecurities. For someone with her life (sort of) and her career (definitely) solidly on track, she shouldn't be having all these doubts. And yet she did. Doubt and self-doubt were tying her insides into knots.

She was grateful. She was grateful. She was . . . desperate for something else.

She sat up. The book slid onto the sand. What was she going to do?

A small voice, the voice that always spoke up when she needed it, said, *You'll keep on doing what you planned. You're right on schedule. Everything is fine.*

"Right," Julie said, and picked up her book. Shook off the sand. "Right."

The next time Julie looked up, she realized that the beach had emptied considerably as it seemed to do every midafternoon. Only the die-hard surfers sat on the surface of the water like seafaring commuters waiting for a wave home.

From the corner of her eye she saw a Jeep drive into the parking lot. She turned her head to watch Alex park at the side of Lucky's and get out. He was carrying his briefcase—again.

What the hell did he do with a briefcase? It was so not everything she knew about him. Maybe he was making legitimate orders with distributors for the bar. So what was with the illicit goods in the middle of the night?

For a second it looked like he might be heading her way, but he went up the steps and into the bar. She ignored the little dip of disappointment in the pit of her stomach, went back to her pirate romance with a vengeance, and lost herself in impossible love.

Felt something wet on her cheek.

She moved away before turning to see Dougie, drool at full steam ahead, looking back at her.

"You again? I suppose Scatter put you up to this."

"Wuff."

"Don't even pretend to know what I'm saying."

Dougie bumped her leg, leaving a slick of saliva on her thigh.

"Gross, Dougie, just gross. Slobbering on people is not the way to win friends. Speaking of which . . ." No sign that Aggie and Kayla had returned. Their beach gear was still lying on the sand near Surf's Up.

Dougie bumped her shoulder, then took off across the sand. Stopped after a few feet. Looked back at her.

"Really? You want me to . . . play fetch? I doubt it. Feed you? The bar is the other way. I know. Take you to the groomers!" she said with false enthusiasm.

Dougie shook his head. Fortunately Julie was out of slobber range. Then he took off toward the private beach.

Oh man. Why did they let him roam loose like this? He probably wasn't even supposed to be on the public beach, and if the less-than-friendly owners of that house caught him, it was dog pound city for the stupid mutt for sure.

"Dougie, come back!"

He paused, looked expectantly at her, then splashed into the rivulet of water.

Julie tried to whistle, but between a dry mouth and the brisk breeze, it was a no-go. "Dougie, come here, boy." She clapped her hands.

He lumbered in a clumsy circle in the water and looked back at her.

Julie knew he would take off the minute she tried to stop him. She dropped her book and hauled herself out of the chair anyway. Of course she had to go after him. It wasn't his fault that he wasn't properly supervised.

He waited for her in the water, but when she got close

enough to reach for his collar—no easy feat since it was buried in a glob of matted fur—he managed to twist out of the way and pranced out of reach.

"Now you get frisky. We are not amused. Get over here now." Dougie backed away.

This time when she reached him, instead of taking off, Dougie leaned against her leg. "What, Doug? Running out of energy? All this frolicking about the beach for at least twenty seconds tired you out?"

"Wuff."

"I was being sarcastic, but you're probably suffering from heat prostration. Why don't you just find a tree—or a tire? Scatter has a nice Jeep for you to pee on. And then you can go back inside the bar where it's dark and cool."

Dougie seemed perfectly content to lean against her leg standing in the little rivulet of water making its way down to the sea. He was probably just hot with all that fur. Standing in the water was going a long way toward cooling her; maybe it was the same for dogs.

And while her feet were cooling, something melted inside her. She'd never had a dog of her own. Lucky often showed up with strays of the canine and human varieties. Her mom would clean their wounds and feed them, sometimes even help Lucky bathe them, but she would never let the dogs stay inside the house. She said it was because they had fleas and were dirty and would wreck the furniture, but for the first time ever, Julie wondered if it was because she was afraid of becoming attached to something who would run away . . . or die.

Julie shuddered in the waning sun.

"Please come on." She turned and started back toward the public beach, but Dougie just stood watching her as she walked away. "Come on, Dougie, you don't want to stay out here in the sun and sand flies."

He just cocked his big head.

"Suit yourself. I'm going to see if Aggie and Kayla are back yet."

Dougie shook himself and took off at a lope, not toward her but toward the private beach.

Julie attempted another whistle with no success. "Dougie. Here, Dougie."

Dougie stopped a few feet from the new PRIVATE sign. Today in the light, she noticed it was only one of three signs positioned along that stretch of beach, two facing the water. The image of Scatter unloading the van and leaving its cargo in the dunes—on the path to this same house—flashed across her mind.

Something fishy was going on here. And Julie was pretty sure it was something she didn't want to get involved in.

"Dougie. You really don't want to go over there. It's private." Like that had stopped her or Scatter the night before. But the night before she hadn't thought about the owners' need for privacy—not just from being overrun with vacationers, but . . . to hide something nefarious.

Maybe I shouldn't be reading about pirates.

"Dougie, please."

Dougie bounded farther away, then turned back to look at her.

Did she have a choice? What if they called the pound, or what if they shot him?

"Dougie, come on, now!" she hissed, keeping her eye on the house.

Dougie was nosing at the bushes that grew along the edge of the dune.

"Dougie, do not pee on these people's bushes." Julie clapped her hands. "Dougie!"

But Dougie's tail had started to wag in frenzied wide sweeps. He'd found some prey or other. A poor sandpiper or turtle? *Please don't let there be skunks at the beach. Arrested for trespassing and skunk odor—now that would be humiliating.* Julie took a breath and hurried toward him.

She managed to grab his collar. He didn't even try to evade her. His attention was trained on the bushes.

Julie leaned over to look. Blinked. Looked again. A pair of frightened dark eyes peered back at her. Not a turtle, not even a skunk, but a small boy.

Poor kid, Dougie had probably scared him.

She knelt down. "Oh, sweetie, it's okay. He won't hurt you."

She glanced at Dougie. Surely he wouldn't hurt him. She eased Dougie aside, which he allowed, and she leaned closer to the child.

"Hello."

The boy cringed farther back into the bushes.

"Were you playing? Dougie found you. He's good at hide-and-seek."

No response.

Someone called out from the house.

The boy's head snapped toward the voice, then back to Julie.

"Someone is looking for you. Why don't you come out? Dougie wants to meet you."

Big, round dark eyes. Not a sound.

"Are you stuck?" Or was he so afraid of Dougie—or whoever was looking for him—that he was afraid to even make a sound? Either way . . . She pushed at Dougie's shoulder. "You need to move away."

To her surprise, Dougie backed away and lay down in the sand.

"Hmm. Good dog," she said skeptically. "Okay. Dougie is lying down. Do you want to go home?"

Still no response.

The same woman she'd seen the other day at the back of the house, and again taking the kids inside, appeared in a break in the bushes and ran onto the beach, shielding her eyes and looking up and down and then out to sea. The woman probably thought the boy had drowned.

"She's looking for you."

The boy's eyes flitted past her but he still didn't come out. Was he afraid of the woman? Julie quickly scanned his skinny little body. There was a discoloration on his cheek. A bruise?

Should she call some authority to check out the situation? As a teacher she was mandated to turn in cases of potential child abuse. So far she hadn't had to, and she really didn't want to start now.

The woman was running back and forth along the shore,

frantic now, calling out some word that might be a name. Caught by the wind, it was impossible to understand.

Julie stood up. Bit her lip. And made a decision. "He's over here!"

The woman didn't hear her.

She waved both arms. "He's over here!"

The woman spun around, and the look of surprise on her face—more than surprise—took Julie's breath away. Fear—raw fear—the same reaction when she'd first seen Julie, only multiplied.

It took only a second for her to run toward them, her short, compact body moving in lurches and tiny catch-up steps until she reached Julie. She stopped long enough to huff out two breaths, looking not at Julie but into the bushes. She let out a cry of such anguish that Julie stepped aside.

"Pablo, niño, ven aqui a Rosie."

Rosie. She must be the housekeeper.

Slowly the kid crawled out of the bushes.

Rosie fell to her knees and he threw his arms around her. She reassured him in Spanish, asking questions: What had scared him? Whom had he seen? Interspersed with "You know not to come out without me," while looking frantically around the beach—but not at Julie—as she spoke.

Hell, no wonder he hadn't answered Julie's questions. The kid didn't speak English. Fortunately, Julie's high school and college Spanish was good enough to pick out a few words in the barrage of excitement, which reassured her that the boy wasn't being mistreated.

The woman finally stood up, lifting the boy, who must have been about five or six, with her.

"I'm sorry if he bothered you, miss. Thank you, thank you for finding him." All this was said as she backed away from Julie, her eyes lowered as if she was afraid to look Julie in the eye. Then she turned and bolted up the path to the house, the boy clutched in her arms, his legs bouncing out to the sides with every step.

Julie cast a look over to Dougie, who looked back at her with such a lugubrious expression that Julie laughed. "Come on, Doug. Let's get you back to the bar."

She'd had enough of kids—and dogs—for one day.

*M*arie stood at the window of Madame Marzetta's, willing any potential customers away, as she waited for Julie Barlow to pass by on her way to the hotel. She was impatient, and her new turban was giving her a headache.

A trio of women passed by and lingered in front of the store. Marie gave them her mother's and grandmother's evil eye. Marie hadn't inherited its power, but she had the look down pat. The three women eased away.

Marie tapped her painted fingernails on the brochure table. She'd just given up a quick sixty bucks minimum because somehow life in Lucky's Beach had suddenly spiraled out of control.

She picked up her cell phone. "Are you sure she's coming this way?"

"That's what she implied when she dropped off Dougie,"

Mike, Lucky's regular bartender, confirmed. "Let me double-check."

She heard his footsteps in the background, a door swing open and shut. "She's not in the parking lot, so she should be there any second. Want me to send out Ike, Corey, or Ron to make sure?"

"No thanks. Here she comes."

Marie ended the call, slipped the cell into one of the voluminous pockets of her caftan, and opened the door to the street.

"Julie."

Julie Barlow stuttered to a stop and turned toward Marie, causing the beach chair she was carrying and the bag hung over her shoulder to swing out like a boardwalk ride. Luckily there were no oncoming pedestrians.

Marie stepped out onto the sidewalk. She didn't really like to stand outside as Madame Marzetta. It took away the allure, made her feel exposed, and she had a sneaking suspicion that the heavy makeup showed every line and wrinkle.

That was vanity for you.

"Yes?" Julie said tentatively.

Marie got a full look at Lucky's niece, standing in a slant of afternoon sun. Her hair after a few days on the beach was sun-kissed the exact color as Lucky's.

The eyes, the cheekbones, the mouth. Julie Barlow had gotten the best of her mother and her uncle. It was a little uncanny. Marie had noticed the resemblance the first day, but her mind had still been reeling. More consumed with worry over Lucky's latest exploit than paying attention to detail, a stupid and dangerous state in the scheme of things.

Fortunately it was not too late to rectify.

"I wanted to invite you to dinner—tonight if it's not too short notice."

"Dinner—with you?"

"And Lucky of course. He's staying at my house. You took him off guard yesterday morning. He was . . . embarrassed that you would have caught him out in such a numbskull thing as a fistfight."

Julie's eyes narrowed. Now she looked more like Louise, studying, weighing, calculating. "Was that him in the alley the other night?"

Marie considered, thought what the hell. "Yes."

"Was he doing something illegal?"

Definitely more like Louise than Lucky. Right to the heart of it all. Was it something illegal? It depended on whom you asked.

"No."

"Okay. I'll come."

That stung, not for Marie herself—she really didn't care whether the girl stayed or not—but for Lucky, who didn't deserve this distrust.

"Thank you. We'd invite your friends, but my place is really small. Maybe sometime early next week, if you're still here," she added cautiously, "we can all get together. Is eight okay? I need to do a few more hours of work."

"Eight is fine. Thank you. Can I bring something?"

Marie almost laughed out loud. It sounded so normal. "No, thanks, we're good. See you then."

Julie started to leave.

"Oh, and Julie? Do you mind coming in the back door?"

Chapter 16

*J*ulie was early as usual. She'd seen Aggie and Kayla off to dinner, then sat in her hotel room, wearing a T-shirt dress she'd bought just for this trip. She'd briefly considered wearing something more stylish, but she'd packed those outfits for clubbing, not dinner in Marie's kitchen with her surfer-bum uncle and possibly a drooling Dougie.

This dress was comfortable, tucked across the front and flaring slightly toward midthigh. She'd added a double shell necklace that she'd bought on her last vacation.

It was fifteen to eight and only a three-minute walk max to Marie's cottage, but Julie couldn't sit still any longer. She locked her door, went downstairs, and headed not down Dune Lane and not out the back service door, since that would make her walk even shorter, but down Main Street toward Lucky's beach parking lot.

Most of the stores were still open, and she considered then

dismissed finding a hostess gift on her way. She had no idea what Marie would appreciate.

She strolled slowly past Madame Marzetta's CLOSED sign, waved at Claire through the window of Beachables. She stopped at the window of the Knitting Knoll, but it was closed and the interior was dark. The show window lacked even a spotlight, giving tourists out for an evening stroll no invitation to return the next day.

As Julie turned away from the window, she wasn't really surprised to see Ike, Ron, and Corey coming down the sidewalk behind her.

"Evening, Julie," Ike said. "We were just on our way to Lucky's for a postprandial beer. You going that way?"

"To Marie's," she said.

"Most people use the alley," Corey said.

"Can't park on Dune Lane," Ike explained.

"We'll walk with you a ways," added Ron.

The four of them continued down the sidewalk together.

"Well, good night, thanks for the escort," Julie told them when they reached the parking lot, and Julie turned toward the alley.

"Good night, Julie," Ike said.

"Enjoy your dinner," Corey added.

"Have a nice time," Ron chimed in.

She didn't look back as she walked away, but she had the feeling that they were still standing in the parking lot watching her.

It was still early and she walked slowly, taking up time, attempting to arrive a couple of minutes after eight so as not to appear too eager. Because suddenly she was eager to see her uncle. She'd like for just a moment to go back in time and sit down, just the two of them, with her Coke and his beer, and ask him what she should do with her life.

She passed the dumpster; Kayla's SUV was gone. She and Aggie must have decided to go out to the highway and hit some nightspots. Julie was relieved to be going to a quiet family dinner instead.

She'd reached Marie's cottage and she was still five minutes early. She could see two people moving around inside even though the half curtains were closed. The crown of Marie's head moved from one side to the other. Lucky, much taller, stood in one place, his profile tracking left and right, following Marie's movements.

Julie felt a frisson of nerves.

"Are you going to stand here all night or are you going inside?"

Julie nearly jumped out of her skin.

Alex "Scatter" Martin had come up behind her and she hadn't heard or felt a thing.

"Sorry, didn't mean to startle you."

"Where did you come from?"

"The bar. Aren't you going to Marie's?"

"Yes. How did you know?"

He grinned at her.

She steeled herself against his smarmy charm. Okay, not so smarmy tonight. *Do not succumb,* she warned herself. "Well?"

"Easy. I'm going there, too." He offered her his elbow.

She knew he was goofing on her, but she took it, felt a little scintillating rush as her hand touched his bare skin. She mentally rolled her eyes.

Scatter knocked on the door but didn't wait before pushing it open and shoving Julie inside. It was a low-down trick, purposefully making her entrance awkward. Which she didn't rectify when she finally collected herself and looked up right into Uncle Lucky's face.

Close up and personal, he still looked startled but not as much as the last time. Of course he hadn't been expecting her then. And she could understand how he might be embarrassed to see her. One whole side of his face was variegated colors of purple, green, and yellow.

She winced just looking at it.

"Don't tell your mother," he said. And the bubble of anxiety burst and she smiled, shook her head. The rest of him was just as she remembered him, except a little older, the tanned skin a little craggier. Still sinewy strong, he looked as if he could ride any wave that came his way.

And Julie was transported back to a time when Lucky would return home late, and her mother would be up waiting just like he was a teenager and had missed curfew. She knew because her mother would worry all night until she sent Julie to bed, where Julie couldn't sleep because her mother was worried and she didn't want Uncle Lucky to get in trouble.

He never did, not then, and he wouldn't now. Her mom would complain and scold and then she'd forgive him for worrying her, until the next time.

He opened his arms and she went in for a hug. And her anxiety melted away, until he let out a little grunt.

She pulled away. "Are you okay?"

"Better than ever," Lucky said. "How about a glass of wine. Red or white?"

"Red, please." She cut Scatter a look that said, *Take a page.*

Marie had been bent over the oven during this exchange, but now she closed the oven door, pushed a strand of hair out of her face, and said, "Welcome," before turning back to stir something on the stove.

She'd changed into a pair of floral slacks and a nubby tee and looked like any other beach community dweller; the mysterious Madame Marzetta had completely disappeared. And Julie wondered which person was the real Marie Simmons.

"Thank you," Julie said. "Can I help with anything?"

"No, just relax, I have a system; a necessity in a cottage kitchen."

"Yeah," Lucky said. "Her system is everybody stay out of her way."

They stood in the kitchen sipping wine, Lucky asking questions about her life, Marie puttering about the stove, and Scatter, who had helped himself to a beer from the fridge, leaning against the doorframe, oblivious.

Maybe he felt as weird as she did. What had she told him last night on the beach? About her mom, how she was sick of teaching. And then she was pretty sure she'd hit on him when he dropped her off at her room. Well, so what?

The conversation moved from initial awkwardness to conge-
niality and back to awkwardness, and Julie was sure everyone
was as relieved as she was when Marie pulled a crusty loaf of
bread from the oven, placed it on the table, and announced dinner was ready.

They sat in the overly warm kitchen around a rectangular
wooden table, eating flank steak over vegetable couscous and a
salad of fresh roquette, picked from Marie's garden.

Lucky poured more wine. "Will you please tell your mother
you've seen me in the flesh? And I'm fine and to please stop
calling the bar since I'm not there. Just tell her I look great.
Don't mention the Technicolor face."

"Which he is embarrassed to show even to the community,"
Marie said. "A grown man in this state."

"I've learned my lesson," Lucky said contritely. "So how *is*
Louise? She's actually on a cruise? Better late than never, I
guess."

"It's a nurses' conference."

Lucky breathed out a laugh. "Figures." He turned to Marie
and Scatter. "There's one who doesn't know how to have fun."

Julie didn't miss the quick look Scatter sent her way. Did
he think she didn't know how to have fun? He was probably
right, at least not the kind of fun he would consider worthy of
the name.

"And what about you, Julie?"

Julie's attention snapped back to her uncle. "I have fun. And
I get ten days at the beach every summer."

"That's all?"

"I have to start a course in three weeks. I'm working on my master's . . . better salary, better job security."

"You sound just like Louise."

"That's not a bad thing," Julie said defensively.

"She's taking surfing lessons with Les," Alex piped in.

"No kidding. How do you like it?"

"So far it's been a lot of waiting around."

"The big waves are farther down the beach."

"With bigger crowds," Alex added.

"Is that why you aren't living there, or Sunset Beach, or Waikiki? The crowds? It's none of my business, but I always thought you'd end up at some big-wave beach."

"We get decent waves down around Ocean City. In winter we have those waves all to ourselves, a ten-minute drive. No crowds. Plus I fell into a great deal for the bar and surf shop. Too good to pass up."

"You own the surf shop, too?"

"I lease out the building to Les. He owns the business."

"And you like running a bar?"

"What's not to like? And I have friends here." The look he gave Marie made Julie's heart hurt. Lucky and Madame Marzetta. Marie had told her they'd been friends in Asbury Park. They were definitely more than childhood friends now.

Marie, seeming to have read her mind, said, "I knew Lucky was looking for a place to invest in, so when I heard about Sam's bar being up for sale, I gave him a heads-up." Marie had moved so smoothly into the story that Julie felt like it was one they'd rehearsed.

"I showed up two days later, took one look, and bought it. Got it for a song." That sounded more like her uncle.

They seemed a strange couple, a fortune teller and a retired surfer, though on second thought . . .

There was something about Marie that always made Julie think of something else, like she wasn't exactly who she wanted people to see. Though the same might be said of most people, Julie realized, including herself.

"So, Marie, you lived here before Lucky?" Julie asked.

"Oh yes, I've been coming on vacation here for years. Bought this little place, then retired here."

"Retired? But you still have your business as Madame Marzetta."

"Yes, but it's really just a hobby now." Marie stood up. "I'll get the dessert. Alex, will you clear the dishes?"

Alex got up with more alacrity than the request required.

It left Lucky and Julie looking at each other.

"So," he said, studying the wine in his glass. "You like teaching?"

Julie hadn't anticipated that question. "Sure. It's steady hours and has possibilities of advancement. And . . ."

"But do you like it?"

"I'm good at it."

"Ju-u-u-liet . . ." Lucky drawled. Her mother always drew out her full name whenever she'd caught her daughter in a white lie, the only kind of lie Julie ever had the courage to attempt. Lucky would echo her "Juliet" with such an exaggerated drawl and hangdog expression that Julie would burst out giggling, ruining her mother's attempt at discipline.

His expression had changed from coaxing to looking at her sort of like her mother, and Julie caved.

"Actually, I think I hate it." She lowered her eyes, noticed a nick in the wood on the edge of the table. Concentrated on it, feeling like she might burst into tears.

Marie placed a bowl piled high with ice cream and peaches before her downcast eyes.

"It's okay," Julie said. "It's no secret." *Except from Mom and my two best friends, the most important people in my life.* "Even Scatter here knows." She cast a glance at him. Had he blabbed to Lucky about the things she said about teaching? Is that why her uncle had asked? What *had* she said? It was a little blurry. But she knew she'd said too much.

"So what do you want to do?" Lucky asked.

Julie shrugged. "Teach. I've put too much into it not to continue. What else could I do? And after all Mom has done to get me through school and started on my career, I can't do that to her."

Scatter made a disgusted sound from where he was looking out the window, where the night had grown dark. A sharp look from Marie and he sat down to eat his ice cream.

"Maybe it's just an exhausting time right now," Marie suggested.

"Bull," Lucky said. "If she doesn't like it, she doesn't like it."

Marie picked up his spoon and handed it to him, giving him a warning look that Julie didn't miss.

"What don't you like about teaching?" Marie asked.

"Pretty much everything," Julie said. "But I'll get over it. I'll have to."

"Well, you have time, right?" asked Lucky. "What kind of lead time do you need to give notice?"

"Notice? I can't give notice. Mom—"

"Will get over it."

Marie stretched out her hand. "Maybe you just need a sabbatical. Look at it from a different perspective."

Julie shook her head, miserable. "I tried that. They turned it down since it failed to meet the requirements of class curriculum." She could apply again in a few years, but she knew what would happen. She'd seen it in the older teachers, planning for this and that, and then waiting to retire to do it. If they ever did it at all. If she kept teaching she would always wonder what might have been out there waiting for her. "It doesn't matter. Marie's right. It's probably just end-of-the-year burnout."

"It might be," Marie agreed, interrupting whatever Scatter had opened his mouth to say. "Just make sure that's what it is. Life is passing, you don't want it to pass you by."

"And try to have a little fun while you're figuring it out," added Lucky.

Fun. Her uncle knew how to have fun. Sometimes it was irritating as hell. Though now Julie suspected it was just what she needed. But how?

She took a bite of ice cream. "This is delicious."

"Lucky made it," Marie said.

"You make ice cream?" Julie said, wondering why she suddenly felt better. Was ice cream the key? That would be too easy.

"Something to do while I was under house arrest."

Julie smiled; Marie and Alex didn't.

"I don't know how you do it," she told Lucky.

"What? Make ice cream?"

"No. Make me feel better." She'd forgotten those times until this week. "Remember you'd give me a Coke and I'd pour out my troubles and then I wouldn't be worried anymore?"

Lucky cracked a laugh. "*You* wouldn't be, you'd go upstairs and sleep like a log. I was the one who tossed and turned all night wondering if I'd said the right thing."

"Did you, really?"

"It was my pleasure."

"I'm sorry."

"Don't be, it was the least I could do, since your mother would never accept any other help."

"What do you mean? You . . ."

"Never offered?"

"I was going to say you were never there, but that isn't true, is it?"

Lucky didn't say anything. Scatter slapped the table, but a quelling look from Marie stopped whatever he was going to say.

"Sunshine, your mother wouldn't accept it, so I stopped trying. And I had other stuff I was doing."

She smiled, said sheepishly, "Catching the big one?"

"Among other things."

"I sometimes wished you'd taken me with you." She touched her fingers to her mouth, surprised at her own admission.

"You did?"

She nodded, forgetting they had an audience. It was suddenly really important to get to the place with her uncle that she'd forgotten. Not the moocher uncle that she remembered, but the other loving, funny, supportive one.

Lucky pointed his spoon at her. "Now don't you worry about a thing. You make your decisions. She'll come along if she has to."

"I can't disappoint her; she did everything for me."

"Look, honey, your mother did everything for everybody, including me. I came to help her, but she wouldn't let me. Your mother is one of those people who can't accept help. If she were in a leaky boat with a dozen able-bodied people, she wouldn't let any of them help bail."

Julie smiled in spite of herself. It was true. "She didn't want to be caught unprepared again after Dad died."

"We all knew that, except her. She might have needed to do that for herself. But not for you. People need friends, and a support system—isn't that right, Scatter?"

Scatter started and nodded. "Uh, yeah, no dude is an island." Then he shoveled a huge spoonful of ice cream into his mouth.

Better than his foot, Julie thought, and rolled her eyes.

Lucky shook his head. "Really, Scat, is that what they teach psychologists these days? That no dude is an island? For that you get the big bucks?"

Scatter's spoon, which had been scraping the sides of his bowl, stopped.

Marie stared at the center of the table into the crystal ball that wasn't there.

"You're a——" Julie choked on the word.

"Family therapist," Lucky said innocently. "Didn't he tell you?"

Alex finally looked at her, his eyes dark, deep, and guilty as charged.

All the things she possibly could have confessed to him tumbled over each other in her mind. The walk to the hotel, standing close, wanting to be closer; the proposition he'd turned down—it all came back to bite her. God, she was such an idiot.

She pulled herself together. "No, he didn't. An interesting pastime for a bartender."

Where did she leave her purse? Hanging on the back of the chair. She'd calmly thank Marie and leave. Ugh, she was *such* an idiot.

"Coffee anyone?" Marie asked into the well of silence.

Julie shook her head, thankful for Marie's women's perspicacity. "But can I help with the dishes?"

"No thanks." Marie smiled, and even though it was forced, Julie clung to it.

"Well, then I'd better be going. Thanks for dinner."

She pulled at her bag and managed to drag the chair several inches before she untangled the strap. She leaned over to give Lucky a kiss, then slipped past Scatter and reached for the doorknob.

"Good night, all. Thanks so much."

And Julie fled.

*A*lex threw his napkin on the table and pushed his chair back, nearly knocking it over as he stood. "You did that on purpose."

"What?" asked Lucky. "You didn't tell me not to mention you were a therapist. I thought she would be interested."

"I was going to tell her—at some point—if she hung around."

"Maybe you should go explain things." Lucky grinned at him.

"Explain what? I thought we agreed you got in a bar fight."

"Not that stuff. I thought you'd like to get to know her better. Aren't you going to tell her anything?"

"We agreed to keep her in the dark. For her own safety."

"About yourself, Scat. About your past. About—"

"You leave my past out of this. It would just complicate things."

"Scared, Mr. Therapist?"

"Marie . . ." Alex pleaded.

Marie looked up from the dishes. "You two duke it out. But really, Alex, you can't spring things like this on vulnerable people."

"I didn't spring it on her. Lucky did."

"For your own good," Lucky said.

"What the hell? She told me all this stuff before I could tell her I was a therapist and then it was too late. Now she probably thinks I was . . . hell, I don't know. Maybe it doesn't matter."

"Sure it does. You used to like her . . . a lot, didn't you?"

"I was twelve. I don't remember. And that's not the point."

"Okay, so what do you think of her now?"

"Don't even go there, Lucky. We have enough on our plate as it is."

"You're at least interested."

"Yeah, I'm interested. Or would be if we weren't in the thick of God knows what. Do you have a problem with that?"

"Not me. You might have to get past Louise, though."

"I don't think it will get that far."

"That'll be a first."

"Well, I think," Marie said, tossing the dish towel to Lucky, "you should go try to explain things to her. I don't know what you two have been talking about, but it was obviously uncomfortable for her. She deserves an explanation."

"Oh hell." Alex yanked the door open and strode outside.

Once he was actually outside, he hesitated. He could see her almost at the end of the alley. Damn Lucky and his twisted sense of humor. He'd have to run to catch up to her—and then what? He'd be out of breath and looking like a fool.

Damn. He took off at a jog. "Julie, wait."

She ignored him. He put on some speed and caught up to her just as she reached the back of the knitting store. Oh, great, all he needed was to run into Stella the conspiracy theorist on her way home.

"Julie, listen."

Julie turned on him.

Okay. He could tell she looked pretty mad even in the motion light of the knitting store door.

"I guess you were really entertained last night, me sitting there spilling my guts about my life; no wonder you acted so smug."

"I wasn't acting smug. I was listening."

"You were therapizing."

"No, I wasn't. And this is just why I didn't say anything. Who wants to have a conversation with a therapist? Unless they're out for free advice."

"Well, you don't need to worry. I don't want either from you."

"Would you just chill? I said I was sorry."

"You let me keep talking like an ass and didn't tell me."

"I didn't want to break the mood."

She just stared at him.

"It's not that big of a deal."

"It is to me. I'm never telling you anything again. I don't know why I told you all that stuff in the first place. You cheated, misrepresented yourself, tricked me."

"No, I didn't. It just never came up." From the corner of his eye, he saw the shades of the knitting storeroom window move slightly. Damn. Stella was watching them.

Julie turned to see, and the shades dropped back into place.

Alex moved her into the shadows, lowered his voice. "Stella is a nosy, unhappy woman. Don't give her ammunition."

She hung her head, and he felt like an ass.

"You let me pour out my most vulnerable secrets and you were analyzing me the whole time."

"I wasn't."

"I don't believe you." She pushed him away and headed for the parking lot.

He grabbed her arm and pulled her back. "You don't? Then believe this." He drew her close, thought, *I am so screwed,* and kissed her.

An eternity passed before they pulled away.

"Does that feel like analyzing to you?"

She shook her head.

"Good." Alex kissed her again.

Chapter 17

He'd left her at the lobby. A kiss like there was no tomorrow, then he drops her off in the lobby? Didn't that kiss warrant at least a drink to prolong the evening? Maybe he had a shabby apartment. Maybe he didn't want gossip if he was seen going upstairs to her room and didn't come back. Maybe he was afraid of Stella. Or maybe he already had a wife or girlfriend. She wouldn't put anything past him. He was charming *and* a bartender; he must meet women all the time.

Well, to hell with him, he'd misrepresented himself, let her spill her innermost fears to him. It was embarrassing, humiliating, and she'd doubled that by running out of Marie's without a proper thanks or planning to meet again.

Then he'd kissed her and left her without a "see ya."

God, what was wrong with her that she kept falling for all the bullshit in the world?

At least Aggie and Kayla were still out when she'd returned

to the hotel, so they didn't see her solo climb up to the third floor.

Still, she wasn't surprised when there was a knock on the door the next morning, earlier than their usual breakfast call. She was already dressed, knowing they would be curious about what had happened with Lucky. And she could tell them about the kiss—the two kisses—over a stack of pancakes and lots of coffee.

"Just a sec." She brushed on some lip gloss and went to answer the door. Maybe they would have some advice.

Yeah, like move on to the next guy.

"Coming." She brightened the smile. Noticed the stack of clothes on the bed she'd been about to pack last night in the throes of embarrassment and disappointment. She grabbed them and quickly shoved them in the drawer before opening the door.

"You guys were late last—" She broke off. It was not her friends.

Scatter Martin held out a takeout coffee. "Large, milk and sugar. I figured you'd need the sugar, and Darinda at the luncheonette said that's the way you took it at breakfast."

Julie took the cup. She didn't know what he wanted, but she'd gladly take his coffee. She pulled back the tab and took a sip. Heaven.

"Thank you. Is there anything else? Does Lucky—" She bit down on the words. She wouldn't further her humiliation by asking.

"Nope."

"Then thank you for the coffee." She started to shut the door.

He merely stepped farther into the room.

"What do you want?"

"Is that the way to talk to someone who just brought you coffee?"

Julie could feel herself caving. *Ugh.* "Look, thanks for the coffee. If this is a peace offering, I accept. I guess."

"Peace offering? You know . . . Forget it. Come on. I want to show you something." He opened the door wider.

"Why?"

"You'll know when we get there."

"Is this about last night?"

"Yes and no. Yes about your life, not about us."

"There is no us."

"Fine. Grab a sweatshirt; you'll need it for the ride."

"What ride?"

"It's not far." He looked around the room. He picked up a sweatshirt off the back of the desk chair. "Here, this will be fine."

She reached for it. "It doesn't go with what I have on."

"That's even better. Are you ready?"

Alex's Jeep was illegally parked outside the hotel. A squad car was parked a few feet in front of it.

"Doesn't look like we'll be going anywhere for a while," she said.

"Them? Nah. Stella reported a burglary. The third time in two weeks, whack job that she is." He opened the door for her.

"Is that the way a psychologist should be talking about a potential client?"

"I wouldn't see her." He stood by while she climbed into the front seat, struggling to balance the coffee cup, shoulder purse, sweatshirt, and phone. He didn't offer to help.

As soon as she was seated, he swung the door shut. While he was going around to the driver's side, she pressed speed dial for Kayla. "Hey, it's me. Evidently I'm going on a drive with the Scatterbrain. If I don't come back by tonight, call the fire department."

Kayla barked out a laugh. "Wait! What? You're with Scatterman? So that's where you got off to last night. Good one, Julie."

"No, it wasn't like—" She broke off as the driver's-side door opened and Alex slid into the seat.

She held up a finger to tell him to wait. "So I don't know how long I'll be gone." She glanced over to Alex, but he just shrugged. "I guess I'll see you at the beach later."

"Cool," Kayla said. "Can't wait, but take your time. We want to hear every detail."

Julie heard Aggie in the background. "What, what?"

There was a struggle over the cell. Then Alex grabbed Julie's out of her hand. "Everything is under control. She'll be back." He ended the call, swiped the phone off, and tossed it under his seat.

"Hey. Give me that. What if there's an emergency?"

"Then someone will call me."

"It better not be wet under there," Julie said. "Or you'll owe me a new phone."

"Deal."

He made a U-turn in the middle of Main Street and drove out of town.

"Just so you know—"

"You're a black belt in karate," he finished. "Good to know I'll be safe as long as you're nearby."

Julie had the most annoying urge to laugh. "So where are you taking me?" she asked. *And why?*

"You'll see. Consider it a field trip. One where you don't have to be responsible for a bus full of kids and can sit back and enjoy the ride."

Once outside of town, the Jeep picked up speed. Julie put her coffee cup in the console while she wrestled with the seat belt to put on her sweatshirt and gather her windblown hair into a ponytail.

Then she sat back to enjoy the view, which was pretty nice, even though they were moving away from the beach. All evidence of tourism gradually disappeared until they were driving along a narrow two-lane country road, surrounded by . . . cornfields?

The corn was about halfway to harvest, high enough to hide any signs of civilization around them. It was a little spooky.

She glanced over at Alex, who seemed to have forgotten her existence. They came to a T junction and Alex took the left fork. The road dipped, and suddenly a manufactured community rose from the midst of the corn like it had been dropped by aliens. There were no cars, no people, and they passed it so quickly that Julie wondered if it had been a figment of her imagination.

More fields, no longer growing corn but with row upon row of low, rounded bushes. And scores of workers bent over, picking the crop.

"Strawberries," Alex called over the engine noise and rush of wind, just as if she'd asked him. Which she hadn't. "Backbreaking work. Near the end of the season. Next is tomatoes, then watermelons, the real backbreakers."

"Don't they have machines for that?" Julie asked.

He just gave her a deadpan look and returned his attention to the road.

I guess not, thought Julie.

They'd been driving about fifteen minutes when Alex turned the Jeep down an even narrower road and into what appeared to be a small—really small—town, then out the other side, where he pulled into an asphalt parking lot. A basketball hoop stood at one end, a dumpster at the other. A narrow one-story cinder-block building sat at the back of the lot and was surrounded by a wide swath of mowed grass that gave way to more fields in the distance. There were a couple of other cars parked in front, and Alex pulled in next to them.

Julie couldn't imagine what it was used for, but she was about to find out. Alex had gotten out and was coming around to open her door. At least his manners were on display. But why? He hadn't gone out of his way to be nice since she'd been there. Well, the kisses were nice, she had to admit. Better than nice.

"Are you going to get out?"

"Sure." She slid off the seat and followed him to a metal door with a glass window embedded with honeycombed security wire. A bit intimidating. A warehouse?

Someone buzzed them in, and Julie felt a frisson of nerves. She sure hoped it wasn't going to be some illegal liquor warehouse. But why would he take her there?

Alex held the door and let her enter first. It was quiet but not deserted. As they stood in what looked like a reception room with no reception, a door opened down the hall, unleashing a rousing rendition of "This Old Man," and a petite, dark-haired young woman wearing black yoga pants and a tie-dyed T-shirt hurried toward them.

"Alex! You made it." She had a killer smile.

"Desiree Hoyes, meet Julie Barlow."

"Pleased to meet you," Julie said, not understanding why she was meeting her. Her name belonged to a thirties movie star. But this Desiree was totally here and now and vibrating with energy. Her smile broadcasted the brightest red lipstick Julie had seen since the parent-teacher Christmas party.

Her eyes sucked in Alex and twinkled at Julie.

"Everyone calls me Dee." She took Julie by the elbow like they were old friends and started down the hall. "I'm so glad you decided to come. I think you'll really like what you see."

Julie opened her mouth to explain that she had no idea why she was here. She managed to look back at Alex, but he merely waved and walked off in the opposite direction.

Dee opened the door she'd just come from to a room painted light green. A double semicircle of children stood in the middle of the room. Off to one side a skinny man in a plaid shirt and work pants was leading the singing at a rickety upright piano. Along one wall were Formica tables with a row of computers, and on the other, two rows of smaller tables, with books and papers and pencils stacked in the center of each.

Two nights ago she'd poured out her feelings to Alex, about love, life, and hating her job. Last night he'd kissed her. Today he'd shown up at her door with coffee.

I want to show you something.

She had to admit, she'd been intrigued, and maybe a little flattered? He wanted to show her something. A surprise. She thought maybe things were looking up and decided to give him one more chance.

And what did that surprise turn out to be? A twenty-minute drive to school.

When would she ever learn?

*A*lex didn't wait around to see what Julie's reaction would be. He'd considered telling her where they were going, but she would have balked. And maybe he should just stay the hell away from her. But she seemed so lost.

Not lost. Hindered. It was a word he had cause to know in counseling. *Hindered.* Kept back from being yourself.

Julie was good at what she did, who she was. He could tell that now. He could tell that she would be, even back then.

Julie Barlow was hindered, not lost. Alex was the one in danger of losing himself if she stuck around.

Maybe Lucky was rubbing off on him. But Alex also thought he saw that little bit of the devil in her. But shit, it was buried under a lot of good girl, good daughter, good teacher, good citizen, good everything. How could someone live with all that goodness?

Not him. He couldn't, and he was pretty sure Julie shouldn't.

He walked out the side door to the mowed field where a soccer game was going on. Two games actually: half a field for the older boys and the other half, more like a quarter, for the younger ones. But it didn't matter to them.

Just having a place to go during the long, hot day while your parents and older siblings worked in the fields was like a slice of heaven. And if you learned a little English and how to read along the way, not shabby.

A third of the older boys would be in the fields themselves next year, maybe even by the end of summer, instead of day camp.

"Alex! Over here!" Tito Burgos waved to him, trapped the ball with one foot, then passed it off as Bobby Garza slid in for a tackle.

The younger boys stopped playing altogether and ran en masse toward Alex. He was glad to see Alberto among them.

"Play with us!"

He gave Tito a wait-a-minute sign and let the little kids drag him toward their side of the field. He wasn't as clueless to think he was an ace soccer player. He hadn't even learned how to play until he was in college.

Both sides wanted a tall guy on their team.

After a few minutes he switched to the other game and spent the next half hour going from one game to the other.

*A*lex said you're Lucky's niece visiting for a while, that you're a schoolteacher, and that you would like to help out with the camp." Dee flashed that Christmas-red smile, then shrugged. "Alex can sometimes be a little forceful."

Julie was thinking more along the lines of sneaky, conniving, and arrogant. "Yes, he can," she agreed.

"But you *did* want to come?"

"Of course," Julie said. Really, what else could she say?

"We're a little shorthanded for the next couple of weeks. Geraldo"—she pointed to the piano player—"is actually the custodian here, but is sitting in on music as a favor.

"We're what you might call a satellite camp; the main camp is about twenty miles away and already bursting at the seams. We take the overflow kids." She looked up at Julie's face. "Oh, it's like a summer day camp, fun and learning. Field trips. They go home every day at five. It's a community effort."

Julie nodded. For a moment the word "camp" had thrown her. She was glad they weren't talking about the other kind of camp. But she still didn't want to be here. It was her vacation and she wanted to escape teaching—at least for ten days.

Alex knew that. But he'd disappeared, probably ditched her and drove off, leaving her here just to get her out of the way.

She brought her attention back to what Dee was saying.

". . . younger, newer to the system . . . most of them have some catching up to do. A few trauma cases. Alex sees them in town away from the others. A mixed bag," she added, smiling even more brightly, if that was possible.

She moved toward one of the tables and Julie followed. She saw right away that the books were used—a lot—and several years out of date.

The song had moved on to "The Ants Go Marching," and Julie remembered why she would never be a kindergarten teacher. Though at her school they were more likely to be singing "Circle of Life" than a number-learning song.

"The little one stops to . . ."

"So after music we divide into groups and have reading and wordplay. Mostly we read, they play."

Julie smiled for the first time since she'd arrived.

Dee raised both eyebrows; they made two perfect arcs. She was very pretty and very dynamic.

And enthusiastic about this, Julie thought, looking around at the depressing surroundings.

"I usually take them outside for that session. More things to relate to in the open. And there's enough shade so that it's not too uncomfortable."

Dee Hoyes was a brave soul.

"Geraldo will take one group today. And you and I'll take

the other. Vicky, who's in the math room, will meet with the older kids." She gathered a stack of books off the table. "How's your Spanish?"

"Basic. Two semesters in college and rarely used."

"That'll do. I'll get you started. Then maybe you could take over while I get some much-needed paperwork done."

"Take over? Wait, I'm not qualified . . ."

"I'm sure you are. Alex said you won teacher of the year at your school."

How did Scatterbrain know that? Julie certainly hadn't divulged that. She could murder him for volunteering her for this. Aggie and Kayla were at the beach, and she was about to sit under a tree teaching reading.

"I'm sure you'll do fine."

Dee looked so hopeful that Julie felt a stab of contrition. The ants were now marching three by three, and she tried to remember how many verses were in the song. She was struck with horror as she realized it might go up to ninety-nine, like bottles of beer on the wall. She'd be a raving lunatic by then.

"I'll start you off. Mainly you just read to them, have them pick out words. Go through the flash cards . . ." She handed Julie an inch-thick stack of cardboard cards bound by a rubber band.

Flash cards. That was so not progressive. Where the hell had Alex gone?

"Then some word games out of the book, then whatever keeps them interested. If they don't engage, go on to the next book. Afterward they'll have lunch and Vicky will reinforce whatever words they learned today and add them to their vocabulary."

Oh, great, no drinks with umbrellas in them for Julie today. Maybe Alex would take pity on her by then. And really, what was the point? Was he trying to get her out of town? For what? To unload more contraband? What did he think? That she'd turn them in?

The ants finally stopped marching at ten, and Julie was introduced to a group of five children—two girls, three boys—who could have been any age from three to six. It was hard to tell.

"Buenos días," they responded. Then Dee mouthed the words, "Good morning," and they repeated that, too.

Julie smiled and did the reverse. "Good morning. Buenos días."

They followed Dee and Julie down the hall and out the back door without question. They passed Alex and a passel of boys all sweaty and dirty coming inside, which answered the question of whether he had driven away and left her stranded. He grinned at her. Several of the others turned to stare, but Scatter fired off something in Spanish and the boys hurried on down the hallway.

As soon as the kids got outside they ran to a large spreading oak tree, one of three that had survived on the edge of planted fields. Dee sat down cross-legged in the dirt. Whatever grass had once grown there had shriveled up and died weeks before.

Julie sat down beside her, wishing she hadn't worn her good shorts. The kids sat in a circle all cross-legged, matching Julie and Dee. Dee picked up one of the books and handed the other two to Julie. The kids broke rank and crowded around the two women, leaning into and over them to get a better look at the book.

Julie couldn't remember having such a captive audience. Dee read the first book, a short ESL primer with a simple story line. She pointed to the pictures, accentuated the specified words and repeated them in English. When she finished the story, she pulled out the flash cards and had them say the English word, then turned the card over to show the accompanying picture.

When they'd made it through the first stack of flash cards, Julie opened the next book. It was going to be a long morning at this rate. The children moved even closer and Dee took the opportunity to slip away.

Julie read through the book, stressing the pertinent words and having them repeat them, but when she put it down and reached for the flash cards, one of the little girls picked up the book and shoved it at her. "Again . . . please."

The others nodded. So with urges of "please," Julie read it again. Again, they pointed to the pictures, recited the words, sometimes talked in enthusiastic Spanish, much of which was too fast for Julie to understand.

"Where is the cat?" she asked to see if they had understood the words of the story.

The boy on her right reached over her and turned the page, pointed to the correct picture. "El gato."

"Yes," said Julie. "'El gato' en español and 'the cat' in English."

"There," the boy next to him said, and took off toward the field.

"Wait!" cried Julie. The other four children jumped up and ran after him.

She caught up to him just as he was about to climb over the irrigation ditch and into the rows of plants. He pointed again.

They all gathered around, standing close to Julie and holding on to her so they could lean over to see.

Two green eyes looked back at them from under what looked like blueberry bushes.

Then the cat jumped out and darted past them toward the building. The kids turned and took off after it. *Shit,* thought Julie, and took off after them.

As she ran, she looked desperately for Dee or anyone else for help. But evidently she'd been left alone with her charges. She was afraid not to join them.

"Cat!" one of the kids squealed, and reached out with both hands.

"Don't touch," Julie warned.

The cat took off again. This time it slinked behind a large, rusted oil drum. Julie didn't even want to imagine what it was used for. "Careful," she called as the kids rounded the drum. *Tetanus . . . stitches . . . letters to the principal . . .*

"Cuidadoso!" she yelled, her college Spanish finally kicking in.

She reached the back of the drum. They were all squatting

in the dirt looking at the bottom rim of the drum. The cat was nowhere to be seen.

Julie huffed out a sigh of relief. But now what were they doing? She leaned over the five who were intently watching . . .

"Ants!" they yelled excitedly, and Julie Barlow had an epiphany.

*W*hat's she doing?" Alex asked, looking out the window of Dee's office. Julie was running after a bunch of kids all looking at the ground.

"Teaching vocabulary."

"Really? It looks like she's just chasing kids to me."

Dee got up from her desk and came to the window.

"Do you think you should intercede?"

"Hell no," Dee said. "I'd hire her if I had a penny to fly with. As it is, I may have to adopt her technique."

"That's a technique?" Alex asked.

Dee smiled her megawatt smile. "Oh yeah. She's a natural."

Chapter 18

"Counting ants," Julie said, still trying to brush off dirt from the seat of her shorts, when Alex and Dee met her in the hallway. The kids ran ahead to wash their hands for lunch.

"Brilliant," said Dee.

Alex just grinned like he hadn't trapped her into substitute teaching for free. Though she'd had a good time, she had to admit. But not to Scatterbrain. He was too smug as it was.

"Well, I appreciate the help. Lunch is being served in the music/math/nap/reading/lunch room if you're not averse to cheese sandwiches and chips. We give them breakfast every day and try to feed them something hot and something green at least once a week. We don't really have kitchen facilities here."

"Where can I . . ." Julie held up her dirty hands.

Dee fished a key from her shirt pocket. "Staff bathroom. One of the many perks of the job. Down that hall and to the left."

Julie took the key and walked down the hall, past a door

that read DIRECTOR, past the supply room, and finally found the staff bathroom.

After a semi-successful cleanup, Julie made her way back to the main hall. As she reached it she heard voices. Scatter and Dee had moved to the far end and were speaking in low tones. Bodies close, Alex's head bent almost as if he were going to kiss her.

Really, she had kisses on the brain. And evidently so did Scatter Martin.

Julie jerked her gaze away and strode to the music room, where she found the space now taken over by long folding tables.

Geraldo was helping three older women pass out sandwiches and drinks. The only other adults in the room were two young women who sat at a separate table. Julie went over to join them.

She had just sat down when Dee and Alex came in. Several of the boys called out to Alex to sit with them. He called back something and went to sit at the table with the younger boys.

Dee snagged a sandwich and soda from the volunteers and made her way over to the staff table. "Hope you all introduced yourselves," she said, and sat down. "And I hope you enjoyed yourself this morning."

"I did," Julie admitted.

"After lunch the younger kids have quiet playtime; there's computer and English for the others. Mary here is helping some with work permits and such. Scatter takes a bunch down to the conference room."

"Group therapy?"

Dee gave her an odd look. "More like they just hang out and talk about stuff. You don't approve?"

"Oh, sure I do. It's just he kind of sprung his profession on me."

"He doesn't like to boast."

"He doesn't?" You could have fooled her. Actually, he hadn't exactly boasted to her, just been a cocky, arrogant know-it-all. And he'd let her embarrass herself in front of him and then in front of Lucky and Marie. Something she would never forgive him for. She was having a serious crisis and he . . . oh well, it didn't matter.

". . . three times a week," Dee was saying. "Then the miniature golf place out on the highway lets us come in on Tuesdays, and swimming at the community center, which gives them a chance to interact with the local kids." She paused. Smiled her high-wattage smile. "And I wouldn't say no if you wanted to come back again. We meet every day until five. But even a couple of hours would be a huge help. And the kids like you."

Julie returned her smile, feeling trapped. Kids liked her. She knew that. It was hardly something to build a life on. She liked them, too, but maybe just not enough.

No, that wasn't true. She liked them; she just didn't feel excited around them. No, that wasn't true, either; she'd really enjoyed watching ants this morning. Maybe she should be teaching younger kids.

No, she'd sat in on Kayla's class one day while Kayla had an evaluation meeting. They were cute, assured, polite, did everything they were told. Not one of them ran off to chase an ant.

Of course, they didn't have ants at Hillsdale Progressive, unless they were in the biology lab inside a plastic ant farm.

This morning had been kind of fun. Would it kill her to do something to help these kids who didn't even have permanent homes, much less schools?

"Sure, I guess I might come back for a day or two. But I'll have to see what my friends are doing. We might be leaving. We were on our way to another beach and just stopped in to see my uncle. I saw him last night so . . . they may want to go on."

"Lucky's a great guy. He's helped more than one of our families."

"He has? Doing what, if you don't mind me asking?"

"Stuff with the authorities and the kids. Most of them are perfectly well behaved, but with so much time on their hands . . . That's why we opened the overflow camp. The county gives us the space rent-free and we have a couple of grants, but for the rest we depend on volunteers and donations.

"He and the guys and the whole town have gotten involved at one time or another. The mayor has been especially helpful getting us through the bureaucracy."

"It's like a do-gooder town, Lucky's Beach?"

"You could say that."

Geraldo stuck his head in the door. "The people with the sports equipment are here."

"Oh good. Come help carry," Dee said, and Julie followed her and Geraldo to the front door.

The sports equipment turned out to be several open boxes of hand-me-down junk left over from the equipment swap at one of the local schools. They carried the boxes back to a large storage room, a rectangular disaster area of boxes, large black garbage bags, a long, battered table, and a few metal utility shelves, several of which looked like they might fall down if someone actually put something on them.

"I've been meaning to get this cleaned up," Dee said. "We had a lot of donations at the beginning of summer and we haven't had time to go through them all. But we've been waiting for this. Fingers crossed." Dee reached into one of the boxes, brought out a lacrosse stick. Leaned it against the wall. A bag of T-shirts with numbers on the back and BENNIE'S BAGELS written across the front.

"A whole team's worth," Dee said delightedly, and put them on one of the metal shelves.

They weren't new. And Julie felt a little burning in her throat, thinking about her own school's uniforms, not T-shirts but real uniforms, with players' names printed on the back.

"Wow!" came voices from the open doorway.

They turned to see several children crowded around the opening.

"Aren't you supposed to be having quiet time?" Dee asked.

"We're being quiet," one said.

"We heard truck," said another.

"We told them people were bringing equipment today," Dee explained.

Several more had joined in the doorway.

"Okay, but be quiet and stay right where you are."

So with half a dozen kids looking on, they pulled out several baseball bats, a bag of scuffed balls. Several mitts. Two pairs of roller skates. Two basketballs, five soccer balls, and one box filled with Hula-Hoops.

"Bless these people," Dee said, and Julie thought of all the times brand-new state-of-the-art equipment had arrived in her classroom or the gym or the science lab and everyone had just taken it for granted. Well, there had been interest in the digital microscopes for sixth-grade biology . . . but no chasing after ants.

Julie didn't think of herself as entitled. She'd worked hard all her life, and her mother had worked hard to give her opportunities. But she felt her world tilting; she didn't know why, she just knew that she had some decisions to make . . . as soon as she recognized what they were.

When they were almost finished unloading the boxes and the mismatched equipment was spread over one long table and several shelves, Geraldo leaned into the last box and pulled out a long rectangular cardboard package. He opened the top and pulled out a metal tube with white bulbs at each end, one large, one small.

"Batons," Dee said quizzically. "How many?"

"Ten," Geraldo said.

"I wonder if anybody knows how to twirl them."

Julie just stared. She knew how, *had* known how. She'd just been remembering. How weird was that?

Geraldo shrugged. "Guess not." He slid the box onto a shelf.

"Me, me," said a little girl, waving her hands.

"You know how to do this?" Dee asked.

She nodded vigorously. Geraldo pulled a baton from the box and handed it to her. She held it in her fist. And twisted her wrist back and forth energetically. Then smiled broadly.

"That's lovely," said Dee, a note of acceptance creeping into her voice. She glanced at her watch. "Okay, fun's over. Time to get back to work. How about some games out in the heat of the day? How's your duck, duck, goose?"

"Not a clue," Julie said. She looked down at the little girl who was eyeing the box where Geraldo had returned the baton. *Oh hell.* "My ducks and geese are pretty bad, but I think maybe I can go around with a baton."

"You twirl?"

"I did. I might be a little rusty. A lot rusty. But I can get them started . . . if anyone's interested."

Dee turned to the group and explained in Spanish, then asked who wanted to try twirling. Several did, boys, too.

"Got yourself a class," Dee said. "Just make sure the boys don't turn them into instruments of destruction."

They all went outside, including Geraldo, who insisted on carrying the Hula-Hoops and the entire box of batons.

Dee took those interested in Hula-Hoops off to the far side of the yard. Geraldo handed out batons to the others, then handed one to Julie, who took a minute to reintroduce her fingers to the lightweight instrument. It was small for her but perfect for little hands. She gave a couple of test twirls. Managed not to drop the thing and turned to her students, who had stopped their mad imitations of drum corps to watch.

"Okay, spread out. Hold it out like this. Thumbs over like this . . ."

A few kids gave up right away and went to join the Hula-Hoop group.

After a few minutes some older girls who had been sitting under the tree came over to give it a try.

It took several minutes just to get them to do the opening pose. Free hand on hip. Baton held in the working hand perpendicular to the ground. They practiced lifting it up and down like a drum major.

The younger kids enjoyed that, but the older ones wanted more splash.

"It takes a long time to learn all those tricks."

"Show us."

"I'm pretty rusty."

Blank looks.

"It's been a long time since I practiced," she tried in Spanish. Still, no one spoke, and she realized they were waiting for her to perform. Oh man, she should never have started this. She would probably be awful. What if she couldn't do it?

And what a stupid reason not to try. She took the baton, gave it a couple more test twirls. Backed away from the group and took her opening stance.

And right there in the dry stubble of the lawn, watched by a handful of children and teenagers, fingering a child-sized metal baton, Julie Barlow twirled like it was her last chance to make the team.

An hour later, when the bus came to pick the kids up to carry them to the community center pool, Julie was still holding a baton.

She watched as Alex gave a young boy a complicated handshake, said, "Dos Als," and lifted him on the bus. Dee and Geraldo waved goodbye as the bus pulled away and went back inside to clean and close up.

"So what's that?" Alex asked, indicating the baton.

"A donation. A whole box of them. I guess some school lost their majorette corps."

"Know how to do it?"

She didn't like the way he was looking at her. Like he already knew the answer. Like maybe he would catch her in a lie. "I learned a little bit when I was nine. The kids wanted to learn how."

"Does that mean you're coming back again?"

Julie shrugged. "Dee asked me; the kids were really enthusiastic about learning. How could I say no?"

"Easily, you should do it because you want to, not because you always do what everyone tells you to do."

"I don't. Besides, I don't know what Aggie and Kayla want to do. It sort of depends on them."

"That's just what I mean. Show me a few moves."

"I don't think so."

"I thought you knew how to twirl. Come on, just a few moves. Or . . ." He had that kind of cocky grin on his face that made her want to lift the baton and brain him with it.

He was daring her. She'd probably make a fool of herself. What did she care? She'd already done that. She didn't have to try to impress him—but she would if she could.

"Psychoanalyze this, buster."

She stepped back, took an opening stance, started with the simple under-over figure eights, moved on to a lunge for pinwheels. It was like riding a bicycle. She stretched to the left then the right, touching the ground with the ball of the baton each time, then turned and threw it up in the air—

And caught Alex's eye. Her stomach dropped and she was ten years old and devastated at not being chosen for the squad.

The baton dropped to the asphalt, bounced, and rolled to Alex's feet. He picked it up and handed it back to her. "You're good at that. Except for that last part. Ready to go?" He didn't wait for an answer but walked over to the Jeep.

Julie watched him go. He turned back to her. His dark eyes were Alex's eyes, but in that split second before she let the baton drop, he'd been that raggedy kid in her backyard.

Julie followed him, the baton suddenly just a cheap aluminum toy in her hand.

They drove back in silence, Julie by choice, and who knew about Alex. She'd felt mildly sure of herself until the baton episode in the parking lot. Why had she fallen for that? She went back over their conversation. He'd been baiting her. But why? Professional curiosity? Some double-blind study that she just happened to stumble into?

Was there anything straightforward about Alex "Scatter" Martin? She glanced over from the passenger seat. He looked back and she quickly looked away. He kisses her, dumps her off at her hotel, picks her up first thing the next morning, then takes her to work all day while he disappears.

But he didn't disappear; he'd played with the kids, held group sessions with them. She wanted to ask about what they did, but she hadn't gotten the opportunity. And that first talk the night of the bonfire had seemed so promising . . . Oh well, not her summer for love.

She shook herself to clear that notion. She had more pressing concerns, like what to do with her life. Something she was never going to discuss again with a therapist unless it was one she hired for the purpose.

She'd just have to kiss Alex "Scatter" Martin goodbye—in a figurative, not literal, way. The thought flashed hot through her. Of course she was hot; it was summer driving over asphalt, she could practically see the road steaming up ahead.

Denial, whispered a little voice. She ignored it.

It seemed faster coming back than it had going out to the camp, and they arrived in town before she was ready. She'd been here five days, her vacation was halfway through, her tan was lagging behind, and she hadn't made it through even one book. The one man she realized she was interested in was a family therapist. *Not touching that one.* The only other man who'd showed any real interest in her was Dougie.

Maybe she'd get a dog.

And who would keep it while she was at school all day? The mere thought of school brought on that empty sinking feeling. What the hell was she going to do?

They had just passed the convenience store, and Julie was about to tell Alex he could just let her off at Lucky's parking lot, when a black SUV came swerving out of the bar's drive-way and hooked a right.

Alex slammed on the brakes, even though it hadn't been close to hitting them. He turned around to watch the SUV speed down the street. Looked back to the opening to the drive.

"Dammit. Get out."

"What?" Julie asked, nonplussed.

"I have to go, can you get back to your hotel by yourself?"

"Of course I can."

"Then go." He didn't wait for her to move, but reached across the seat and opened the door.

She jumped out and barely had time to slam the door before Alex made a U-turn in the middle of the street, nearly clipping a truck that had pulled up behind them, and sped off in the direction they had just come. In the direction that SUV had just taken.

He was chasing the SUV? What the hell had she wandered into?

Julie stood watching until both vehicles were out of sight.

Realized she'd left the baton in his Jeep. Fine, he could take it back to camp without her. Julie was pretty sure she shouldn't be going anyplace with him. Therapist or no, the man definitely lived a questionable life.

But a car chase? And what would he do if he caught up to the SUV? Julie shuddered, horrified at the thought. Then realized it wasn't horror at all. It was excitement. *Possibly dangerous excitement,* she reminded herself, dousing that bit of her imagination that was saying, *Yeah!* and she turned resolutely toward her hotel.

But as she passed Madame Marzetta's, she slowed. She should really apologize for her abrupt exit last night. She'd been so humiliated and embarrassed she could think only of getting away. But that was no excuse for her rudeness. It was only right that she apologize to Marie.

And what about Lucky? She'd ask Marie what she should do. Lucky had seemed glad to see her. She'd had a good time. But was that all it would be? Should she continue on with her vacation and leave him to whatever fix he was in? Because even though Julie dealt with children most of her days, she could still recognize an adult lie when she heard one. And it seemed she'd been hearing plenty of those since she came to town.

She stepped into the psychic's lair and found the vestibule free of waiting clients. She listened but didn't hear Marie's voice.

But the curtains suddenly parted, and there was Marie dressed like a cross between a nomad and a Moroccan belly dancer. She was wearing a veil. It was pulled back from her face, but still . . .

"Hi," Julie said, and could have kicked herself. She sounded like one of her kids. "I came to apologize for leaving the way I did."

"No need. I don't know what's wrong with Scatter." Marie smiled briefly, an odd expression that didn't fit her words. "Lucky shouldn't have sprung that on you. He didn't realize— actually, he did—he did it on purpose. Alex isn't one to talk about himself."

Marie waited for a reaction, but Julie didn't know how to react.

"Well, you can imagine how hard it is for a therapist to get a date. Either women are repelled, like you were, or they glom on to him like barnacles."

"I didn't think about that. And I wasn't repelled exactly. Still, he should have told me."

"That's what upset you?"

"Yeah. I guess I was already on overload, but that was kind of the last straw."

"I hope not."

"I mean we had this long talk on the beach—well, actually, I did all the talking, I was kind of drunk or I would never have said so much."

"So why did you? I don't believe for a minute you couldn't control what you said. No offense, but you are Louise's daughter and, for that matter, Lucky's niece."

Julie frowned at her.

"Don't be offended."

"I'm not. There's no disputing my mother taught me to control my life, but Lucky? I just never thought about him being in control. He did whatever he wanted."

Marie laughed. "Lucky? Lucky is like a juggler of odd objects. He rarely loses focus. That's what made him a world champion surfer and good at . . . well, the other things he does."

"What does he do? Is it something illegal? Is he in trouble? Are you busy? I'd just like to talk for a minute. I'll even pay you for a reading. But I just want to talk."

"Don't be ridiculous. Come." Marie turned over the CLOSED sign and pulled back the curtains.

Julie stepped through. "How do you know when people come into your shop?"

"Trade secret."

Marie smiled her Marzetta smile, and Julie felt a jolt of disappointment. She hoped she wasn't setting herself up for another con, because she felt like she was straddling the lunatic fringe as it was.

"Do you mind sitting at the table? I don't have enough space for a sitting area."

"No," Julie said, "but no fortune-telling, psychoanalyzing, or anything, okay?"

"Agreed." Marie pulled a chair over so that Julie was sitting to her right rather than across from her. It was easier to ignore the crystal ball that sat dark on the table.

Julie sat down.

"Now what would you like to talk about?"

"I just have a few questions."

"Yes?"

"Is Lucky in trouble?"

Marie gazed into the crystal ball; nothing happened.

"Everything since I arrived has seemed out of kilter. No one fessing up to where he was. Him arriving in the dark of night. That was him in the van, wasn't it?" She didn't wait for Marie to come up with an answer. She'd figured that much. "And now Alex chasing after that SUV—"

"What?" Marie asked, sounding alarmed.

"When we were driving into town just now. He'd pretty much kidnapped me this morning to go out to that county day camp, and we were coming back down the street when this SUV pulls out of the drive to the bar and speeds off. Scatter ordered me out of the Jeep and took off after it."

"Where is he now?"

"I don't know, I was just walking back to my hotel when I decided to stop here. Marie, please, what is going on? I feel like there's a secret that the whole town's privy to but not me."

Marie looked down at the table and its swirls of paisley as if she might divine an answer there. The crystal ball stayed dark.

"What is it?" Julie pleaded, fear curling inside her.

"Wait here while I lock up. We need to talk to Lucky."

Chapter 19

Julie didn't miss the pause Marie made when they left through the back door of the psychic's shop. She was making sure the coast was clear, and Julie felt a buzz of fear as they walked down the alley to Marie's cottage.

Marie went inside first, Julie on her heels. She heard Lucky snap, "Cease and desist. Now!" into the phone before he saw them and hastily shoved the phone behind him.

Not a landline, a cell phone. So much for his excuses for why he hadn't called.

Dougie, who had been lying under the table, lugged himself to his feet and came to greet Julie. But at a hand gesture from Lucky he dropped to the floor and stayed. Julie stared at him. The drool machine was down but alert as all get-out. Even the pets in this town were acting weird.

Lucky shot a questioning look to Marie. She shut the door behind Julie—since Julie in her surprise hadn't thought to—and turned on Lucky. "Julie was just with Alex. She said he dumped her in the middle of the street and took off after a black SUV."

Lucky's lips tightened. "I know. Mike just called me." He grinned suddenly as if he were picking up a part in a play, which Julie was beginning to believe was the case. "Scat shouldn't have dumped you like that. Damn boy, always forgetting his manners."

"Uncle Lucky. What is going on? It's not a dead phone battery or a dead-zone convention room or a simple barroom brawl. I don't believe any of it."

Lucky exchanged looks with Marie.

"I need to know. Mom is worried . . . and so am I."

"Listen, Julie, I seem to have gotten mixed up with some unsavory people, nothing to worry about, but it might be best if you and your friends—"

"Lucky," Marie interjected.

"Me and my friends . . . what? Leave you to these . . . What kind of unsavory people? Did you call the police?"

"It's not the kind of trouble the police can fix."

"Did you do something illegal?"

"No. Well, not exactly. Once again, not something the police would be interested in."

"Gambling?"

"No, of course not."

"Smuggling?"

"What on earth would I smuggle?"

"Liquor comes to mind."

"Nope. I have a distributor. Scat orders and he delivers. I sign for the goods. All aboveboard, I assure you."

"Then what is it?"

"It's nothing I want you involved in. You need to get out of here. When it gets straightened out, I'll come for a nice visit. Or you can come back here. I'm sure *everyone* will be happy to see you."

Not like now, when everyone was trying to get rid of her, Julie thought. "And what am I supposed to tell Mom?"

"Lucky, dammit . . ." Marie began.

Lucky cut her a defiant look, shook his head. "Tell her we had a nice visit and I'll come to see you later in the season."

"No." Julie heard herself say it, couldn't really believe it. "I won't. I won't lie to her and I—Mom wouldn't desert you, and neither will I."

Lucky smiled, warm and a little sad. "I was supposed to be taking care of you, but Louise would never let me. Let me do it now."

Julie stopped, taken off guard. She wanted to ask what he meant, but the words wouldn't form.

"Go. Tell Aggie and Kayla I'll see them next trip. I always liked those two."

"But—"

"Now, please do as I ask. I'll explain it when we're together again."

Before she could protest, he scooped her up in a big hug, then abruptly released her.

"Now go. I'll tell the hotel you're checking out."

"Lucky, we agreed—" Marie began.

"Stay out of this." He opened the back door and, like Marie, checked the alley before motioning Julie outside.

Marie only had time to give Julie her own quick hug before Lucky closed the door behind her. Julie stood for a moment, perusing the alley, not knowing what she was looking for except possibly the black SUV from earlier. She felt unease in her gut, but also a strange urge to laugh. She didn't want to believe she had brought her friends into something that might end badly. That was so not her life.

But the only people she saw were Ron and Ike standing at the end of the lane, passing the time of day with Stella Killready. And even though she wasn't dying to confront Stella again, she hurried toward them.

$\mathcal{D}$ougie whined at the door.

Lucky snapped his fingers. "You can't go with her, boy. Wish you could. I'd feel a lot easier if she had a bodyguard."

Dougie looked back at him and Marie lost it. "That was really stupid, Lucky." Marie paced away from him and back again. "You tell her half the story, then jettison her to deal with whatever happens by herself. That's your idea of taking care of her?"

"She'll be safer away from me. She won't have to deal with anything if she just goes to Dewey Beach or wherever they were going in the first place. Not that I think anything will come of this."

"Really? That's why Scatter is off chasing thugs? That's why half the town is on red alert?"

"It's not half the—"

"That's why you're holed up here like a criminal on the lam? Not because you're embarrassed to be seen with a shiner or you're afraid of those assholes. It's because you think you'll be harder to find and Ana and the children will be safer.

"Well, if that SUV was carrying any of Raymond's men, it's a little late for subterfuge. You better talk with your contacts and get them to move on that paperwork."

Lucky coughed out a laugh. "I've been on them. But hell can freeze over before the wheels of bureaucracy muster up enough energy to file paperwork." He scrubbed his face with his hands. "I think they should move Rosie and the kids to a safe house."

"It's a little late for that, too. If they've found her here, they can follow her anywhere. You're not thinking straight. And, love, let's face it. There are no safe houses in this world."

"I've put my family and friends in jeopardy."

She crossed the space between them, put her arms around him. "We are all in this for the long haul. Julie just had bad timing."

"Just because I didn't call Louise. But I forgot all about her weekly call until I was in the thick of things. I didn't dare use my cell to call her. These jackasses are pretty sophisticated. They would have picked up my signal and waylaid us before I got them back here."

"You're beginning to sound a lot like Louise."

He pulled away to look at her. "My way or the highway?"

"No. Take-care-of-the-world-or-bust complex."

He breathed out a laugh. "God, what a mess."

"Pretty much, love."

"I guess I better have Corey send over some more phones. We may be in for a long few weeks."

"And what about Julie?"

"Julie's out of the equation."

"The fruit doesn't fall far from the tree. I don't think she'll walk away. And even if she leaves right now, if Raymond finds out about her, he might use her to get to you and Ana."

"Shit. I'm not thinking clearly." He dropped his arms from around her. "You're right. Time to call in reinforcements. And hope they don't haul me off and throw away the key."

Lucky picked up his burner phone.

$\mathcal{A}$lex parked the Jeep by the side of the bar, bounded up the steps, and went inside. Mike was pulling a beer for Corey. Ike and Ron were missing.

"Out in the alley," Corey said. "Seems Julie told Marie about you dumping her in the middle of the street, then Marie took Julie to Lucky, and the shit hit. He's sending Julie and her friends away and calling in the big guns. Ike and Ron are on lookout to make sure she doesn't get nabbed off the street."

"Oh shit!" Alex shot his fingers through his hair in sheer impotent rage. What had he been thinking?

"That bad, huh?"

"I followed them out of town, but they headed straight to the highway, took the exit north. I decided I better get back here. They came to the bar? Did they ask about Lucky?"

"Yeah, two of them. Nice enough if you like hired thugs. Didn't threaten or shove their weight around, though I gotta tell you one of them had plenty to shove. But shit, these guys will never learn, I can still spot a gang man a mile away."

"What did they want?"

Mike pulled another beer and placed it in front of Alex. "Looking for Rosie. Said they were headed south to do some bass fishing. That they were friends of hers and thought they'd stop and say hello."

"My arse," Corey said. "Any fisherman knows the bass have already run and would be headed up to Jersey."

"Yeah," Mike said. "I told them she'd quit last week, no notice or anything, and it pissed me off. And that when they did see her, to tell her not to bother to ask for her old job back."

"Did they believe you?"

Mike gave him a look. "Just because I'm living like a hermit in the back of beyond don't mean I've lost my street smarts."

"No, you haven't."

"He was pretty convincing," Corey said.

"Yeah," Mike said, "but I got a feeling they'll be back. Their boss must have gotten into the mother's phone and traced Rosie to here. I sent Ike and Ron out to see if they talked to anybody in town, but I had to divert them to tail Julie."

"I stayed here as backup," Corey said, and finished off his beer. "I'll walk you out."

Alex took a swig of beer and got up.

"And, Scat," Mike said. "Rosie is having a hard time keeping the kids inside. They see the sand and the water and they want to play. Julie's seen them. Don't know about anybody else."

"I know. I don't think it'll be much longer." Though even if they managed to nab Raymond, they might not be safe for a long time.

Corey hoisted himself off the barstool. "Then I'd better drop by the store and pick up some extra equipment. Tell Lucky to stick to runaways, cults, and abusive families from now on. I'm getting too old for all this excitement." He moseyed full speed to the door.

Mike slid his empty stein off the bar top. "This is going to take more than a few burner phones and walkie-talkies. Somebody official needs to move on this."

"Don't I know it. Lucky and Marie are both pushing, but getting these people to expedite things is near impossible."

"I remember. Hard to know who to contact without having it come back to bite us in the ass."

"Can't trust anybody."

"That sounds like you in the old days," Mike said.

"I feel like me in the old days." Alex caught up to Corey at the door. "Sorry you guys got caught up in all this."

"You kidding? We were doing this shit long before you came to town. We would've done this anyway." Corey held the door for Alex to go out.

Julie nodded to Ron and Ike as she passed. Stella didn't slow down in her heated explanation of why she believed someone was breaking into her knitting store. Stella might have called wolf one too many times, because Julie had actually seen someone looking out the window of the shop last night. But had it been Stella working late or someone up to mischief? It was none of her business, Julie reminded herself, and she certainly didn't want to be the brunt of Stella's hostilities.

She stood on the edge of the parking lot, scanning the beach, and made herself not glance toward Lucky's, even though the Jeep was parked in its usual spot. So he was back from whatever mission he was on.

What had she gotten herself and her friends into? And how could she explain to them that they had to leave just when it was clear they were both enjoying their stay here? Julie didn't even want to leave, which went against every piece of good sense she'd ever had, and she'd had a lot.

She was just beginning to understand that there was a lot more to her uncle than riding waves and following the sun. She just didn't know what it was. And he wasn't about to tell her.

One thing she did know was that she didn't want to get her friends or her mother involved.

It was late afternoon and the beach had begun to clear out. Everyone would be getting ready for dinner and whatever other entertainments were available up and down the highway.

She looked over the last few groups spread out on the beach but didn't see Aggie and Kayla among them. Didn't even see their beach chairs.

She reached in her bag for her cell to call Aggie. Damn, it was underneath the seat in the Jeep. The Jeep was still parked by the side of the bar. She could just retrieve her phone and leave without having to face Scatter.

She glanced toward the bar. No one was coming out. She hurried over to the Jeep, opened the driver's door, and leaned over to reach beneath the seat.

"Julie! Stop!"

Julie automatically drew back.

Alex and Corey were running toward her from the bar. Scatter got there first.

He grabbed her by both hands. "What the hell are you doing?"

"Getting my phone."

"Oh. Well . . . you should never . . ."

"It's the beach," Corey broke in. "You never should reach for something without looking first."

Julie frowned, glanced back at the Jeep. Her eyes narrowed. "Scorpions? Alligators?"

Corey chuckled. "Gators don't usually get this far north. Not unless someone smuggled them in as a pet. But other things sting or bite. Scat, get Julie's phone for her."

Scatter, who seemed to be playing statue, suddenly eased her aside and leaned over to retrieve her phone. "Here, like new." He shoved it at her.

"See you later," Corey said, but instead of walking away, the two men stood, obviously waiting for her to leave.

When it was clear they weren't going to move, Julie gave up and headed toward the beach. She called Aggie; it went to voice mail. "I'm at the beach," she said, and ended the call.

She saw that the door to Surf's Up was open. She'd ask whoever was manning the register if they knew where her friends were.

As she reached the porch, CeeJay stepped out, saw Julie, and slouched into one hip. Julie gritted her teeth. CeeJay acted more like a hormonal teenager than a young woman.

Julie pasted on a smile. "Hey, have you seen my friends this afternoon?"

CeeJay shrugged. "Out with Bjorn and Les. They waited for you but you didn't show."

"I know. I got busy."

CeeJay glanced toward the parking lot. "Yeah. I know."

"Did they happen to say when they thought they'd be back? Aggie's not answering her phone."

CeeJay took time to slouch into her other hip. "Les has to close up. So . . . soon."

"Thanks," Julie said. Maybe she'd text them to meet her in town. They had things to discuss and they couldn't do it at Lucky's with everyone obviously knowing what was going on but them. She turned to go.

"Whatever."

Maybe it was her ambivalence about her future, maybe it was the confusion at not knowing what was happening, maybe it was just twirling a baton too long in the sun, but dammit, she'd had enough from the surly CeeJay. She turned around.

"I don't know why you don't like us. We're leaving soon, so don't bother going out of your way to be nasty." Julie smiled her best you're-so-in-trouble fourth-grade teacher smile. It was the best she could do after the day she'd had.

"He'll never go for the likes of you. You're such an uptight bitch."

Julie told herself to keep walking, but she'd been pushed around, cut off, yelled at, lied to, and it was her vacation. "What is your problem? I have absolutely no interest in Les or Bjorn, which you would know if you halfway paid attention."

CeeJay didn't seem to be attending. She was looking over Julie's shoulder. And Julie took the bait. She glanced behind her. Alex was still standing by the Jeep. Corey had gone.

"Scatter? Is that what you think? Then relax. I assure you, you have nothing to fear from me."

CeeJay jutted out her chin. "I'm not afraid of you or anybody."

"Well, good for you. I'm afraid of just about everything." Julie left CeeJay staring openmouthed and she trudged across the beach toward the street. It was getting late and she was hungry. She was definitely in need of happy hour, and she didn't dare go into Lucky's with Alex shooting daggers at her across the pavement.

And where were her friends? She'd ditched them to go off with Alex, so she couldn't blame them for ditching her, but they had some decisions to make.

Chapter 20

Julie stood between a rock and a hard place: CeeJay staring daggers from the beach, Scatter doing the same from the bar. Julie stuck in the parking lot.

Her phone pinged.

A text from Aggie. *We're walking to the beach from the marina. Wait for us at Lucky's.*

Julie texted back. *I'll wait in parking lot.*

She walked over to the sand and tried to look occupied with staring out to sea. A few minutes later she saw Kayla and Aggie trudging up the beach from the marina. They appeared to be loaded down with shopping bags.

"We had so much fun!" Aggie said. "There is the cutest shopping area down shore. And restaurants. And we drove there in a boat. Marina parking. How cool is that?"

"We kind of went crazy with the shopping," Kayla said, sounding like she already regretted the splurge.

"And Les said we could take the boat out tomorrow since he and Bjorn are going to be busy all day doing some kind of work for Lucky."

Julie's heart sank. Were they all in this—whatever it was—together?

"Don't worry," Kayla said. "Bjorn showed me the finer points of steering and docking. And how to work the anchor so we could picnic and swim from the boat."

"But," Aggie said, "we're in dire need of happy hour." She started in the direction of Lucky's.

"Fine," Julie said, running to catch up. "But not at Lucky's. I have something to tell you."

Aggie stopped. "About the scrumptious Scatterman?"

"Indirectly," Julie said.

"So why can't you tell us at Lucky's? We can go on the deck if it's too noisy inside."

"It's not something I want overheard."

Kayla frowned. "What is it?"

"Something bad?" Aggie asked. "Please say it isn't something bad."

Julie hesitated. So much had happened since dinner at Marie's the night before that her head was spinning. How would she explain what she didn't understand herself?

"Okay," Kayla said. "What if we go back to the hotel, you can tell us what it is, and then we can clean up for the evening."

Julie nodded. She was getting a deep, painful feeling in her stomach. As they turned to go, Julie saw a gray pickup turn from the street and make the hard right into the alley. Corey was at the wheel.

Jeez, she was getting as bad as Stella, suspecting conspiracies everywhere. As far as she knew Corey lived on Dune Lane and was going home.

They were almost to the street, but Julie couldn't keep from glancing down the alley toward Marie's and Lucky's cottages. Corey's truck was parked in back of Marie's. As she watched, Lucky came out of the cottage, took the keys from Corey, and climbed inside.

Julie stopped midstep.

Lucky was supposed to be hiding out, so where was he going?

"Julie, what are you stopping for?"

Julie bit her lip, thinking furiously. Why would Marie let him drive away? Did she know what he was doing? Surely not. She'd been the one who was adamant about Lucky continuing to hide out.

Corey stood in the alley until the truck drove away. Then he shook his head and went through the back entrance to the bar.

Julie grabbed Kayla's arm. "Do you have your car keys?"

"What?"

"Car keys. I need your keys. Now."

Kayla didn't ask again but rummaged in the side pocket of her beach bag and pulled out a ring of keys. Julie practically snatched them out of her hands.

"Thanks. If something happens to it, I'll pay for it."

"What's going to happen? Where are you going?"

"We'll all go," Aggie said.

"Just me," Julie said. "I'll meet you back at the hotel." She was already running down the alley toward the dumpster where Kayla's SUV was parked.

"Julie! Wait! What are you doing?"

She didn't stop but beeped the SUV open, jumped in, and sped down the alley after Lucky.

"Please be a false alarm," she said, not knowing what a real alarm would look like; she might not even know the difference. Though if he pulled in front of the convenience store and came out with a carton of milk, she'd know she'd jumped the gun.

She veered left at the end of the alley, hesitated. What did she think she was doing? It was one thing for Scatter to peel off after an SUV, but she didn't do things like that.

She didn't even know which way Lucky had turned. Right or left. There was a fair amount of traffic on Main Street. Even if she managed to find him, she would never catch up to him. It was really none of her business.

Coward. It's Uncle Lucky. She looked right and left, back to the right. And then she saw it, a gray truck moving over the slight rise of the bridge to the highway.

She stepped on the accelerator and turned right.

*M*arie turned from the window. She had always hoped that this day would never come, but since it had . . .

She left the kitchen, got the stepladder out of the hall closet and carried it to her bedroom. She paused at the sight of her open double closets, crammed with the tools of her trade: flowing robes and sashes, jewelry and headpieces. False eyelashes, makeup. All meant to camouflage, intrigue, heighten the senses. To entice the unsuspecting.

She opened the ladder, pressed down the spreaders until they locked in place, and shifted it closer to the hanging garments, overly aware of every move she made, hoping that she'd hear the back door open and Lucky's voice from the kitchen saying, "False alarm. It's over."

But no voice came. They were out there making plans without her. She'd left that behind long ago.

And yet, she'd known this time might come . . .

And she knew what she would do, because it was for Lucky. Not just for Lucky, but for Rosie and Ana and her kids. For whoever asked for their help.

Where did you stop? Where was too far? What could make you say no to people who needed you?

She put her foot on the first step, climbed to the second and the third, then slid her hand beneath a bolt of pink gauze, its glittered fabric catching at the dry skin on her hand. Stretched until her fingers felt the cold, hard steel and closed around the patterned grip, a sensation so familiar, so sensual, so . . . no going back now. She pulled it out and, without looking at it, climbed back to the floor.

It surprised her how natural it felt in her hand, like a part of her, and it made her kind of sick to realize that. It had been a long time. Never again would not have been long enough.

She placed it on the bed, returned the ladder to the hall closet, then went back to her room. She kept a magazine safely tucked in a bottom drawer of her dresser, one that she didn't use except for storage of things she didn't want but couldn't bring herself to throw away.

She rummaged among the other castoffs, even though she knew exactly where it was. Found it sooner than she wanted to and carried it to the bed, where she fitted it into the grip.

Her stomach threatened to revolt. But she had already stepped into that no-man's-land of unfeeling, where she'd been trained to make the most horrible decisions without hesitation.

She didn't once think about dismantling it and putting the parts back, because she knew that when it came to protecting those she loved, she would not hesitate. She had never hesitated before; she wouldn't start now.

A tear escaped from her eye; she let it roll down her face as a tribute to the enormity of what she was doing. She hated how comfortable the heft of it in her hand made her feel. Competent. Powerful. It was a false feeling.

She placed the government-issued Glock in the pocket of her caftan. It was old, but it still worked. She went back to the kitchen to wait.

Julie drove out of town in a state of disbelief. She might have passed Aggie and Kayla as she followed Lucky to the bridge, but she wasn't sure. Everything but the gray pickup was a blur.

It was slow going; no one but her and Lucky seemed to be in a hurry. She lost sight of him, found him, lost him again as they neared the highway and traffic became more dense. She was ready to scream with impatience when she had to slow down as the cars in front of her merged onto the main road. The truck kept going straight.

She followed at a safe distance, at least about the same as she'd seen on *NCIS*. She'd never followed anyone before. And she was shaking from adrenaline, maybe fear. She'd stopped asking herself what she was doing or what she hoped to accomplish. Something totally alien had taken over. If she'd had the sangfroid to question it, she might think it was that little spark of the devil Lucky had said she had.

But she didn't have it. Had never felt it before. But she'd never felt this driven before.

Every boundary she'd ever made for herself seemed to be falling away, urging her on to do stupid, self-defeating things. But she couldn't stop.

She kept a safe distance behind. When he turned right into a beach neighborhood, she turned right; when he drove straight through and out the other side, she did, too. They were on another county road; he turned off that a mile later.

He'd been traveling west toward the setting sun, but now he turned east again, into another little community, and Julie wondered if he knew she was behind him and he was trying to teach her a lesson. Even she knew that an electric-blue SUV was not exactly a stakeout kind of car, but it was the best she could do.

She slowed down until there were a good two blocks between them. If she lost him, so be it. But it was clear to her now that wherever he was going, he was taking a circuitous route to get there. She had to slow at each intersection to make sure he hadn't turned onto one of the side streets.

Once, she almost missed him and had to back up to make the turn.

He didn't seem to be in a hurry now. But she noticed they were getting farther from civilization. In fact, for the last minute or so, they had entered some kind of backwater, surrounded by marsh and grasses. "Lonely" was the word that came to mind. She wished she had Aggie and Kayla by her side, but she couldn't jeopardize their safety.

And what about yours? Uncle Lucky wouldn't let any harm come to her. She wouldn't let any harm come to him, if she could help it.

He turned onto a narrow, sandy road; Julie stopped and waited. They were the only two vehicles in sight. Lucky, Julie, and marshland. She cringed, imagining what or who might be waiting for them at the end of the line.

The end of the line. She began to rue the moment that she'd taken the keys from Kayla. But it was too late to go back now. She wouldn't even know the way. She had no idea where they were.

And what if there was no way back?

The road, such that it was, had narrowed to one stingy lane. It was surrounded by wetlands, the marsh grass encroaching almost to the road. It was too narrow to turn around, without even a shoulder on which to park.

There must be a way out or at least a turnaround at the end, but whoever was there would run head-on into her unless she started backing out now.

Why hadn't she just left well enough alone? Minded her own business. She could be with her friends at happy hour with the question of what to do about her future her only worry. It seemed like a small problem now, in light of what might be ahead.

Just back out and go home, she told herself. But for once the doggedness that had kept her on the straight and narrow in life was preventing her from returning there. On the road and in her life, there was only one way to go, and that was forward.

She pulled as far to the side of the road as seemed safe, stopped the car, turned off the engine. Opened the door and slid to the ground. She stood listening for the sound of another car, and hearing nothing, she eased the car door shut and slipped the keys into her shorts pocket.

She started down the road hugging the edge; the sand was soft—and wet, she realized. She neared a turn in the road, stopped long enough to stand on tiptoe to see over the grasses, and caught a glint of car roofs. Two of them.

He was meeting someone. Now she knew for sure it was not good. You didn't meet friends in the marshes unless maybe you were going fishing. And she hadn't seen any fishing gear in Corey's truck.

She couldn't keep going along the road without walking right into whatever it was. She looked around, saw something that a huge imagination might call a path. She headed for it but stopped to test the strength of it. She didn't want to die in quicksand. Did they have quicksand in Delaware?

It seemed firm enough, so testing each step she crept closer and suddenly heard voices ahead. She crouched down and eased nearer. She tried not to think about what she was doing. One thing kept her moving toward them: she had to know the truth.

She peered over the tall grasses. There were at least two other men: one about the same height as Lucky and one a head shorter. She could just see the top of his navy-blue bandanna as it moved above the grasses.

She crept just a tiny bit forward. They had stopped talking.

Then suddenly everyone was returning to their vehicles. Julie turned and rushed to the SUV, sliding in the loose sand. *Is it getting wetter?*

And what would she do when she got to the SUV? No way in hell could she back out before they passed her on their way to the highway. But they would probably have to turn around before they could leave. She'd just have to back out and hope for a miracle.

She ran across the road, turned on the SUV, and put it in reverse; the tires sputtered out sand but didn't budge. She changed to four-wheel drive but only managed to get both front and back wheels stuck.

She banged on the steering wheel and considered throwing herself onto the floorboards, hoping they wouldn't associate her with the blue SUV parked in the alley. They hadn't really used it since they arrived. If she hid they might mistake her for a fisherman out on the catch.

What the hell. She slipped onto the floor and held her breath, which was stupid. It wasn't like she was going to drown or even give herself away with a sneeze.

She waited . . . and waited . . . and waited, and no one passed by. Still, she was afraid to get up. She turned her head so she could see out the window, half expecting to find the face of a desperado staring back at her, imagined being dragged out of the car and kidnapped. Still she waited . . .

Finally when she'd grown stiff with waiting, she sat up. No one had passed; there must be another way out. They probably just kept going down the road and were on a highway by now.

And here she was stuck in the sand. Did AAA pick up in the middle of nowhere? She didn't even know where nowhere was. She started the SUV again, tried rocking it back and forth to no avail.

She was hopelessly stuck.

Then another, more horrible thought struck her. What happened when the tide came in? Did the road flood? She stuck her head out the window. Her makeshift path had definitely taken on water since she'd started down it.

She got out of the car, scanned her surroundings. If Kayla's car flooded, it would be ruined. And Julie could never afford to replace it.

She'd have to walk back to the main road and call a Lyft. Or she'd hitch to town. And have someone send out a tow truck.

That sounded crazy.

Or you can sit here and watch Kayla's car be destroyed.

She reached back inside and snagged the keys from the ignition, dragged out her bag, pulled it across her body, and started down the road. She'd been walking for less than five minutes when she heard a vehicle coming toward her.

She stiffened—they were coming back for her, to what ends God only knew. She considered throwing herself in the tall beach grass and hoping for the best, but before she even moved, a familiar Jeep appeared ahead of her. She stepped to the side of the narrow road.

The Jeep pulled to a stop beside her and a very exasperated Scatter Martin said, "Lucky called. He said you might need a tow. Get in. Where did you leave the SUV?"

Her first impulse was to refuse. But that would be incredibly stupid. She swallowed her gall, pride, self-esteem, and whatever other qualities that were still hanging by a thread and walked around the front to the passenger side and got in.

She pointed ahead and he took off.

He pulled to a stop beside the SUV, shook his head, and stuck out his hand. She hesitated, dug the key ring out of her pocket and handed it to him, then got out of the Jeep and followed him to the SUV. He started it up; sand spurted out from the tires, stinging her legs, as he rocked the SUV back and forth. It seemed to Julie it only dug the wheels in deeper.

If that's the best he could do, she could have done that.

Then something happened; the wheels caught and the SUV shot onto the road. When it was dead center, Alex jumped out, leaving the door open.

"Thanks," she mumbled.

He barely slowed down as he passed her. "I hope you don't expect to make a habit of having me bail you out of stupid situations."

She shook her head and walked, mortified, to the SUV.

"Follow me and stay in the middle of the road."

She followed him exactly, continuing to the place where Lucky had met those other people, and where she saw that the road curved and divided, one leg continuing farther into the marshland, the other hooking back toward the road. Scatter took that fork, and soon they were back on the highway. The Jeep shot forward; he probably was not even looking to see if she continued to follow him. She did, but at a slower speed. She didn't want to have to deal with him again today.

And how was she going to avoid facing Uncle Lucky?

Scatter, not Lucky, was waiting for her at the dumpster. He didn't even give her time to get out of the SUV before he started yelling.

"Do you know how stupid that was? What if they had been criminals? You could be dead by now." He walked away, turned back. "What were you thinking?"

Julie shrugged. She hadn't been thinking; she'd been going on pure instinct. Her instincts were pretty lousy. "I just wanted to help."

"By going blindly into a situation without knowing anything? Anything?" he repeated several decibels louder.

She finally found her voice. "Well, no one else went with him or after him. You let him drive into a possibly dangerous situation. Where were you?"

He grabbed his hair with both hands. "Minding my own business. Doing what I was supposed to do. Not interfering in something that could get us all killed!"

She stared at him. Took a step back. "Killed?"

"No. No. I didn't mean that." He walked away, back again. It must be some anger management thing. "Actually, yes, I did. You don't have a clue as to what is going on here. You just nearly messed it up big time."

"Well, if someone had bothered to tell me what was going on. What *is* going on? What is so dangerous? Who were those men?"

"None of your business. So take your friends and get the hell away from here. No, wait, that won't work. God, I don't know, what will it take to get rid of you?"

"Don't worry, I'm going, and I'm sorry I bothered to care."

He blinked, frowned, then turned and walked away.

"I just wanted to help him," she said to his back as he reached the bar. He didn't stop, but went inside. The door slammed. She turned away and didn't look back.

Chapter 21

If Julie had been thinking, she would have run straight to the hotel's service door. It had been unlocked since they'd arrived, but in her shame and unhappiness she'd just wanted to get as far away as possible, so she ran in the direction of Lucky's parking lot, not slowing down until she reached the street. Even then she had to force herself not to race-walk to the hotel.

But there was no respite there. Kayla and Aggie were waiting for her on the front porch, sitting in two of the rocking chairs and looking anything but relaxed.

"Henry said we were checking out. Did you tell him that?" Kayla asked.

"That's Lucky's doing. He wants us gone."

"Why? What happened?"

"I don't know exactly. But he's into something weird." She quickly looked around and lowered her voice. "I'm not sure what. Nobody's talking."

"All right, tell us everything you do know, or think."

"Okay, but not here. Let's go upstairs. I need water and I feel like even the rocking chairs might have ears."

Once upstairs in Julie's room, Aggie and Kayla took their places on the bed, a practice begun years ago, where monumental decisions were made, where heartbreaks were mended, where sympathy and understanding and sometimes swift kicks were administered.

"Where did you just go?"

"I was following Lucky. He met some men in the marshes, then I got stuck and Scatter got me out—your car's fine—but he was furious with me and said I was stupid—"

"That creep," Aggie said. "I take back all the hot things I said about him."

"—and that I could have gotten killed."

"No!" exclaimed Kayla.

"What's Lucky got himself into?" Aggie asked.

Julie breathed out. "The thing is, I still don't know. At first I thought it was something illegal, but now I don't know, because evidently the men he was meeting weren't the bad guys, according to Scatter."

"Can we put this on hold a minute and start at the beginning?" said Kayla. "None of this is making sense. The last time we talked you were going to dinner with Marie and Lucky."

Julie took a deep breath, organizing her thoughts as best she could. "I did." She told them about dinner at Marie's and finding out that Scatter was a therapist.

"Scatterman?" Aggie said. "He's a psychologist?"

"Yeah. And I had just spilled my guts about the most embarrassing things to him in a drunken stupor the night of the bonfire."

"You? In a drunken stupor?" Aggie asked incredulously.

"Aggie," Kayla said. "Don't interrupt."

"Well, slightly buzzed. Anyway it seemed so right, sitting on the rocks on the beach, under the moon. It was so easy to talk to him, like I knew him. For a nanosecond I actually wondered if we'd met before."

Kayla and Aggie sighed.

"You know, it's weird. I didn't want to come here in the first place, and I have to admit, I've been ambivalent about seeing Lucky the whole time. Then when I first saw him, he kept saying that he wanted me to leave town, that he's in some kind of trouble that could get dicey. He'd definitely been in a fight.

"But last night at dinner, everything seemed fine, just like it always was. Until he let slip about Scatter being a therapist. I was so mortified after everything else, that I cut the evening short and left. Scatter came after me."

"Is *this* the good part?" Aggie prodded.

"Yeah, the only good part. He stopped me, yelled at me for being upset, then he kissed me."

"At last," Kayla said.

"Twice," Julie added.

"That good?" Aggie said.

"Pretty much."

"And then?"

"And then he dropped me at the hotel and left. It seems to be the MO with him."

"Weird."

"Yeah, it was. Then this morning he shows up at my door with coffee and takes me out to this summer camp for migrant kids, run by this woman named Dee who's very pretty and, I might add, he seems awfully chummy with."

"What's she like?"

"Very nice and dedicated. Pretty, petite, dark hair, wears red lipstick. But that's not important right now."

"Do you think you and Scatterman will get together?" asked Aggie.

Julie stared at her and realized that she hadn't told them the most important news. She'd gotten swept away in remembering Scatter and her kissing in the alley.

"No. On our way back from the camp, he sees this SUV coming out of the parking lot, practically shoves me out the door, and takes off after it. Then Lucky jumps in a truck and drives away. He'd said he was involved with some unsavory characters. I thought he might be in danger. So I followed him. What else was I supposed to do?"

Neither of them had an answer.

"Lucky wants us to leave. Scatter wants us to leave. He made that perfectly clear. Everybody wants us to leave."

"Not Les and Bjorn," Aggie said.

"Well, actually," Kayla said, "Bjorn said something about it when we were shopping today. He said he and Les wouldn't have much free time anymore and that if we decided to leave they would understand."

All three of them sighed.

"Have you told Louise?"

"God, no," Julie said. "She'd be on the next helicopter here. We're not telling her anything."

"So what are we going to do?" asked Aggie.

Julie tried to smile at her two best friends in the world. She knew she couldn't get her friends involved, but she also knew she couldn't leave until she knew what was going on.

"We can't split up," Aggie said, a tinge of anxiety in her voice. "Louise would know something was up for sure."

"I'll call her tonight. Tell her we're moving on to Dewey Beach and I'll call her in a few days." Julie winced. "I just hope her cruise lasts until whatever is happening is over."

"What do you mean by danger?" Kayla asked. "How dangerous? He might get hurt? He doesn't want you around to see him get arrested? He thinks you might be collateral damage?"

"Don't be hysterical," Aggie snapped.

"I have kids," Kayla reminded her.

"Kayla's right," Julie said. "She has responsibilities."

"But you should come with us," Kayla said.

"Yes," Aggie said. "If something does happen, we don't want to be the ones who have to tell Louise we let you stay behind."

Julie smiled. "You both are the best of besties. It's funny, I've been trying to get us to leave since we got here, and now that there's a real reason to go, I want to stay . . ."

"Because you have a better reason to stay," Aggie finished for her.

Julie shot her a questioning look. "If you mean Scatter . . ."

"She means Lucky," Kayla said. "Maybe we should all stay and just be cautious."

"No. I can't ask you to do that. And I won't let you. You go to Dewey. If this just blows over, I'll join you there in a day or two. And we'll still have a little vacation to enjoy."

"We were enjoying it here," Aggie said.

"We were," agreed Kayla. "But we're not leaving without you."

"Are Les and Bjorn involved?" Aggie looked close to tears.

"I don't know. I just know that it has to do with whatever was delivered in the alley the first night we were here. I wish I had never seen that." *Or followed Lucky to his meeting, which evidently put us all in danger.* And yet she hadn't felt so alive in years—maybe ever.

"It'll be okay," Aggie said. "Les says everyone in the town is loyal to Lucky. They won't let anything happen to him. And what could possibly happen?"

"Hopefully nothing," Julie said. "But . . ."

"We're not going without you," Kayla said.

Julie bit her lip. "You're right. I'm being selfish. If it is something bad, they'll do better dealing with it without us. I guess we'd better start packing."

I'm kind of proud of her," Lucky said.

"Give me an effing break," Alex said. "She could jeopardize our little bundles of joy, not to mention get all of us killed. Not to mention get herself killed."

"I know but . . . I hate that it had to happen this way."

"It's for her own good."

"I know, but listen. And listen good. If for some weird reason something happens to me—"

"Nothing's going to happen."

"Yeah, but if it does, tell her I was proud of her. I've always been proud of her. And to live her life the way she wants to."

"You tell her." Alex walked away, then walked back toward the man he loved like a father, more than a father. Lucky was the only father he'd ever known and the best friend a man could have. "So do these guys have a plan?"

"Yeah, but it hasn't been okayed by their superiors. They're going out on a limb."

"They owe you."

"Only because I drove a van and extracted the goods. They owe Marie for a lifetime of service, let's not forget that."

"She's going to be pretty upset."

"She already is. I wish I could send her away, too."

Alex laughed, mirthless and defeated. This was going down with or without them. "She was here first, remember," Alex reminded him. "What do we do?"

"Two of our favorite things: sit and wait. Ana evidently has regained consciousness but can't remember anything. It's temporary, hopefully. Raymond will have to get to the kids pretty soon to prevent her from talking."

"We're ready."

"Do not confront him, any of you."

"You can't ask that, especially if you're planning to use those kids as bait."

"Good God, no. I would never jeopardize their safety."

"And how are you going to stop him?"

"I'm guessing he'll have to come himself, possibly with some paid coppers. He'll have paperwork. But when he tries to take them, and if we have any luck on our side, our guys will move in to arrest him."

Alex walked away again. He was so frustrated he could cry. If he could cry. Though he was pretty sure he'd used all his tears up as a kid. He turned back to Lucky. "I was pretty vicious to her."

"Marie?"

"Don't be dense. Julie."

"Feeling bad about that?" Lucky flashed him a quick grin.

"What do you think?"

"I always thought you two could learn a lot from each other."

"Don't get your hopes up. I'm pretty sure I screwed that possibility. Plus, I'm pretty sure it's an oil and water situation."

"But I was right. Right?" Another of Lucky's irritating grins.

"Maybe."

Lucky slapped the bar in triumph.

"I don't know how you can be worrying about my relationship with anybody when we're teetering on the brink of disaster."

"Sometimes you just have to see the humor," Lucky said.

Or make it up where none existed, Alex thought, and wondered if he would ever really understand what made people tick.

*A*s soon as Kayla, somewhat relieved, and Aggie, more reluctantly, left, Julie pulled her suitcase once again out of the closet.

This time she studiously avoided looking out her window; she didn't want to see anything that would sway her back into irrational actions.

She tossed the suitcase on the bed, unzipped it, and began taking things out of the chest of drawers. The new bikini she hadn't yet worn. The bikini, she admitted to herself, that she'd been saving for something special. And a betraying little voice whispered, *I wonder how Scatter would like you in this.*

It didn't matter, he wasn't going to see her in it. Still, it took all her good sense to empty the third drawer into her suitcase. Back to the closet. Just fold everything over and worry about wrinkles when they got to the next hotel.

Every impulse she'd been fighting for the last few years was pulling at her.

Stay.

No, take him at his word and leave.

He might need you, you're family.

You're responsible for your friends' safety. Don't poke your nose where it doesn't belong. Leave.

Her arms closed around the dresses she'd been about to dump on top, as she thought of the girls at camp twirling their cheap batons. Of kissing Alex. Of seeing Lucky get into that truck and knowing she had to follow. The thrill of driving after him.

It was the stuff of movies, not real life. She was being totally unrealistic and stupid. She would leave, go home and take her summer course, return to her job in the fall like nothing had happened. Because nothing *had* happened.

But something had happened, she realized. In a few short days something inside her had changed. Not because Alex "Scatter" Martin had kissed her or because Lucky was involved in some kind of scheme gone wrong.

But because for the first time in her life, Julie was forced to think for herself, make her own decisions, rational or irrational, while fighting herself all the way.

She looked at her half-packed suitcase. She'd never stepped out of the box before, doggedly following what should be her dream, hardly ever allowing herself to wonder what if, what if . . .

One foot in that world and one foot not quite in the other. All she had to do was take a step left or right, forward or back, to decide her future.

She knew what she had to do.

A knock at the door. Julie opened it to find Aggie, face tear streaked. She slipped past Julie and Julie shut the door.

"I'm going to stay," Aggie said. "I'm sorry, but . . ."

"Is this because of Les?"

"Sort of. Lucky, too, but Les mainly."

"Aggie, not to be mean-spirited, but can I remind you this is vacation and you hate to leave every year?"

"I know. And I know it sounds crazy, but this is different."

It was always different with Aggie, but Julie, who was living in a glass house herself at the moment, was not about to throw stones. "Are you sure?" she asked.

"Of course I'm not sure. I'm always looking for Mr. Right. I know that. And yeah, I know, there is no Mr. Right."

"Hey. Don't say that. You're our last holdout for believing there is."

"I know, stupid."

"No, I'm just jealous. But are you sure this isn't just your biological clock sounding the alarm?"

"Maybe, but I'm listening to it."

Another knock sounded at the door.

Julie went to open it and wasn't at all surprised to see Kayla, looking worried and not at all resolved. "I went to your room, and when you didn't answer, I knew you must be here."

Aggie shrugged, for once speechless.

"You don't want to leave."

Aggie shook her head, her eyes beginning to swim with tears that would soon overflow.

"I figured as much." She turned to Julie. "You, too."

Julie nodded.

"Then count me in. But at the first sign of trouble I'm heading for the hills. My kids will kill me if something happens and they have to live with deadbeat Dad."

"You don't have to do this," Julie said.

"I know, but we're not sure there will be bodily damage kind of trouble, and besides . . . sometimes you have to take a stand for your friends."

Julie swallowed the big fat lump in her throat and resisted the urge to pull her friends into a group hug. Aggie, however, felt no such compunction. She threw her arms around both of them. Group hugs were not uncommon among them— congratulatory hugs, sympathetic hugs—usually announced with a cheery, "Group hug!" This one was quiet and solemn—a promise.

Julie was the first to ease away. "Guess I'd better call downstairs and confront the manager."

It took six rings before he picked up.

"We've decided to stay," Julie announced.

Silence.

"Is that a problem?"

"Uh . . ." More silence. "I'll have to check the bookings."

"I can wait, though I doubt if you've already booked the rooms we're already booked in and, I might add, that we haven't checked out of yet." Getting no response, she continued. "I'd hate to have to report you to the Better Business Bureau about double-booking."

"Well . . ."

"I take that to mean we're good? Great! And when you call my uncle to inform him, tell him that we'll be here at least till Friday, either in your hotel or one right down the road. I'd really hate for you to lose three rooms of income to a competitor. Good night."

She hung up.

"Wow," Aggie said.

"Is there a hotel right down the road?" asked Kayla.

Julie beamed at them. "I have no idea."

$\mathcal{T}$he back room of Lucky's was packed, standing room only. The air-conditioning was pumping just enough to keep people from passing out, but they were sweating. Handkerchiefs had come out of pockets. Notepads had been commandeered as hand fans.

Marie was only slightly surprised at the number of people who had turned out. The fact that the room was barely larger than a storeroom didn't make her feel any less proud. It seemed like a third of the town was there. And there were others who weren't close to the operation but were on the alert for anything unusual.

Since the day she'd been sent to bust an offshore drug ring that was using Lucky's Beach as a drop point, she'd fallen in love . . . with the beach, the people, and, once the drug runners had been arrested, the lifestyle. Of course it hadn't been Lucky's Beach then, just a crossroads community not large enough to be a town.

She'd bought the cottage and began spending her vacations here. Got to know the people and helped them out when she could. Took an early retirement and moved here permanently.

She was accepted as one of them. Pitched in where she could. Took up a second profession—one she had run from in the first place—and became Madame Marzetta like the women in her family before her.

And what better way to keep an eye on the town than as the local fortune teller? On two separate occasions, she'd uncovered small-time operators—one drugs, one illegal firearms related—both perps having spilled everything while having their palms read. Marie notified one of her friends in the agency, was thanked accordingly, and settled down to life at the shore.

Then came Lucky, awakening tamped-down feelings and upending her well-ordered retirement.

Marie had been reluctantly pulled into his world. And back into her old life.

When Rosie's niece, Ana, was beaten and her kids were kidnapped, Lucky was determined to help her. And the town was right behind him.

She scanned the room.

Darinda Kumar and her eldest son, Vihaan, sat upright halfway back among the jumble of chairs. Lucky had helped them with work papers years before.

Les stood next to Bjorn, both alert and ready for a fight.

Corey, Ron, and Ike sat together on the front bench. Those three had frequented Lucky's when it was Sam's Beach Bar and Grill. With their pool of expertise, they'd been helping folks long before Lucky or even Marie had arrived on the scene.

Marie made her way toward Lucky and Scatter, who stood leaning against the wall, both with their arms crossed. Lucky looked as if he bore the weight of the world; Scatter, determined to risk anything for his mentor and friend.

None of them, except Marie and a couple of others, had ever been asked to be a part of something this volatile, a sting that could so easily go off the rails. Marie was immensely proud to be among them all.

Two serious-looking men, longtime colleagues, entered the room and took their places at the front, where they would give last-minute instructions and give anyone who was having second thoughts the opportunity to leave.

No one left. It was their town, their reputation, their Rosie.

They were instructed not to engage, to stay far away from the actual confrontation if it came. They were merely to report anything out of the ordinary and leave it at that.

It was a piecemeal undercover operation—a handful of volunteers and two agents, off the clock—and Marie couldn't wait until it was over.

Chapter 22

With a cheese sandwich for lunch and pizza ordered for dinner the night before, Julie was all too ready to go to Darinda's the next morning for breakfast. Still, it took all the courage she had to walk into the diner.

And she wasn't mistaken in her apprehension. The entire crowded, noisy place fell silent, before picking up again. Word must be that she was on Lucky's get-out-of-town list. She hadn't even considered that when she'd jumped in Kayla's car and driven after him.

Corey, Ike, and Ron were sitting in their regular booth. Their eyes rounded as the three women followed the silent waitress to their "regular" table. She smiled and handed out menus, recited the breakfast specials, and left to bring them coffee.

In the booth behind the three guys, four policemen were enjoying a hearty breakfast. They only paused long enough to check out the newcomers, nod, and return to their plates.

"I guess everyone's surprised to see us," Aggie whispered.

"I guess," Julie said, looking over to the booth where Ron, Ike, and Corey sat looking suspiciously innocent.

"Morning, Julie, ladies," Corey said.

Ron and Ike nodded, and they all went back to their breakfasts.

Darinda herself brought the coffees to the table. "How are you this morning?"

They were fine, they assured her.

"It's a lovely day. Do you girls have any special plans? We're just a few miles away from the lighthouse museum and some nice boutique shopping if you're tired of the beach."

"Sounds like fun," Julie said.

Darinda lingered, smiling at them, before finally going away.

The waitress returned and took their order. Two tables away, the mayor nodded and went back to his breakfast.

It was obvious to Julie that something had changed overnight—and it was because of her. She began to wish they hadn't come. "Is it me, or is everyone acting kind of strange this morning?"

"I think we're just a little paranoid," Kayla said. "We don't even know most of these people, and why would they care what we do?"

They were halfway through plates of eggs, bacon, and Darinda's currant and saffron rolls when Stella Killready burst through the door. She stopped just inside, looked around, then zeroed in on the four policemen. She plowed past the busboy and headed for their booth.

"I saw your squad car outside. I knew you would be in here.

I want you to come over and look at my store. Someone keeps breaking into it. And I demand something be done."

"Good morning, Ms. Killready," the youngest looking of the four said. "We were there just yesterday. And you said nothing was missing, remember?"

He sounded sympathetic, but Stella was having none of it. "A body isn't safe in this town anymore. Someone's vandalizing my store and you're not doing one darned thing to stop them."

"*Is* something missing?" asked a second cop.

Stella glowered at him. "Why else would they break in?"

Two of the cops looked away, a third stood. "Is there something missing *this* time?"

"Most likely. But everything is all different. They break in and wreck everything. They're vandalizing my shop. Am I going to have to start sleeping there to protect my merchandise? When are you going to do something? When you find my dead body?"

"Now, Ms. Killready, there are not going to be any dead bodies. But Rex and I will go over with you now and check things out. Isn't that right, Rex?"

"Sure, no problem." Rex slid out of his seat. "Come with us, Ms. Killready, and let's see what we can do."

The two policemen still seated hurriedly finished their coffees and followed the others out.

As soon as Stella had left with the policemen, another two men who were seated several tables away stood and left. They had surfer-length hair and were dressed for the beach in wrinkled clothes. There was nothing strange about the timing of their leaving. It was Julie who was definitely feeling paranoid.

"I swear, that Stella is going to drive us all over the edge," Ron said, and pushed his plate away.

A couple of minutes later Corey, Ike, and Ron got up to leave.

"Been nice seeing you, Julie," Ike said. "Ladies."

Corey gave him a nudge out the door. "Have a nice day," he said in the direction of their table.

Ron went to the cash register to pay their bill.

Julie had to sneak a peek and turned her head just enough to catch Darinda and Ron looking back at her.

Ron left, and Darinda grabbed a coffeepot and came to refill their mugs. "Those three," she said softly. "You've really made an impression on them. I think they're a little smitten with you girls. But don't pay them any mind. They won't bother you."

"They're sweet," Aggie said, and Kayla murmured her agreement.

Julie buried her nose in her coffee mug. She had been conjuring all sorts of crazy scenarios, but maybe they were just three older men trying to be charming. She was such a dunce. Everything was fine.

"Darinda," Julie said, "yesterday Alex, um, Scatter, took me to see a camp for migrant children. I was telling my friends about it, but I forgot the name."

"Out the county road? I don't know that it has a name; it's a local project, put together through the mayor's department."

Darinda paused to nod at the mayor, who was getting up from his table. "He is a good man. He's very helpful to those in need."

"The whole town seems to be," Julie said.

"Yes," Darinda said. "We take care of our own. Excuse me." She hurried back to the cash register to take the mayor's check.

Julie was almost relieved when breakfast was over and they were standing outside on the sidewalk. "So now what?" she said.

"Well, I just got a text from Les," Aggie said, returning her phone to her shorts pocket. "He and Bjorn and some of the other guys are gone for the morning. So it's just us and the beach. Or we could go shopping, except that we've sort of done all the shops in Lucky's Beach."

"I really should go out to the camp for an hour or so," Julie told them. "I promised to come back, and I'd feel bad about letting them down. Can I use the SUV? I promise to bring it right back. No car chases or anything."

Kayla, who had been consulting her phone, returned it to her pocket. "What? Sure, but since the guys are gone for the morning, why don't we all go? I wouldn't mind seeing this paragon of community programs."

"She means she wants to give twirling a whirl," Aggie said.

So, after a brief cleanup in their rooms, they all climbed into Kayla's SUV.

"I remember the first part of the drive," Julie said. "Straight across the intersection on the highway, about another five minutes or so, then . . ." She pulled her phone out of her bag. "I don't suppose GPS will be any more helpful finding the camp than it was finding Lucky's Beach. But at least I can consult the map."

"Hey, we got here, didn't we?" Aggie said. "Holy smoke. Is that corn growing?"

"Yep," Julie said.

They passed more fields and made more turns until Julie recognized the concrete building that housed the camp. Julie breathed a sigh of relief. She'd been half expecting to find Alex's Jeep already there.

Dee Hoyes answered the door. "Hey, I'm surprised to see you. Alex said he wouldn't be out today because you were leaving."

"We had a change of plans at the last minute," Julie said. "And Kayla and Aggie wanted to see the camp. They're teachers, too, and Kayla also coaches girls' sports."

"Perfect, I'll show you around and maybe you can hang out for a bit."

*A*lex was setting up the bar for the day, when Corey, Ike, and Ron came in. It was pretty early even for those three.

"Their SUV is gone," Corey said.

Alex nodded, trying to quell the betraying disappointment he felt. Totally self-involved bullshit, but still . . . "That's good. One less thing to worry about."

"I wouldn't bet your reputation on it," Ron said. "They were at Darinda's for breakfast. They didn't look like girls who were packed and ready to go."

"I thought you said they left."

"The car is gone," Ron said. "So to make sure, I popped into the hotel on our way over. Seems like they decided to stay after all."

"But Henry was supposed to—"

"He did, but Julie threatened to call the Better Business Bureau on him. So what could he do?" Corey chuckled.

"The Better—?" Alex felt three parts pissed and edgy and two parts . . . Well, he didn't want to name it, but he was glad in a very self-serving way. Though it killed him to admit it, he couldn't seem to get that kiss out of his head. It had started out as a means to make her feel less vulnerable, a kind of apology for not being straight with her from the get-go.

It turned out to be a dumb idea, because it immediately turned into something else. If he were honest with himself, he'd admit that he'd been curious to see if it would be good. He wanted it to be good. He wasn't disappointed. But now he was totally screwed.

"Hey, Scatter, you taking a nap back there?"

"What?"

Corey was frowning at him. "Something the matter?"

"You don't think those girls are really in danger, do you?" Ron asked.

"If anything sours, we'll make sure to keep them out of harm's way," added Ike.

Alex looked from one to the other. Local guys, retired, who still hung out together to enjoy their golden years. But they'd helped Marie with a few saves before Lucky even came, and long before Alex found his way back to where he belonged.

Alex didn't believe in magic—that hope had died a violent

death before his tenth birthday, when he started living on the streets. At first he'd just prayed not to be found and taken home. Then he prayed for a superhero, even a fairy godmother, to come and take him someplace safe. Someplace magic. Someplace where he would be clean and not hungry, with a bed instead of a stairwell to sleep in. With no gangs and no guns and no beatings by parents or other boys or the men who controlled them.

And finally he stopped praying. There was no magic.

But there was Lucky. And now Alex would do anything for him.

"Man, what's the matter with you? You gotta get your head on straight. Things are moving," Ike said.

"Yeah, I know," Alex said. "I'm cool. I was just trying to figure out what to tell Lucky about Julie staying. And if he wants us to . . ." He shrugged.

"Kidnap her and her friends?"

"Ain't doing it," said Corey. "Those girls have minds of their own, and if I'm not a total dummy . . ."

"Not total," Ron said, and punched him in the ribs. "Just valedictorian of the county high school."

"Oh man." Corey rubbed his thick fingers across his face. "Didn't think I'd ever live that one down."

"And honor society," Ron continued. "And here was me and Ike, happy to get B minuses."

"Hell," said Ike. "I was over the moon to see a C."

Alex laughed. He loved these people. They knew when to laugh, when to cry, when to bolster you up or bring you down a peg. And none of them had ever been farther than a car ride away from home.

If anyone could keep Julie and her friends out of harm's way, it was these three and Les and Bjorn. Hell, they were probably safer here than they would be in Dewey Beach or anywhere, if Raymond decided to use them as pawns to get to Lucky.

"Next round's on the house," Alex said.

The three men simultaneously slid their mugs across the bar.

*Y*ou sure you guys don't want to stay all summer?" Dee said to Julie as they watched Kayla put a group of girls through a series of soccer drills. She'd taken one look at the boys playing outside and formed a girls' team on the spot. And enlisted Aggie to help her run drills while Dee and Julie and Mary took the rest of the kids into science.

"In my defense," Dee said with a laugh, "I hardly know the difference between a soccer ball and a basketball." A quiet expression crossed her face and Julie waited. "I worked most days in the fields myself. When my father died—he collapsed in the midday sun between two rows of cantaloupes—my mother had had enough. She took us to child services. Told them to take me and my sister and give us to someone who could send us to school.

"They got her on a work program instead, and we were registered in the local school. It wasn't easy, but we were lucky."

"So now you're paying it forward?"

"In my little way."

I was lucky, too, thought Julie, and she was appreciative, not ungrateful—just dissatisfied. If she put off taking a course this summer, there was really no reason she couldn't stay and help out at camp.

She immediately shot down that idea. For one, she couldn't pay rent at home and rent another place in Lucky's Beach. The hotel would be too expensive, and she wouldn't ask Lucky or Marie to put her up. Lucky obviously had had enough of the Julie experiment.

A stream of girls came through the door and made a beeline toward Julie.

"Your twirling squad has arrived. I swear, by the end of summer, we'll be having intramural soccer games and a pep squad. Who would've thought? I'll get the batons out."

After lunch, they climbed back in the SUV to continue their adults-only vacation on the beach.

"There's still a few good hours of sun," Aggie said.

"Hope I didn't finagle you into wasting a day," Julie said.

"Don't apologize. I had a blast," Kayla said. "And with the workout we had, we can eat more at dinner."

"True," said Aggie. "After five days of indulgence, I was beginning to have to hold my stomach in every time I got out of my beach chair."

"Speaking of which," Kayla added, "I need lunch. They should get a better chef at chez summer camp."

"And newer computers," Aggie added. "I wonder what Hillsdale does with their old ones."

"I think it's a shoestring budget," said Julie. "They're the overflow day camp for the kids who weren't able to get into the regular county program, so I'm betting they don't get a lot of extras."

"Well, at least it's a nice place to spend the day: a little learning, a little friendship, a little play," Kayla said.

They stopped at the deli to get sandwiches for the beach and stopped by the hotel long enough to return the SUV to its spot by the dumpster and, making use of the hotel's service door, run upstairs to change into their suits.

Ten minutes later they were heading toward Surf's Up to see if anyone wanted to join them for a picnic on the beach. The only person who seemed to be there was CeeJay, who stood in the open doorway, leaning against the frame, arms crossed and looking crosser.

"Scatter said you were leaving," she announced without even saying hello.

"Changed our minds," Aggie said. "Where are the boys?"

"Out."

"Where did they go?" Aggie asked.

CeeJay shrugged, dropped her shoulders. "They didn't tell me. It's a big secret. Ask Scatter. But he probably won't tell you, either." She bit her lip and added, "They said you could take the boat out if you want."

"We'll do that," Aggie said, and started up the beach. Kayla followed.

"You coming, Julie?"

"Sure." Anything to stay away from Lucky and Scatter. "You guys know what you're doing?"

"Yep," Kayla said.

"Oh," CeeJay called. "And Les said to stay near the shore if you want to swim. There's a big riptide."

"Thanks," said Kayla, and they headed toward the marina. "That's the most words she's said in the last five days."

"Makes you wonder," Julie said, pausing long enough to look over her shoulder to where CeeJay was standing on the sand, arms crossed as usual and still watching them.

"She should get a life," Aggie said.

"I think she thinks we're encroaching on hers," Kayla said.

"Oh, come on. We're not the first women who have come for surf lessons. And Les and Bjorn definitely don't act like they're interested in her."

"I think it's about Scatter," Julie said.

"No, really?" Aggie asked.

"Let's get out on the water first," Kayla said. "That girl is beginning to give me goose bumps."

"But at least now we know why," Aggie said. "She's jealous of Julie."

The marina seemed busier today, but Kayla knew exactly where she was going. She untied Les's boat and held it steady while Julie and Aggie climbed over the side. Kayla had no trouble maneuvering the boat out of the slip, avoiding a couple of sailboats, and they headed out to sea, laughing at the spray that hit them in the face, bracing themselves as the boat crested a swell and dropped into a trough.

"I'll head into shore," Kayla called. "Look for a nice place to anchor, and we can have our lunch."

She cut the craft back toward the shoreline, hugging the

slight curve of the surfer beach, and slowed and rounded the point that separated the public beach from the private one.

"How about here?" Aggie said. "Get in a little closer. The dunes will protect us from the wind so we don't have to scream to have a conversation, and maybe we'll get a peek at the mysterious owners of *the house.*"

Kayla nosed the boat toward the shore.

"And they might greet us with a shotgun," Julie said. "I don't think this is a good idea. There are signs posted everywhere."

"Oh, come on. Just a little closer. Nobody owns the ocean, do they?"

"I have no idea," Julie said.

"I wish I had binoculars," Aggie said, her eyes bright. "Maybe we could see what evil lurks there."

"Julie's right," Kayla said. "We don't know who lives there or why they don't like people. I'm taking us back out."

Kayla started a turn back to the sea; the nose lifted, and the boat lurched, then seemed to drag. The engine made a strange noise. Kayla quickly cut it off. "Shit—"

"What?" asked Julie, eyeing the house.

"I think we hit something." Kayla left the console and hurried toward the engine, pulled it up, checked the propellers. "Whew! Doesn't look like we bent anything."

"We need to get out of here before the surf takes us into the beach," Julie said. *There is no reason to panic,* she told herself. She'd been on the beach more than once and so far she'd encountered only a little boy and a housekeeper . . . and Scatter.

"Why aren't we moving?" Aggie asked.

Kayla was looking over the side, hands on her hips. "That little be-otch. A sandbar. We're stuck on a sandbar. And Cee-Jay led us right here. Wait till we get back. I'm going to give her what for. She could have wrecked the boat, even caused bodily injury. I've just about had it with her bad attitude." She straightened up, looked toward shore. "We'll have to get out and try to push her off." She threw one leg over the side.

"Wait!" Aggie grabbed her and pulled her back.

"What the—?"

"There." Aggie pointed to the sign nearest to them on the point.

"I know, 'Private: Keep Out.' Whoever lives there is crazy. He doesn't own the ocean."

"Read it!"

All three of them turned toward the sign and read.

Julie blinked, read the words again.

DANGER: SHARK BREEDING GROUNDS.

Chapter 23

They stared at the sign. Even Kayla seemed at a loss of how to fix the situation.

Julie's first thought was *No wonder the housekeeper was so frantic to find the little boy, she thought he was shark bait.* Her second thought was *I might be shark bait myself.*

"What are we going to do?" Aggie's question broke their silence.

"Hell if I know." Kayla looked around, gauging the situation. If there was an obvious action, she would figure it out.

"It's not that far to shore . . ." Aggie said.

"Except for the sharks," Julie said.

"Academic, because we can't leave the boat to drift out to sea at high tide." Kayla leaned over and lifted two emergency oars from the hull, handed one to Aggie, and motioned her to the opposite side.

"Julie, go forward to take the weight out of the back of the boat."

Julie moved past them, climbed onto the bow, and hung on for dear life, thinking, *Shark bait, shark bait, shark bait.*

Kayla and Aggie lowered the oars into the water. "Use it like a gondola pole," Kayla ordered.

She and Aggie pushed and pushed, but after much grunting and heaving, they were still stuck.

"Okay, you two in the back and I'll see if I can get the front pointed out to sea."

Julie scrambled to the back next to Aggie.

Kayla pushed the oar into the sand, trying to dislodge the nose of the boat. After a few seconds she gave up. "Try calling Les and see if he can send us a tow."

"He and Bjorn are probably still gone, but I'll try." Aggie searched in her beach bag for her phone. The call went to voice mail.

"The coast guard?" Julie suggested.

"Too embarrassing," said Kayla. "I guess we'll have to call Surf's Up. Maybe there's someone there who can help us."

"CeeJay?" Aggie said. "That little bitch told us to stay near shore in the first place."

"You think she did it on purpose?" Julie asked. "No, don't answer that. It's to pay us back because she thinks I'm moving in on Scatter."

"She said that? You didn't tell us that part."

"I didn't think it was important. I assured her I had no interest and to get over it."

"*Are* you and Scatter . . . ?"

"No."

"There was that night of kissing," Aggie reminded her.

Julie held up two fingers. "Two. Exactly two kisses. And besides, I think he and Dee at the community camp are pretty tight."

"The Scatman is pretty damn popular."

"Yeah," said Julie, trying to ignore the niggle of disappointment she felt over that near miss. But it had been all wrong from the get-go.

"Well, I'm calling CeeJay." Aggie made the call. Mouthed, "No answer." "CeeJay, we know you're there. And yes, we're stuck on the sandbar like you wanted. Ha ha, cute. We're having lunch. Screw you. There will be repercussions." Aggie ended the call.

"Aggie," Kayla and Julie said simultaneously.

"Well, I've had it with that little punk. She's not even eighteen. So she can forget any of the guys hitting on her."

"What?" Julie asked.

"Yeah. Les told me in strictest confidence. She's on the run. Abusive father—physically abusive and not just hitting, if you get my meaning. I was feeling a little sorry for her, but really?"

"She's underage?" Kayla said.

"She has ID and work papers, most probably fake, but everyone here pretty much looks the other way. They give her a little work where they can. She rents an apartment in town with several other girls. So at least she's not on the streets or anything. You'd think she would be nicer to people."

"Isn't that illegal?" Julie asked.

"You would send her back?" Aggie asked.

Julie thought about it. "Nope."

"We'll just have to wait for high tide to lift us off," Kayla said.

"When is that?"

Kayla consulted her watch. "Four hours?" She looked up and shrugged. "There's an app for that."

"Oh well," Aggie said, and reached for the deli bag. "So who's ready for a sandwich?"

They ate their sandwiches and chips, but went easy on the sodas after Aggie pointed out that no one wanted to have to hang her butt off the side to pee and risk a shark coming up for a bite. That made them laugh. They sunscreened and stretched out to enjoy the wait.

"The next time we get stuck on a sandbar," Kayla said lazily, "let's remember to bring cosmos or margaritas to help pass the time."

Several times they tried to unmoor the boat to no avail. On the third try Julie was in the prow when she saw the little boy standing on the house's deck.

"Thank you, thank you." She cupped her hands, called out, "Hola. Estamos atrapados. Um . . . Necesitamos . . ." She groped for the word for "help." Looked at the others.

"Sorry, French," Aggie said.

"Latin," said Kayla.

Julie made a stab. "Necesitamos ayudó?"

The boy stood there.

"Maybe he didn't hear you."

"Maybe I asked for avocado." She cupped her hands again. "Por favor—"

He disappeared.

"Do you think he'll come back with help?" Aggie asked.

"I don't know," Julie said. "Hopefully he'll tell the house-keeper. She seemed nice enough, but if the owners come out and they accuse us of trespassing, just say we drifted and got stuck."

Julie was just about to give up hoping for a rescue when she saw a solitary figure walking, not from the house, but from the public beach. Even at a distance with the sun in her eyes, Julie recognized him and groaned. Of course, it would have to be him.

"My hero," said Aggie, as the three of them watched Scatter stride across the beach.

"A barefoot knight without armor," said Kayla.

"Oh, he has armor," Julie said. "Plenty of it."

He stopped at the edge of the surf and called out. "What seems to be the problem?"

He was too far away for Julie to see his actual expression, but she was certain he was trying not to laugh. Kayla and Aggie looked at her.

"We're stuck on the sandbar," Julie called.

"Get out and push," he called back.

"What about the sharks?"

"What sharks?"

At least she'd gotten his attention. "The ones the sign warns about."

He started splashing toward them.

"Stop! Go back!" Aggie yelled.

He stopped when he was a few feet from the boat.

Now Julie could see he was grinning. "There's no shark breeding ground here, is there?"

"Nope, though we do get an occasional sighting."

"But the signs," Aggie said.

"Posted to keep nosy tourists away."

"Nice guy, whoever owns this house," said Kayla. "Fortunately one of his kids escaped long enough to go get help. They called you?"

He held out both hands. "As you see . . . as they say."

Aggie snorted a giggle.

Julie was not amused. "Why did he call you?"

"Do you want to get off this sandbar or not?"

"Yes. But we can probably manage. Sorry to have bothered you. Better get back before Ike, Corey, and Ron start handing out free beer." Julie swung her legs over the side and slid into the water, then threw her full weight against the nose of the boat.

He was laughing outright now. "Chill for a sec, and let's use a little science. Ladies, out of the boat."

Kayla dropped a ladder over the side, and she and Aggie climbed down to the water. Without their weight in the boat and with Scatter helping, they managed to push the boat into the rising tide.

"Thanks," Kayla said, and scrambled back up the ladder to take the helm. Aggie quickly followed, but when Julie started up, he pulled her back into the water.

"Not you. We have to talk."

Aggie and Kayla shot Julie knowing looks, blatant enough for Scatter to see. Kayla dropped the engine back into position and they roared out into the open sea.

Julie and Scatter stood in the water looking at each other.

"After you," he said finally, gesturing one hand toward shore.

They were waist-deep in water and the undertow was strong. Julie struggled not to go down, until Scatter slipped his arm around her waist, adding his strength to hers.

"Thanks, but I can manage."

"The way you've managed everything else so far? You've been here less than a week and I've had to rescue you twice already."

"Let go!" She pushed at his hand.

He let go suddenly and she was knocked back into the water. She floundered, trying to regain her feet.

He leaned over and hauled her up. "What do you do when there's no one to save you?"

"I save myself." She trudged through the surf toward solid sand. "Though I don't usually need saving."

"I can believe that," he said, coming to walk beside her. "Nothing ventured . . ."

"Oh, shut up." She made it only a few more feet before he spun her around.

"So what are you gonna do now?"

"Me? What do you mean?" Julie looked up at him—sucked

in her breath. That flash of recognition again: immediate, visceral, and totally unsettling.

Scatter frowned down at her. "Now what?"

"Nothing . . . it's just . . . I keep thinking we've met before."

"Christ Almighty."

"I know, ridiculous, right?"

He walked over to the boulder where she'd been sitting the night of the bonfire. "Sit."

"So you can stand hulking over me? No thanks."

"We'll both sit." He pushed her down on the rock, sat down beside her. "Why won't you just leave like Lucky asked? Why can't you and Louise just leave him alone?"

That stung. "He's family. I've left him alone for six years—he left me alone before that. Now I'm trying to help. And my mother is worried. She's always felt responsible for him."

Scatter barked out a laugh so harsh that it made Julie flinch. "Did it ever occur to you that he didn't need her to do that? He doesn't need you now. You're more of a hindrance than a help. Just like your mother. I thought you might grow up to have that spark of the devil Lucky imagined, but you haven't. God, the two of you are suffocating."

"How do you know how I've grown up? How dare you insult my mother or me. You don't know anything about us."

"I'm not insulting her, she did what she thought he needed; it just wasn't always right."

"You have no idea, you and your piece of paper from a university. If it was even a real university."

He bolted to his feet and she thought he might leave. But he turned back to her; his eyes flared, and she got that same jolt of recognition she'd gotten before. The molten anger and hurt. *He's just like a caged animal.* Her mother's words ripped through her from the past.

And a flash of a bleeding, skinny street kid exploded in her mind. Late at night, Julie in her princess pj's, mud on the kitchen floor, the smell of unwashed body and blood. A sullen, dirty, angry boy, his filthy fingers curved as claws, as he struggled in Lucky's grasp. Body tense with aggression, or could it have been fear? Her mother told her to go back to bed, but his black eyes cut into her as she backed away.

Like they were doing now.

Julie looked up and saw the man the boy had become.

"So you finally remembered."

Julie shook her head. But she did remember. Scatter. *Scatter.* "Scatter. I thought it sounded familiar the other day, but I figured it was a surfer moniker. But it isn't." *My name's Scatter 'cause I warn the gang when the cops are coming.* "It was your street name."

Scatter turned slightly, as if he were expecting a blow.

"Wow," she said.

Slowly he turned to look at her. "Wow?" He blew out a laugh. "I've been waiting all week for you to figure it out, and now that you finally have, I get a wow?"

"What do you want, fanfare? The cancan? Fireworks? I'm still processing."

He looked down at her. "Cancan sounds good."

"You're really that kid?"

"Yep."

She smiled. "You got taller."

"So did you."

"Why didn't you just tell me up front? Why did you try to keep me away from Lucky?"

"Because I didn't know what Lucky would want. At first we didn't know where he was, or if he would bring trouble with him when he did return."

"But he's back now."

"Yeah, he is. We're pretty sure things are about to come to a head."

"Are Les and Bjorn part of Lucky's posse, too?"

"We're all in this together."

"I figured as much. Well, Aggie refuses to leave Les. Kayla agrees. You guys aren't the only ones who love my uncle. So you can count us in, too."

He let out an exasperated sigh. "You're not understanding this. Just stay out of it. I have to get back to work."

"Which one?"

"I left Corey in charge of the taps while I came after you. I need to get back."

"Okay, but I expect you to come clean about everything since you sneaked out of our house, taking a whole peach pie as I recall."

He smiled.

"And you didn't even leave a note."

"I was screwed up, okay?"

"I guessed that much." She looked down at the sand. "I missed you."

When he didn't say anything she glanced up at him.

He was just looking back at her.

She swallowed. "Anyway. You never told me who lives in this house."

He shrugged, obviously relieved to have the subject changed. "I do."

"No way."

"I don't own it. I'm just house-sitting for a guy we helped out last year."

"And are those your kids or his?" She nodded to where the boy and a girl stood at the edge of the dunes.

He let out an audible sigh. "Mine, for the moment. They're staying with me." He lifted his chin and they ran forward to stand behind him, peering out at Julie.

"Es bonita," the boy whispered into Alex's ear.

"Yes, she is, and she speaks Spanish, remember?"

The boy nodded and broke into a quick smile that was gone almost as quickly as it had appeared. He pressed closer to Alex's back. The little girl was younger, smaller, and, if possible, thinner.

"Oh my—" Julie blurted out with a bolt of understanding. "They're the 'contraband' I saw Lucky delivering the first night we were here."

"Contraband," he echoed like it was a bad taste in his mouth.

"I thought they were bootlegged liquor."

"It would've been easier for everyone if you'd left it at that."

"We just stopped to say hello. Then I thought you were ripping Lucky off. That's why I stayed."

"So you could protect him against me and Marie and two kids?"

"I didn't know they were kids."

From the corner of her eye, Julie saw the housekeeper standing on the path between the dunes.

"Is she their mother?"

"Rosie? She's their aunt. She's taking care of them until their mother is out of the hospital. She takes care of the rest of us full-time."

"But why sneak them here in the middle of the night?"

"It's a long story, and the less you know the better. Lucky had to extract them from some bad people. They'll be looking for them."

"What about the police?"

"Out of their expertise."

"So you're just going to wait until these guys show up and what?" Her blood seized up. "Gunfight at the O.K. Corral?"

"Not if we can prevent it. But Lucky doesn't need you as a distraction."

She stood to face him. "Well, I won't be a distraction, but I'm not leaving." She smiled down at the kids. "Como se llaman?"

"Pablo," the boy said.

The girl buried her head behind Scatter's leg. "Cecilia," he said for her.

Julie knelt down. "Seremos amigos, okay?" Julie said. "Friends?"

She saw Aggie and Kayla hurrying across the rivulet toward them.

"I'm being rescued," Julie said.

Aggie and Kayla slashed through the water, then slowed, hesitating, probably not wanting to interrupt anything.

Julie called them over. "I think we all deserve an explanation."

For a second Scatter looked like he might bolt. It was an expression Julie remembered all too well.

And one day he had.

"Why did you run away?"

"What?"

"You ran away after all Lucky and my mom did for you."

"Can we discuss this later?"

Aggie and Kayla had stopped on the sand.

"Permission to come aboard, Captain," Kayla said.

Scatter looked down at the kids, then back to her friends. He nodded and they slowly moved closer.

"Hi," Aggie said when she saw the two children. Kayla gave Julie a questioning look.

"The loot I thought was contraband."

"You're smuggling children?" Aggie blurted out, frowning at Scatter. "Does Les know?"

"Yes. Everyone knows and now you do, too. But please, don't give them away. They're in danger."

Julie's attention snapped back to Scatter. It was the first time he had ever sounded like a caring human being. *He actually cared.*

"We would never give them away," Julie said. "I'll clue them in. Tell Lucky we're still here. And ready to help."

She wiggled her fingers at the children. The girl bent two fingers back at her and hid her face.

Julie joined her two friends. And they turned back toward the public beach.

"Just so you know," Scatter called out. "I went to a real university. My degree is on my office wall."

Julie smiled, before turning back. "Good to know, you can tell me all about it over a drink tonight."

Chapter 24

𝒜lex walked the kids back to the house. They were reluctant to go and he couldn't blame them. It was a sunny, warm day, and they were tired of being cooped up inside.

He knelt down on the dune path, pulled them close. "Soon we can play in the water and build a sand castle."

"Y la señorita también?"

"Maybe. Maybe she'll come and play."

"Ella me gusta."

"I like her, too," Alex said.

"Like her, too," the boy agreed.

Alex smiled. Children were amazing. These two, torn from their mother, kidnapped by a man who told them he was going to be their father, and kidnapped again by Lucky, were already adapting. It gave him hope.

They would survive. Like Alex had.

Rosie was waiting for them on the stairs to the deck.

"You let them come down," Alex said. He thought he understood why.

"I thought she should know about them," Rosie said. "She is kind to them and doesn't even know who they are. They need to learn they can trust more than just you and me."

"You were right," he said. "She has a lot of Lucky in her."

"So do you."

Alex shrugged and they walked toward the house. "I think I have a date tonight. You better help me pick out a clean shirt."

Rosie flashed her big smile. "It's about time."

"Yeah. I hope you're right." He called Lucky and explained what had happened and that Julie and her friends already knew enough to get them in trouble without understanding the rest.

"How?" Lucky asked.

"Asking questions. Pillow talk." He hurried on. "Not mine, but Les and Bjorn. I think they were right to confide in Kayla and Aggie. Julie is determined to stand by you no matter what. And her friends will stand by her."

"As stubborn as her mother," Lucky said.

"And you," Alex reminded him.

"Yeah. It just seems like one too many loose ends to worry about."

"That's why I think I should explain so they won't blunder into something they aren't equipped to handle."

"I should have sent them away the first day."

"And if Raymond had decided to come after them to force your hand, they would be without backup. At least here, they've got us."

"Oh Christ, what a mess."

"It's bound to break soon. But until then, what do you want me to do?"

A sigh. "I guess bring them up to date without specifics and just warn them to stay away from me and those kids."

"Okay," Alex said, though he doubted if Julie would stick to those orders. For a nonconfrontational, do-what-she-was-told elementary school teacher, she had just done a big flip-flop. Alex guessed he had to accept partial blame for that one. He was glad in a way, but damn, he had no idea what to expect now.

"And, Scat . . ."

"Yeah, Lucky?"

"If you're waiting for my permission to court my niece, I'm giving it."

"Jeez, Lucky, we have bigger things to worry about." Alex swore he could hear Marie laughing in the background.

"Nothing's so major that you can't take time for love," Lucky said.

"You've been listening to too much country-and-western music at the bar. Tonight is all business." *And a confession,* he reminded himself. He was interested in Julie. What guy wouldn't be? But not unless she really understood what he was—had been. He'd tell her and give her the opportunity to tell him to get lost.

$\mathcal{W}$ow, I can't believe you said that to Scatterman. He looked totally gobsmacked," Kayla said as they walked across the beach to gather up their stuff.

"I know, I was kind of crazed. You're not going to believe what he told me."

"Maybe not, but let's wait until we're away from prying ears." Aggie jerked her head toward Surf's Up, where CeeJay had once again taken up residence in the doorway.

"Did she say anything when you came back?"

"No, she hurried inside when she saw us coming."

"Something tells me the Scatman may have reamed her for it before he rescued us," Kayla added.

"Don't remind me," Julie said. "But some good did come from it, which I'll tell you about, if you'll hurry up."

They returned to the hotel and stopped at Julie's room.

Aggie opened the cooler. "Just let me get out some water and snacks and we're all ears."

"And while she's doing that, let's focus on what's really important." Kayla went to the closet, Rolodexed through the hangers, and pulled out Julie's new dress. She held it up for the other two to see. "Thumbs-up or -down?"

"I think it's a little dressy for the ambience," Julie said. "Especially after I tell you what I found out after you left."

Kayla returned the dress to the closet. "So tell us what happened."

"Every detail," Aggie added, and handed Julie a bottle of water. "He sweeps you out of the boat and into his arms . . ."

"He hauled me out of the water, said we have to talk, dragged me across the beach—okay, perhaps I exaggerate—sits me down, and proceeds to confess that he . . . Well, do you remember when Lucky brought that street kid home? He stayed with us for a while?"

"Yeah. Lucky found him in an alley. He was the lookout for some street gang."

"Well . . ." Julie waited.

"No-o-o," Aggie said.

"Scatterman?" Kayla asked.

"One and the same," said Julie. "How could I have not recognized him?"

"Wow," Aggie said. "Maybe because then he was a dirty, foulmouthed delinquent and now he's Mr. Hunkadorable."

Julie snorted water out her nose. "I wouldn't go that far. But he has cleaned up rather well."

"Still has an edge," Kayla pointed out. "As long as he's learned to tame his temper."

"Well, he still has one of those, too, but it hasn't turned violent that I've seen."

"Yet," said Kayla.

"He's totally loyal to Lucky so that's in his favor."

"They've been together all this time?"

"I don't know. He started telling me and then the kids—the ones I saw on the beach before—appeared on the deck and came running to him. They were the 'contraband' I saw them delivering in the middle of the night. Someone had kidnapped them from the mother. Lucky extracted them from the kidnappers and brought them here to their aunt, who's Scatter's housekeeper. They're hiding them here."

"Hiding?" said Kayla. "They're expecting trouble?"

"It sounds that way."

"So that's why they've been trying to get rid of us," Aggie said.

"They? Les and Bjorn, too?"

Kayla and Aggie nodded.

"Not at first," Aggie said.

"But in the last day or two. That's probably why they've made themselves scarce lately," Kayla said.

Aggie nodded. "Les told me some stuff but not that. I guess he didn't trust me."

Julie studied Aggie's face. She was always up for a lark, ready to roll with the punches, but now she seemed genuinely hurt. "Because he cares about your safety."

"Sure," said Aggie, but she didn't sound convinced.

"So are we about to be under attack?" Kayla asked.

"I was going to make him tell me the specifics," Julie said, "but between the kids and then you guys showing up, I didn't have a chance to ask him. That's why I invited him for a drink."

"Jules, that wasn't an invitation, that was a command."

"Man, how the tables have turned. Scatter was that crazy kid? I can't get over it. He was like a wild animal," Aggie said.

"You thought he was cute," Kayla reminded her.

"I did not. Or maybe I did. In those days I thought most guys were cute."

"We were only nine."

Aggie looked down her nose at Kayla. "Evidently I saw his potential." Her cell rang; she picked it up, listened. Ended the call. "Looks like it's going to be a triple date tonight."

"See. Business, like I said." Though Julie had to admit she felt a smidge of disappointment.

"More like he brought in reinforcements," Kayla said, and reached back into the closet. "So . . . maybe leggings and a T-shirt."

As it turned out, Julie's "date" was a three-couple powwow on the state of things in Lucky's Beach. Julie was okay with that. Having thought about it, she wasn't quite ready to pry Scatter's life story out of him. She had a feeling that it hadn't been pretty, even after Lucky pulled him off the streets the first time. It might be easier to take in the company of friends, but right now she wanted to find out what was happening in Lucky's Beach.

Scatter wasn't the least bit surprised that they were being joined by Julie's "posse" as well as his.

Aggie and Kayla stopped a few feet away, shook their heads.

"I would have never guessed," Aggie said, giving Scatter the once-over.

"Pretty amazing," Kayla said. "You look really different."

"Yeah, I've been told already," Alex said. "Taller. And cleaner."

They both zeroed in on Julie. "You didn't say that."

Julie shrugged. "I'm afraid I did, but it's true."

"We thought it was about time we filled you guys in on what is going on," Les said.

Scatter looked like he might argue, but after a long silence he walked past them, took Julie's arm, and steered her across the parking lot. For a charming bartender and working therapist who dealt with people all day long, his own social skills were a little rough around the edges.

The other four fell in behind Julie and Scatter, Les and Bjorn ushering the girls along as if they all knew where they were going.

Evidently they did. A block later in the opposite direction from the hotel, they turned down an alley and into the doorway of what appeared to be a pub, though there was no obvious sign outside. It was a smallish room, with dark paneling and a darker wooden bar. The bartender nodded and pointed to a round corner booth in the back.

They scooted into the banquette, not the usual alternating male and female, but Les in the middle and Bjorn and Scatter on the outsides. Julie kept telling herself not to read more into their actions than there was, but she couldn't help but notice that Les had a full view of the front door.

Stop it, she told herself. It did absolutely no good. This whole trip had suddenly taken on an air of undeniable intensity, and she wondered if she had done the right thing in deciding to stay.

They ordered drinks and food, then Aggie and Kayla told them about their visit to the day camp, which brought a look of surprise to Scatter's otherwise deadpan expression, and about getting stuck on the sandbar.

"It was CeeJay's suggestion."

"For which she's been duly reprimanded," Les said.

Dinner came and they fell silent. The pub might be run-down, but the burgers were excellent. Several customers left; it seemed the pub catered to locals and most of its diners were early birds. A few people lingered at the bar.

"Since you won't leave town," Les said without preamble, "we think you should know what's going on. We're expecting a certain individual to show up to collect a . . . package."

Julie didn't know whether to duck and cover or roll her eyes.

"I don't think it will lead to . . . any serious altercation . . . but you girls need to stay mum, and don't get in the way."

"Jeez, Les," Aggie said. "Why did you bring us someplace where you have to talk in code?"

"He enjoys it," Bjorn said. "Besides, this is the safest public place we have."

Les gave him a look. "Look, girls, just keep your eyes out for one ugly mother, and go to ground when you see him."

"How will we know if it's him?" Aggie asked.

"The air will grow cold."

"Metaphorically," Bjorn said. "It's probably not going to happen; it's been a week and he hasn't come after the kids yet. He may have just cut his losses, but we haven't heard anything, so we're playing it safe, as you should."

Julie looked to Alex, who hadn't said anything.

He caught her eye. "But if he does, go straight to your hotel and stay there until you're given the all clear. Do not try to intercede or help. Everything is in place. Any variable could unravel the whole operation. Understand?"

Julie nodded.

"Maybe we should just leave town," Kayla said.

"A little late for that," Scatter said.

"Okay, that's it," Julie said. "Are you trying to scare us?"

"Yes."

"Anyone for dessert?" Les asked.

No one was.

The conversation evidently was over. The guys didn't even quibble over who was paying the check. Alex just told the bartender to put it on his tab and they went out into the night.

Les and Aggie and Kayla and Bjorn walked down the street like couples out to dinner, their arms around each other, laughing and enjoying the late-evening air. Alex and Julie walked side by side not speaking. She was having trouble shifting gears from beach vacation to cloak-and-dagger operation.

And what she'd wanted to do tonight was sit down just the two of them. Hear about how he and Lucky and these guys all ended up in the same town and in all this trouble. But mostly she wanted to hear about what had happened to him since he'd run away all those years before.

They fell behind the other two couples.

Finally Julie said, "Are you really worried?"

"Nothing we can't handle."

"Then why is Lucky acting so furtive and adamant that we leave?"

"He's just overprotective."

Julie groaned. "I figured as much. For two people so unalike, my mother and uncle are two of a kind when it comes to me."

"You should be thankful."

"I am," she said, taken aback. "It's just he was always such a free spirit."

"He still is, but not when it comes to people who need him."

"I don't exactly need him, I just . . . love him." There, she'd said it. Since seeing him again, even with all the baggage he seemed to be carrying, she'd realized she loved her uncle and she wanted him to love her, too.

He'd always been so elusive when she was young, had disappointed her so many times. It wasn't until she'd come to Lucky's Beach that she'd begun to remember the good times, the supportive times.

"Why did he always take care of others first?"

"I don't understand the question."

"It seemed like he cared more about people like Bjorn and Les and runaways like you than he cared about us. Mom said he came to take care of us, but she ended up taking care of him."

Alex stopped. "Is that what you think?"

"Was I wrong?"

"The first intelligent question you've asked since you came here."

"Don't talk like a therapist."

"I'm talking like someone who Lucky pulled out of an alley before I was beaten to death by my own gang. I needed him."

"We needed him, too."

"No, you didn't. Louise wouldn't let him do anything to help her or you. She wanted to be the one taking care of both of you. So he helped people who needed help. Real help."

"Like you."

Alex shrugged.

"Then why did you run away?"

They started walking again. "I didn't think you'd notice."

"I did. It was such a shit thing to do after all he and Mom had done for you."

"I don't expect you to understand."

"Try me. I teach fourth grade, you'd be surprised at the things I understand."

He hesitated, breathed out slowly, controlled. "It was too much temptation."

"Huh." She tried to see his face, but he'd turned away, looking into the shadows.

"I wanted to belong there more than anything I'd ever wanted. I wanted you to be my family. It wasn't going to happen. Even in the state I was in I knew that, so I left before it became more . . . painful . . . the idea of it ending, as I knew it would."

"You made sure it did."

"Yeah."

"Lucky left soon after that."

"He came after me. Took me to California with him."

"You were a minor. He could have gone to jail for kidnapping."

He gave her a patient look. "It didn't matter to Lucky. He took a chance. *He's* never been afraid of taking a chance."

"Unlike me you mean."

"Maybe. It didn't really matter. No one was looking for me.

A throwaway. That's what they called us. Kids dropped off on a corner, the side of a highway—left by parents or whoever used you last."

He said it matter-of-factly, as if it had happened to someone else and not him. It made it sound even more awful. *Throwaways.* Marie had mentioned them before.

Julie thought of her own comfortable life. The children in her classes. She was beginning to think a dose of reality of how others were sometimes forced to live would go a lot further in molding useful adults than all the apps you could fit on an iPhone.

Her students deserved mentoring and love, too, but just not from Julie. She was like them. She was beginning to understand that now. She was just too much like them.

"I kept running away," Alex said. "Hell, I've lost count of the times, but he always came after me."

"Why?"

"'Cause that's the way he is."

"What I mean is, why you?"

"Dunno. He just did and finally it worked. And FYI, I wasn't the only one. Eventually I gave up trying to destroy my life, got my GED, a part-time job, went to community college, and got a degree in psychology."

"To pay him back?"

"To pay the world back." He breathed out a low laugh. "Anyway, it was the least I could do, don't you think?"

"And you moved back here to follow in his footsteps?"

"It's just what I do."

"Except is it what you want to do? It sounds—and don't get mad—a little like a hostage situation."

"What are you talking about?"

"You living your life to pay back Lucky."

"Isn't that exactly what you're doing? Paying back Louise?"

"No—I'm preparing myself for my future."

"Louise's idea of your future."

Julie's breath stuck. Was that what she was doing? All that work and preparation, was she living her own life or—

Without warning Alex grabbed her, pushed her into the shadows, pinned her body with his. She didn't have time to react, lash out, or even wonder what was happening.

"Shh," he whispered into her ear. "Don't move, don't make a sound."

He released her and was gone. Julie didn't move. She couldn't hear footsteps or breathing, only the sound of waves echoing through the silence. And for the first time ever, Julie Barlow feared for her life.

Chapter 25

*A*lex slid through the night; the others had moved far ahead while he and Julie had been talking. His hearing, honed during his time as a juvenile lookout, had saved him from walking Julie right into the thing Lucky was trying to keep her from.

He hadn't wanted to leave her, but he couldn't take a chance of losing the two men he'd spotted lurking in the street, and he couldn't bring her along; she would have given them away for sure. But things were moving. If there were two of them, there would be more not far behind.

He heard a sound off to the left, slipped into the shadow of a building, waited until the two men stepped out of the passageway between the deli and the souvenir shop. *The same two men? Theirs or ours?*

It was too dark to identify them. They were traveling silently, and Alex felt that old gut-stabbing feeling that things were about to go south. They should have moved the kids. In spite of Rosie, in spite of the takedown plan of Marie's "friends" in the agency. He didn't like depending on outsiders to keep them safe. Too many variables. But Lucky was adamant about not going rogue.

Alex hoped to hell he was right.

He stepped out of the shadows and saw them up ahead. They turned into the bar and grill's parking lot. Good. Corey and Ron would take over from there. He'd have time to get Julie to a safer place.

*L*ucky ended the call and turned to Marie.

"It's starting?"

Lucky nodded. He was standing on the other side of the kitchen table. A physical separation to mimic the mental and emotional separation that was a necessary part of getting a job done.

"Don't you dare get yourself killed."

He grinned. "Would you miss me?"

"What do you think?"

"Stay here until it's over."

She smiled and felt her caftan pocket.

As soon as he slipped out the back door, she went to the front window. She'd drawn the curtains earlier, turned out the lights. She lifted a corner of the curtain to the side and peered out, watching for any movement. She knew there were men watching from the Crosbys' darkened house across the street. Next to them, the Venturas' television was blinking through the open drapes, but the Venturas had gone to stay at the hotel until this evening was over.

She was supposed to be there, too, but she had refused to leave her home. Besides, she was far more equipped than any of them to deal with these crooks. A little rusty maybe and loath to involve herself, but she had no choice, did she?

Marie was hoping for a peaceful encounter. They'd identified four men who probably belonged to Raymond. There might be more, but they were waiting for Raymond himself to make a personal appearance.

This time, instead of snatching the children off the street and beating their mother to near death, he would be armed with legal papers that some crooked judge filed to give him custody. It would all be aboveboard. And if Ana survived, either she would crawl back to him and become the mule he demanded she be, or she would meet with an unfortunate accident and the kids would become his employees.

And there would be nothing any of them could do about it.

Lucky had decided to extract the children himself, since the agency couldn't, due to the usual bureaucratic nonsense. It would look the other way and let Lucky break the law, then make the bust and forget he was any part of it.

That was the deal, but the deal depended on catching Raymond in the act, bringing him down on drug charges and kidnapping.

It was how things worked in the murkier waters of law enforcement, caught up in the world of informants, snitches, and anonymous sources, late-night meetings in less than reputable places. Marie had once been addicted to the thrill and the sense of justice. Not anymore.

It had been a long time since those days. She'd retired here to take up her former livelihood of town psychic like her mother and grandmother before her. Then Lucky came and all that changed.

He got her interested in helping again—this time out in the light, on the safe side of the law, mostly. Lots of paperwork, contacting the right agencies, finding a good pro bono lawyer. It had been enough because it had been Lucky calling the shots. But this . . .

You have to take the good with the bad, her mother, the real psychic, always said.

But not this kind of bad, Marie thought, and dropped the curtain.

Julie didn't move until her feet started to go to sleep. She tried wiggling her toes, eased away from the brick facade of whatever store they'd stopped at. She strained to hear the sound of anything but the waves. Heard nothing. Took a deep breath and realized she'd been taking shallow breaths, afraid to even disturb the air.

She didn't feel him come up beside her. She choked back a scream even as she realized it was Alex.

"The street is clear for the moment. Go straight back to your hotel, don't stop anywhere, and stay there until it's all clear. I can't take you myself. Just do it. Now." He pushed her out into the street.

She deliberated, turned back. "What's—?"

But he'd disappeared.

She didn't stop to look for him but hurried on, wondering what she had gotten herself—all three of them—into. This was something right out of prime-time television—without the commercials. Something she could use right now to try to figure out what the hell was going on.

She hugged the storefronts as she raced toward the hotel. It was only two blocks away. Only two blocks. The longest two blocks she could imagine. She tried not to run, not to call attention to herself. But it was hard. And where were Aggie and Kayla? Had Les and Bjorn taken them to the hotel? Or were they still together? At the bar and grill for a final nightcap?

She went straight toward the hotel. She had no intention of possibly screwing up Lucky's plans, and she was desperate to know if her friends were safe. But as she reached the entrance to Lucky's parking lot, she saw a figure running toward her from the direction of Surf's Up.

Aggie? Kayla? Had they split up? Julie automatically ran to meet her, to tell her to hurry to the hotel.

But it wasn't either of her friends. The girl stopped, gasping for breath.

Julie grabbed her by the shoulders. "CeeJay, where did you come from?"

"Let me go, I have to—" The girl looked back, suddenly looking younger and more vulnerable than Julie had ever seen her. "It's started, hasn't it?"

Julie nodded. She didn't know what CeeJay knew, and she wasn't going to be the one to enlighten her.

"I heard them. They're going to search Scatter's house. Are the kids still there?"

Julie put her fingers to her lips as two men stepped out from behind Surf's Up.

"Let me go, I have to warn—"

"Shh."

The men were coming their way, not hurrying; maybe it was a false alarm.

Julie leaned close to CeeJay. "Don't panic, but two men are coming this way."

CeeJay tightened, tried to pull away.

They were getting closer.

Julie straightened but kept hold of CeeJay's shoulders. She raised her voice. "Mom is going to be so mad at you for being late. You better run all the way home. You are so going to get in trouble."

The men had slowed down. What were the chances that they had heard CeeJay's questions?

Julie leaned into her. "Go tell Lucky or somebody they might have heard and to hide the kids."

CeeJay was looking like she thought Julie had lost her mind. Julie was feeling like she had, too.

Then, louder: "Oh, don't worry about it, I'll go check the register and lock up for you. So what if you were a couple of dollars short? You were never great at math. You go on home now."

The men had almost reached them; they were definitely on an intercept course.

"Get." Julie shoved CeeJay toward the street and CeeJay took off at a run.

Julie took a breath. *Please don't let me die,* she thought, and went to meet the two men.

"I'm sorry," she said, stopping directly in front of them. "Are you interested in surfing lessons?"

Stupid, but it was the only thing she could think of to give CeeJay time to get away. Why didn't someone come out of the bar? Why was everything so quiet? She didn't want to wonder about that too closely.

"The surf store is closed, but if you're interested in lessons, there will be someone here around nine in the morning," she said in her brightest the-field-trip-has-been-canceled-because-of-the-rain voice. Her heart was pounding so loudly she could hardly hear her own words.

The men started to step aside; she stepped with them.

"Or if you'd like to leave your number, I'll have someone call you first thing in the morning. I have paper and a pen here somewhere."

They pushed past her, none too gently.

Julie turned to watch them. "Really, it's no trouble."

CeeJay was out of sight.

"Have a nice night," she called after them.

At least they were striding toward the street, not toward the alley.

Damn. She couldn't go to the hotel—the men might see her. She didn't have anyone's phone numbers.

The men reached the street and turned left, and Julie headed across the parking lot to the bar. Once inside, she hesitated, glanced around the crowd. Smiled like she was looking for her friends. Actually, she was, but she was really looking for someone who could help her.

She walked up to the bar, leaned over the bar top until she got the bartender's attention. It was Mike; he would have to do.

"What can I do you?" Mike asked, and mopped the bar top in front of her.

"I need to talk to Lucky."

Mike rubbed harder, not looking at her. "He's not here. Talk to me and look happy about it."

Shit, she hadn't thought that there might be spies everywhere.

"A glass of cabernet." She smiled. "It's an emergency."

Mike leaned beneath the bar top, and Julie took the opportunity to look in the mirror that ran behind the bar. There were a good number of patrons, but who was friend and who was foe?

He placed a glass of wine in front of her. "The ladies' is through that door and to the left," Mike said. "I'll save your place for you."

She looked from Mike to the door near the bar. "I'll be right back."

It took all of Julie's discipline not to run toward that door. But she measured her steps until the door closed behind her. She walked past the door that said MEN and opened the door to the ladies' on the outside chance there was any clandestine meeting going on, but except for two girls talking to each other in the mirror while they reapplied their lipstick, the room was empty. She walked to the next door. Put her ear to the wood. Heard muffled voices.

Now what? Did she knock? Just burst in? What if it was locked? She had to do something.

But before she could decide, the door opened and Corey, smiling, pulled her inside.

"How did you know I was there?"

"Security camera. Put it in myself. Why are you here?"

"Because CeeJay overheard two men saying they were looking for the kids. She saw me in the parking lot and ran to tell me to get someone to move them from Scatter's house. I think they might have heard her. I told her to get help, and I tried to keep them from following her, but I don't know how successful I was."

"Holy Toledo, Julie. You oughta be at the hotel with your friends."

"Are they there?"

"Yes, but . . ." He turned to the other two men in the room, who were sitting in front of several monitors that seemed to be connected to security cameras.

Ron turned from the monitor he was watching. "Ha, I told Lucky you were his niece," he said as if he'd just won a bet. "But don't you worry. We got one more camera out front, three in the alley out back, and two at Scatter's house. Corey knows what he's doing. We're cool."

"All quiet so far," said a dark young man Julie recognized as Darinda's oldest son, Vihaan. They nodded at each other. It seemed like the whole town was in on this mission.

"Uh-oh, here we go." Ron motioned Corey and Julie over.

One screen showed a van, moving slow, then it shot forward and out of frame. Another camera picked it up.

"Where are they—? Never mind." Julie spotted the dumpster and Kayla's SUV. "They're going down the alley. Do they know about Scatter's house?"

"Don't know," Corey said. "Better ping Ike and tell him and A.J. to zero in on the driveway."

"There's a driveway?" Julie asked. She'd only been on the path through the dunes.

"Of course. Farther down the alleyway."

"I just picked them up," Vihaan said.

They all crowded around his monitor. A vehicle turned, and suddenly they were watching a head-on view of the same van.

"Oh no," Julie cried, and covered her mouth with both hands.

"Damn, that was fast," said Corey.

"We have to stop them," Julie said, and started for the door.

"Just a minute, young lady. We're not in the apprehension business."

"You're just going to let them take the children?"

"Rosie knows what to do."

"How can she keep them safe?"

"There's a security detail," Corey said.

"Of two men," Ron said. "I don't like this. Where is Raymond? Lucky was sure he would show."

"He's somewhere close," Corey said. "We'll just have to wait. Let's just hope he shows before anything goes down."

"What are you talking about?" Julie asked. "Who is Raymond? Where are Lucky and Scatter?"

"We have people all over. Not in dangerous places—please God, don't let it come to that. Did CeeJay know where to go?" He looked at Julie.

"I don't know. I just told her to find somebody and tell them what she'd overheard."

"Sometimes that girl is more trouble than she's worth. Just hope she doesn't get caught in the middle of something nasty."

"Too late," Ron said. "Sounds to me like she's stepped in it big time."

They all watched the monitor.

"I've got something," Ron said. He pointed to his right screen. They were back in the alley. Someone slipped out of the bushes—the path to Scatter's house—looked around, then reached back and hoisted . . . Julie leaned closer to see. It was CeeJay, and she hoisted the little girl, Cecilia, to her hip. She grasped CeeJay around the neck, and CeeJay reached back in and grabbed the boy, Pablo, by the hand and sprinted across the alley.

"Damnation. What the hell is she doing? What happened to security? Where the hell is she going with those two?" Corey picked up what Julie assumed was a radio. Spoke into it.

CeeJay ran diagonally across the alleyway, past the hotel's service entrance.

"Maybe she's going to Marie's shop." But she passed Madame Marzetta's and disappeared under the eaves of the next building.

"Gotta get somebody to intercept her," Corey said.

They all watched intently, waiting for CeeJay to reappear again. But she didn't.

"What's happening?" asked Julie. "Where is she?"

"Damned if I know," Ron said. "All the stores are closed."

"You don't think they got her, do you?" Vihaan asked.

"No, we would've seen."

"Unless they dragged them into one of the stores."

"The knitting store," said Corey. "Damn. Stella Killready's been complaining about people breaking into her store. Maybe it was those thugs setting up an escape route. And nobody took her seriously. That van going up to Scatter's may have been a decoy."

"What if they've got a van waiting on Main Street?" asked Vihaan, getting up from his seat. "Who's posted there?"

"I'm on it." Corey went back to his radio and motioned Ron out the door.

"I'll go," Vihaan said. "I'm faster."

He was already headed for the door. Julie didn't wait but followed him out and down the hall toward the alley. They stopped in the doorway. Ron caught up.

"Mike's taking over in the control room. Come on."

He opened the door, and they all peered out. Two men were converging on the back door of the knitting store.

"Ours?" Vihaan asked.

"Ours. Come on." Ron took off, Vihaan and Julie right behind. He didn't follow the men but ran to the parking lot and out into Main Street. But there didn't seem to be a waiting car, SUV, or van at the front.

"Now what?" Vihaan asked Ron.

"We act like nothing's happened. Oh hell's bells. Here comes

Stella. I forgot Corey put one of those surveillance cameras in her store, so she could monitor it at home. So she'd rest easy, dammit. Excuse me." He hurried forward and stopped Stella just as she was unlocking the door to the Knitting Knoll.

Julie started to follow, but Vihaan stopped her. She looked up at him, but he was scanning the street. He looked so serious, so professional, that Julie shuddered. He couldn't be more than eighteen, if that.

It was like she'd entered an alternate universe, where normal people were more than they seemed.

Small business people by day, but at night . . .

Vihaan lifted his chin. "There, down the street. It comes."

His words sent a chill up Julie's spine. At first all she saw was one man walking toward them. Just as he reached Madame Marzetta's the door opened, and Marie in full regalia stepped out and slipped in front of him, slowing his progress. And though Julie couldn't hear what she was saying, she recognized that boardwalk stance of solicitation. Marie was trying to lure the man inside.

Julie was so intent on Marie's actions that she didn't see the silent sedan, lights off like in every gangster movie she'd ever seen, drive slowly up the street, heading their way. It stopped in front of the Knitting Knoll just as Ron and Stella went inside.

Vihaan reached in his pocket, pulled out a small walkie-talkie, and said something into it, then turned to Julie. "Stay here," he said, and started toward the knitting store himself.

Julie couldn't have stayed put if she'd wanted to, but she would stay out of their way.

Across the street Lucky, Bjorn, and two other men stepped out of the dry cleaners.

One of the rear car doors opened. A man, dressed in a summer suit, climbed out and stepped onto the sidewalk and walked into the knitting store.

The driver's door opened, and the driver got out of the car, right into the arms of the two men who had crossed the street with Lucky and Bjorn.

One man flashed something—a badge—while the other motioned the driver to turn around, before he pushed him up against the car and proceeded to handcuff him.

Thank God, Julie thought. There were real policemen here. At least she hoped they were real.

The man who had been trying to skirt around Marie lurched forward. Marie stood her ground and stuck out her finger. He stopped dead. Julie's principal could stop kids with a point like that.

Neither of them moved, and that's when Julie saw that it wasn't just a finger that Marie was pointing at him. Julie blinked, looked again. Marie Simmons was holding a gun. Julie shrank back, trying to make sense of the situation. Marie? She was an active part of all this? The woman with the crystal ball and the tarot cards and the beautiful garden?

Two more men appeared to take the man into custody. Everyone else converged on the Knitting Knoll.

Chapter 26

They never got inside the door. The man who had just entered the knitting store burst out again, knocking the crowd aside.

Julie scanned the street for the plainclothes police officers, but they were gone. Vihaan started to go after the fleeing man, but Ron yanked him back, just as something dropped in front of them and knocked the man to the ground.

Lucky and Bjorn rushed to add themselves to the melee, and it was over in a matter of seconds. Everyone else had crowded around the door.

Lucky hauled Scatter off the prone man and helped him to his feet. Bjorn and Les, who had appeared from a door down the street, held the man who must be Raymond to the ground.

A local police car cruised up the street and came to a stop in front of the Knitting Knoll, and two of the officers from the diner got out.

"We got a call from Ms. Killready that there was a B and E. This the perp?"

"No. He belongs to these fellas," Lucky said as the two plain-clothesmen who made the first arrests returned. They flashed badges at the two local police.

"Wow," said the younger one.

The two plainclothesmen dragged Raymond to his feet, started to take him away as they read him his rights.

But he balked as he passed Lucky. "I know your face."

"Yeah, but you won't be seeing it for, say, ten to twenty," Lucky returned. "If you last that long. They don't like men who hurt children inside."

The two men took him away to a waiting van.

"Wow," Julie said.

"Are you okay?" Scatter said, limping over to her and cradling his left wrist.

"I am, but . . . where did you come from?"

Scatter looked up.

Julie followed his gaze. "You were on the roof?"

"Yeah."

Lucky joined them, gave Scatter a long look. "That was very stupid."

"Yeah. I think I broke my wrist."

"Serves you right."

"Yeah, I know. But all the agents were busy. I was afraid he might get away, then we would be up the creek."

"You did good. Just don't get into the habit."

"No problem."

"Then you better go over to the hospital and get it looked at."

"First, are the kids okay?"

"Where are they?" Lucky asked.

"Rosie said CeeJay came and warned them that Raymond's men were coming. Security sent CeeJay and the kids to hide in the back bedroom—it's pretty safe—but they sneaked out."

"Ah. Billy, Casey, I think you'll find your culprits in here."

They all followed Lucky into the Knitting Knoll, where a crowd had gathered and was talking excitedly.

"They're in the storeroom, officers," Stella said. "They've got the door barricaded."

Lucky motioned the police and Stella back and moved toward the barricaded door. He leaned close to the wood. "CeeJay, it's Lucky. It's all over; it's safe to come out."

For a full minute no one moved. Finally they heard the scrape of something heavy being pushed across the floor on the other side of the door. The door creaked open and CeeJay peeked out, opened it a little wider, and guided two small, frightened children forward.

As soon as they saw the crowd, they both threw up their hands, and Pablo cried, "Don't shoot. Don't shoot."

And Julie thought, *They don't speak English.* But someone had taught them to say one thing. Her stomach heaved, and she breathed hard trying to quell the bile that rose to her throat. *Don't shoot.*

There was a communal gasp, then Stella's voice rose in the silence. "No one's gonna shoot you. We don't shoot people here. I never heard of such a thing. But what are you doing hiding in my storeroom?"

Julie wasn't so sure. Not after all she'd seen tonight. And she wanted to run to those kids and protect them from she didn't know what. But she would just frighten them further. She looked around for Lucky. Where was he?

"Well, I'm waiting for an answer, CeeJay," Stella said. "And you children, put your hands down. I think I have . . ."

She opened her purse and rummaged through it. The kids cried out and cowered behind CeeJay.

"Here," Stella said, pulling her hand from her purse. "Have a Life Saver." She jabbed it at the kids.

"Wonders never cease," said Marie, coming to stand on the other side of Julie. "The old girl has a heart after all. Albeit a small one."

Scatter, who had been standing beside Julie and was still cradling his wrist, pushed through the others, who were now all staring, and knelt down by the kids. Talked to them in low tones, then reached back to take the roll of candy from Stella.

He couldn't quite manage the packaging, so CeeJay took it and gave a candy to each of the kids, looked at the pack, then, with a defiant look at Stella, took one for herself.

The back door opened, and Rosie hurried in, followed by two men—her security detail?—and Ike and Corey. Rosie stopped when she saw the crowd, looked around, saw the kids, and knelt down. The kids ran into her arms. The two men who'd entered with her frowned at CeeJay.

"We told you to wait in the bedroom. That was a very foolish thing to do."

The local cops looked at each other, then at the other guys, who must be some kind of agent, because they made no bones about taking over.

The two men took out ID cards and flashed them around, not that Julie could see what they were. She had a feeling everyone but her and possibly Stella knew what agency they were from.

"If everyone will just stay put while we take your information. And you." One of the agents turned to CeeJay. "We'll need a statement from you, if you want to call your parents."

CeeJay's eyes shifted toward the door. No one said a word.

Julie willed her not to try to run.

"You won't be in trouble, unless you weren't supposed to be out at this hour. That's between you and Mom and Dad."

CeeJay set her teeth. "I'm twenty-one."

The agent dipped his chin and gave her a try-again look that Julie had used a few times herself. CeeJay's whole over-the-top jaded-young-woman-of-the-world act was pure compensation, though Julie suspected the jealousy was real.

"Then give me a phone number and address where you can be reached."

CeeJay stared back defiantly.

"You're a material witness in an attempted kidnapping."

CeeJay's eyes rounded just long enough for Julie to see real fear. And to suddenly understand. Julie looked around for her uncle, saw him stepping out of the crowd. "Lucky, do something."

He strode over to the man standing with CeeJay. "Agent

Harrison—Danny—she's living with some girls who share a place in town. I'll make sure she's available to you. You have my information."

"Ah." The agent turned back to CeeJay, studied her for a minute. "Don't disappoint us. This is very important. Lucky will be in big trouble if you bolt."

One of the local cops stepped forward. "We'll make sure she's available when you need her."

CeeJay's eyes widened, then glanced at Lucky. Nodded.

"So just give your name to my buddy here and we're cool," said Agent Harrison. "You're now a witness. All your info is confidential."

A nanosecond of relief before CeeJay reverted to her normal sullen self.

She's one of Lucky's, too? Amazing.

They all followed the agents out to the street, where an even larger crowd was waiting. For a laid-back beach town, the place was hopping.

Agent Harrison stopped by Lucky and Marie. "Thanks, we couldn't have done it without you. We've been after that piece of trash for years. I hope the kids aren't traumatized after tonight."

"They were traumatized before we got them." Lucky looked over to Scatter, who was nursing his wrist. "But we have an excellent resident therapist. And now that we know their mother will survive and be with them soon, they'll be okay."

"Good."

His colleague came up. "Sir, we're ready."

The agent nodded. "Thanks again," he said to Lucky, then turned to Marie, touched two fingers to his forehead, and strode away.

"I knew he would be perfect for the agency," Lucky said.

Julie had heard and seen enough. She went over to them. "Did that guy just salute you?" she asked Marie.

Marie snorted. "Me?"

"Yes. He did, didn't he? Who is he?"

"An old acquaintance of ours," Lucky said.

Julie's eyes narrowed. "How do you know federal agents? He is an agent, right?"

"Yes, Ms. Nosy, and Marie will tell you all about it while I drive Scatter over to the ER. I think he might need a cast on that wrist. Jumping off the roof at his age," Lucky added, with a wink to Marie.

Raised voices from inside the store got their attention.

"Oh no," Marie said. "And after the Life Saver event I actually hoped . . ."

They followed Marie back into the store, where Stella was lecturing the two local police. She had CeeJay by the arm.

"Stella, is this necessary?" Marie asked.

"It most certainly is. How did she get into my store if she didn't break in? And what has she stolen?"

"Well, CeeJay," Marie said. "It's a valid question, though I must say it was a brilliant hiding place." She countered Stella's scowl with a raised eyebrow. "How did you get into the knitting store?"

"I didn't break in."

The two policemen, Lucky, and Alex, who had joined them, waited for her to enlighten them.

CeeJay shrugged. "I borrowed the extra key." She grinned.

"See, officers," Stella said. "The girl is incorrigible. She should be locked up. And you'll pay back everything you took."

"I didn't take anything," CeeJay said. She turned to Lucky. "I swear."

"Then why did you borrow the key?" Marie asked.

"I—I needed a place to sleep."

"I thought you had a room over on Third Street," Lucky said.

"They kicked us out. Said there were too many people for one bedroom. I didn't have enough money to get another place." She shrugged again. "And this place was an easy commute."

She'd tried for a joke, tough girl, but she was on the verge of breaking. Julie saw it and so did Marie, though she was smart enough not to show sympathy.

"She's got you there. Roll out of bed and into Surf's Up." Marie walked past them and turned on the light to the store-room, peered inside. "Where's your stuff?"

"They'd tossed most of it before I got home from work. The rest is in the bottom cabinet behind some boxes."

Marie disappeared inside, came back with two plastic gro-cery bags and a rolled blanket. "You slept on this?" Marie asked, holding up the blanket.

CeeJay nodded. "But I didn't steal anything. I paid you back by reorganizing your yarn. This place is a dump. No won-der nobody ever comes in here. Everything's stuffed in those baskets and it's impossible to find anything. If you'd turn on some lights ever you'd see what I'd done."

The store *was* pretty dark, Julie thought, even though the agents had turned on the front part of the store after the children had been found.

"Where's the light switch?" Marie asked. "Never mind, I see it."

She walked to the back entranceway and flipped a switch. Light invaded the store. Not brilliant, but at least enough to be impressed by the back corner of shelving, where a rainbow of color-coordinated skeins of yarn shone like the way to a pot of gold. It only served to show the disarray of the rest of the shop.

"Well," said Marie, "I think this more than pays for a place on the floor in your storeroom."

Stella for once was speechless. She walked over to the yarns and looked up, then across. "This is what I do. I've always done this."

"No, you don't, Stella." Corey came up from behind them. "You won't use the electricity, the heat, the air conditioner. What you think you're seeing is the way the store used to be. You let it go to pot because you were too cheap to hire help. You should thank CeeJay for reminding you what you could be doing."

"I don't have enough customers to pay for all that."

"You would if you made an effort." Corey walked over to the wall of colorful yarns. "Look at this." He lifted his arm in an electronics store owner's version of Vanna White. "All this could be yours."

"Well, she can't sleep in my storeroom and that's final."

"Fine." CeeJay took her bags and blanket from Marie.

"You're about to lose the best chance of revitalizing this store you'll ever have," Corey said.

"Humph." Stella turned away, glanced around, looked back at the wall. "She can't sleep on the floor. But I guess . . . I do have that spare room in my attic. Gets hot, but I suppose somebody could donate a fan if they wanted to."

Corey grinned. "I'm sure they would."

"But I'm having no shenanigans in my house, and no loud music, and no—"

"It doesn't matter, I can't pay," CeeJay said.

Marie sighed.

"Don't have to," said Corey. "You can reorganize the knitting shop in exchange for your room—"

"And board," added Ike from the sidelines.

"Room *and* board?" Stella exclaimed.

"You're absolutely right, Stella," Corey said. "I knew you'd insist. Room and board it is. Ike, you and Ron help CeeJay with her things, and we'll walk them over to Stella's house and get her settled."

"Whoa," Julie said as they left.

"You've just watched the residents of Lucky's Beach in action," Marie said. "Wonder why I retired here?"

Julie shook her head. "Makes me wonder if this is all Lucky's operation or yours."

Marie laughed. "It's everybody's. This town—Ike, Corey, Ron, the mayor, Claire Doyle—they were helping each other out long before I or Lucky or any of the others settled here. It's grown since.

"What you witnessed tonight was a one-off. At least I hope it was. Usually it's just lots of paperwork and court battles. This was different. But they'd been trying to get Joseph Raymond out of hiding for a long time. Once Lucky got the kids out it was just a matter of time until Raymond came looking for them. They were his bargaining chip to keep Ana, Rosie's niece, from testifying against him."

"But it wasn't just a rogue operation," Julie said. "It had to be coordinated by some government agency, right?"

"Well, I wouldn't call it coordinated. More of a you-scratch-my-back-and-I'll-drop-a-criminal-in-your-lap situation. It's a long story."

"I've got another four days of vacation."

"Oh, fine, but while Lucky and Scatter are over at the ER, I'm going to get out of these clothes and I need a glass of wine."

The Knitting Knoll was locked up, so they took the shortcut through the hotel lobby and out the service door to the alley. Julie slowed down as they traversed the way to Marie's kitchen door. So much had happened in the last few hours, in the last few days. "Heads really do spin," Julie said out loud.

"That's to be expected when Lucky's calling the shots."

"How did you and Lucky get back together, if you don't mind my asking?"

"Depends on what you mean by getting back together. If you're asking about how we ended up in the same town after all those years, it's simple. I was here. Lucky looked for me. He had a protégé, one of his many, that he wanted to get started in the 'business.'" She made air quotes. Julie didn't interrupt. "So he ran me to ground and asked me if I might be able to give Danny a leg up. Nothing under the table, just sponsor him when he applied to the program. Danny did it all himself. I just helped him get his foot in the door. You saw him in action tonight."

"What door?" Julie asked. "FBI? CIA? DEA? Those agents were with the DEA, right?"

"They were."

"How do you know them?"

"A lot of the agents used to vacation here. Close to D.C. Not expensive. You get to know each other."

"Then you really are just Madame Marzetta?"

"Just like my mother before me and her mother before her."

"Are you really psychic?"

Marie gave her a Madame Marzetta smile. "That's a family secret."

They'd come to Marie's cottage and could see Dougie's head and paws pressed to the kitchen door's window. Marie let them in the door. He jumped and sniffed and drooled and finally whined at the door once Marie had closed it behind them.

"He'll be back soon, Doug. Just relax." Marie pulled the turban from her head and threw it on the table, opened a bottom cabinet, and came out with a superlarge bone-shaped dog biscuit.

Dougie sat long enough to snap the biscuit from her hand, then went to lie down under the table.

Marie reached back into the cabinet and pulled out a bottle of wine. "A nice cabernet, or would you prefer something stronger? I can do Scotch or bourbon, but anything else we'll have to go over to Lucky's."

"Cab is good," said Julie, thinking of Scatter and his attitude toward girlie drinks.

"I suppose you have more questions."

"I do," said Julie. "But first I want to make sure Kayla and Aggie know what's going on."

"Good idea. I'll just go get out of these Marzetta clothes."

Julie made the call. She was just hanging up when Marie returned wearing jeans and a T-shirt.

"They're at the bar. Les and Bjorn have filled them in on all the pertinent details. I told them I'd meet them there later." It had been such a scary, thrilling night, but now that it was over, Julie was feeling a little sad or something.

"It's the adrenaline letdown," Marie said as if reading her thoughts. "We all suffer from it. Occupational hazard."

"Speaking of which, what is your real occupation?"

"I told you. My *real* occupation is being Lucky's Beach's sole psychic."

"You didn't stop that thug by pointing your all-seeing finger at him."

"Nah. I just stood in his way until somebody came to get him."

"I saw you, you had a gun."

"Me? What would I be doing with a gun?"

"I don't know, but you're one of them, right?"

Marie scoffed, then looked Julie in the eye. "If you must know, I might have at one time been part of a quasi, loosely connected, this-tape-will-self-destruct sort of subgroup."

"This whole town isn't what it seems."

"Of course it is. It's exactly what it seems. We're just like people in any town who care about each other; we lend a hand when we're needed, look the other way when we're not."

"Most towns aren't that friendly or compassionate toward others. And they certainly don't have the skills."

"Their loss, which is what makes Lucky's Beach that much more special."

"So special that they can take on drug traffickers in order to save a couple of children?"

"Lucky just poked the wrong bear. He didn't have a choice. Rosie asked, and what could he do but try?"

"And who is Rosie? Besides a lot of people's housekeeper."

"Haven't you met her? She's the housekeeper to several people in the community, plus she keeps the bar in mint condition."

"That's all?"

"She takes care of a lot of people. Does it seem odd to you that we would try to help her?"

Julie thought about it. "I guess not . . . It's just most people don't seem to go out of their way to do something extraordinary to help others, at least not these days."

"You just have to look."

Julie nodded, but she didn't think it was as simple as that. It seemed like there were two different worlds out there, one where success was everything—no matter what you considered success—and one like Lucky's Beach, where people managed to get beyond petty squabbles and differences of opinion, envy and even greed.

It was something Julie had been missing. She had her

friends, people did, but this was something that went beyond your "posse." Lucky's Beach was its own posse.

"Do you think CeeJay and Stella living together will work out?"

"Who knows? I doubt it. CeeJay has been on her own a long time, seen stuff a kid should never see."

"How old is she?"

Marie shrugged. "My guess is fifteen, maybe sixteen. I hope she isn't younger."

"Hasn't someone asked her?"

"Nope. We know better. We know she was in the system for a while, that her foster family was bad. That much we were told. Services looked the other way and let her slip through the safety net. It's easier to do than it should be, but in CeeJay's case, she's safer on the streets. At least on the streets of Lucky's Beach. No one's come looking for her yet, thank God.

"So, to answer your question, I hope it lasts long enough for her to get used to sleeping in a real bed, and for Stella to get her groove back, before she moves on. By then, who knows, we may have found her a place to move on to."

"It must be hard for the guys to work around her. It's sort of jailbait territory."

"The guys know better than to mess with her, and they keep anyone else from going over the line, when they can. On her own time, who knows? She's not an innocent."

They sat silent for a while, Julie pondering the state of children in the world, Marie thinking thoughts that only Marie could know.

"I'm not going back."

Marie looked up. Poured them more wine.

"I don't know why it isn't working. Well, I think I might be getting an idea. I'm . . . superfluous there."

Marie nodded. She didn't try to dissuade or encourage her. She just let Julie talk, and Julie did, saying all the things that had been tumbling around in her mind that she hadn't yet put together into coherent thoughts.

But when she finally stopped, the bottle was empty and Julie was pretty sure she had made her decision.

Dougie clambered to his feet and went to the back door. "Guys are here," Marie said, and got up to take some beers out of the fridge.

Lucky opened the door and moved aside to say hello to Dougie and let Alex through.

"Que pasa?" Alex said, his arm in a soft cast.

Julie just shook her head.

Alex shrugged. "Don't say it, Lucky has already reamed me. I don't know what came over me."

"I think I do," said Julie.

"Yeah, so old habits are hard to break."

"Harder than your arm, evidently."

"Well, what choice did I have?"

"I can think of several."

Lucky just leaned back in his chair and smiled. "Already fighting like an old—"

Marie rolled her eyes. "Don't even say it."

Chapter 27

They tried to talk Scatter into letting Lucky take him home, but he insisted on going to the bar before taking the painkillers the doctor had prescribed.

"I think I deserve a beer at least," he groused.

"Then you're stuck with ibuprofen," Julie told him.

"One beer won't—" Lucky broke off as Marie punched him. "What?"

Marie sighed. "You want her to be her own person. Then let her. Honestly, between you and Louise, I don't know how she grew up to be as independent as she is."

"What did I do?"

Marie shook her head. "Come on if we're going. It's past my bedtime."

He gave her a dopey smile. "Mine, too?"

"Honestly, men and their adrenaline."

They crossed the alleyway and entered the bar through the back door, mainly, Julie thought, to save Scatter from any more jarring of his wrist. He insisted on having a beer and checking on everything before he "crashed under the influence," but if Julie thought it was because he wanted to be greeted as a hero, she was wrong.

They entered the bar, which was crowded to capacity and perhaps beyond. Everyone greeted them or raised their glasses as they passed. Mike slid mugs of beer to Lucky and Scatter, but not before shaking his head.

"I guess you expect me to do all the heavy lifting for the next few weeks," he yelled over the buzz of conversation and music.

Scatter took his beer. Two glasses of wine appeared for Marie and Julie, and they waded their way through the revelers to a table where their friends sat.

Les pulled Aggie onto his lap so Scatter could sit, which he did, gratefully, Julie thought. Probably he was hurting in more places than his wrist. Luckily, the building was only one story, or he could have broken a lot more. Bjorn ceded his seat to Marie, and Lucky pulled up a chair for Julie. Three polite surfer dudes, still basking in their success.

"Wow, what a night," Aggie said. "Les and Bjorn dropped us at the hotel, told us to stay put, and disappeared into the night." She patted Les's cheek. "Thank heavens for the hotel's front porch. We saw everything that happened on the street. It was so exciting."

"Yeah," said Kayla. "Just glad it turned out all right."

"Me, too," Julie said.

"So the kids really are safe?"

Julie looked to Lucky.

"Yep. Free to be kids, and their mother will be out of the hospital soon and will join them." Lucky raised his hand, not for another round, but to high-five Corey, Ike, and Ron. "Where's Vihaan?"

"Darinda made him come home to bed," Corey said. "She's expecting a big crowd at the diner for breakfast tomorrow. Besides, he's not old enough to drink. These kids run rings around us oldsters with that online stuff. He did a stellar job tonight. I wonder if I can lure him away from the diner and get him to come work for me."

"On peril of your breakfast," Marie said. "She wants him to get a full education."

More people came, and everyone told and retold their favorite highlights from the evening.

Julie was more than ready for bed, and Scatter looked like he might pass out any second, when Marie took the dregs of his first beer away, called over to Mike for a glass of water, and opened the bottle of pills Lucky had in his pocket. Scatter didn't argue but downed them dry.

"I'll take him home," Lucky said.

"I'm good," Scatter said.

"Right, just don't want you to break anything else stumbling over the dunes at night. It would be anticlimactic."

Scatter stood up, winced, and let Lucky lead him off. They had gone two feet before he turned back, zeroing in on Julie.

"Tell Dee . . ." He seemed to lose his train of thought, the painkillers kicking in.

"I will," Julie said. "I'll call her tomorrow."

"Swim . . ."

"We've got it covered. Don't worry."

He pointed his finger at her.

"Mañana," Lucky said, and steered him away.

Julie left soon after that. Marie was right, adrenaline had deserted her an hour ago and she was dead on her feet. She said good night to Kayla and Aggie, who were still going strong, and headed for the door.

"I'll see you to the hotel," Marie said.

"You're not expecting more trouble, are you?" Julie asked.

"No, but still, it's late."

"We would be honored to see Julie home," said Corey, flanked by Ron and Ike. "We'll see you home, too, Marie."

"Thanks, fellas, but I'm just going to run out the back door to my back door. Take good care of Julie."

Corey offered his elbow to Julie, which she was too tired not to take.

The three guys saw her to the hotel lobby, where Henry was waiting to press the elevator button for her. Though she didn't relish the idea of being alone in that creaky box, she thanked him and stepped inside.

She took a shower and headed for bed, stopping to crank up the air conditioner and look out the window. The alley was dark and deserted; no cars without headlights on cruised past. She did have a moment of panic when a figure stepped out of the shadows, but tonight she recognized her uncle, upright, with a jaunt to his step, headed back to Marie's.

She pulled down the shade. All was right with the world at least for tonight.

$\mathcal{M}$arie was in bed when she heard the kitchen door click open and Dougie's nails move across the tile as he went out for the last time of the evening.

A few minutes later, Lucky appeared in the doorway of the bedroom. He braced his elbows on the doorframe and looked down at her. "Damn, I'm tired."

"I know," Marie agreed. "We're getting too old for all this running around."

"Yeah," he said, cocking his head and really looking at her. "Fortunately we've got a second generation to take over."

Marie narrowed her eyes at him. "What second generation would that be? Just what do you have in mind?"

Lucky grinned sleepily at her. "I do have an idea." He pushed through the door and leaned over to kiss her. "This, and perhaps this."

She pushed his hand away. "About the second generation?"

"Well, you gotta admit, they're perfect together."

Marie sat up against the headboard. "Stop it right now. You don't know that. You just want it to be true."

He eased forward until she could feel his breath on her neck. He smelled like beer and sweat and truth. "I knew the minute I saw them together, almost twenty years ago, her standing there in Louise's kitchen in her little pink pj's, with her clean hair and her perfect manners. And me hanging on to Scat bleeding and half dead, fighting with every last bit of his energy like some wild creature raised by wolves and smelling like it."

He chuckled. "I knew then that, just like yin and yang, they were a match."

Marie stroked his hair, still thick and blond like his niece's. "You are more full of shit than Madame Marzetta," she said.

"You wait and see."

"I'll wait and see once Louise gets back from her cruise and gets wind of Julie's intention to quit her job."

Lucky sat up. "She wants to quit?"

"Yes, but I didn't tell you. And you're staying out of it. That's an order."

"Yes, ma'am."

"I mean it. Don't interfere."

"We'll worry about it tomorrow. We had enough work cut out for us tonight to last me awhile. Help the old man to bed."

He grinned again, this time not so sleepily.

*D*arinda was right. The luncheonette was packed the next morning when Julie, Aggie, and Kayla stopped for breakfast. Vihaan still managed to see them when they entered and threaded his way through the patrons to greet them.

"I thought you might be coming. We saved you your table."

They sat down at their usual table, nodded to Corey, Ron, and Ike and to Claire Doyle, who was sitting a few tables away.

Even the two cops who had been on duty the night before were back in their usual booth.

They filled up on the day's specials: chocolate orange cardamom pancakes for Julie and Aggie and a curried egg and goat cheese scramble for Kayla.

The police officers got up to leave.

"Billy," Ron called out, "come over here and meet Julie and the girls; you didn't get a chance to in all the excitement last night."

The policeman came over and Ron stood up.

"Julie, Aggie, Kayla, meet my son, Officer William Petry. One of the heroes of last night."

"Thanks, Dad." He nodded at the three women, his cheeks scarlet. "Nice to meet you all." He turned on his heel and strode out the door.

"Just love doing that to him," Ron said. "He's made me proud."

When they'd finished breakfast and were on their way to the hotel, Aggie said, "Tell me again what six degrees of separation means?"

"It has something to do with people knowing the same six people or . . ." Kayla stopped. "Julie, do you know?"

"Not really, but if you're talking about this town, yeah. It sure seems like everybody is connected to everybody else."

They went into the hotel.

"Swimsuits in fifteen minutes," Kayla said.

"Ugh," said Aggie. "After that breakfast, I hope it still fits."

"Not to worry, it's so small, no one will notice if your stomach is hanging out."

"Har har, I'll take the stairs."

They all took the stairs. And a half hour later they were sitting in their beach chairs in the sand.

"Now this is the life," Kayla said.

"More than half of our vacation is already gone," Aggie pointed out.

"I know," Kayla said. "And the kids haven't even called this morning to complain about how bored they are. But what a week," she added. "One to remember. Hand me the sunscreen, will you?"

Aggie tossed it to her. "What next I wonder."

So did Julie. She hadn't heard from Lucky or Marie or Scatter. They were all probably sleeping in. Les and Bjorn and two new guys were already at work when the girls set up their chairs.

"Nothing, hopefully," Aggie continued. "All this excitement makes time go too fast. Though I did volunteer us for swim lessons on Thursday, since the Scatterman can't get his cast wet."

"Have you heard from him today?" Kayla asked, looking at Julie.

Julie shook her head. "I imagine Rosie has him and the kids cosseted indoors."

"I would like to take a couple more trips to the camp," Kayla said. "I've got the makings of a kick-ass girls' soccer team. Hope they can find someone to take over for me." She sighed.

Aggie sighed.

Julie sighed, but probably for different reasons.

"This is the life," Kayla said.

"Are you going to miss Bjorn when we leave?" Aggie asked.

"Sure, for a few days. He's really nice. But I have to admit I'm kind of missing my kids. Are you going to miss Les?"

"Yes." Aggie's voice was wobbly.

Kayla sat up. "Spill."

"It's nothing. I was just thinking."

"On vacation? That's a first. Did you and Les have a fight?"

"No, just the opposite."

"So what's the problem?" asked Julie.

"It's just that we only have a few days left."

"We always only have ten days."

"I don't know . . ."

Kayla rolled her eyes. "Well, I do. You do this every vacation."

"But she usually waits until we're in the car driving home," Julie reminded her.

"This is different," Aggie said.

"They always are," Kayla said.

"No really. This is really different."

Julie dropped her feet to the sand. "Do you want to talk about it?"

"Not yet. For now I'm going to pretend that I have all summer."

Julie totally felt the same. Decisions were easier to make when the sun wasn't shining, the waves weren't lulling her to sleep, and there were no cute surfer dudes telling them to chill and enjoy, even though one was missing.

"What about you, Jules?" asked Kayla.

"What about me?"

"You and Scatterman."

Julie shrugged. "I have no idea, but . . ."

Aggie sat up. "But what?" They both leaned toward Julie.

She couldn't do it. "Nothing."

"You're not still upset about your sabbatical, are you?"

"No, actually I'm not."

"Then it is something about Scatterman."

"Maybe."

"Maybe? Yes or no? What's going on?"

Julie took a deep breath. It didn't give her any more courage.

"Jules?"

"I don't know . . . yet. But I'm thinking of sticking around for a while."

"Wow," said Aggie.

"What about your master's course?" Kayla asked.

"It will still be there next summer." *And the summer after, and the summer after that.*

"Wow," Aggie repeated.

"Well, why not?" Kayla said. "You deserve some time off. You think you'll spend the whole summer here?"

"I'm thinking about it." Hell, it was the only thing she'd been thinking about when she wasn't worried about kidnappers and special agents. She looked at her pirate romance, facedown on the chaise beside her. It had nothing over the excitement of Lucky's Beach. But she could already feel herself backing down, the old panic setting in, the indecision. "But keep it to yourselves until I decide, okay?"

"Sure."

"Not a word."

Julie lay back. She had plenty of time to decide—or not. "For now we have three more glorious days to do nothing but relax. And that's just what I plan to do." She closed her eyes. "Ah, perfect."

"Yoo-hoo, girls! Over here!"

Julie's eyes flew open. It couldn't be. She sat up. Kayla and Aggie sat up, too.

"Is that—?" Aggie began.

Julie nodded. "I'm afraid so." She turned in her chair, waved. "Hey, Mom, we're over here."

Chapter 28

$\mathcal{M}$arie stood in the hallway of her cottage, listening. Louise had been here for two days and they couldn't keep Julie's plans from her any longer. It was inevitable that it would come out somehow. Which it had, when Ike, Corey, and Ron met Louise and the first thing out of Ike's mouth was "We sure hope Julie decides to stay."

Ron's kick came too late for any of them to salvage the situation, though God knew they had tried.

Marie had insisted Lucky stay out of it. There was no way he wasn't going to get in trouble with either his sister or his niece. Now Julie was out helping with the community camp's swim hour, and Louise and Lucky were in her kitchen. Marie was prepared for whatever would come, but she had no intentions of becoming a party to it.

It wasn't that she was a coward; she just thought that what Lucky and Louise had to say to each other should be private.

Besides, Julie might need her support later no matter what decision she made.

Lucky still hadn't moved back to his own cottage, and Marie had wondered momentarily if that was any kind of sign. She doubted it, but she was glad that he was still here for the inevitable showdown between Julie and her mother.

Marie had tried not to influence Julie either way, not even as Madame Marzetta, when she'd encouraged her to leave; but that had been to get her out of harm's way.

Now that Raymond was behind bars awaiting trial, and Ana and her children were about to be reunited as soon as she was able to leave the hospital, there was no danger to worry about . . . until the next thing happened.

She wouldn't interfere, just let Julie make her decision and then support her either way.

She leaned closer to the door. The voices had grown quieter, the calm before the storm. Or at least that was Lucky's way. She imagined Louise could hold her own.

"There's nothing wrong with her taking a year off. And if she finds something she likes better—"

"Like what? Running a bar?"

Marie leaned up against the wall. If Louise thought running a bar was bad . . . She willed Lucky not to mention the other things he did.

"I'm sorry, Lucky, but she has a good job, one with benefits and job security."

"And one that might not be the right one for her. But it's up to her, not us."

"I don't want her to have to live the way we did. It was hard."

"It was hard, sis, only because you wouldn't accept help."

Total silence. There went the calm, thought Marie, and braced herself.

"You think I should have gone on welfare after my husband died?"

"I think you could have accepted more than condolences from your friends. Let your neighbors watch Julie a few afternoons until you got your life together."

"I did get my life together," Louise said, her voice rising.

"You did. And did a damn good job of it. But you lost your joy, Lou. It was all hard work, even after I came to help out—because you asked me to—"

Marie closed her eyes. It was all going to come out. *Be kind. Be kind. Be kind.*

"—but you didn't want me to help. I didn't realize it right away. I thought you needed to be able to lean a little on your brother for a bit and I was more than willing, but you didn't."

"You had your own life."

"I did. I still do, but you and Julie are a part of that life. But I couldn't be what you really needed me to be, the little brother that you'd always taken care of. I didn't need taking care of. I wasn't just some bum roaming aimlessly from one beach to another." He laughed. "At least most of the time. I made a good living at surfing. I've made a better living since."

"Running a bar? Really, Lucky."

"Owning a bar on a beautiful beach is pretty lucrative. Plus,

I'm paid very well for reconnecting families who come to me for help."

"But it's dangerous, and I don't want Julie involved."

Do not engage, Marie telegraphed mentally. Not that she had any illusions about being successful.

"Sometimes it is dangerous, but usually it's just a question of finding them and persuading them to go home, convincing people to forgive. This latest one was highly unusual."

"Promise me you won't do anything like this again."

Marie would love to add her plea to Louise's. She'd had enough danger and adventure for one lifetime, maybe two. But she would never turn her back on Lucky or anyone else who came to them for help.

"I can't. But who's to say Julie is even planning to stay here or even keep in contact with me? She only came here because you . . ."

Don't push your luck, thought Marie.

"You were worried about me."

Marie let out her breath.

"But what will she do? How will she survive?"

"Oh, Lou, just like you did. By being the incredible woman you are and she is."

*C*ome on, Julie, the bus will be here in a few minutes and I promised Les we would be there to meet it."

Julie looked up from her beach chair. "What? I must have dozed off."

She didn't want to get out of her chair. She was exhausted with indecision. Her mother had been here for two whole days; she was leaving with Kayla and Aggie the next day, since Julie "wanted to spend some time with Lucky and Marie."

And that part was true.

Still, Julie felt like time was running out to make her big decision. She wanted her mother to know before she left.

Sure, she could wait, take a few more weeks before handing in her resignation, leaving the school in the lurch and scrambling to find her replacement. But she wouldn't do that to them. It wasn't their fault that she hadn't worked out. They were pleased with her work.

She wasn't. She'd rewritten her resignation and printed it out on the hotel's printer. It was sitting in her hotel room, still waiting to be mailed.

But was she strong enough to do this on her own? Call her a wuss, but she needed her posse around her or she was afraid she might give in to her mother's fears—and hers.

Time was running out, and she still couldn't get herself to pull the trigger. A terrible metaphor, considering their close call with Joseph Raymond.

What was she going to do?

"Yo, Julie."

"Right." She got up, looked over to the private beach. Still no sign of people. Then she saw two little faces on the deck. And Rosie standing next to them.

"I'll be right there," she told the others, and walked across the beach to say hello. "Morning," she said. "We're going to help out with the camp's beach time. Do you think it's too soon for Cecilia and Pablo to come?"

Rosie bit her lip.

Julie understood. "You can come with them. They can just play in the sand if they're afraid of the water. They might meet some friends." Then she stopped herself. "There's no reason for them to hide anymore, is there?"

Rosie shook her head. Held up a finger, then bent down to talk to the children. "I will bring them. We will see."

"Great, we're looking forward to it." Julie waved and trotted off across the sand just as the bus arrived.

The first person off the bus was Dee Hoyes.

There were eighteen children today, all in various degrees of excitement, from ready to float off on a wave to clinging to Les's leg as he walked them toward the water.

Dee saw Julie and came over. "Usually Geraldo comes, but I wanted to have a beach day, too. And really I was hoping Alex would at least get down to say hello."

Julie smiled.

"Because," Dee continued, "I have his other half here at last."

"His other half?" Julie said, astonished.

"Yes, his abuela finally agreed to let him come, though I'm afraid he's even less enthusiastic than she was. Ven aca, Alberto."

A small boy standing near the bus, head bent, eyes down, came slowly toward her.

"Do you remember Ms. Julie? She's Dos Al's friend."

"Ah," said Julie. "Dos Als. He hurt his hand," she attempted in Spanish. "Did I say that correctly?"

"Close enough," Dee said, and explained to Alberto that Alex had fallen down and hurt his hand. And that he couldn't come today. "And then again, he just made me a liar."

Scatter was walking across the beach with Rosie and the two kids in tow.

The rest of the adults organized the other kids and led them off to various activities.

Julie, Dee, and Alberto waited for Scatter to reach them. He knelt down and went through some goofy handshake with his good hand. Alberto at first didn't appear very enthusiastic. But by the third try he laughed, and little Pablo, who had been holding Rosie's hand, came over to try it himself.

Scatter left the two boys trying to accomplish the handshake with each other.

"How are you?" Dee and Julie asked simultaneously.

"Fine," Scatter said. "Do you have enough people in the water?"

"Trying to get rid of me?" Julie asked, only half kidding. "Anybody for the water?"

She didn't get any volunteers from Alberto, Pablo, or Cecilia, so feeling slightly disappointed, she waded into the waves by herself.

Julie made herself not look toward Dee and Scatter; she still wasn't sure of what their relationship was, and it didn't matter, she chided herself. She had more important issues to deal with than a beach fling.

Soon she was totally involved in beach ball volleyball in

ankle-deep surf. When she did look over, Scatter and Dee were still standing together with Alberto silently sitting in the sand between them. Rosie was standing at the edge of the water, holding on to Pablo and Cecilia in a death grip.

Julie waded over. "Want me to take one?"

"No. They do not swim."

"Maybe they would like to play." Julie rummaged in the cart for three sets of beach pails and shovels. She brought them close to the water, just where the sand was wet enough to make a castle.

Rosie brought the children and stood feet braced in the sand, arms crossed like a guardian figure, while Julie showed them how to pack the sand. The first efforts were pretty unrecognizable, but Cecilia and Pablo didn't seem to care.

Soon Julie became aware of Alberto watching the proceedings with a keen eye. She smiled and motioned him over.

He shook his head.

She nodded hers.

Scatter gave him a nudge with his toe. He reluctantly walked over to where Julie was overseeing the growing mound of sand. She handed him a shovel; he looked at Pablo, then Cecilia, wary as if they might snatch it away.

"It's fun," Julie said, and kept an eagle eye out for any sign of trouble.

Which was ridiculous, she told herself, they couldn't be more than five or six. And yet bands of the same-age children roamed the streets of Central and South America, she knew. Probably even in the States. Scatter had been a pro at twelve.

Julie had always made sand castles imagining the prince and princess inside. She wondered what these children were imagining as they shoveled and patted and the pile of sand grew. Were they thinking of home far away or of mountains—or was it just a pile of sand to while away some time in the sun?

She took a shovel and began digging a moat around the lopsided castle, then took a pail and poured water into the moat.

"Safe now," she said. The water would protect those inside. "Salvo ahora."

When it was time to leave, Alberto waved goodbye and got on the bus with the others. Dee counted heads and started to get on, but ran back at the last minute. "Julie, if you're still here tomorrow, get Alex to bring you to my engagement party. I want you to meet my fiancé, John."

Julie smiled. "Thank you. I'd love to come."

The bus drove away.

"Got time for a glass of cabernet?" Scatter said.

"Yes, but not right now. There's something I have to do. I really am a teacher after all."

"Oh." Scatter watched the bus drive out of the parking lot. "Well . . . it's good you figured things out. See you later. Rosie! Leave those pails for someone else to pick up. Let's get these kids back home."

$\mathcal{A}$lex reluctantly walked over the dunes path to Marie's cottage. He was not happy about the phone call. Julie had just said to meet her at Marie's cottage. He didn't hold out hope that she was going to stay. Her words to him when she'd left the beach pretty much said it all.

Well, of course she was a teacher. She'd always trained to be a teacher. Was good at it, had the rest of her life planned. What did he expect? That she'd see him, reconnect with Lucky, and live happily ever after at Lucky's Beach?

He hadn't expected that. He wouldn't even want that. But she had so much more to give. He mentally kicked himself. What was he talking about? She was a teacher; she gave every day of her life. It's the way it should be.

Unfortunately it made him feel like shit.

Dougie was sitting at the door looking depressed. Julie was right. He was probably uncomfortable in the heat with all that fur. If she had decided to stay he would have told her to take him to the groomers or whatever. Maybe he could get Rosie to give him a bath. That would help.

"What's up, Doug? Did they throw you outside?"

Dougie didn't even give him a welcoming thump of his tail. They both probably wore the same hangdog expression.

"Yeah, me, too," Alex said, and knocked on the door.

He walked in to find Louise and Lucky standing in the middle of the kitchen, scowling at each other across the table. Marie was seated and staring at a teapot as if she were conjuring spirits.

Dougie shuffled past him, sniffed at Lucky, looked at Louise, and kept going through the kitchen and into the front room.

Great, even Dougie knew when to cut his losses.

"Have a seat, Scatter," Marie said. "Would you like tea or maybe a beer?"

"No thanks." Alex sat down at the table, looked around at the three of them. "Julie called and told me to meet her here. She's not here yet?"

"No, not yet," said Marie, who seemed to be the only one who had a voice.

They heard Dougie's bark before they heard the front door open and close. Marie smiled at the others and left the room. She returned in less time than it took to turn around, being pushed back into the room by Dougie and Julie, looking somber.

Alex's stomach plummeted. It was the pills, he told himself. He would stop taking them as soon as she left; his pain would keep his mind off Julie. He'd welcome a little wrist pain, in comparison to the way he felt at this moment.

Julie was carrying a stack of papers and she put it down on the table. "Is that tea? Could I have a cup?"

"Sure." Marie went to the cupboard, brought down a mug.

"Are those your school papers?" Louise asked.

"Yes," said Julie.

"So you decided to go back and take your summer course as planned," Louise said, her face brightening.

"No, Mom, I just sent in my resignation. This is just some paperwork that I needed to fax over to them."

"Oh, Julie." Louise gathered up the papers as if maybe she could put the genie back in the bottle.

But it was too late.

Alex was almost afraid to breathe.

"I've turned in my resignation and I'm going to stay here."

She's staying here. Alex thought he'd heard it but he wasn't sure. He stared at her, willing her to look at him, but she kept focused on Louise.

"I'm sorry, Mom, I know you're disappointed. But I can't live the life you envisioned for me. I thought I could, but I can't. I'm still going to be a teacher, but I want to help those who really need me. Somewhere where I can make a difference. My kind of difference."

Lucky squeezed Louise's shoulder. "It'll be okay, Lou. I'll take care of her for a change."

"You don't have to," Julie said. "I can look after myself; I always could. You guys gave me the tools to do that, now it's my turn to take care of myself."

Now she looked at Alex.

Well, finally.

"But what will you do?" Louise pressed.

"I have some money saved. I'm going to finish out the summer helping Dee Hoyes over at the county camp, and I'll look around for something more permanent for the fall."

Louise groaned and sank into a chair.

"It's going to be fine, Mom."

It at least will be okay, Alex thought. Who knew where things might go.

"I'll just put on water for more tea," Marie said, and moved to the stove.

"I think, Marie," Louise said, "I may need something a little stronger."

The next day, Aggie and Kayla departed for home, taking Louise with them and leaving Julie behind.

"I'm sorry I have to leave," Louise said, taking Julie by the shoulders. "I only had two weeks off. I shouldn't have frittered away two days in Bermuda."

"But you had a good time," Julie reminded her.

"I did, but I should have . . ."

"Mom, I think it's great. I'll call you tonight to make sure you got home okay."

"Okay. Love you."

"Love you, too."

Louise climbed into the back seat where she'd insisted on sitting.

Kayla closed the trunk. "Thanks for helping us pack. I thought it would be a breeze without your stuff, but Louise . . . What do you think she has in all those suitcases?"

"Not a clue. I'm guessing clean uniforms?"

Aggie teared up. "We're going to miss you."

"I'll be back in a week or two for a few days to get some more clothes and deal with the moving and stuff. I'll let you know when. You can help me pack," Julie said brightly, then her lip quivered.

Aggie's tears spilled over, but Julie thought they were as much because of leaving Les as they were for leaving Julie.

"We're only a few hours away," Julie reminded them. "We can visit."

"It won't be the same," Kayla said, "but I'm glad for you. Besides, the kids are already planning a vacation here since we'll have a place to stay."

"You know you do," Julie told her, and gave her a hug. "I'm definitely going to get a place that has room for everybody." She turned to Aggie and hugged her. "You okay?"

Aggie nodded as tears streamed down her cheeks. "Like you said, we're really close." Her mouth twisted. "I knew it would be this way. Les won't leave his job, and I won't leave mine. I guess it was just another summer fling. But I'll still come to visit you."

"And who knows?" Kayla said, pushing her friend into the front seat. "Stranger things have happened, right, Jules?"

"Right." Stranger things had happened. Julie was headed toward an un-thought-out future. You couldn't get much stranger than that. Actually, that wasn't exactly true. There was the summer camp, the swimming lessons. She still planned to get her master's. And Dee had already promised to put her in contact with several of the schools where she had subbed during the school year.

Then there was Lucky and Marie and Scatter.

And yeah, she pretty much decided to go where Julie had never gone before. And go there without a plan.

She blew her mom a kiss, silently thanking the cosmos that she wasn't riding back with them, and watched until the SUV crossed the bridge and drove out of sight. Then she looked at her phone.

As always, they had been late leaving, and she'd be late if she didn't hurry. She sprinted across the parking lot and into the bar. "Can I borrow the Jeep?"

Alex looked up from where he was helping Lucky dry beer steins with one hand and having little success from the looks of things. He tossed her the keys with his good hand.

"Thanks." She headed to the door.

"Where are you going in such a hurry?"

"Out to the camp," she called back. "I have ants to count."

Acknowledgments

Sometimes we all need to step out of our comfort zone as a person or as a writer. In *Lucky's Beach* I wanted to explore characters as opposite as they could be and yet tied to one another. It was a roller coaster of a ride.

Thanks to my reading pals, Gail Freeman and Lois Winston, who were ready to take on all questions from the nature of good and evil to character motivations and questionable fashion sense. You certainly made it interesting.

And thanks to my editors, Tessa Woodward and Elle Keck at William Morrow, for kneading this story into shape. And special thanks to my agent, Kevan Lyon, ever brilliant, energetic, and indefatigable.

And finally a big thank-you to the people of Rehoboth Beach, Bethany Beach, and Lewes, Delaware, for their hospitality and their passion for their communities and the people who live there.

Reading Group Guide

1. Sometimes it takes great courage to step out of the person we think we are and accept the person we may become. Why do you think Julie decided it was time to take a chance on a different self? Is she being smart or naive or ungrateful?

2. Julie, Kayla, and Aggie have been friends since childhood. They still do a lot of things together. Do you think they've grown together or differently? Has their friendship developed as they matured as people, or are they still together out of habit? Can friends change in major ways and still connect?

3. Our friends can be great supporters, cheerleaders, shoulders to cry on. Sometimes they're the ones to give us a quick reality check. What do you think are the most important characteristics of good friends? Which characteristics do

you think Aggie and Kayla have? Are they good friends to Julie, and is she to them?

4. Sometimes love can be smothering. Julie's mother has always tried to control things. When she and Lucky were kids, she took it upon herself to take care of her younger twin brother. When her husband died, she made sure that Julie would have a secure future. What do you think drove her to be so fiercely independent and to protect her loved ones? Why do you think she couldn't let go? Do you think she will still oversee Julie even in her new choices?

5. As a little girl Julie wanted Lucky to be a father, but Lucky was often gone and disappointed her. Lucky tried to do what he could but was sometimes thwarted by his sister. Do you think Louise was afraid of his way of life? His freedom? Was she afraid it might encourage Julie to take dangerous chances? What is Louise afraid of?

6. The way we see people is not always as they really are, whether it be by their choice, our choice, or just circumstances. How did perception play a part in the estrangement between Lucky and Julie?

7. Alex had a very stark, violent, and traumatic childhood. What part do you think his loyalty to Lucky plays in his desire to help children? Do you think he can be a good

therapist and a good friend, or is his past bound to trip him up somewhere along the way?

8. Lucky says that from the first time he saw Alex and Julie together as children he knew they were made for each other. What made him think this? What strengths and weaknesses might Julie and Alex share that help to make the other whole?

9. Marie has a somewhat vague past. As a writer I found her interesting because of that. We meet so many people in daily life and have no idea what they might have done with their lives, how they adapt to changes. Marie doesn't want to be dragged back into the past, but she agrees. Why do you think she was willing to be a part of the operation? Do you think it will change her life going forward, or her relationship with Lucky?

10. Do you think Julie will find fulfillment in a different way of teaching? Or will she return to the classroom, bringing something more to her students than she understood before? Is one choice better than the other for Julie?

About the Author

Shelley Noble is the *New York Times* and *USA Today* best-selling author of *Whisper Beach* and *Beach Colors*. Other titles include *Stargazey Point, Breakwater Bay, Forever Beach, The Beach at Painter's Cove, Lighthouse Beach, A Beach Wish,* and four spin-off novellas. A former professional dancer and choreographer, she lives on the Jersey Shore and loves to discover new beaches and indulge in her passion for lighthouses and vintage carousels. Shelley is a member of Sisters in Crime, Mystery Writers of America, and Women's Fiction Writers Association.

BOOKS BY
SHELLEY NOBLE

**LUCKY'S
BEACH**

**A BEACH
WISH**

**LIGHTHOUSE
BEACH**

**THE BEACH AT
PAINTER'S COVE**

**FOREVER
BEACH**

**WHISPER
BEACH**

**BREAKWATER
BAY**

**STARGAZEY
POINT**

**BEACH
COLORS**

ALSO AVAILABLE • E-NOVELLAS BY SHELLEY NOBLE

Stargazey Nights
Holidays at Crescent Cove
Newport Dreams: A Breakwater Bay Novella
A Newport Christmas Wedding

Available in Paperback and E-Book Wherever Books Are Sold